The Witchfinder's Well

JONATHAN POSNER

CONTENTS

ACKNOWLEDGMENTS

I would like to offer my heartfelt thanks to those who helped make this book happen.

My son Henry for his kind and helpful comments, and the same to Helen Day, Kathryn Collinson and Sue Bond, as well as my friends on the Windsor Writers' Group.

Also to Sinead Fitzgibbon for her thorough review and encouragement.

This book is dedicated to the memory of John Gauntley, who, together with Chris Smellie and myself created the original musical Spirit of History – without which this book would never have happened. My thanks also to the cast of the Riverside Players' premiere production for having such faith in the story.

CHAPTER ONE

As she surveyed the royal banquet from her high vantage point in the Minstrel's Gallery, Justine Parker twisted slightly to get more comfortable in the tight bodice of her gown.

All things considered, the banquet was going pretty well.

An army of servants had brought exotic dishes up from the kitchens into the Great Hall and presented them to the assembled ladies, gentlemen, knights and courtiers for their appreciation and amazement.

There were dishes such as the noble roast peacock with its plumage dancing in the light, guinea fowl in a deep crusty pie and legs of mutton surrounded by mountains of peas and carrots. Fine red claret was drunk copiously from silver goblets, with the servants replenishing them from silver pitchers as they weaved around the tables.

Justine leaned on the railing of the gallery and let the warm sound of conversation and laughter wash over her; the rich hubbub of noise that rose up to the furthest corners of the magnificent ornate plaster roof. Down below her, the face of every guest was bright with enjoyment, bathed in the golden glow of a thousand flickering candles.

In the middle of the high table, Her Majesty Queen Elizabeth sat bolt upright, her bright eyes dancing round the room as the courtier to her right engaged her in conversation.

Justine admired her pale beauty, set off by her striking bodice of red velvet edged with gold lace and sparkling with a thousand shimmering pearls, together with the single flashing emerald at her neck that brought out the green fire in her eyes. Then there was her red-bronze hair adorned with its simple, elegant gold crown, framed by the high pearl-edged lace ruff that flared up from her shoulders.

With a small raise of her hand, the Queen paused the conversation with the courtier beside her and looked up at the gallery. Maybe Justine's small twisting movement had caught her eye. She held Justine's gaze a moment, then gave the smallest nod of her head – so small that it could easily have been missed – as if to congratulate Justine on the success of the banquet she had organised.

With a smile Justine bowed her own head and gave a gentle curtsey. The Queen nodded again, then turned back to the courtier and resumed their conversation.

In the gallery Justine smiled again, this time to herself.

Yes, all things considered, the banquet was going pretty well.

She looked down across the room, taking in the full scene. The long high table ran along the back wall under the big windows with the Queen in the centre. On either side Justine had seated her most important courtiers, looking resplendent in their richly-coloured silk doublets with slashed sleeves and fine white ruffs. Beyond the courtiers she had seated the women, elegant in their low-cut gowns, their hair carefully parted in the centre and tucked under their French hoods – a style introduced originally by Elizabeth's mother, Anne Boleyn.

Justine's gaze moved to the table down the left side of the room. The people here were less important and their clothes reflected this – the men wore plain doublets and the women wore their hair in simple cotton coifs rather than the more elaborate French hoods of the high table. Their behaviour was no less exuberant, if anything slightly more so, and Justine smiled as they all laughed at a joke from the jester who had been moving round the tables. His brightly-coloured motley costume consisted of a tunic split into a red half and a yellow half, while his hose had one red leg and one yellow leg on the opposite sides. In his hand was a small jester head on a stick, which he was using to entertain the guests.

From behind her came the sound of the minstrels; four elderly men with lutes playing light-hearted music that was all but lost against the loud noise of the room. Their piece came to an end, and she turned to them.

"You play well, good sirs," she said with a twinkling smile. "What is next?"

"We have not yet played Greensleeves," said the eldest minstrel. "But first we need a drink." All four reached down for the tankards by their stools and drained them with great satisfaction. The oldest man then examined the bottom of his empty tankard and looked up at Justine expectantly. She laughed and reached for the large pewter jug ready by her feet, then went to each in turn, pouring more beer into their proffered tankards.

"Ahh, thank you my girl," said the oldest man, "it is always a pleasure to play at one of your banquets."

Justine curtseyed in reply. The men drank some more, then put down their tankards and launched into Greensleeves.

She turned and resumed her gaze across the Great Hall.

To her right was a smaller table seating more people, with a carving table beside it. On the wall above was a large portrait of a handsome knight in a shining breastplate standing with a white stag in the background. Her gaze stopped on this portrait, as it so often did, and she gave a small sigh as she studied the man's long blond hair and trim beard.

The jester turned from the table he'd been entertaining and looked up, catching sight of Justine as she stared across at the portrait.

His gaze took in her shoulder-length cascade of russet-coloured ringlets trying to escape from under her French hood; her small, slightly snub nose, her pale blue eyes under thick, dark eyebrows staring with a faraway look at the portrait…

He gave a little dance and waved his stick to catch her eye.

She spotted him and gave a small wave back. He raised an enquiring eyebrow, then flicked the stick up behind his back so the little jester head on the end popped up on his shoulder.

He turned to it and appeared to have a brief conversation, then pointed up at her. The little head on his shoulder nodded. He made a 'doe-eyed' face – a gross over-exaggeration of hers, with a sickly grin and fluttering eyelashes – then pointed back at her. The head nodded again, then both the jester and the head turned to look up at her, with the jester smiling broadly.

She couldn't help but laugh and he laughed back. Then he gave a low courtly bow, while she applauded.

The jester turned back to the room and started dancing sideways up towards the high table.

Still chuckling, Justine's gaze moved upwards to the large tapestries depicting heroic scenes of hunts that were hanging round the hall between the sconces. In one scene knights attacked a stag with spears and arrows in a green forest; in another a different stag was running from a pack of baying hounds, followed by nobles on horses.

Justine looked back down at the hall. The servants had cleared the main courses away and were now circulating with bowls of fruit and more wine.

'Only an hour more and we'll be cleared and finished,' she thought, as she twisted once more in the tight bodice of her gown.

Just then she became aware of an insistent beeping sound over the noise of the room. Fishing her mobile from the pocket of her gown, she swiped the screen.

"Hello, Justine Parker here."

"The taxis have started arriving," said a voice. "They're early."

"Oh, bother. I put half-eleven on the schedule." She nudged up the end of her lace sleeve with her elbow, to reveal her watch. "It's only eleven fifteen. We've just served the fruit. Would you be a sweetie and tell them they'll have to wait?"

"OK."

"And please can you tell them to turn their meters off. I don't want one of their silly waiting charges when it's all their fault." Justine thought a moment. "It is their fault, isn't it? Oh bother and blast it, it had better be. I'll check the email I sent them. Can you be an absolute poppet and bluff it out or something?"

"Sure, no problem."

Justine tapped the email app on her phone and scrolled through to find the relevant message. There it was – 'please make sure the taxis arrive at 11:30pm'.

Tucking her mobile back into her pocket with a satisfied smile, Justine looked back down at the hall.

The Queen was dispensing her wisdom to the courtiers on either side, who were hanging on her every word and laughing sycophantically, even though Justine didn't think the Queen was actually trying to be funny.

Justine sighed deeply. For all that she liked to pretend to herself that events such as this were real, in truth this was just a modern-day re-enactment of a Tudor banquet. The setting was real enough – the magnificent Grangedean Manor genuinely dated back to the late 1400s – but now it was a National Trust property, purposefully restored to its Tudor period as a 'living museum'.

The costumes were all hired from the special fancy dress store in the old stables, and were held together with Velcro and poppers, not laced and tied as they should have been. They were a modern-day approximation of the Tudor costume; made for ease of putting on, not authenticity.

The dishes that had been served for the meal were cooked in a modern-day kitchen set up to standards demanded by the environmental health officer, and while the dishes were close enough to the Tudor recipes, the reality was that they were only interpretations for 21st century tastes. Even the peacock had really been a pheasant in disguise.

The 'courtiers' were the CEO and Board of an American corporate with offices in the UK, while the other guests were members of their teams. They had signed up for the Genuine Tudor Banquet Experience at Grangedean Manor – Complete with Her Majesty Queen Elizabeth I and as the events manager, Justine had been determined to give them their money's worth.

Looking down at the glow of the candles on the bright, happy faces, she thought she'd done OK.

She had wanted to welcome them on arrival with a full tour of the magnificent 15th century manor house and grounds, so a week before she had sought out Mrs Warburton, National Trust volunteer tour guide and retired schoolteacher, whose knowledge of Grangedean Manor was encyclopaedic and whose no-nonsense disciplined approach meant she could be relied upon to keep control of such a large party.

Justine had found Mrs. Warburton in the Master Bedroom; she was a tall, ramrod-straight woman with iron-grey hair wearing a tweed twinset that looked like it was straight out of the 1950s. She was in the middle of explaining to a family how Tudor people managed their clothing.

"Clothes were kept in wooden chests like these," she was saying, "rather than hanging in wardrobes like we do now."

"They couldn't have got much in there," said the mother, looking dubiously at the metal-bound oak chest at the end of the bed. It was about five feet long by three feet high and three feet wide.

"There may have been more than one chest in a bedroom, particularly for the nobility like Sir William de Beauvais, who owned the manor in the 1560s," explained Mrs. Warburton. "But the truth is they didn't have anywhere near as many clothes as we do now, and only really changed their underclothes to keep clean. Sometimes all they did was unlace the sleeves on their outfit and lace on new ones."

"Ugh!" exclaimed the daughter, who looked about fourteen. "Didn't they smell rank?"

"Very possibly," said Mrs. Warburton matter-of-factly, "but that would have been the same for most. Certainly the poorer people."

"So didn't they, like, have baths and stuff?" asked the girl incredulously.

"Occasionally, but only the nobility. A copper or wooden tub would be brought into the bedroom and filled with water heated on the fire. Herbs would be sprinkled on the water to make it smell good, and soap for the rich would be made with olive oil. The poor – they would wash in a stream or with a bucket of water and soap made of animal fat."

"Eww, gross," said the girl.

Justine couldn't let this go unchallenged. "No, no, no!" she interjected, her eyes shining brightly. "The Tudors were absolutely wonderful people!"

The family and Mrs. Warburton all turned to look at her in surprise.

"Sorry to butt in, Mrs. Warburton," she went on, "but I wouldn't want this young lady to think the Tudors were ghastly at all. Imagine you were in Tudor times," she said brightly. "There would be lots of dancing, great banquets that lasted for hours, riding in the park and handsome young men just itching to go out with you! It would be such fun!"

"Suppose," said the girl, not looking convinced.

"And beautiful gowns to wear and jewellery and dainty shoes…"

Just then the girl's father intervened. Casting concerned glances at Justine, he said, "Come, Shaz, time to go, I think."

The girl Shaz said, "But didn't they, like…?" then caught the expression on her father's face, and shut her mouth. The family shuffled quickly out, leaving Justine alone with Mrs. Warburton.

"You are very enthusiastic, my dear," observed the older lady drily. "Maybe just a little too much, perhaps? Although I am not sure that the girl,

Shaz, wasn't starting to become just a tiny bit more interested in the Tudors."

Justine laughed. "Maybe. Maybe not. But Grangedean Manor can have that effect, can't it?"

Mrs. Warburton thought about this a moment, her hands clasped together and her lips pursed. "Yes, it can. It can certainly make you feel like the Tudors are alive, and may come through a door at any moment. But only if you're that kind of person. I am not sure that Shaz was really that kind of person." She smiled. "Anyway. Did you want me, Miss Parker?"

"Oh yes," said Justine, "Yes, yes, I did. In fact, you're absolutely the very person I wanted. I have a large party of Americans coming next Thursday for a banquet, and I would really love it if you could very kindly show them round before we get them changed into their Tudor outfits?" Justine smiled warmly. "I am sure you'll be absolutely brilliant at keeping them together and giving them a really wonderful tour. There's no one who knows more about Grangedean Manor than you."

"I suspect you actually know at least as much as I do, Miss Parker," observed Mrs. Warburton with just a hint of amusement in her voice. "But no matter. Of course I'll show them round."

"That's great! Great! Thanks!" said Justine happily. "I'm putting the schedule together and I'll email it to you later."

"I don't really look at emails," said Mrs. Warburton. "Can you not print it out for me?"

"Yes, of course," said Justine. Then she added, "But you really should use emails – they're so easy." She held up her phone. "I get them on my PC and on this phone, so I have them wherever I go."

"I am sure that works well for you, but I prefer the old fashioned methods of communication," observed Mrs. Warburton, "such as writing," she shook her head, "and talking."

"Ahh, but this talks as well," said Justine opening up the battered cover protecting her phone.

"It is a phone, so I suppose it does. Although it is actually the other person that does the talking, is it not?"

"No, no, it's the phone," Justine insisted. She tapped to open an app and held up the screen for Mrs. Warburton to peer at vaguely. "It actually talks if you want it to! It's brilliant! You can type text into this special app, then tap on a button here and it says what you've written. You can choose what voice you want it to talk in, as well. Look…" She quickly typed and tapped the screen. The phone said, "Hello, Missus Warburton." It was slightly robotic, but reasonably clear. Justine looked at the older lady in triumph, challenging her not to be impressed.

"What will they think of next?" said Mrs. Warburton politely.

Justine closed her phone cover and dropped it back in her pocket. "Anyway, I must be getting on. Thanks, Mrs. Warburton. I'll send you the schedule for next week." She turned to leave.

"Miss Parker," Mrs Warburton stopped her. "These Americans. Is there anything particular" – she emphasised the 'tic' in the middle – "that they want to see?"

Justine considered. "No – the standard tour should be fine. The CEO told me in one of his emails, that he wants to 'absorb all your English history'."

"He sounds fascinating. I very much look forward to meeting him."

"Me too," said Justine, brightly. "Me too!"

CHAPTER TWO

It was the following Thursday afternoon; Justine and Mrs Warburton were in the Great Hall, having greeted the corporate guests on their arrival.

The CEO stood in the middle of the hall, his hands thrust deep into the pockets of his jeans as he looked around him. He looked in his mid-forties, tall with short grey hair and small round glasses. His gaze stopped on the picture of the blond knight with the white stag.

"Who's that guy?" he asked

"That's Sir William de Beauvais, the owner of Grangedean Manor in the 1560s," said Justine. "A very interesting man indeed."

"Why so?"

"He never married for starters," she answered, "which was very unusual in those days."

"The guy was gay?"

"That's very unlikely," she said defensively. "In fact it is rumoured that he was very much the ladies' man and had many lovers."

The CEO studied Sir William's portrait. "Certainly looks gay," he observed. "Long blond hair and little beard..."

"No, no!" said Justine indignantly. "Of course, he was very handsome and apparently quite charming, but he was also rumoured to be a strong, rugged fighting man. In fact," she continued, as the CEO glanced at her with a raised eyebrow, "he actually died in a fight on the 31st July 1565, when he was only in his late 20s."

"Hence he never married."

"Exactly."

"Hmm." The CEO studied Sir William again. "How'd he die?"

Mrs. Warburton answered, "It is said he was stabbed in a brawl in a tavern."

"Over a woman?"

"We don't know," said Justine, "but maybe it was. Wouldn't that be just so romantic?"

"Waste of a young guy," said the CEO. "Think what he could have achieved if he'd lived a longer life."

"Oh yes," breathed Justine. "Such a waste."

The CEO chuckled and leaned in conspiratorially to Mrs. Warburton. "The kid's sweet on the dead guy," he said, then turned and moved on.

It was deliberately loud enough for Justine to hear and she felt her face flushing red as she stood rooted to the spot. What a strange idea – how could he possibly think she had anything other than purely historical interest in Sir William de Beauvais? She shook her head to clear the thought, then trotted after the CEO and Mrs. Warburton.

He was walking briskly; his Converse sneakers squeaking on the flagstones as he stared intently at each of the tapestries and the leaded windows in turn.

"Place like this has gotta be haunted?" he demanded.

"Certainly not," said Mrs. Warburton sharply. "Why does everyone assume old houses like this are always haunted? There are no spirits here apart from the spirit of history," she paused, "and the whisky in the private wing, of course." The CEO was sharp enough to recognise that this was meant as a joke and gave a polite laugh. "Sure. Whisky in the private wing. Cool. Yeah."

He turned to Justine. "Right," he said briskly, "let's get this Tudor show on the road. What's first on the agenda?"

Justine took out her phone and opened the notes app. "Mrs. Warburton will take you all around the manor for the full tour. She will finish in the tea rooms so you can grab a cup of tea and some scones, before I take you over to the stable block where we'll fit you into your Tudor costumes."

"Tea and scones?" asked the CEO. "How quaintly English. Do they do coffee and cookies there for us Yanks?"

"Of course," said Justine, trying to ignore Mrs. Warburton's derisive snort behind her. "And they do lovely cakes and tarts as well." She consulted her phone again. "After tea, we have archery, jousting, falconry and sword-fighting, then into the Great Hall for the Royal Banquet at 7pm. Taxis are at 11:30pm." She put her phone back in her pocket. "A full afternoon and evening living the life of the Tudors. Won't that be such great fun?"

---0---

And now it was nearly 11:30pm; the banquet was all but over and the taxis were ready to take the guests away.

Justine stood up from leaning on the gallery balcony and decided to pop down and see if all was well in the kitchens.

She turned and ducked through a low doorway and went down the short stairway into the hall. Then she went through another door and took the final flight of stone stairs down to the kitchens.

As she ran lightly down the stairs she marvelled as always at the sophistication of the Tudor builders who had constructed the magnificent Grangedean Manor over 500 years ago. Every stone fitted together perfectly and such was its quality that even after all this time and use there was only an inch or two of wear on each step. The wood panelling in the private rooms was still in excellent shape, and only in the Great Hall had there been any real renovation – mainly to correct some disastrous redecoration done by the Victorians.

Months of painstaking work had been undertaken under the watchful eye of the National Trust. They were keen to ensure that every detail was correct, even down to the position of the sconces on the wall – although these now had electric bulbs and silk 'flames' rather than actual candles due to health and safety concerns.

Arriving in the kitchens, Justine soon located Rick, the manager from the contract catering company that provided food for the banquets, as well as the lunches and teas for the day trippers in the canteen and tea rooms. He was an unshaven man in his late thirties, with dark spiky hair and large tattoos on both arms; a Colt 45 on the left arm and a pair of crossed hunting rifles on the right. Justine had never made a secret of her dislike of these tattoos, which she thought were unnecessarily aggressive.

"How's it going?" Justine asked neutrally.

"OK," he replied. "The fruit is out but they're hardly touching it. We're going to start clearing the tables now." He shrugged. "Serve them up effing burger and fries and they'd find room, believe me." Behind him a line of serving staff was forming to go out into the hall, all dressed as Tudor servants in smocks bearing the Grangedean Manor coat of arms. "OK, you lot," he barked as they moved past him and started up the stairs to the hall, "get out there and clear the effing tables."

Justine watched them go past. "This lot are quite good. Where d'you get them?"

"Acting school in West London graduated a couple of weeks ago," he answered. "I put a notice up on the board and got the pick of the effing bunch." His gaze lingered on the bottom of the last girl going past. "They were pathetically grateful for any job – especially one where they get to wear a costume."

Justine bit her lip to stop herself being provoked by his typically crass comment. She would be professional, she told herself. She would not let him get to her.

"Talking of actresses, the one playing the Queen has been a perfect darling," she said to change the subject. "Much better than the last one we tried. I'll have a word with her agent tomorrow and see if we can get her again. She's had the CEO eating out of the palm of her hand."

"Too bad they don't eat the effing food as well," muttered Rick.

"Rick, my sweet," said Justine with a forced smile, "they're here to make believe that this is a real Tudor banquet. We put them in Tudor clothes, we pretend the Queen is here and we serve them up the closest thing we can to Tudor food. We try and make it as lovely as we can for them, so they think it is real."

"Yeah. But if this was a real Tudor banquet, Justine, my hopeless little romantic, there'd be more meat than they could possibly stomach; whole deer, hares, pigs, rabbits, stuffed partridges – and that's just for starters. There'd be sugared fruits and marzipan, plums stewed in rose-water – all washed down with a thin ale for the riff-raff because the water was undrinkable, and wine for the nobles. Believe me, if we served them that lot we'd be seriously out of pocket and they'd be as sick as pigs."

"Oh for goodness sake, Rick, don't be such a party pooper," she snapped. She took a breath to steady herself, unsure as to whether she was annoyed with him for being a jerk, or for trying to out-do her on knowledge of the Tudors. "They have a lovely time and that's all that matters," she finished lamely.

"Yeah, well enough," he muttered with a small triumphant grin, then turned away as the first of the Tudor servants started coming back down into the kitchens with the plates.

Still annoyed with herself, Justine went to go back up the narrow stairs to the hall, but first she had to wait for one of the servants to come down carrying a big stack of pewter plates. The serving girl smiled as she went past and said "thanks", but then completely missed her footing on the bottom step; falling headlong and throwing all her plates into the air like an acrobat tossing a fellow performer up to a trapeze.

The plates and cutlery came tumbling down to the flagstone floor in a series of ear-splitting crashes, closely followed by the girl herself. Leftover food was splattered across the stainless steel units; while plates and cutlery spun off in all directions across the kitchens.

Everyone stopped what they were doing and turned to stare. One last plate rolled unsteadily across the flagstones with an unnaturally loud trundling noise, then slowed and toppled over like a drunk, flopping noisily around on its rim a couple of times before coming to rest.

There was a moment's shocked silence.

Then Rick barked out, "Oh effing, effing hell! What the frigging heck was that?"

The girl got up painfully. Justine caught a glimpse of blood on her leg before she smoothed her skirts down. "Sorry, Rick," the girl muttered.

"Sorry?" he said grimly. "Sorry? You'll be effing sorry if you don't clear up that effing mess. You'll be out on your effing ear!"

"Sorry," the girl repeated, and limped forward to pick up the first plate.

"Oh for goodness sake, Rick, that was totally and utterly uncalled for," Justine snapped, "now you've gone too far!" She rushed forward and started picking up plates as well. "It was only an accident!"

"Yeah, right…" Rick snapped back, "and it has to be effing cleared up!"

"You don't need to be such a pig about it." Justine grabbed a cloth and started wiping splattered food off the units. "Why do you always have to be so bolshie?" she hissed at him when she went to the sink to rinse it out.

Rick looked the anger flashing in her eyes. Some of the fight went out of him.

"Yeah. Well, sorry."

"Don't apologise to me," growled Justine. "Apologise to her."

"Yeah, whatever."

"I mean it, Rick. Now!"

Rick went over to the girl, who was standing alone in the centre of the kitchen, clutching some plates and quivering like a hunted stag.

"Sorry," he muttered.

"S'all right," she whispered.

Normal activity and noise levels were resumed in the kitchens. Justine went over to the girl.

"Thanks," the girl said quietly as she put the plates on the worktop.

"It wasn't your fault," said Justine, her voice equally low.

"I'm just a bit clumsy, that's all," the girl said, wincing as she shifted the weight on her leg.

"What's your name?"

"Rachael."

"Well, Rachael," said Justine, putting her hand on the girl's shoulder "I should get that leg bandaged up if I were you. Why don't you pop upstairs to the first aid cupboard? I'll meet you there in five minutes and see what I can do."

---0---

It was after one in the morning when Justine finally got out into the cold night air and made her way across the gravel at the rear of the manor, past the ancient well to where her battered little Ford was standing alone and forlorn in the staff car park. Its windows were misted white in the light of the modern overhead lamps.

She got in and started the car, put the demist on full blast to clear the windows then settled down for the usual long wait until they were clear enough to drive.

Often she would find herself falling asleep, but on this night, she took out her phone and flicked open its case. Scrolling through the screens of apps, she got to the book-reader app and tapped it. It opened where she'd last left off in one of her favourite books – a series of adventures featuring a courageous Tudor heroine called Mary Fox. This book was Mary Fox and the Broken Sword; the first in the series.

"Where was I…?" she muttered to herself. She scanned the first few lines of the chapter. The story quickly came back; Mary Fox has just escaped from the wicked Sir Reginald de Courtney and his henchmen once again…

She settled back in her seat to read, and was quickly absorbed in the story.

She had first come across the series of Mary Fox adventures in the Grangedean library, when she had been exploring the house by herself one summer's evening after work. The library was a lovely peaceful room with a central stone fireplace, which had oak panelling above and barley-twist columns supporting the great mantelpiece. Either side of the fireplace were two large alcoves, each with a gothic arch reaching right up to the white plaster ceiling, and each featuring a richly-decorated oak bookcase with shelves above a cabinet base.

Justine was fascinated by the rows and rows of beautiful leather-bound books, with their musty but evocative smell. There were complete sets of Shakespeare's plays, as well as the works of Jane Austen, Charles Dickens and George Eliot. She selected Middlemarch by George Eliot and opened it to read a random page. She quickly decided that Dorothea Brooke seemed a bit too worthy to hold her interest, so she put the book back. Idly she bent down and opened one of the cabinets. Inside were more books, but these were modern paperbacks. Justine crouched down level with the books for a closer look. Immediately she spotted a series of matching paperbacks with gold leaf titles in a mediaeval typeface. She twisted her head to one side to read them. Mary Fox and the River of Fire. Mary Fox and the Broken Sword. Mary Fox and the Tudor Prince. Fascinated, Justine pulled out the first book – The Broken Sword. She read the blurb on the back. It promised adventure, romance and intrigue, all in a Tudor period setting, with an all-action heroine called Mary Fox who had perilous challenges to face, a curse to defeat and a man's heart to win.

Walking over to a high-backed armchair by the window, Justine sat down, opened the book and started to read.

Two hours later, she finished the last page, closed the book slowly and sat back with a deep sigh. Never before had she read a book that had so completely absorbed her; so completely immersed her in its world, its plot and its characters. Mary Fox was the perfect heroine – idealistic, honest, clever, resourceful and never afraid to fight for what she thought was right. She also had a wide romantic streak – and her honesty, courage and integrity meant she had won the heart of the young man by the end of the book.

Justine then borrowed and read each of the books several times, before deciding that she wanted her own personal copies. She downloaded them all onto her phone so she could dip into any of them whenever she had a few minutes to spare.

Justine glanced up from her phone and saw that the windscreen had now fully cleared. With a small sigh she bade farewell to Mary, switched off her phone and dropped it back in her bag. Then she let out the clutch and the little car juddered forward out of the Grangedean Manor car park.

It was the darkest part of the night with not a star in the sky, or another car on the road, and soon Justine's headlights swept around the corner of her block of flats in Hammersmith, West London, before she parked in her designated space.

She got out and locked the car, then let herself into the flat, kicked off her shoes and changed into an old t-shirt. She padded into the kitchen and opened the fridge door, then peered in for half a minute without being really aware of what she was looking for.

With a grunt of annoyance at herself, she closed the fridge, went to her room and climbed into bed.

Lying on her back, she chuckled drowsily as she remembered the words of the CEO before getting into his taxi to go home.

"Good job, Justine," he had said. "The team bonded well, and having the Queen was a great piece of theatre. Only thing…" he had looked her squarely in the eye "…not sure about the food. A bit rich, even for us Yanks. I don't suppose next time you could bend history a bit and lay on some burger and fries?"

CHAPTER THREE

Justine's drive from her flat in Hammersmith back to Grangedean Manor the next morning was considerably slower in the busy traffic, until she got to the leafy lanes of the countryside. The sun shone weakly overhead, but out to the west she could see an ominous dark grey storm cloud approaching.

She turned into the car park and slowed to drive round the large ancient well before parking.

Seeing it brought back memories of the day she had first driven into the Grangedean Manor car park for her job interview a year before. She'd been working as an events manager for a corporate hospitality firm, organising events like lunches at Ascot and Henley – but she'd been feeling more and more disillusioned with these. Where was the satisfaction in delivering yet more smoked salmon to hordes of racegoers? How could she possibly get excited about catering to people who were really there just to 'see and be seen'? There must be more interesting events to organise, she had thought – a chance to create something with passion, something that people would remember for years to come. So when she saw the advert for the job of events manager at Grangedean Manor, she'd applied straight away.

On the morning of the interview, the ancient well had fascinated her as she had driven in, optimistically choosing the car park marked 'Staff'.

Once she'd parked, she walked up onto the raised dais to get a closer look. The well was built of thin red bricks that were worn down through years of weathering. Above it was a pitched roof finished with orange clay tiles, supported by two thick wooden struts. It stood on a raised dais that ran all the way round, lifting it up above the main cobbled car park.

She ran her hand over the worn bricks, wondering how many different people had done just that over the centuries. What had happened here – was it like a Tudor 'water cooler' where people would meet and gossip? What stories could this humble brick, wood and clay structure tell? What dramas had taken place beside it; what events had it witnessed?

She peered over the edge. There was a wooden board set a couple of feet below the lip, capping off the void below. She leaned over and tapped it curiously. There was a hollow, echoing sound that suggested great depth underneath.

Suddenly a wave of dizziness swept over her and she felt as if she was tipping forward into the well. Then it seemed like the wooden board had disappeared and all she could see below her was a dreadful blackness, rising up to swallow her. In terror she scrabbled at the sides and after a moment, managed to get a grip. With an effort she pushed herself back upright.

As she stood up, breathing hard, she looked back down at the well.

The wooden board was firmly in place – very solid and very real. There was no black void and she could never have been in any actual danger.

"Are you all right?"

She turned to see a tall, iron-haired lady in a tweed skirt and sensible brogues striding towards her across the courtyard.

"Yes, yes I'm fine," she said, glancing back into the well. The board was still there. Still solid. She took a deep breath and smiled. "Just a dizzy turn." She stepped down from the dais.

"This is the staff car park," said the lady, sounding as if she was trying to be helpful but betraying annoyance with her sharp tone. "The public car park is round the corner and on the other side of the cedars." She pointed across towards the exit.

"I'm actually here for an interview – for events manager."

"Oh, right. I see." The lady paused, looking Justine up and down, and seemed to soften. "Are you really all right? You look green."

"Really, I'm fine."

The lady shook her head. "Well, you don't look it. Quite green. Come into the house and we'll find you some water."

Justine suddenly felt very thirsty. "OK, thanks," she said.

"And I'll show you where to go. Is it Susan Holmes you're seeing? The general manager?"

"Yes."

"Right. Come on then." The lady turned and strode across the car park towards the house. "Mrs. Warburton," she said suddenly over her shoulder.

"I beg your pardon?"

"My name. Mrs. Warburton."

"Oh. Right. Justine. Justine Parker."

Mrs. Warburton stopped and turned, then shook Justine by the hand. Her handshake was very firm.

18

"Pleased to meet you, Miss Parker."

"And you, Mrs. Warburton," answered Justine, trying to restore feeling in her hand by flexing her fingers rapidly.

A few moments later Mrs. Warburton led Justine up a few steps through the front door and into the main entrance of the house.

Justine caught her breath as she took in the scene. They were in an imposing hallway with a single wooden staircase leading up to a gallery corridor. The wood of the banister finials and gallery vault posts was a fine dark oak, turned in a barley-twist style. The stair treads were also oak, with only the slightest wear in the centre of each tread. At the back of the hallway under the gallery was a hanging tapestry showing a hunting scene and next to it was a burnished suit of amour by a pair of imposing double doors.

"What a magnificent, lovely place," Justine whispered, letting her gaze move slowly up the stairs and onto the gallery. "So romantic."

As she looked around, she felt the house work its magic on her – she felt that this house belonged in the past, not the present. Its true reality was the golden age of the Tudors; an age of chivalrous men and romantic women, of intrigue and love, of beautiful clothes and fine foods. An age when the concerns of modern life – of mobile phones, traffic, televisions and social media – didn't matter anymore; when all that mattered was romance and a love of life. In this reality there were no electric bulbs lighting the hallway, the suit of armour was for battle not display, the tread on the stairs was new and there were no information leaflets on display for tourists...

What this reality needed was a romantic love scene.

Justine gazed up at the gallery. In this scene a beautiful girl in a narrow-waisted gown would open the door and step serenely onto the gallery. Justine half-closed her eyes and let several hundred years roll away. In the bright sunlight of a fresh Tudor morning, she imagined such a girl appearing.

Justine admired the elegant simplicity of the girl's green velvet gown with its lace trimmings at the sleeves, the wide neckline with a single pearl on a chain, the fine jeweled velvet French hood that framed her face, as she swept effortlessly to the top of the stairs and seemed to glide down. As she did so a tall, handsome man with curly blond hair and a trim beard stepped out to receive her. He gave a low bow. Justine admired his fine doublet, the deep slashes over red velvet in his breeches and sleeves, the grey hose and soft leather boots. He had a sword hanging from his left hip and a red silk cape on his shoulder.

Justine held her breath as the girl gazed into the man's eyes, then looked down demurely and curtseyed low. The girl held out her hand and he took it, brought it to his lips and kissed it gently as he raised her up. She lifted her eyes and smiled at him, a look of deep love that Justine knew was forever. The girl took the man's arm and swept her away through the double doors.

Justine sighed deeply.

"It's beautiful," she said. "I love it."

"Indeed," said Mrs. Warburton matter-of-factly. "Fascinating people, the Tudors." She pointed at the double doors. "You go through to the Great Hall while I'll get you some water." She marched off across the hall and disappeared through a side door.

Justine picked up a leaflet from a rack. 'Grangedean Manor was built in 1498 by a wealthy landowner called Sir Thomas de Beauvais and extended in 1560 when his grandson Sir William inherited it,' she read. 'The house has twelve bedrooms, a great hall, extensive kitchens and has its own chapel. Much of the original Tudor décor is still intact, and, while not on the scale of Tudor houses such as Burghley or Hatfield, Grangedean represents a significant historical insight into the lives of Tudor nobility. It is understood that Shakespeare stayed here in 1594 and that Charles I stopped here during the Civil War.'

Justine walked through into the Great Hall.

If the entrance had been beautiful, then this place was doubly magnificent. Light burst in through the leaded panes of square, clear glass in three main windows. The central window was a gothic arch that ran right up to the ornate plaster-decorated ceiling, and the two side windows each reached to about three quarters of its height.

Justine looked up and saw that she was standing under a minstrels' gallery. A large portrait of a Tudor knight caught her eye. He was wearing a burnished silver breastplate and was holding his sword up in his right hand. There was a noble-looking white stag standing behind him.

Justine moved closer to look at this man.

Suddenly she caught her breath. There was no mistaking the blond hair and beard – he was absolutely the romantic hero she'd imagined in the hallway…

"Sir William de Beauvais," said Mrs. Warburton from behind her. "Born 1539, died on the night of the 31st of July 1565; stabbed while in a tavern. He was reputed to be something of a wild man." Mrs. Warburton held out a glass. "Your water."

Suddenly the peace was broken by the sound of loud voices, the squeak of trainers on the flagstones and the clicking of smartphone cameras. Justine took the water, then turned and saw a party of tourists being led in by a woman in her mid-thirties with blond highlights. The woman was talking to the group.

"This is the Great Hall. Come on, everyone in? Good. The great hall was the heart of a Tudor manor and would have been used for banquets, dancing and entertaining. The painting on the wall is of Sir William de Beauvais, the squire who owned the house in the 1560s. The hall is undergoing restoration work to bring it to exactly how we believe it would have looked to Sir William. Except, of course, the electric light there," the woman pointed at the sconces, "would have been real candles."

There were appreciative noises from the tourists as they gazed around the hall. One of them walked to the wall for a closer look at some restoration work on the plaster mouldings.

"We frequently hold Tudor banquets ourselves, with authentic costumes, food and entertainment," continued the woman. "Very popular in the corporate entertainment market. If anyone is interested, I can let you have a leaflet on the way out."

She turned and noticed Justine and Mrs. Warburton. "Justine Parker? Here for the interview?"

"Yes."

"Good. This is the last room we're doing. I'll see you in my office in a few minutes; just to the right of the front door. Has Mrs. Warburton been giving you the tour?"

"Yes," said Justine, wondering if Mrs. Warburton actually had a first name.

"Good." She moved to the other end of the hall with her party and started telling them about the decorative plaster work above the large ornate fireplace, before leading them back out into the hallway. She could be heard saying goodbye to them, then a door closed and there was silence.

"I think that's your cue to go in for the interview," observed Mrs. Warburton.

"Yes," said Justine. "Thanks for the tour. The house is so lovely."

"Indeed it is," agreed Mrs. Warburton. Together they went back to the entrance hall, where Mrs. Warburton pointed to a door marked 'Office'. Justine took a deep breath to steady her nerves, and knocked.

"Come."

She pushed open the door and went in. The blond woman was sitting behind an antique oak desk holding Justine's CV. She gestured to the chair opposite.

"Hello. I'm Susan – general manager at Grangedean Manor," she said when Justine was seated.

"Hello."

"Look, I've read your CV – looks fine. Events co-ordinator at university, events administrator at your last place, promoted to events manager – blah blah blah. Fine. Just fine." She tapped the CV on the table a couple of times, as if considering her options, then deliberately put it face down on the table. "But I'm not interested in that – I'm much more interested in you, Justine – you as a person."

"Oh, right. OK." This was not how she expected the interview to start.

Or any interview, for that matter.

"I have one question. What is it about Grangedean Manor that appeals to you, and why?"

Fighting down the instinct to point out that that was two questions, Justine thought a moment and said: "My previous job was all about money. Events were purely about the numbers – numbers of people through the door, numbers of pounds profit made. And while I know that's important, for me it's about the event itself. Here at Grangedean Manor you can give people a taste of what it must have been like in historical times. I want to be able to make history come alive for them – that's really special." Justine's eyes sparkled as she went on, "Grangedean Manor is such a fantastic place – I mean, when the restoration is complete, we will be able to see the house just as people like Sir William de Beauvais would have seen it. How amazing is that? To look at a wall, or a window, or a fireplace, and to know that people 450 years ago would have seen just the same thing – it's like they just walked out the room and will walk back in any moment!" She stopped. Susan was looking at her with a quizzical expression. "Sorry – got a bit carried away there. Yeah – it's a lovely house. I'd love to work here…" she tailed off.

Susan carried on looking quizzically at her.

Justine thought she must have blown it.

"I see… When can you start?"

CHAPTER FOUR

It was 6 o'clock in the evening, the day after the big banquet. Justine had now been working at Grangedean Manor for over a year.

She finished some last emails and switched off her PC. The storm which had been threatening all day had now finally arrived. The rain was lashing down, with frequent rumbles of thunder and flashes of lightning that seared across the office with harsh white light.

She grabbed her bag, unplugged her phone from its charging cable and threw it in. She then grabbed her Bluetooth portable speaker and threw that in as well – she liked to have it filling her kitchen with its loud, pure sound while she was cooking and had even been known to do some serious karaoke, dancing round using her wooden spoon as a microphone.

The joys of living alone.

Something caught her eye in her bag and curiously she fished it out. It was an unopened box containing a solar charger for her phone and speaker. For a moment she couldn't think how it had got in her bag, then she recalled buying it on a whim when she'd last been in the phone shop – attracted by the thought of being able to charge her batteries even if there wasn't a plug handy. With a shrug she tossed it back in her bag and left her office.

She made her way towards the kitchens, with the sound of thunder echoing along the long basement corridor, then climbed the steps and went through the door into the Great Hall. Out of the windows she could see the sky was so dark it was almost as if it was a winter's night, as sheets of rain battered the ancient leaded windows.

A few of the electric candle lights were on in the Great Hall, and Justine's eye caught the picture of Sir William on the wall. As usual, she walked over and gazed up at the portrait. As she did so a flash of lightning lit up the room with a burning intensity that seared a negative of the painting into her brain. Immediately afterwards, there was a deep blast of thunder that made the windows shake and the whole room resonate like a giant drum.

At the same moment, the lights went out.

With the image of the picture dancing in front of her unseeing eyes, she turned and made her way by feel and force of habit to the main doors, as another roar of thunder shook the room and a searing flash of lighting lit it up as if it were broad daylight. She reached the main double doors and pulled – but they remained stuck. Starting to feel scared, she pulled again and again, as yet another flash of lightning illuminated the room, followed by another crash of thunder. This one was so loud, that Justine thought her ears had burst. Now screaming, she pulled at the door again, but it remained stuck firm. She pummelled on it, shouting, but she knew it was no use. How would anyone hear her above the driving rain and roaring thunder?

Another bolt of lightning flashed and she ran to the door to the kitchens that she had come through only a few moments ago. She knew it couldn't be locked – it didn't have a lock on it at all. But like the main doors, it too was firmly closed. She beat on it screaming till her fists hurt, but no one came.

Another bolt of lightning.

Another immediate massive blast of thunder – the loudest yet.

After this came further loud secondary rumbles. They rolled on, one after another, but seeming to get louder and louder so that soon she was sure they were louder than the original crash...

Then she heard the voices.

At first they were indistinct against the lashing rain and roar of the thunder, but increasingly they became clear. Voices from the past, beating against the inside of her head: Queen Elizabeth's Annus Horribilis speech; Churchill's rousing call to 'fight them on the beaches;' Chamberlain's ultimatum that launched World War 2; snatches of speech referring to Queen Victoria, the American Civil War, Waterloo, the slave trade, the Fire of London, the Spanish Armada... with her head spinning and her eyes tight shut, Justine slid down the door and curled up in a foetal ball on the floor, wishing it would stop, sobbing for it to stop, becoming nothing more than a shrivelled bundle of anguish as the noise and the voices spun round and round in her head...

A crash of thunder – even louder than the last.

Then total, wonderful, silence.

Peace.

Justine uncurled herself slowly and opened her eyes.

The Great Hall appeared bright and fresh, as summer sunshine poured in through the great window. Carefully she got to her feet. Everything looked normal as she turned round and round, seeking some confirmation of the traumatic events of a few moments ago. But there was no sign of the storm or any physical evidence that it had ever happened. Just peace and quiet, with dust drifting gently down through the shafts of sunlight, birds singing outside and the soft sound of trees rustling in a light breeze.

She turned back to the double doors and reached out to try them again. At that moment they burst open.

A man strode in, in full Tudor clothing.

He was wearing a muddy doublet, muddier boots and a dusty cloak. His tousled blond hair fell over his forehead and was streaked with dirt, but there was no mistaking the trim beard and aristocratic bearing from the painting on the wall.

The man was every inch Sir William de Beauvais.

He stopped at the sight of Justine standing in the hall. Three more men were entering behind him, all dressed in similar clothes to his. One was in the middle of a conversation.

"So I said, 'Damn me, sir, if the horse founders under me, get me another!'" He laughed. "The scoundrel would have none of it, though..."

He and the other two stopped short at the sight of Justine.

"Well, well, well," said the man, "what have we here, Sir William?"

"I cannot tell, Dowland, except that it is a wench who is wearing the strangest garments I have ever seen." The blond man stopped and studied her closely, his expression one of amused curiosity as he walked all round her, staring at her short pleated skirt, plain sweater and soft leather boots.

"Do you pretend to be a man, wench? For if you do, you have the sorriest excuse for clothing. Your doublet has no shape, your breeches are unfinished and your hose is so thin you would sooner be barelegged."

He paused.

"Who are you and what are you doing in my house?"

CHAPTER FIVE

Justine had always felt that underneath her slightly fluffy exterior, there beat a reasonably rational heart. She wasn't superstitious; she made a point of walking under ladders and delighted in seeing a single magpie. These things proved how sensible she could be. Sure, she had a romantic streak as wide as an ocean, and often found herself disappointed when people she thought were nice turned out not to be, but no one could accuse her of believing in magic, or witchcraft, or even time-travel...

So there must be a perfectly rational explanation for this strange turn of events. What was the conversation she'd had the night before with Rick? He'd mentioned the local drama school providing actors – that must be it.

So she clapped slowly. "Very good! Love it! You're meant to be Sir William de Beauvais!"

"Aye, I am Sir William de Beauvais. And this is Master Dowland, Master Stanmore and Master Melrose." He indicated the three other men.

"Right. OK. Sir William de Beauvais, Master Dowland, Master Stanmore and Master Melrose. OK, guys, you can drop it now. I'm on the staff. You're very good, honestly. Who booked you? Why wasn't I told? I usually get the actors..."

"Actors?" Sir William barked. "By thunder, you think we are lowly mummers or strolling players?" He folded his arms. "I can assure you, we are nothing of the sort!"

"Yeah, right – so these beards are..." She grabbed Dowland's beard and gave a sharp pull. It stayed resolutely attached to his chin and he gave a wounded yelp. "...real, then. Sorry."

"By heaven, Sir William, turn her out! She is mad!" snapped Dowland, rubbing his chin.

"You are too easily frighted." Sir William chuckled at his friend's discomfort. "I feel she possesses an elfin charm. What is your name, wench?"

But Justine wasn't listening. She had just noticed the sconces had fat wax candles burning in them instead of light bulbs and flappy silk. And now she looked through the double doors, she could see that there was no literature rack, no suit of armour, and out through the open front door there was no driveway or gravel, just open lawns. 'OK, so maybe it's a dream,' she thought, 'a very vivid, very real dream. I must have banged my head during the storm. So that's all right then. Just a dream.'

She looked back at the men standing before her.

The man identified as Sir William, for all his muddy clothes and dusty cloak, carried himself with an easy, aristocratic charm, and it was clear to see that he was the man in the picture on the wall behind him. The man called Dowland was short and dark, with a swarthy, almost Hispanic look, and a gold earring in his left ear. Stanmore was tall and blond and was regarding her with a look of deep suspicion.

Justine looked at Melrose and saw that he was different from the others – a dry, cold man, with strange, almost lifeless eyes. He seemed to be dressed less for hunting than for a formal occasion; even his clothes were less dusty and muddy than the others. His doublet and breeches were dark grey, with slashes revealing a darker material beneath, and his black hose disappeared into boots that were stiff and shiny whereas the others were of soft brown leather. Yet, for all his formality, Justine thought he was actually less well off than the others, as if he was the poor relation allowed to tag along.

She became aware that Sir William was waiting his answer.

"Your name, wench?" he repeated.

"Oh, sorry, yeah. Justine. Justine Parker."

"Justine?" This was Stanmore. "Is that a French name? She is French? By heaven, turn her out, Sir William!"

"Are you French?" asked Sir William.

"No, I'm from London. From Hammersmith," she added, feeling that a bit of extra geographical accuracy may help. Although as it was her dream, did that matter?

"Come, wench," said Dowland, "you cannot be from London and from Hammersmith. They are many miles apart."

"Give her to me, Sir William. I will put her to use in my house," said Melrose.

Sir William glanced at him, and Justine could see that this had touched a nerve. "No, Tom, I will keep her here. Martha has told me that we are short-handed in the kitchens. She can work there."

"If you please, my lord," muttered Melrose, his cold formality from a few moments ago briefly stripped away to reveal something more visceral under the surface.

28

"I do please, Tom," replied Sir William, seeming not to notice.

'I think I was right about Tom Melrose,' thought Justine. 'Definitely the poor relation – there's no doubt who is the lord and master in this house. Fascinating dream – very interesting.'

Sir William threw off his cloak and shouted out, "Martha! Martha! Here, I say!" Then he turned to the other men. "I think some hard labour in the kitchens should knock sense into this little madam, and teach her not to pull at men's beards."

The door under the gallery opened and a girl in her early twenties appeared. She was wearing a plain black dress and a simple cotton coif on her head. "Yes, Sir William?" she said with a warm smile.

"This girl is to be put to work in the kitchens, Martha. Cook can see to her tasks. Take her down."

Martha looked hard at Justine. "A strange girl, Sir William," she said with a confident smile. "I wouldn't have her in the house."

"By thunder, woman! I don't ask for your opinion, and I don't expect it!" barked Sir William. "Were you my wife, I would expect less of the carping concerns I get from you all day long. Now take her down!"

The smile froze on Martha's face. Justine felt that she had been put firmly in her place. "As you wish, Sir William," she said coldly. She grabbed Justine's arm and started dragging her to the door. "Now you come with me, missy, and we'll soon find out what you're made of."

The pain of Martha's grip on her arm was a shock to Justine. It was exactly the kind of pain which would normally make her wake up from a dream – but in this case it didn't; the pain, and the situation, continued.

As she was dragged to the door, Justine was forced to the terrifying conclusion – indeed the only conclusion.

This was actually happening.

This was real.

Martha pushed her through the door and down the stairs. In the flickering light of the torches on the walls, Justine could see that the stairs were completely flat, with no wear on them at all.

Oh yes, this was real all right. Somehow, time in Grangedean Manor had turned back hundreds of years and she was now a part of actual Tudor history.

'Oh Christ. Oh hell,' she thought, fighting down the panic that was starting to twist her stomach. 'I'm really back in Tudor England. What do I do now?'

---0---

Back in the Great Hall, Richard Stanmore settled himself with a deep sigh on one of the chairs at the high table, while Sir William sat at the head.

Dowland and Melrose sat on the other side of Sir William.

"You are hard on your housekeeper, Sir William," observed Stanmore as he stretched his legs out to ease them after many hours in the saddle. "I think she has perhaps set her sights on you."

"My dear Stanmore," responded Sir William. "Martha is a housekeeper – a passable housekeeper – that is all. She should no more think to rise above her station than to fly over the chimneys." He paused and gave a broad grin. "Just because a man has known a woman in his bedchamber this very night past, it does not mean he has opened the door of his heart to her knocking."

On the other side of the table Dowland laughed loudly. "Will, you dog! Is there any woman of this house you do not 'know'?" He accompanied the word with an obscene gesture which gave Stanmore no doubt about its meaning.

"I'll admit the cook is not to my taste – that is all," responded Sir William. "Nor has this strange wench from Hammersmith been explored – as yet."

"And these girls have no cause for complaint?" asked Stanmore levelly, wanting to enter into the spirit of this humour, but not wishing to stoop to Dowland's levels of obscenity.

"My dear Stanmore – if by that you mean that the girls I employ do not object to my attentions before I carry them through, then I say I neither know nor care. If, however, you are referring to any concerns they may have afterwards…" Sir William paused for effect, "…then they are quite past caring!"

When the laughter had subsided, Melrose observed dryly, "Gentlemen, here you see the man with everything; good looks, good land, a fine house, wealth – and a form of droit de seigneur with all the women of his household. Except, of course, the cook. What more could a man ask for?"

"You do me proud," responded Sir William. He glanced at Melrose, then added casually, "it is too bad only one of us can enjoy such good fortune."

A chill suddenly descended on the room, despite the bright sunshine.

Stanmore could see instinctively that Sir William had touched the rawest of nerves in Thomas Melrose, although he did not know why these words had produced such a strong reaction.

Melrose's thin mouth was working and his eyes were narrowed as he struggled to contain himself. Stanmore found himself automatically looking down at Melrose's hand in case it went to his sword. Stanmore's own hand moved closer to his own sword, ready to draw it and spring to his master's defence if necessary.

Then the moment passed. Melrose smiled; a thin, humourless smile. "Indeed, my lord, it is too bad. But such is fortune."

"Aye," said Sir William, with a most guileless look. "Such is fortune." He turned and said to Dowland on the other side, "Come, we have all enjoyed a magnificent hunt. Shall we not have a pint of beer, some cake, and relive the glories of the chase?"

"My lord, I was sure you would never suggest it!" responded Dowland impishly, forcing Stanmore to conclude that neither Sir William nor Dowland had understood the depth of Melrose's anger just then. Maybe he'd imagined it? But then, over Sir William's shoulder, he caught sight of Melrose shooting a glance of pure loathing at his master, before composing his face into its more usual mask of urbane civility. 'No,' thought Stanmore, 'that was real.'

"Excellent," said Sir William and called out, "Martha! Here, I say!"

There was silence for a short while, then the door opened and Martha came in. "Yes, my lord?" she said coldly.

"Some cakes and ale."

"Yes, my lord."

"And the girl – she is put to work?"

"Yes, my lord." Martha turned to go back through the door. "And I don't warrant she's up to it, either, the little slattern," she muttered. She closed the door behind her.

"It pleases you to pull that woman along?" Stanmore asked.

"She is a servant," said Sir William. "And she cleaves to her position in life. There's no more to say on the matter."

"Indeed," cut in Melrose quietly. "But be sure to keep a watch on your back, Sir William, lest one who is in your service sees fit to attack it."

"Nay, Tom," responded Sir William, turning to him. "Upon my honour, no one in my service would attack my back. Not when I have such upright, steadfast and loyal bondsmen as yourself to look out for it." The challenge hung in the air between them.

"Indeed, my Master," answered Melrose. It seemed to Stanmore that his lips formed a thinner line and his eyes were even more lifeless than before. "You are fortunate in this matter."

"Excellent!" exclaimed Sir William. "There is no more fortunate knight in the county than myself." He spread his arms wide. "To have friends such as you – that is true wealth!" He smiled at each in turn. "I am indeed blessed!"

The door opened and a man in black breeches and a blue jerkin entered, carrying a wooden tray with a jug, four tankards and a large baked loaf. He set these down on the table in front of the four men and bowed low.

"Thank you, Simon," said Sir William.

"Master," muttered the servant in acknowledgement, then retired backwards through the door and closed it after himself.

CHAPTER SIX

At one end of the kitchens was a large metal spit, standing over head height. On the spit was the carcass of a boar and under it was a large brazier filled with blazing coals. The spit needed to be kept turning in order to ensure the boar cooked evenly, so it was linked by a series of chains and pulleys to a handle. And to work the handle, a dedicated person – known as a spit-boy – was needed.

Justine Parker, events manager at Grangedean Manor in the 21st century, was now its 16th century spit-boy.

Filthy with sweat and soot in the unbearable heat, Justine was sullenly turning the handle under the watchful eye of a small, shrewish woman called Margaret. When the servant Simon entered down the stairs from the Great Hall it distracted Margaret briefly, so Justine took the opportunity to rest. Immediately there was a shout from the cook.

"Hey, you girl! No stopping!"

Margaret looked up, saw what had happened, and as Justine pushed the handle round again, she stepped up and hit Justine in the side with a birch stick she was carrying.

"Oi, girl!" she shouted. "Don't you be stopping!"

Justine resisted the temptation to break the birch stick across Margaret's forehead. She had quickly learned that such defiance did not lead anywhere. This had been a lesson courtesy of the cook, a fearsome woman with teeth like an old graveyard and breath to match.

As she turned the spit, Justine recalled her introduction to the kitchens.

At first the kitchens had been a source of great wonder – her first glimpse of the reality of Tudor life, even blowing away her initial panic. She had simply stood and looked round in amazement, her mind almost exploding with the enormity of seeing at first-hand the lives she could only have imagined before.

People in smocks were chopping vegetables, pounding substances in pestles, kneading dough and rolling out pastry. They were all working at a large wooden table running the full length of the room. There was no natural light – some braziers on the walls and the fire under the roasting spit providing all the light and considerable heat.

Justine wanted to run up to each person and ask them what they were doing. What foods were they preparing? What tools were they using? She wanted to find out what they thought about the dishes they were making – dishes for the nobility that they would never be allowed to enjoy themselves. Did they like their jobs? What were their hours? What was the part of the job they liked best? What was the worst?

She wanted to ask them about their lives at Grangedean Manor and what life was like at their homes. How did they feed themselves and their families? Where did they get their own food...? So many questions – so many interesting facts to learn first-hand from real people in their very own words, instead of out of a history book...

But she hung back, because stationed at the centre of the table was a large, red-faced woman with straggly straw-like hair escaping from under a grubby white woollen cap, small, piggy eyes and a large nose covered in broken veins. The woman was attacking a joint of meat with a cleaver. Her air of authority and menace was palpable and Justine decided she must be the head cook.

Martha went over and leaned across the table, talking to the woman in a low voice. Justine couldn't hear the words, but there was no mistaking the meaning as the woman stopped chopping, and turned to stare at Justine.

"Where is this girl? Bring her here so I can see her better – me eyes ain't what they once were."

Martha pushed Justine up to the table in front of the woman, who put her cleaver down and peered myopically at her.

"I'll leave her to you, Cook," said Martha. "Menial tasks only, mind. Nothing better than scullion or spit-boy." She gave Justine a hard look and swept out, leaving Justine face to face with the cook.

"Ha!" exclaimed the cook and Justine got a full blast of the worst breath she had ever smelt. It was all Justine could do not to faint; instead she brought her hand up and rubbed her nose, trying to use the smell of her hand to mask the foul breath of the cook.

"A delicate little madam is this, I fear," the cook continued, addressing the room in general. "We shall have to knock some of the silk and lace out of her." The kitchen servants all nodded and made approving noises.

Justine decided to try a reasonable approach. "Look," she said "I'm sorry to bother you and all that, but I think there's been some sort of mistake..."

"Mistake?" responded the cook, in an ominously sweet-sounding voice. "Mistake?" she repeated softly. "I don't think my ears is gone." She inclined her head slightly at a small, weasel-faced woman standing next to her, while her eyes never left Justine's. "Margaret, is my ears gone?"

Justine noticed the kitchen servants now start to back cautiously away from the three of them at the centre of the table.

"Goodness, no, Cook," responded Margaret silkily, seeming to play along. "Better than those of a bat, they are. Begging your pardon, Cook."

"So, madam, think you my ears is gone?" the cook asked Justine, as the kitchen servants backed away further.

"Well, no, but..."

The cook gave a sickly smile and dropped into an even silkier voice. "And blow me," she purred, "if I didn't hear Mistress Martha say you was to work in the kitchens. That not so?" She paused. "Was I mistaken?"

The kitchen servants were now spread around the edges of the room, leaving Justine, Margaret and the cook quite alone at the centre of the table.

"Well, no, but..."

Then the explosion came, on a blast of stomach-churning foul breath.

"So you're to work! Hear me?" the cook bellowed, leaning forward so her face was inches from Justine's. "You're to work in my kitchen, doing work that I give you and thank me for it!" She paused to draw breath. "And if I hear so much as a whisper of complaint from you, you no good little piece of baggage, you'll find I'm not so reasonable no more, and you'll be begging me for mercy. You like that, girl?"

Justine tried to formulate a reply, but waves of nausea were making her feel she was going to throw up any moment.

"I don't like you, girl, I don't like you at all. But I've got you, so I'll use you. Margaret! Put her to the spit. And if she slacks a moment, sharpen her up with your birch."

Margaret ducked under the table and emerged next to Justine. She grabbed Justine's arm. "You come with me, missy," she said as she dragged Justine to the handle of the spit. A teenage boy was already turning it. "You, boy – go gather parsley from the gardens." The boy looked up and Justine caught a glimpse of white eyes in a soot-blackened face before he scampered quickly away. Margaret pushed her to the spit handle. "You'll be the spit-boy and turn that, missy, and don't you stop – or you'll have my birch here to smarten you up."

Justine put her bag down near the spit and started to turn the handle. It moved with difficulty and creaked loudly, but everyone had returned to their tasks and no one seemed to be particularly bothered as she got into a rhythm; turning the handle at the right speed to make the boar cook all round. In the searing heat of the fire, with a prize blister soon starting to come up on her thumb and an ache building in her back and arms, Justine watched them go about their work in wonder…

That was until the moment when Simon's entrance had brought her the birch stick in her side.

Maybe Tudor life wasn't quite as fun as she had originally thought? Maybe she had been a bit too enthusiastic, as Mrs. Warburton had pointed out? Maybe history was only fun when you looked back on it… Maybe, being stuck in history was actually rather scary…

Justine suddenly became aware of the foul reek of dead cat, and looked up to see the cook standing over her.

"You girl, stop now! The roast is done – can you not see?"

"But you said…" Justine started, then caught the look in the cook's eye and held her tongue.

The cook turned away and was bellowing orders. "You, you and you," she pointed at three of the servants, "come with me to the gardens to gather herbs. The rest of you can go up and start to prepare the Great Hall. Margaret, go up first and be sure the room is clear and the master is gone. You," she turned back to Justine, "dowse the fire and wait here."

Margaret immediately gathered her skirts and ran out. She could be heard pattering up the stairs to the Great Hall, as the cook gathered the three designated herb-pickers. When the cook was happy that everyone was in place, she marched out with them, like a mother duck with her ducklings in tow. Those who were to prepare the Great Hall were running around gathering up knives, wooden platters and pewter plates onto old blackened wood trays, and were making ready to take them upstairs.

Justine suddenly had a flashback to the night before; a line of actors playing at being Tudor servants, holding trays of food and preparing to go up into the Great Hall to serve…

…only this time the servants were real Tudors…

…the food was real Tudor food…

…and that fire was really blackening the belly of the roast…

Justine looked around in a panic for something to dowse it and saw an old earthenware jug standing by a tub of water. She ran over to it. The water was brown and smelt rank. She wondered if it might actually be the soup, but she filled the jug to the brim anyway and ran back to throw it on the fire. There was a whoosh of steam and a few sparks flew onto the flagstones. She stood back and looked at the remaining kitchen servants to see if there would be a shout of annoyance, but no one commented so she ran back, re-filled the jug and repeated the operation several times, with more steam and whooshing noises until the flames were gone and the fire was down to just glowing embers.

Breathing a sigh of relief she studied the belly of the boar and decided that it might, at a pinch, not be too obvious that it was burned – in the dark, with the light behind, perhaps. Relieved, she rubbed her hands over her face and through her hair, unaware she was leaving further black streaks on her already filthy face.

Margaret reappeared and announced that the Great Hall was clear. The remaining servants ran out with their trays and suddenly there was silence, broken only by the gentle hissing and popping of the fire as it died.

Margaret stood still and eyed Justine suspiciously. She still had her birch stick, which she held in one hand and tapped menacingly against the open palm of her other. "You, girl. You finished turning the roast?"

Justine nodded.

Margaret walked over and inspected it. "You burned it," she said coldly. "Cook will have to decide what's to be used and what's to be thrown to the dogs, as the Lord is my witness."

Justine remained silent, eyeing the birch stick suspiciously.

"You got a tongue in your head, girl?" demanded Margaret, an unpleasant sneer across her small face.

Justine didn't answer immediately – she was thinking hard. What would Mary Fox do now? Most probably she would snatch the birch stick with a defiant yell, give Margaret a few hard thumps with it – to pay her back for the earlier beating – then sprint across the kitchen and make good her adventurous escape, stealing the horse that just happened to be conveniently tethered outside. Yes, that's what Mary Fox would do.

But back in the real world, Justine Parker simply smiled weakly and said, "I am so sorry, Margaret. This is all a bit new to me, but I'm sure I'll get the hang of it soon. Is there anything else I can do to help?"

Margaret looked a bit taken aback but seemed to rally quickly. "If you cannot even perform duties as a spit-boy, why should you be given anything else to do?" She paused a moment. "You was only to do menial duties, anyhow." She glanced around the kitchens as if looking for the most unpleasant job she could find. "Yes," she said with a slow smile, "you can scrub the hearth."

Justine followed her gaze across to the blackened hearth under the arched stone chimney breast and her heart sank. The hearth was around six feet wide and three feet deep, with a black metal grate standing in the middle. All round the grate thick soot had piled up like black snow drifts, clinging to the legs of the grate, spilling over the front of the hearth, and streaking up the stone wall behind.

Margaret tapped Justine with her stick to walk her over to the hearth. "There, girl," she said when they were in front of it. "Clean that well – I'll be back presently to see how you have progressed." She turned to walk out, but then paused by a large tub full of a nasty-looking grey-green substance. "And when you have finished, you can empty out this tub of old tallow. It is no longer fit for anything but spreading on the land outside." She gave a small chuckle. "Fare thee well, girl," she said, and walked out, leaving Justine alone in the kitchens.

Justine stood in front of the hearth. "Welcome to Tudor England, Cinderella," she muttered to herself, then looked around for something to use on the hearth. After poking around the back of the kitchens for a few minutes, she came across a wooden broom standing in a wooden bucket. The broom looked just like the classic witch's broomstick, with hundreds of very thin pliable branches bound onto a long wooden handle and cut straight across at the end.

She took it back to the hearth and started sweeping, but the soot was so fine that all she succeeded in doing was stirring up great clouds of it, which then settled back onto the hearth – and also quite liberally onto her clothes and skin.

With a frustrated curse and some heavy coughing, she put the broom down and looked around for some other means of cleaning – such as maybe a damp cloth. Then her eye fell on the tub of rancid animal fat that Margaret had told her to clear. With an idea forming, she walked over and took a closer look. The fat smelt dreadful, but if her idea was good, it might just be what she needed. Gingerly, she put a finger into the fat to test the consistency. As she hoped, it was quite thick and glutinous – more so than one would expect from old animal fat. Goodness only knew what was in it.

She dragged the tub over to the hearth, as well as another empty tub she found nearby, then knelt down and, with an expression of pure disgust, scooped out a handful of the fat. She slapped it down onto a pile of soot, then rolled it around until as much soot as possible had been bound into the fat. With the same expression of disgust, she dropped the soot-filled ball of fat into the empty tub and looked at the grate. There was a clear dip in the pile of soot. The idea was working.

With grim determination, she set to work shifting all the soot by the same means; emptying the first tub and transferring all the fat and soot into the second.

Soon she had cleared the hearth completely. She managed to find a rough linen cloth to wipe down her hands and all the surfaces – leaving the hearth clean, if slightly greasy.

With a satisfied smile, she stood back and admired her work. 'Nice job, Cinders,' she thought, 'jolly nice job.' She picked up the now full tub of sooty fat and staggered with it along the corridor and out of the back door. There was a patch of dark brown earth nearby, so she upended the tub onto it, then carried the empty tub back into the kitchens.

She was just using the brush to sweep out the very last bits of soot when Margaret came back in.

Speechlessly, the serving girl took in the scene – Justine, her white eyes blinking guilelessly in a face blacker than a chimney sweep, standing with the brush by a clean and very shiny hearth. By her feet was the tub that had held the rancid fat, now completely empty.

"You done that, then?" Margaret asked suspiciously.

"Yes," replied Justine, and couldn't help adding, "it wasn't difficult."

"That's fine soot – no brush cleans that up."

"You asked me to clean the hearth and I cleaned it."

"But it's not a half hour passed…" Margaret fell silent and again looked suspiciously at the clean hearth and back at the sooty girl holding the broom.

"What's your name then, girl?" she muttered eventually.

"It's Justine."

"Justine? I ain't never heard that name before, as the Lord is my witness. What kind of name is that?"

"It's my name. It's not unusual where I come from."

"Where you from, then, strange girl?" Margaret looked at Justine's sooty sweater, skirt and boots. "Does everyone wear them strange clothes? Think you to dress like a man?"

"I'm from Hammersmith," said Justine.

"Where's that, then?" Margaret asked, suspiciously.

"It's in… it's near London," answered Justine.

"Out the parish, then." Margaret said, slowly. "I thought as much. Them's as out the parish is no good, my Ma says."

"I'm sure she does," responded Justine, slightly too glibly.

"You know my Ma, then?" Margaret said, her eyes narrowing, her voice sounding even more suspicious.

"Of course not."

"So how you know she says that, then?"

"I don't."

"But you said you were sure she does. You must have known that, else, how would you have known…" Margaret stopped, staring hard at Justine.

"You cleaned that hearth faster than a body could ever clean it…" she said slowly, as if starting to list out Justine's peculiarities.

"You claim to know what my Ma says when you've not met her yet… You wear strange clothes and you're from out the parish…"

Suddenly Margaret stepped back, staring wildly, then started to cross herself repeatedly. "Lord a' mercy – Lord a' mercy! I know you now! I know you, Satan! You're a… you're a… a witch!"

"Oh Christ! Hell, no…" Justine said, thinking fast as to what she could say to refute this dangerous allegation, but of all the things she could have said, this was possibly the very worst. Margaret immediately gave a small scream and put her hands to her ears. Her jaw dropped and her eyes opened so wide, Justine couldn't help but think they might pop out.

"Blaspheming the Lord?" Margaret said in a strangled whisper. "Invocation to your master the Devil? Oh mercy, mercy! I cannot tarry a moment in the presence of such evil!" She turned and made to run out of the kitchens, but stopped by the stairs. "I will fetch Master Hopkirk, the witchfinder. He'll know how to deal with you – witch!"

She ran up the stairs, leaving Justine staring after her, with the growing realisation that if time-travelling unexpectedly back to Tudor England was bad in itself, she had now made the situation considerably worse.

Almost immediately she heard the sound of heavy boots coming down the stairs. Quickly she looked around for somewhere to hide, but before she could conceal herself, a man appeared in the archway.

Could the witchfinder have been found so fast?

Then her heart gave a small jump of relief, as she saw that it was Sir William.

He had changed his clothes after the hunt and was now resplendent in a trim ivory doublet, with deep slashes over red velvet in his breeches and sleeves, grey hose and soft leather boots. He had a sword hanging from his left hip and a red silk cape on his shoulder.

"Ah, wench. There you are," he said with a broad smile. "Alone in the kitchens, I see. What did you say to that girl who would as like have knocked me over as she ran past me on the stairs?" He chuckled. "Ah, but 'tis no matter." He studied her in the dim light. "I see the soot of the kitchens has attached itself to you." He looked at her more closely. "By heaven, there is more soot here than girl!" He laughed. "Aye, you have a novel look about you – the look of a vagrant."

Aware that she cut more of a miserable figure than a novel one in her soot-blackened clothes and face, Justine couldn't think of a single thing to say. Frankly, she had to admit, not only did she look like a vagrant, but that was exactly what she had become – a stranger.

Out of place, out of time – and in a very dangerous, very frightening situation.

This wasn't a Mary Fox adventure. This was actually happening.

And with no guarantee of a happy ending.

"Come girl, why do you make sounds like a frightened mouse? And why do you pale beneath your soot? Am I a ghost?" asked Sir William genially. "Nay, withal – I am all too real." He put his hands on his thighs and pushed back his shoulders and roared with laughter. "Although parts of me are to be wondered at, as you shall discover ere too long!"

He grabbed her arm and started to pull her out of the kitchen. "Come now, girl, let me put you from your misery!" Justine's immediate thought was to get her bag from where she had put it near the spit, and she tried to get her arm free. "Do not struggle, girl, you're quite safe with me," said Sir William, still maintaining his jovial temper.

"My bag!" muttered Justine. "Let me get my bag." She broke free and grabbed it from the floor. After being accused of witchcraft, the last thing she wanted was curious Tudor eyes peering at its contents. Goodness knew what they would make of her phone, solar charger and Bluetooth speaker.

"Aye," said Sir William. "Take whatever you must." He laughed and grabbed her arm a second time. "I'll warrant that the sword of de Beauvais will cut and parry with honour tonight!"

He looked her up and down.

"Though we may need to have you washed first."

CHAPTER SEVEN

It was a quiet afternoon in the large taproom of the village tavern, situated on the edge of the green around two miles from Grangedean Manor.

A few villagers were sitting on stools or benches at the rough wooden tables dotted around the room. On every table was a fat tallow candle; each one pushed into the remains of the previous candle that had burned down to a hard yellow ring that was forever stuck to the table.

The only sound was the buzzing of two flies, darting in and out of the shafts of light from the small leaded windows. A couple of villagers waved them casually away if they got too close to their tankards of ale and crusts of bread.

The flies moved over to the corner and tried their luck with a small, dour man in grey, sitting on his own. They landed on his crust of dry bread and began to eat.

Unlike the other villagers, the man made no movement.

Growing bolder, the flies settled down to gorge themselves on the bread. Still the man made no overt movement, although an observant onlooker would have seen his eyes lower slowly and focus without any emotion on the flies.

They say that flies can see the approach of a threatening movement in two-tenths of a second, and their 360-degree vision means that they can fly directly away from the direction of attack. It was unfortunate for these two flies that while the hand that struck them came from behind, it was aimed at a point around one inch in front of them – so they flew straight into the path of its crushing blow.

The man flicked the bodies of the flies to the floor. Still without emotion he ate the rest of his bread and finished his tankard of ale. Leaving a silver three-farthing coin on the table, he stood up, pulled his hat lower over his eyes, walked to the door and stepped out into the summer sunshine.

---O---

Margaret ran across the village green and arrived at the front of the tavern, just as the grey man was starting to walk away from it.

"Master Hopkirk?" she panted, running up behind him and grabbing at his cloak. The man stopped, but did not turn round. "Master Hopkirk?" she repeated.

"Yes?" he said, his voice barely rising above a whisper. "I am Hopkirk." He turned round slowly, then fixed her with a pair of cold grey eyes that seemed to suck every ounce of resolve out of her. "What is your business?"

Margaret swallowed and forced herself to look away from the eyes. "I was told you are to be contacted if a w... if a wi..." She could not bring herself to say the word.

"If a witch is found?" asked Hopkirk. She nodded. "Indeed. I am not only the magistrate, but am also charged to identify those who practice the work of the devil in witchcraft." He paused to let Margaret's breathing slow down. "Do I take it from your agitated state that you have identified a witch?"

Margaret nodded again.

"Then we will go inside the tavern and you may tell me about this witch, that I may know better who she is and how she may be identified."

Hopkirk led her inside the tavern and indicated a table. Margaret sat down. "But first," he whispered, "you will regain your breath and have some ale, so we may converse more easily."

Hopkirk sat opposite Margaret, raised his hand and clicked his fingers. A large, heavily-bearded man in an old white smock appeared out of the shadows at the far end of the taproom and approached the table. "Yes, Master Hopkirk?" the man asked in a deep, coarse voice.

"A pitcher of ale and a pair of tankards, Jake." He put another three-farthing coin on the table.

"Yes, Master Hopkirk." The innkeeper Jake padded back to the shadows, and could be heard pouring ale into an earthenware pitcher from a barrel. He reappeared with the pitcher and two pewter tankards, which he put down and filled. Then he slid the three-farthing coin off the table into his pocket and padded away.

Margaret forced herself to slow her breathing, while Hopkirk's cold grey eyes never left her face. Margaret found this deeply uncomfortable, particularly as he never seemed to blink.

Gradually her breathing slowed to normal levels. She gulped down some ale while Hopkirk maintained his silent stare. Margaret felt sure she should say something, but decided to wait until spoken to.

Eventually Hopkirk cleared his throat. "We'll start with your name," he said.

"It's Margaret, sir," she replied, with a weak grin. This seemed to have no effect whatsoever on the man opposite. She continued, "I work in Grangedean Manor – in the kitchens, mostly, and in the hall when there's a banquet."

"I see," he replied. "Then pray, good Mistress Margaret, tell me your tale."

Now that the moment had come to tell her story, Margaret felt very nervous. It had seemed so clear to her as she had run from the manor to the village – a witch had been identified, so the proper authorities must be informed. But now she was here it didn't seem so clear-cut. What if this grey man with his air of menacing power didn't believe her? What if he thought she was covering up her own satanic practices by pointing the finger at another woman? The risks of her position were now becoming clear to Margaret, and her resolve was weakening. The strange girl had blasphemed – there could be no doubt about that. But had she really known what Margaret's mother would say? Was that really evidence of the dark arts? And what about the fast work in cleaning the hearth – was that in itself proof of witchcraft? Silently Margaret offered up a prayer, 'Sweet Lord, oh Lord Jesus, guide my tongue to speak the truth and this man's heart to receive it.' She gulped and crossed herself, then finished in her head with a silent 'amen'.

"Oh, Master Hopkirk," she began, "a strange girl from out the parish comes to work in the kitchens at the manor. She wears clothes that are like a man's and she was able to clean the hearth faster than is natural, and she knows things she shouldn't know..." She faltered and stopped. Even to her it sounded thin. There was a silence as Hopkirk's grey eyes bored into hers.

"I will need more proof than this," he whispered. "Do you have more?"

Margaret felt her stomach knotting in tension. This was what she had feared the most; that she would have to repeat the girl's words – her blasphemy – in order to provide the unassailable proof that the colourless man in front of her was seeking. Would this make her a blasphemer too? Could she risk her immortal soul by repeating such words?

"Oh, Master Hopkirk," she blurted, crossing herself again and again, "I can give you such proof of this girl's wickedness, but I cannot say it! Such blasphemy will be to endanger my own immortal soul!"

"I shall be the judge of that," said Hopkirk, some colour coming unexpectedly into his cheeks. He licked his lips. "Blasphemy, you say? This is your proof?" Margaret nodded, wide-eyed. "Then I must hear it. I must."

"Oh, Master Hopkirk. She said... she said..."

"Yes?"

"She said... when I accused her of being a witch, she said..." Margaret's voice dropped to a hoarse whisper and again she crossed herself repeatedly.

"She said... 'oh Christ in hell, no' – oh sweet Lord forgive me!"

The colour in Hopkirk's cheeks deepened and he licked his lips again. "She said that?"

"Those very words, Lord forgive me."

"And she dresses as a man, and can use magic to clean things and knows things she couldn't have known?" asked Hopkirk.

"Yes!" Margaret was relieved – it seemed like he was believing her. Jesus had heard her prayers!

Hopkirk's next words confirmed this thought.

"Then you were quite right to tell me – this is an envoy of Satan and we must be rid of her. Her name?"

"It is a strange name – not one I had ever heard."

"And it is?"

Margaret took a gulp of ale to steady herself, then another longer one that drained her tankard. She reached for the pitcher to top up, but it was empty. "Maybe it is a devil name?" she said. "Maybe if I say it, I'll conjure up her familiars, her evil spirits?"

"That I doubt. I'll need a name," answered Hopkirk, his grey eyes boring into hers.

"It is... it is... Justine," whispered Margaret. She paused and looked around, fearful for some evil spirits to materialise out of the shadows.

At that exact moment, a large white figure appeared and silently floated towards them.

Margaret gave a little scream and clutched at the edge of the table.

Then she realised it was only Jake the landlord in his white smock, padding towards them with another pitcher of ale.

"And how can she be known?" asked Hopkirk, ignoring Margaret's little drama. Margaret got her breath back, poured some more ale and took a drink. "She is tall, with dark red curly hair and bare head, and can easily be known by the strangeness of her dress."

"Which is?"

"She wears a badly-finished doublet, unfinished breeches, thin hose and man's boots."

Hopkirk considered this for a moment. "Aye, then we will work on this information, and we will find her and we will test her."

He gave a thin smile that didn't seem to reach as far as his eyes. Margaret felt the tension leave her body. A great weight lifted from her mind.

Hopkirk's voice dropped to the softest whisper, but there was no doubting the strength of his intent.

"We will test her," he repeated. "And if we find she is indeed a witch, then we will submit her to death by fire."

CHAPTER EIGHT

As Sir William de Beauvais led the girl out of the kitchens and up the stairs to the Great Hall, he was pleasantly surprised to find that she was accompanying him most willingly. Indeed, she was almost unseemly in her haste to get quickly away from the kitchens. Conveniently forgetting that it was he who had sent her there in the first place, he saw himself as her rescuer; a dashing knight saving the girl from the heat and the soot.

'Aye, they all submit in the end,' he thought happily, anticipating the afternoon's pleasures to come. 'No matter that their dress is bizarre, their speech is outlandish and their face...' he glanced back at the girl behind him and was rewarded with a nervous sooty grin '...their face is blackened with grime – they all submit in the end.'

They reached the top of the stairs and he looked back at her again, lit by the sunlight bursting through the door from the Great Hall. 'A comely face, despite the soot,' he thought as he led her into the Great Hall.

There they were greeted by the sight of the kitchen servants sent up by the cook, laying the tables for the evening meal.

To Sir William's surprise, the girl gave a sharp gasp and muttered something which sounded like "can't let them see me", then let go of his hand, shot past him in a cloud of soot and darted out through the main doors into the hallway.

Sir William ran out after her, just in time to see her cannon full tilt into his mother, who had just stepped into the hallway from a side room.

The force of the girl's impact made his mother stagger back; a large sooty mark appearing on the front of her beautiful red silk gown. The girl bounced off in the opposite direction, straight out of the open front door and onto the steps above the lawns, her hands waving like windmills as she tried to keep her balance. In this she was unsuccessful; she lost her footing, tripped down the steps and disappeared from view.

Sir William and his mother rushed out to stand on the top step, staring in amazement at the dirty figure lying spread-eagled on her back on the lawn below them.

Lady de Beauvais turned slowly to her son and asked, "Who..." she paused, staring hard at him, "...or what... is that extraordinary creature?"

"New serving girl, Mother," replied Sir William, with what he hoped was a sufficiently casual tone.

"And why, pray, was she running around the hallway in that dangerous fashion, knocking into me, leaving much soot on my gown and flapping her hands like a duck learning to fly?"

"High spirits, Mother?"

"High spirits indeed, William. You must take more care about the serving girls."

"Yes, Mother."

"What are her tasks?"

"I was going to have her... er... clean my chamber."

"I see. Clean your chamber? Is that indeed so?"

"Indeed."

"Let me see her." Lady de Beauvais stepped carefully down to the lawn, lifting her skirts to avoid the trail of soot. "Why does she dress like an unfinished lad? And she is filthy. You could not possibly allow such a girl in your chamber. Certainly not for cleaning, nor for..." a further pause, "...any other reason."

"I'm not sure what you mean, Mother."

But Sir William knew exactly what she meant. He also knew that his mother was very different to most Tudor nobles in the very important matter that was his love life.

Most noble families would have promised a first-born son like him to the daughter of a suitable family while both were just children, with the marriage taking place while they were teenagers. Not so his mother, Lady de Beauvais. Her own marriage had not been arranged. She was in fact the daughter of a merchant, and had married his late father, Sir Henry de Beauvais, for love. This had been despite the opposition of Sir Henry's parents, who thought she was beneath them, and her parents, who thought she was too ambitious.

As a result she had become convinced that arranged marriages were wrong. She had insisted that William should be allowed to meet a girl in his own time and to his own liking. As she had explained many times to the nobility of the county, she was only following the example of the Princess Elizabeth – now the Queen – and it was only right to let her son make his own choice.

So he had been encouraged to meet as many young girls as possible, in order that he should find one to his liking. Most of the really eligible girls had been promised to others and were now married, but there were still enough for Lady de Beauvais to arrange meetings so that love might take its course. But the only part of love that did take its course was his insatiable carnal appetite, followed by his immediate boredom with each of the girls once he had conquered them.

So there had been an unending procession of girls, from those of noble families down to Martha the housekeeper, who made the journey to his chamber – but so far not a single one had made it twice.

---0---

Justine groaned and slowly sat up. Immediately there was a sharp pain in her hip, which made her yelp. She felt it would ease if she could move it around and maybe put some weight on it, so she struggled to her feet and stamped around on the lawn, alternately bouncing her weight on her leg then shaking it out, while mother and son watched her speechlessly.

After a few moments the pain subsided, and Justine knew there was nothing broken.

She turned to Sir William's mother and said, "I am so sorry, Lady de Beauvais." She guessed that this aristocratic and beautifully-dressed woman would have such a title. "I was totally at fault. I was stupid and clumsy. Please," she added what she hoped was a winning smile, "will you forgive me?"

Lady de Beauvais stared at her. "You are no serving girl," she observed. "No serving girl would talk that way, or look me in the eye like that. Where are you from, girl?"

"I come from Hammersmith," answered Justine.

"And your name?"

"Justine Parker."

"Justine? Eh bien, vous êtes Française?"

"Er, no," answered Justine. "I'm English."

"Indeed. And you are obviously of a good family. Does your family have land? Are they at Court?"

"My father is... he, er... was... a doctor."

"An apothecary? A noble profession and an educated one. It would account for your own intelligent speech. He is dead, I assume, from your use of the past tense?"

"Yes, sort of."

"And your mother?"

"Much the same."

"You poor child." Lady de Beauvais considered her a moment in silence. Then she asked, "So how did you come to be in my house?"

Justine thought fast, trying to come up with a plausible story. In desperation she looked around, and in the distance she saw some horses in a field.

"I was out riding and I fell, and my horse ran off," she said, looking Lady de Beauvais in the eye with a maybe a little too much intensity. Lady de Beauvais gave a little snort. "A single girl out riding? Indeed, very independent. I have not heard of such a thing. Hmm. And what of your strange clothing?"

"I, er, ruined my gown when I fell, so I borrowed these from an empty cottage I found. I don't know what sort of clothes they are." She smiled rigidly at the older lady, as if to make her believe this by sheer force of will.

"Hmm," murmured Lady de Beauvais, "maybe some woodman's wife has made them." Justine couldn't help recalling that she had actually bought the skirt from a major department store only a few weeks ago.

Or in roughly 450 years' time.

She continued to smile, although now it was starting to feel very uncomfortable.

"And how came you covered in soot?"

"I was in the kitchens."

Sir William walked down the steps to join them and spoke up. "We were a girl short, Mother."

"This is an educated girl, and you put her to work in the kitchens?" asked Lady de Beauvais, turning to look at him in surprise. "Shame on you, William."

"Now look, Mother..."

Lady de Beauvais ignored him and turned back to Justine.

"Well, we cannot have you running around the house in such a state. It is not seemly." She turned to her son. "William, this girl will come with me. We will bathe her and dress her in proper clothes. She is a rather comely under the soot. You would do well to mark it."

"I have marked it, Mother," he replied.

"Aye, William, mark it well. And her spirit. Mark that well also."

"That, too, Mother."

She turned and swept up the steps into the house. "Come, girl," she called to Justine.

Justine started after her, then stopped and looked back at Sir William. She raised an eyebrow in enquiry, seeking his reassurance that she was now under his mother's charge. He smiled and made a small movement of his hand, indicating she should follow his mother, so she turned and loped up the steps into the house after the retreating figure of Lady de Beauvais.

CHAPTER NINE

The afternoon sun streamed in through the main doors of Grangedean Manor as Lady de Beauvais swept inside. Justine, who had stopped outside and had been studying the façade of the building, stepped in after her.

Lady de Beauvais rang a bell standing on a table. After a few moments a serving girl appeared from a side door.

"Prepare a bath upstairs immediately," ordered Lady de Beauvais.

"Yes, madam," said the serving girl, curtseying with her eyes down. She disappeared again through the same door.

Lady de Beauvais started up the stairs without looking back. Justine assumed she was supposed to follow and limped up after her.

There were pictures of worthy-looking family members all the way up the stairs. At the very top was a stern, uncompromising-looking man in his sixties with short-cropped iron-grey hair under a felt cap. His long luxuriant beard offset a plain black doublet and fur mantle round his shoulders. A magnificent gold chain was hung across his chest. Justine felt this was the most important portrait – not only was it at the top of the stairs, but there was something about the man that suggested both raw power and unquestioned authority.

"Sir Thomas de Beauvais," said her hostess from behind her shoulder. "He came here from Brittany with Henry Tudor and fought with him in the Battle of Bosworth against the usurper Richard of York. This land was his reward."

Justine stared at Sir Thomas de Beauvais – a man who had fought a historical battle a mere seventy years before. 'Am I mad?' she thought. 'This can't be real. It really can't.'

She winced as the pain in her hip flared up again, making it clear that this was all too real. Instinctively she shook her leg out to try and clear the pain.

There was a snort of amusement from behind her and she turned. "You perhaps have an ague," Lady de Beauvais observed, "that you must dance like you are possessed by St. Vitus?"

"It's my hip," said Justine. "I hurt it when I fell. Shaking it out helps"

"Indeed. I trust it is so, and not some madness or the plague."

Lady de Beauvais then did something sudden and unexpected. Frowning, she reached out and grabbed the bottom of Justine's sweater. In one movement she pulled it up, pushing Justine's arm above her head and leaving her armpit exposed. Lady de Beauvais studied Justine's armpit a moment, then looked down her side and across her stomach.

"What in God's name is this garment?" Justine felt her bra strap being tugged but said nothing. "Most unusual."

Thankfully Lady de Beauvais then lost interest in her bra and let her sweater fall back. She peered at Justine's face and neck, then crouched and looked intently at her legs.

"Hmmm," she muttered. "No buboes." She stood. "No sneezes?"

"Certainly not," answered Justine.

"Good. No plague. You'll do. Very well." Lady de Beauvais turned and walked briskly down the gallery towards the door at the end.

She turned and looked back at Justine, who had not moved from the spot. "Come, girl, do not tarry," said the older woman. "And do not touch anything until we have removed the grime of the kitchens from you."

They walked along the gallery and through the door at the end, into the long wood-panelled corridor which ran the length of the East Wing. Justine recognised it from her time; there were four bedrooms off to the right and on the left there were windows overlooking the front lawn. She glanced out of the leaded window. The view seemed at first familiar as she looked down at the lawns, but then she looked up and gasped.

There was nothing beyond the rolling Grangedean lawns but thick, green trees as far as the eye could see, swaying in the summer breeze with rooks circling and calling above them; covering the distant hills like a cloth of deep green velvet. Where were the big, ugly electricity pylons on the horizon, with the thundering lorries running along the dual carriageway, past the long, low warehouses and on to the sprawling estate of little box-like houses?

Now, Justine suddenly felt faint and put a hand down to the windowsill to steady herself.

The pylons, the lorries – they were all part of a familiar world; her world. Would she ever get back to it? Would she ever get back to the Grangedean Manor that was a museum, not a home? Would she ever see Mrs Warburton again, or Susan, or even Rick the grumpy catering manager? Did they even know she'd gone? Maybe she no longer existed in their world, as if she'd never been born...

"Come girl, I said not to tarry." Lady de Beauvais' voice brought her back to this world; the one where she did exist and was covered in soot.

The older woman was waiting for her in the doorway of one of the bedrooms.

Taking a deep breath, Justine straightened her back and walked into the room.

In the 21st century these rooms were open to the public and each was decorated as it was believed they would have been in the Tudor age – with a four-poster bed, a wooden chair and table and an oak clothes chest at the foot of the bed. True, the furniture had all come from various different houses and not Grangedean Manor, but it had been assumed that as it was authentic Tudor furniture, this would be acceptable.

So Justine was pleased as she walked in, to see that they had got it pretty much correct. A large four-poster bed stood against one wall; at its foot was a large clothes chest. An oak table and chair were placed under the leaded window, with a fireplace on the opposite wall. Even though it was a warm afternoon, the fire was lit. Suspended on a hanging frame above the flames was a copper tub and Justine could see there was water starting to boil inside.

Justine took off her bag and put it on the bed. She realised that in one respect they had got it wrong in the future – the bed was a mass of bright gaudy colours – from the painted wooden carvings through to the glorious tapestries hanging along the side of the tester at the top. In the Grangedean Manor of the future, they had assumed that wooden furniture would have been unpainted natural colours – but as Justine studied the bed she could see carvings of human figures, animals and foliage, all painted riotous reds, golds, greens and blues. It was a magnificent sight.

A large bow and a quiver of arrows was propped up in a corner. Justine smiled to herself – this was the Tudor equivalent to a set of golf clubs that had been left there for want of a better place. It made her realise the mundane normality of this historical way of life.

Next to the fire there was a copper bath, one that looked suitable for sitting in only, but a bath nonetheless. Justine smiled to herself; after falling back through time into the grime and heat of the kitchens, what she wanted now more than anything else in the world was a bath.

The door opened and the serving girl entered, carrying a similar copper tub to the one on the fire. She put it down on the floor in front of the fire, then took some rough sacking material from round her waist. Wrapping the sacking round her hands as mitts, she lifted the hot water tub off the fire and carried it to the bath, then tipped it in. She then hooked the new tub in its place over the fire.

Catching sight of Justine as she turned to leave, the girl's eyes widened and she put her hand to her mouth with a small gasp. Justine smiled warmly at the girl, but this just caused her to look even more alarmed and scurry out.

"She thinks you are a vagrant," observed Lady de Beauvais. "That makes her scared of you – you might carry the plague."

"I mean no one any harm – and as you said, 'no plague'" replied Justine.

"I know that, but they do not." Lady de Beauvais considered her a moment. "We will shortly bathe you and dress you in proper clothes. We will tidy your hair and cover your head. You will no longer look like a vagrant, but I think we need to be sure. You will need to change your name as well, so that no connection can be made with the dirty young woman who arrived here." She paused, staring at Justine intently. "Do you have any name you would like to be given?"

There was only one name – only one possible name.

"Mary Fox."

Lady de Beauvais smiled. "Yes, good. So you will be Mary Fox. Let me see; you are the daughter of my old friend, Richard Fox, a London merchant. You are recently returned from France."

"Thank you, Lady de Beauvais," Justine said. "I will do my best to justify your faith in me."

"Indeed you will," said the older woman with a smile. "I shall see to it." She paused. "You will accompany my son, Sir William, to dinner tonight. He will escort you in, in sight of all our guests. You will do your best to please him."

"I will try."

Lady de Beauvais nodded and considered her a moment. "My son is a good man," she said. "He has taken on the estates and the house well since his father died."

"I can see that," answered Justine, not sure where this was going.

"Many, many girls have excited his interest, looking to be the next Lady de Beauvais. They enter his bed with that prize in front of them. But they do not hold his interest once they leave it. None have succeeded in entering his heart." She smiled again. "At least none so far."

Justine let the challenge hang in the air between them for a moment.

"As you say, Lady de Beauvais," she said carefully, "he is a good man. I will do my best to be worthy of him."

Lady de Beauvais nodded.

"But as to his heart," Justine said, "and as to mine – only time can tell."

Just then the door opened again and the serving girl came in with another tub of water.

"Sarah," said Lady de Beauvais, "this is Mary Fox, the daughter of an old friend. She has been lately in France and on her journey here has suffered a fall from her horse into a pile of soot. See to her bathing and dress her as befits the daughter of a merchant."

"Yes madam," answered the girl Sarah, looking at Justine, but now without fear in her eyes.

"Good. Go to it. She will accompany Sir William to dinner." With that, Lady de Beauvais turned and swept out of the room.

There was an uncomfortable silence, then Sarah said, "Begging your pardon, Mistress Fox. I had thought you were…"

"A vagrant?"

"I am so sorry."

"Please don't worry." Justine smiled. "Is the bath ready? I can't wait."

"Nearly, mistress." Sarah poured the hot water from the fire into the bath as before, then tested the temperature with her hand. "A mite too warm, mistress." She added the cold water she had brought, then tested the temperature again. "Perfect, mistress." She then produced a muslin bag from the pocket of her dress and opened it. Justine caught the scent of herbs – lavender, thyme and rosemary – as Sarah emptied the bag into the bath.

"There, mistress, that will restore your humours nicely."

Not sure quite what to make of this comment, and fearful of saying something to Sarah that would have the same effect as her earlier comment to Margaret, Justine limited herself to saying only "thank you Sarah, that's lovely." It seemed prudent to be as nice as possible to this serving girl.

And to avoid any references to Christ or hell.

Sarah fished around in the pocket of her apron again. She produced a small yellow ball, about the size of an egg. "The soap, Mistress Fox," she said triumphantly, as she dropped it in the bath, before going over to the oak chest at the foot of the bed and rummaging around. She selected a large piece of rough fabric that Justine assumed was a towel and handed it over.

Sarah then rummaged some more and lifted out a large green dress, something that looked like a wooden frame, and various other garments. She put them on the bed. Then she noticed Justine's bag and picked it up.

"Is this your bag, mistress?" asked Sarah. "Shall I sort out what is held inside for you?" She tried to open the bag, fumbling with the unfamiliar clasp.

"No," said Justine quickly, still fearful of letting anyone see her modern-day things. "Thank you." She held out her hand for the bag. "I'll sort it myself."

Sarah handed it over with a puzzled look. "My work is to help you, mistress," she observed, "but if you must sort it yourself…?" She left the question hanging.

"Yes, Sarah, if you don't mind. It's really nice of you to offer. I'll do it."

"As you wish, mistress," replied Sarah hesitantly. "You are being most kind, but I am only here to serve and to help you."

"And I really do appreciate it."

"Thank you, mistress – it is nice to be told that." Sarah turned and left the room.

For a moment Justine stayed stock-still, clutching the towel and her bag. The silence in the room was broken only by the crackling of the fire. Intently she listened out for the sounds of anyone coming down the corridor, but there were none. It did seem she was genuinely alone in this wing of the house.

She opened her bag and checked that the phone, charger and Bluetooth speaker were still there, then closed it and looked for a safe hiding place. She decided the best option was to tuck it under the deep layer of plump goose-down pillows.

Then she undressed and rolled her clothes up into a ball. She wondered what to do with them; they needed to be disposed of quickly – their very presence linked Mary Fox, the respectable merchant's daughter, to Justine Parker, the vagrant girl who was probably even now being sought for witchcraft. And if Lady de Beauvais thought her bra was unusual, what would anyone else make of it?

She looked at the fire, then back at the clothes in her hand. It seemed the obvious solution – but she hesitated. To burn these clothes meant she was severing her links with the future – denying who she really was – and maybe, reducing her chances of getting back again?

'Oh, come on,' she thought, 'it's only some clothes. Get a grip, girl. The real Mary Fox – or at least the real one in the books – wouldn't hesitate a second.'

With that, she stepped up to the fire and placed the ball of clothes onto it. For a moment nothing happened, except that the ball started to open out as it settled, then the flames took hold and the fire flared up as first her skirt, then her sweater, t-shirt, knickers, bra and tights caught fire. She watched as the fire quickly turned them to blackened, charred remains, except the wires from her bra which glowed bright orange before eventually bending and melting down into the coals.

She turned to the bath and was about to get in, when she noticed her boots were still standing by the bed. She picked them up and was about to throw them on the fire as well, when again she hesitated. 'My favourite boots,' she thought. 'I can't burn them, I just can't.' She put them back by the bed and climbed into the bath.

It was warm, not hot, but sheer bliss as she slid down into the bath and splashed the water up her body. She found the soap which smelled of olive oil, but she could not get it to lather, so she abandoned it. Instead she grabbed the towel, dipped one corner in the bath and used it as a flannel, scrubbing her face until the fabric was black with soot. She then used another corner to wipe her face until it was clean.

She wished she could wash her hair, but the bath didn't allow her to slide low enough and anyway the soap wouldn't work as a shampoo. She decided to let that one go for now – although her head did feel dry, sooty and a bit itchy. 'Oh, golly – I hope I don't have lice,' she thought, and spent a few minutes picking at the roots of her hair and examining anything that felt suspicious. Apart from some grass seeds, probably from her fall in the garden, there was nothing that could be cause for concern.

She wriggled her bottom a bit so she could slide further down the bath and get more comfortable, then she gave a deep sigh, relaxed her head back and stared up at the white plaster ceiling with its dark oak beams.

'I am lying in a copper bath in a Tudor house in Tudor times, and I have absolutely no idea how on earth I actually got here,' she thought. 'If it wasn't so definitely real, I'd never have believed it possible.' She wiggled her toes absently, finding herself starting to come to terms more with her situation. 'It must have been some kind of magic.' She stopped wiggling her toes. 'But that would be thinking like a superstitious Tudor; like Margaret. If you don't understand something, it must be magic – that's just a cop-out.'

Then she noticed a spider running along one of the beams and watched as it scuttled along. 'That spider might think everything is magic, because he probably doesn't understand anything. That's fine for him, but not me.'

The spider stopped, then scuttled along a bit further, then suddenly it disappeared.

Justine gave a small gasp. One second it was there; the next it was gone.

She studied the beam closely, and spotted a small dark patch around where the spider had disappeared. 'Maybe that's a hole,' she thought, 'and he just popped inside.'

A sudden thought hit her.

"That's it!" she said out loud. "That's jolly well it! A wormhole! I fell into a wormhole!"

Of course! It must have been a freak wormhole caused by the electrical storm – that for a split second linked the Grangedean Manor of 2015 with the Grangedean Manor of its Tudor heyday. She'd just happened to have been in the wrong place at the wrong time, and she'd fallen through it.

This seemed to make good sense. She'd seen plenty of episodes of sci-fi programmes like Doctor Who, Red Dwarf and Star Trek, where that sort of thing was accepted as perfectly rational. She'd also read A Brief History of Time and while she couldn't remember much because it seemed a bit jumbled in her memory (although it had seemed quite understandable when she was reading it), she thought there might have been something there about wormholes.

'I wonder if I'm the first person to fall through a wormhole?' she thought. An amazing thought occurred to her. 'Probably not – people disappear all the time and the police search for them for years and never find them; maybe they haven't actually been murdered or gone to Spain or something. Maybe, they've simply gone back to another time.'

This seemed to make excellent sense. Except for one thing. 'Then why don't they tell all when they get back?'

A sudden thought hit her, like a cold wave of inevitability crashing in. 'They don't come back, do they? Or we'd all know everything there is to know about wormholes and time travel…'

Justine sat up and put her arms round her knees as the wave of realisation made her head spin. She stared blankly into the distance.

'I'm never going back to my time, am I? I'm stuck here for the rest of my life…'

Slowly, she unclasped her knees, deciding she was not going to give in to despair. 'There's always hope,' she thought. 'If I got here, then surely I can get back again? Yes – there's always hope.'

She sank back into the bath and looked up at the ceiling, just as the spider emerged from his hole and started to scuttle along the beam again.

"Hello again," she said aloud with a smile. "You're a persistent little bugger, aren't you? Looks like I'll need to be as well."

A few minutes later she stepped out of the bath. Thankfully now the pain in her hip had gone.

'OK, so I'm Mary Fox, and a fine Tudor woman,' she thought. She towelled dry, then stood by the bed, looking at the clothes Sarah had laid out. 'No Velcro here. This time, it's the real deal.'

She put on the cotton stockings first, then the chemise – a sort of shirt. Then she put on the red petticoat, and was starting to try and put on the farthingale – a willow frame that would allow the skirts to be pushed out, when the door opened and Sarah came in.

"I thought you would want some help getting clothed, mistress," she said.

"Thank you Sarah, yes please," answered Justine.

Sarah helped Justine secure the farthingale, then laced her into a stiff corset that made her waist appear tiny and almost completely stopped her breathing.

Then Sarah tied a rolled-up piece of padded material around Justine's waist. "Got to get the bumroll right, mistress. Not sure how they do this in France," she said as she pulled it tight and did up the laces. Justine didn't answer – that would be wasting precious breath.

Sarah then pulled a grey skirt over Justine's head and down onto her waist. "Kirtle, mistress. I thought grey would look nice with the gown."

Again, Justine didn't answer. She was too busy focussing on breathing from her upper chest in short, shallow breaths.

Sarah lifted the heavy green velvet gown over Justine's head and pulled it down into place. Justine couldn't believe the weight of all this material and wood she was carrying. Suddenly the fake Tudor gowns she'd worn at the modern-day banquets didn't seem so bad – she'd give anything to be able to wear one now, with its soft padding and Velcro fastening…

Finally Sarah produced two grey velvet sleeves with delicate lace trimming and pulled each one up Justine's arm; lacing them under the shoulder of the gown. She stood back, looking Justine up and down, then nodded with approval. Justine wondered how she looked, but as there was no mirror in the room, she had to assume from Sarah's satisfaction, that Mary Fox would do.

"Now mistress," said Sarah, "your hair. Wait while I get a comb and a hood for you." She turned and went out of the door, leaving Justine standing in the centre of the room, her breathing now starting to come under control. After a moment, Justine shuffled over to her boots and tried to bend over to pick them up. This proved very difficult; only being achieved by sinking down like a hovercraft coming to rest and grabbing them in one hand. Justine decided that she had no chance of getting them on, just as Sarah came back into the room.

"Boots, mistress?" she asked, seeing Justine standing with the boots in her hand. "Oh, no – I have the prettiest slippers for you." She went to the oak chest and produced a pair of ivory coloured shoes, which she placed on the floor in front of Justine. Justine tried to step into the right shoe, but it was far too small. She nearly made a comment about Cinderella, but stopped herself just in time.

"No matter, mistress," said Sarah, and went back to the chest. She came back with another pair – with no better luck at getting them on. A further pair were tried with as little success.

"Maybe those boots are a better fit," said Sarah reluctantly. She picked one up and studied it closely. It had a flat heel and was made of brown leather. The pair had cost Justine over £60 from a leading high street store and she loved them. "A man's boot, mistress," Sarah said disapprovingly, before getting on her knees in front of Justine and holding it out. Resting her hand on Sarah's shoulder, Justine got her foot into the boot and wriggled it on. The other boot followed and Sarah stood back. "I suppose they cannot be seen under the gown," she observed after a moment. "Make small steps and they will stay hidden."

"I'll try," whispered Justine.

"Come mistress, we will do your hair and your hood." Sarah led Justine to the chair, and indicated that she should sit. 'How can I sit in this get-up?' thought Justine, but she did her best and managed to get her bottom onto the chair. It wasn't easy; the bumroll pushed her towards the front edge of the chair, while the farthingale dug in sharply.

Sarah produced a narrow comb with long teeth and started working through Justine's russet hair, pulling at the ringlets until it was all but straight, then pinning it back. She fitted a cotton cap over Justine's head and tied it at the back with laces. Then she produced a green velvet hood studded with fine pearls and trimmed with black ribbon, which she fitted over the cotton cap and secured with a pin.

Sarah then produced a small wooden pot containing white paste, which she rubbed all over Justine's face as a form of foundation, before applying some rouge powder to Justine's lips. 'I'm being made-up,' thought Justine. 'Goodness knows what's in this stuff.'

Finally, Sarah produced a fine silver necklace with a single pearl pendant and fastened it round Justine's neck.

"There, Mistress Fox. You are made truly beautiful. The master will no more resist you than fly across the heavens. He is waiting for you at the foot of the stairs."

Sarah then pressed something into Justine's hand. Looking down, Justine saw it was a hand mirror, made of polished metal. Slowly, and with some trepidation, she brought it up to her face.

She gasped. There, looking back at her, was a face she simply did not recognise. It was not even the face she was accustomed to seeing when she had put on Tudor costume in her own time – no, this was the face of a true Tudor beauty – and not one that could easily be connected with the grubby girl in the 21st century clothes who had been shown up to the room a couple of hours earlier.

Justine stood up. "Thank you, Sarah. You have done magnificent work," she said and smiled warmly at the serving girl.

"You have a wondrous beauty, mistress," said Sarah. "I have just made it known."

Justine took some small steps towards the door, and Sarah opened it for her, curtseying as she went through. 'Now I'm a Tudor lady, she curtseys,' thought Justine. 'Just remember, I'm now Mary Fox, who is a merchant's daughter from London.'

Justine walked carefully down the corridor, then opened the door out onto the gallery.

As she walked down the gallery, she saw Sir William at the foot of the stairs, his blond curls glowing in the evening sun, his beard trimmed and neat.

Justine admired his fine doublet, the deep slashes over red velvet in his breeches and sleeves, the grey hose and soft leather boots. He had a sword hanging from his left hip and a red silk cape on his shoulder.

She passed along the gallery and turned to walk down the stairs. As she glanced at the portrait of Sir Thomas, it seemed to her that he was a little less stern, and maybe even had a twinkle of approval in his eye.

She turned her gaze onto Sir William standing at the foot of the stairs and slowly, deliberately, she stepped down towards him.

She reached the foot of the stairs and looked down demurely as she curtseyed low. She held out her hand and he took it, brought it to his lips and kissed it gently as he raised her up. She lifted her eyes and smiled at him.

As she took his arm, she saw his mother standing in the corner and caught her eye. Lady de Beauvais gave a tiny nod of satisfaction, as Sir William swept her away through the double doors and into the Great Hall.

CHAPTER TEN

Justine caught her breath as she entered the Great Hall; her hand tightening on Sir William's arm in delighted surprise. She stopped a moment and took in the beauty of the room.

The Great Hall was a sparkling sea of brilliant light.

It seemed like there were a thousand candles all ablaze – set in silver candlesticks on the tables, in black metal sconces on the walls and hanging from large iron fittings on the ceiling. There were even a couple of elegant braziers in the corners; tall barley-twist metal posts with a bowl on the top and fat yellow beeswax candles throwing light up the grey stone walls. Justine looked up; the candlelight cast black flickering shadows in the gaps between the stones that made them look very deep and mysterious.

"It's beautiful," she whispered to Sir William, and was rewarded with a deep smile. "Indeed," he answered. "As befits your own radiant beauty."

She smiled back and they proceeded into the hall together, followed by Lady de Beauvais.

There were about thirty people in the hall, all standing at their places waiting for Sir William, Justine and Lady de Beauvais to take their seats. The tables were arranged in a horseshoe shape, just as they would be in Justine's time, with the top table running under the large windows, looking back to the entrance and the gallery above it. That meant the three of them had to walk the length of the hall and round the side of the top table to sit down.

As they were walking down the hall, Justine heard music – and when she reached the other side of the top table, she allowed herself a quick glance up at the gallery. There were four old men playing instruments, just as she had for her banquets. Justine smiled to herself – she'd certainly got one thing right.

Satisfying though that was, it did not dispel the fear, as she took her seat on the right of Sir William, that she would be recognised by one of the kitchen servants. Would they connect the grubby, bare-headed, strangely-dressed girl who had been turning the spit in the kitchens with Mary Fox, resplendent in her green velvet gown and French hood; the elegant daughter of a London merchant and special guest of the master of the house?

Justine also savoured the irony of her situation. For many months she had been the organiser of fake Tudor banquets, creating an experience for her guests that would only ever be a pale shadow of the real thing. Now here she was, a guest of honour and about to experience it for herself.

A long, low gurgling noise from somewhere under her restrictive corset brought her back to this particular time. She realised she hadn't eaten since she'd had a sandwich at her desk at lunchtime, many hours before the storm. That lunchtime may be over 400 years in the future, but according to her stomach it was way too long in the past. She hadn't given it a moment's thought while she'd been in the kitchens, with Sir William and his mother, bathing, getting dressed and made up – but now she could see the servants marching in with plate after plate of delicious looking roast birds, hams, vegetables, fruit pies and many other enticing dishes – she realised just how desperately hungry she was.

Beside her, Sir William picked up a cotton napkin and threw it across his left shoulder. She glanced around the room. Everyone else was doing the same, so she did as well.

Then a servant approached Sir William with a silver bowl full of water and held it out to him. He washed his hands in it, thanked the servant and wiped his hands on the napkin. Another servant brought a bowl to Lady de Beauvais, and she did the same. Finally, a third servant brought a bowl to Justine, so she washed her hands and wiped them on her own napkin. As she looked up to thank the servant, her blood turned to ice in her veins.

It was Margaret.

Justine forced a quick smile, then looked down, trying to seem unconcerned. She fiddled with the pewter plate in front of her for a moment, then looked up again. Margaret was moving off, but as Justine looked, the serving girl glanced back over her shoulder with a small frown, then turned and disappeared into the kitchens.

Justine let her breath out slowly, trying to calm herself down. It had been such a shock to come face-to-face with Margaret. Had she been recognised? Would Margaret make good her threat to call the witchfinder if she recognised Mary Fox, the grand lady at the top table, as Justine, the girl she'd called a witch?

"What ails you?" asked Sir William. "You look like you have seen a spirit."

"It's nothing," she replied. "Really, it's nothing." Even to her it didn't sound all that convincing.

He pulled a roast peacock on a platter towards him. It looked as if it had not been cooked; its feathers and magnificent tail plumage were still in place. He pushed his knife into its side and lifted the entire skin off in one move, revealing the roast body underneath. "Was it that serving girl? he asked. "Did she upset you?"

"Oh no," she replied, more to convince herself than him.

"Good." The matter settled, he applied himself to cutting off the leg of the peacock.

For Justine the matter was far from settled. 'Maybe Margaret didn't recognise me,' she thought at first. 'Why should she? She only saw me with a dirty face in the half-light of the kitchens, and even I didn't recognise me in this outfit.' But then the image of Margaret glancing over her shoulder and frowning came up, forcing its way into her mind like an unwelcome guest at a party. 'She looked back. She definitely looked back. She frowned. She must have recognised me.'

Justine looked round the room, searching out for Margaret, until she caught sight of the girl bringing a silver jug of wine to Lady de Beauvais. Justine stared intently at her, but after Margaret had poured the wine and put the jug down, she turned and went through the door to the kitchens without so much as a glance in Justine's direction.

Justine realised she'd been holding her breath, and she let it out slowly in relief.

"I would have an answer?"

Justine became aware Sir William was staring at her, the half-eaten peacock leg in his hand and one eyebrow raised. He must have asked her a question while she was so preoccupied with Margaret.

"I am sorry, my lord," she replied.

"I had asked if you would eat." He waved the peacock leg at her empty plate. "The finest meats and vegetables have been prepared for your pleasure. The finest wines, too. Are they not to your liking?"

"Indeed my lord, I am not hungry."

Just at that moment, another long, deep gurgle came from under her corset. Sir William couldn't fail to hear it, even over the noise of the banquet.

"Verily," he observed drily. "Your stomach tells a different tale."

Yet another gurgle; this one even louder.

He smiled and took a bite of his peacock leg. "It has much to say on this matter," he added out of the side of his mouth.

Justine blushed. "I am sorry, my lord. Maybe I will have a little something."

"Indeed," he answered. "A good appetite at the table bespeaks a good one in the bedroom." He cut some slices of peacock and put them on her plate, added some carrots and beans, then fixed her with a twinkle in his eye. "I would you feed yourself well."

Justine looked back at him levelly. "I will have a little of this peacock, my lord. And that is all." She gave him what she hoped was an icy stare, "For now."

He gave her a deep, warm smile. Her heart did a little somersault.

"Of course," he observed. "Time is our friend in this." But Justine sensed he didn't really believe it, confident he would get his way when the time came.

She was about to respond, when two elegant men came up to the table. One was tall and blond; the other shorter, dark and swarthy. Justine recognised Stanmore and Dowland from that morning.

"Good evening, my lord," said Dowland, bowing low.

"We have not had the honour of an introduction to this good lady," said Stanmore. He bowed to Justine. "Madam, I am Richard Stanmore, at your service."

"And Oliver Dowland, likewise." Dowland also bowed low, but as he stood up, his eyes didn't get any higher than Justine's chest.

"Mary Fox," said Sir William, indicating Justine. "Daughter of Richard Fox, a merchant of London."

"Delighted, madam," said Dowland to Justine's chest "You grace us with your bounteous beauty.

"Richard Fox is an old friend of mine," said Lady de Beauvais, who had observed the two men's approach and was leaning across her son to join the conversation. "Mary will be staying with us while he travels abroad."

Dowland acknowledged her with a nod of his head, his eyes still fixed.

Justine gave an icy smile. She said, with all the grace she could muster, "I am honoured to meet you, Master Dowland. And you too, Master Stanmore. I am sure I shall have a generous welcome here in Grangedean Manor."

"Most generous," said Dowland. "Sir William is well known for his attentiveness."

"We look forward to better making your acquaintance," said Stanmore.

"Are we to join the hunt on the morrow, my lord?" asked Dowland. Much to Justine's relief, he finally dragged his gaze over to Sir William.

"Yes," answered Sir William. "The white stag has once again been sighted near Briar's Copse. We will seek it out."

"Very good, my lord," said Stanmore. "We will attend."

Again he bowed to Sir William, then to Lady de Beauvais, and finally to Justine. Dowland did the same, appearing to use the bow to steal one last look down Justine's cleavage, then they both backed away from the table and resumed their seats further down the hall.

Justine took the opportunity to eat some of the meat and vegetables on her plate. Hungry as she was, she ate slowly, conscious of the restricted access to her stomach under her gown. When she had finished, she took a sip of wine and sat back as best she could.

"They did not recognise you," observed Sir William slowly. "Even though you would have removed Dowland's beard this morning with your hand, and you called us common players."

He took a draught of wine and considered Justine with a smile. "With the removal of your outlandish clothes and the proper attire of a lady, you have been rendered a different person. It is remarkable."

"As you say, my lord, I am now Mary Fox. It is better that I should be her, not Justine Parker."

"Why, what dark secret does Justine Parker have to hide?" Seeing her eyes widen momentarily, he added, "Nay, do not answer. As I said before, time is our friend. You can tell me your dark secrets – as you may have them – at your leisure."

Justine considered this.

"If I tell my story, it will be to you alone," she said.

"Aye," he answered, laughing. "Pray never share a secret with Dowland. It would be to tell the whole of the county." He raised an eyebrow. "Stanmore – you could tell him, but in truth he would probably have guessed it already." He took another drink of wine. "Now Thomas Melrose – the third man you met this morning – there is a man you should watch. A secret shared with him would stay a secret only if it does not further his ambition."

Justine remembered the saturnine man of the morning's hunt, who would have had her as his servant if Sir William had not intervened.

"Is Master Melrose not here?" she asked.

"Nay, he has gone home early, complaining of a gripe in his stomach. Though I warrant it is in his heart instead."

Sir William poured himself some wine and drank deeply, as if to put a full stop to the topic of Melrose, Dowland and Stanmore.

"Let us turn to you, Mistress Mary Fox," he said, putting down his goblet and stroking the stem with his finger. "What is your ambition?"

Justine slowly reached out to the bowl in front of her and scooped what looked like some fruit compote onto her plate, giving herself precious time to think. If the question had been asked earlier that afternoon, her ambition would have been quite simple – to avoid being tried for witchcraft and to somehow reverse the time-shift that had brought her to the Tudor era.

But now, things had begun to change. Now she had actually met the man in the picture. How could she want to escape back to the modern world, knowing she was leaving him behind? Seeing his picture every day on the wall? And how could she organise fake Tudor banquets, knowing how magical the real thing could be?

"Well?"

"My lord," she said, with what she hoped was the right amount of sincerity, "my ambition is to marry well, to be a good wife and to be a good mother to many children." She took a dainty mouthful of the compote to emphasise the point and was pleasantly surprised – it was raspberries, blackberries and apples, although maybe with a bit too much sugar.

Sir William smiled and touched her hand. "It is an honourable ambition, Mary, and one I would see you fulfil."

Lady de Beauvais, who had been leaning forward and listening attentively to this exchange, smiled and sat back.

Sir William stood up. Immediately the whole room fell silent and stood as well. Justine quickly stood with them. As she stood, she felt Sir William's hand seek out hers.

"Thank you all for your attendance this evening. I shall now retire to my rooms. Goodnight, all."

He kicked back his chair. Still holding Justine's hand, he led her out of the hall past all the standing guests. Justine tried not to catch anyone's eyes, preferring to look demurely down, although she did glance up briefly to see if Margaret was there. There was a line of servants along the wall under the gallery, but Margaret was not among them.

Still, she was glad when they made it out of the hall, before starting up the stairs towards the bedrooms.

CHAPTER ELEVEN

The evening shadows were lengthening as Thomas Melrose rode slowly along the narrow dusty lane towards his house.

He was tired, he was thirsty and he was very, very angry.

He was angry with Arthur, his horse, who would insist on this leisurely plodding pace. Despite frequent sharp kicks in the flanks, Arthur continued with his head down and heavy hooves, seeming tired after the hunt. His pace was punctuated with an occasional snort, as if to show his master just what he thought of him and his boots.

'Even my horse will not bend to my will,' thought Melrose.

Yes, he was angry with his horse, but what was really working him up, what was really making his blood boil, was Sir William.

The casual arrogance of the man.

All the way home the scene in the Great Hall at Grangedean had been replaying in his head. Each time he relived Sir William's vile words, the wound they made had got ever bigger, ever more deadly, like a dagger probing ever closer to his heart.

"You do me proud. It is too bad only one of us can enjoy such good fortune."

"Yes indeed," Melrose muttered aloud. "It is too bad. By the Lord's wounds, it is too bad." He kicked at the horse again, but this achieved nothing more than a particularly contemptuous snort. If anything, Arthur slowed down a fraction, as if to make his opinion even clearer.

"Aye, well you may snort old fellow," observed Melrose. "But you have not been slighted every day by a man who is not worthy to clean your boots; a man who by his slightest action will blight the life of honest folk and lead them to their ruin."

Arthur curled his head back and looked up at his rider. It seemed to Melrose there was a look of enquiry in Arthur's large brown eyes.

"Every day I must endure these taunts and insults from this man," he explained. Arthur shook his head up and down and snorted again. "A man I once regarded as my closest friend – aye, a friend I held in the highest esteem since we were boys. Though he was the son of landed nobility and I was the son of a yeoman farmer." Melrose leaned forward and whispered in Arthur's ear, "A man whose life I even saved once, God forgive me."

Each lost in their own thoughts, the pair plodded slowly along the dusty lane.

---0---

It was a bright afternoon eighteen summers before.

Ten-year-old William de Beauvais was exploring a copse in the woods to the south of the Grangedean Manor parklands.

He was using a long branch as a beater's stick, trying to get conies out from their underground warren, so he could take a shot at them with his specially-made half-sized bow and arrows. This had involved pushing through the thick undergrowth and bashing the base of trees to try and startle the conies out of their burrows. He had been hitting trees in this way for more than half an hour, but had not released a single cony.

Getting bored, he started swinging his stick in a more casual fashion, in ever-wider arcs. Then he saw a dirty-looking brown log by the base of a tree. In his boredom and frustration, he gave it a particularly strong hit with all the backswing he had generated. He was surprised to find that instead of a solid 'thwack' as he would have expected, it made more of a soft 'thump' on contact. He was even more surprised, however, when it stood up and revealed itself to be a boy of his own age, yelling and clutching at the back of his legs in pain.

"What did you do that for?" yelled the boy, as William jumped back, startled.

William recovered himself.

"What were you doing hiding in my copse?" he asked in return, thinking that this was far more important than a mere tap with a branch. Besides, he could see from the boy's clothes that he was not from a noble family.

"You can't go round hitting people with a stick," responded the boy, who was trying to peer round at the back of his legs to assess the damage.

"Actually I can," said William, determined to stamp his authority on the proceedings. "I am William de Beauvais, son of Sir Henry de Beauvais, master of Grangedean Manor. Whereas you," he added, looking the other boy up and down, "are nobody."

The other boy paused in the act of lifting one leg for inspection. He slowly put the leg down and turned to fix William with a firm brown eye and defiant chin, as he said in a steady voice, "I am Thomas Melrose, and my pa farms them fields across the woods with wheat and barley. So if my pa didn't grow his crops, you'd not have bread on your table or beer in your cellar."

William felt this conversation needed bringing back to the key issue. "Doesn't mean you can go grubbing around in my copse, though. Hey," he said, as a thought hit him, "you were looking for conies weren't you? That's poaching. I can have you jailed for that. Or beaten," he added.

"You beat me already, ain't you? Then that's settled it," the other boy observed. Then he added quickly and with an edge of defiance, "Anyway, ain't caught no conies, so I've done no wrong."

"True," admitted William reluctantly. He decided to move on to something much more interesting. "See that tree over there?"

Thomas followed his pointing finger. "Yes?"

"See that large leaf under that branch?"

"Yes?"

"I bet you can't hit it with an arrow."

"I never used an arrow. Pa says I'm too young." Thomas studied the leaf, measuring distance. "But I can throw a stone and hit it, clean."

"Go on, then."

Thomas looked around the undergrowth, but there were no stones on the rough earth. Then he saw a small section of stick, about the width of his wrist and the length of his forearm. He picked it up and hefted it in his hand to test the weight. Then he pulled back his arm, took aim, and threw. The stick swung in a low arc towards the tree, spinning end over end. It just missed the leaf.

"Missed," shouted William. "My turn."

He pulled an arrow out of the small quiver on his belt and picked his bow out of the harness on his back. He slotted the arrow between his forefingers as he'd been taught, pulled back, took careful aim, held his breath, and fired.

The arrow flew straight and true, piercing the leaf close to its stem and detaching it cleanly from the branch.

William stood back; his triumph absolute, his mastery proven beyond doubt.

"I would have hit it, if I'd had a stone," observed Thomas casually.

"Never."

"Would so. I can hit anything with a stone."

"Look, that was the best shot I've ever done," said William, petulantly.

"Not bad, I suppose."

"Not bad? It was masterful. Say it was masterful, or I'll hit you again with my stick."

"I'll knock you down first."

"You'd never."

"Try me."

In response, William launched at Thomas, wrestling him to the ground. A fight ensued, involving punching and kicking. Eventually it ended, with no clear victor and two exhausted boys lying on the ground catching their breaths and rubbing their bruises.

After a short while, William stood up. After such an intense fight, his thoughts turned naturally to his stomach.

"You want to come back to the manor for some food and drink?" he asked.

"Yes," answered Thomas, "I would."

And so their friendship, forged in battle, began that day.

---0---

At first, Lady de Beauvais was unsure about allowing William to mix with the son of a yeoman farmer, but she soon realised that there were very few boys of William's age in the area – and their friendship seemed genuine. So Thomas was allowed to come up to the manor regularly as a companion for William. At first he was only allowed up when William was not at his lessons with his tutor, a splendid old man from the village called Frobisher, who had a white beard so long he could almost step on it, and which he parted in the middle to make two separate beards that hung down either side of his ample belly.

After a couple of months, Lady de Beauvais decided that William's lessons would be more productive if he had another boy in class with him, and agreement was reached that Thomas could be tutored by Frobisher as well. So together they learned Latin, Scriptures, Greek and Mathematics; sitting at dusty desks while Frobisher lectured them for up to eight hours a day. By the time they were twelve, Thomas's quick brain and exceptional ability to learn meant he had caught up with William, and by the time they were fourteen, he had pulled well ahead. Frobisher was full of praise for the boy, continually remarking on his quick grasp of new concepts, and drawing unfavourable comparisons with William's lesser academic abilities.

Thomas loved to run home after lessons, to tell his father what he'd learned, and to see his father's eyes light up as he shared in his son's joy of learning.

"You're getting what few other men in this realm can boast, my son – an education," his father once said. "Use it wisely and maybe one day you'll make a fine gentleman."

"Don't give the boy airs," was his mother's reply. "Boys like Thomas have a place in life and must know it well."

"Nay, Jane, don't stop him trying to better himself," said his father. "Thomas has a talent for learning – and friends in high places. That's a powerful combination." He turned to Thomas and put his arm round his shoulder. "I know you'll make it son. I couldn't be prouder of you than I am today."

Thomas looked up at his father and smiled. "I'm proud of you, too, Pa, and I tell anyone who asks it."

Where Thomas had his books, William made up for his lower intellectual ability with athletic prowess. He could run faster, shoot straighter and fight better with a sword than Thomas, and would seek out any opportunity to take part in such pursuits.

More and more William sought to accompany his own father Sir Henry de Beauvais on his frequent hunts in the forests and fields, seeking out stags and wild boars.

As a yeoman's son, Thomas would not normally be considered eligible to join them – conies and hares would be all he would be allowed to hunt, but such was the companionship between the two boys, his participation was not only allowed, it was actively encouraged.

And so it might have continued – a friendship forged between boys in the hunting grounds, gardens and schoolroom of Grangedean Manor should have blossomed into a lifelong companionship of men. And indeed it would have done, had an unfortunate situation not occurred – a desperate tragedy that neither was responsible for, yet which led to a misunderstanding that left a deep scar on their youthful friendship.

It was after a fine hunt one golden autumn afternoon when William and Thomas, now in their late teens, were riding slowly back to the manor. They were highly elated following a protracted chase after a particularly fine roan stag, which had culminated in a momentous climax that neither could have predicted.

They had cornered the stag in a copse about a mile from the manor. It had stood just inside the copse, snorting and puffing with exhaustion after a long chase.

The two young men quietly dismounted upwind of the stag and crept slowly to the edge of the copse, William fitting an arrow to his bow as he went.

The sun was dropping behind the fine old elm trees, lengthening the shadows and creating dappled shapes that gave the hunters ideal cover as they moved.

They dropped to their knees into the soft undergrowth behind one of the elms, taking care not to snap a twig or make a noise to cause the animal to take flight. Keeping their breathing shallow and communicating only by hand signals, they carefully took position either side of the tree. Thomas hefted a short throwing spear in his hand and pulled it back, ready to throw. The plan was for William to aim an arrow for the sweet spot just above the foreleg where the heart could be pierced, and for Thomas to follow up with the spear if the animal was not killed cleanly.

Thomas watched as William pulled back on the bow so that the grey goose-feathered flight of the birch arrow drew level with his ear; the tension crackling in the yew wood and the tightly-twisted hemp strings humming under the strain.

William took a slow, careful breath as he stared down the shaft of the arrow, sighted it on the stag's haunch, then lifted it slightly to give it the arc it needed to find its target. He exhaled gently through his teeth to steady his nerve, paused a moment, then opened his fingers. It was the smallest of movements, but enough for the strings to snap forward as the tension unwound the bow in a fraction of a second, sending the iron-tipped arrow across the copse at over a hundred miles an hour to pierce deep into the stag's chest.

Enraged, the great stag lifted its head and roared in agony, its hooves carving deep gouges in the soft ground in front of it. The arrow had missed the heart by no more than a finger's width and it was still very much alive. It cast around, seeking the source of its pain, and its large angry eyes narrowed as they fixed on the two young men at the edge of the copse.

With an anguished bellow, it dropped its head, bringing its great pointed antlers down into position so they could inflict the maximum damage on the two young men.

Then it charged.

Thomas knelt and steadied himself, his spear pulled back over his shoulder ready to throw, as the great stag sped across the copse with William's arrow buried deep in its chest. It thundered towards them, snorting and roaring, clearly having every intention of skewering them on the points of its antlers. Then suddenly it clattered to a stop, just before it got in range of Thomas's spear and stood, pawing the ground and snorting great clouds of steam while its eyes flicked either side of the tree at each of them in turn.

It narrowed its eyes on William, then seemed to make up its mind. With a roar of pain and anger, it charged towards him.

"Die, damn you," shouted William, "die!"

Ignoring him, Thomas was totally focussed on throwing his spear as hard and true as he could. He held his breath, seeking out the ideal spot – on the chest just below the soft throat where the spear could fell the great beast in an instant.

He waited for his moment – when the stag would lift its head to expose the lethal spot. But the stag kept its head down as it closed the gap – until the last moment when it lifted it up to fix its aim on William – and Thomas snapped his arm forward with all his strength and let the heavy-tipped spear fly, straight into the stag's chest.

Dead before it even hit the ground, the great beast's momentum brought it crashing towards the pair, the great antlers gouging deep furrows in the soft undergrowth like a plough in a field, before coming to rest just inches in front of William.

Thomas found himself breathing hard and fast as the stag came to a stop, and it was some moments before he could bring his breath under control and turn to his friend.

William's eyes were wide, his cheeks red and Thomas was surprised to see him start to laugh; deep bellowing laughs of exhilaration and release of tension.

"Oh my friend, you throw straight and true indeed!" William stood up. "You must retrieve the spear that has done such noble work this day!"

Thomas stood up as well. "You also shoot true, my friend."

"Nay, my arrow failed to find the heart. But you found it, by God's good fortune, and I am not to be finding myself skewered on the antlers of that beast."

William looked at the twitching corpse before them. "On the day we first met, it was my arrow that was true, and your stick failed to hit its mark. Now we have changed sides completely!"

He laughed again. "Come, let us go back to the manor. We must send for servants to bring this beast back for the table – and we must tell the story of your bravery!"

---0---

Arriving back at the manor, they were still elated with the hunt and the stories they had to tell. Thomas was deeply happy – he had proven himself on the hunt and won the admiration of his friend, and he longed to return home to tell the tale to his father. Already he could see the old man's shining eyes and proud smile as he was taken through the tale of his son's bravery and skill with the spear in the face of such danger.

They rode into the stable courtyard and two servants ran forward to take their horses. They dismounted and strode through to the Great Hall.

As they got there, Thomas could see immediately that something was wrong.

Sir Henry and Lady de Beauvais we sitting at the table, with Jane Melrose, Thomas's mother, sitting by them. She was looking both uncomfortable and deeply upset at the same time.

"Oh, Thomas!" she said as he stopped in front of the table.

"Mother?" he asked. "What is the matter? Why are you here?"

"Your mother has some very bad news, Thomas," said Lady de Beauvais, her voice breaking.

Thomas looked at his mother, who was now in tears. "It's your father, Thomas. He's... he's..." The tears took over and she stopped, gulping and fighting for breath.

Thomas found his own breath catching in his throat.

"He's dead, Thomas. I'm sorry," said Sir Henry.

Thomas clutched at the edge of the table and dropped to his knees.

He stared up at his crying mother, then suddenly she seemed to disintegrate in front of him as his own tears flooded his eyes.

"It's not true," he whispered, blinking furiously. "If this is a jest, it is in the very poorest taste."

"It is true, Thomas," said his mother.

"Then how did it happen?"

There was a long pause.

"He has taken his own life," said Sir Henry, crossing himself.

Sir Henry and Lady de Beauvais looked briefly at each other, then at Jane Melrose. Thomas couldn't be sure, but it was almost as if they were confirming a previously-agreed story.

"We have no knowledge as to why he would do such a thing," Sir Henry finished.

Again, the look.

Thomas knew he was lying, but couldn't find it within himself to make the accusation. He stared at the man. Sir Henry had a look of pity carefully applied to his face, and Thomas, in that instant, despised him.

He turned to Lady de Beauvais. She too was looking back at him with a look of sad pity that made him sick.

He looked at his mother. She was looking down, with tears streaming down her cheeks.

"Come, mother," he said, finding his strength as he stood up, "we must go back home and make such arrangements as must be made."

He turned and made to walk out of the Great Hall. As he did so, he caught sight of William, who had been leaning against the wall behind him with arms folded. Their eyes met.

Thomas stopped with a jolt as a further dreadful truth was revealed in William's eyes.

"You knew," he whispered. "You knew all along."

William said nothing. Thomas shook his head, as if to deny the awfulness of this final revelation, and walked out of the Great Hall.

Once outside he quickened his stride into a run, as his anger took hold.

"My horse! My horse!" he shouted, running into the Grangedean stable yard. Arthur was produced and saddled up, while Thomas stamped with impatience.

As soon as he was ready, Thomas leapt onto Arthur's back, his anger communicating itself to the horse so Arthur reared up, neighing, before Thomas got him under control. Then he wheeled the horse round and together they thundered out of the gates. Arthur, who at that time was young and full of high spirits, shook his mane as he galloped down the forest paths towards Thomas's family farmhouse.

Clattering into his own courtyard, he leapt off Arthur's back and left the horse to trot into the stable alone, as he strode into his own small hall.

"Father!" he cried, "Father! Are you home?"

There was a silence.

"Father!"

Again, silence. No large comforting figure of the old man to throw his arms around his son and welcome him home.

"Father…"

Thomas sank into one of the high-backed oak chairs and let his head fall onto the table. Great, tortured sobs welled up and broke out of him as he grieved for his father, for his youth, and for the friendship he had come to value so greatly.

He sobbed until he felt he no longer had any tears left inside him; until he was as dry as an old, grey bone.

He was still slumped over the table when his mother entered.

"Oh, my son," she said "I am so sorry."

He looked up.

"So he is gone."

"Yes."

"But why, Mother?" he asked quietly, as she sank onto the chair next to him and put her hand on his arm. "What possessed him to do it? I mean, what pressure must he have been under?"

"Great pressure, my son," she replied. "He was facing ruin from the enclosure of the lands."

"Enclosure?" He turned and faced her. He felt his anger start to rise again, like lava in a rumbling volcano. "What enclosure?"

"Sir Henry. He has forced enclosure of your father's lands. It means we may no longer farm them."

"But that is our livelihood."

"Indeed."

"And this is why my father took his life?"

There was a small hesitation before the reply. "Indeed."

"And it is by Sir Henry's doing?"

Again, the small hesitation. "Indeed."

Thomas pushed back his chair and stood up. He could no longer contain his anger, and he strode to the fireplace, kicking aside the protective grass rushes on the floor. He turned back and faced his mother.

"Then we must starve?" he snarled.

"You will need to take service with Sir Henry's household."

"I shall not."

"You must." She paused and fixed him with a piercing stare, "or we shall surely starve."

"This is William's doing," said Thomas, softly.

He was exhausted; his anger had gone as quickly as it had come. "The man is as false a friend as has ever drawn breath," he said. "I shall never forgive him. Never."

---0---

And now it was seven years later, and Thomas Melrose and Arthur were finally plodding into the courtyard of the farmhouse.

Arthur's ears pricked up and he snorted at the familiar smell of his oat mash.

Melrose slipped off his back and tied him to a railing, then walked through into the hall to find his mother with some bread and ale on the table.

"How was the hunt?"

"As ever." He sat at the table, pulled off a piece of bread and ate. "The man must hunt so frequently," he said after a mouthful, "that he will lay waste to all the county if he can." His mother poured him a tankard of ale and he took a long draft. "But the arrogance of the man – that is what I cannot take. He must needle me at every turn."

He turned to his mother and looked her in the eye. "Isn't it enough that I must serve him – that I must attend him along with those imbeciles, Dowland and Stanmore, so he can maintain his lordly status?" He put his tankard down on the table. "I would do him to death, Mother, so help me God. I would do it without a moment's pity, as one kills a beetle."

"Shush, my son," she replied. "Do not suggest such a thing." She poured him some more ale. "And never in the name of the Lord."

"I would do it, Mother. Would I have the chance, I would do it."

"Nay – I would not lose my son as well as my husband. The justices would have your life for de Beauvais. I would not see you hang for him."

"Indeed, Mother." He smiled, a hollow smile. "It was a jest. He is not worthy, even of my hatred."

---0---

Jane Melrose stood up and walked to the door, not reassured in the least. "I will retire to my chamber. You may bid me goodnight shortly." He nodded to her, eating some more bread.

She turned in the doorway and looked back at her son.

'He does not know the truth of this,' she thought. 'Poor William de Beauvais is no more guilty in this than he is.'

She turned back and walked slowly to her chamber, her heart heavy.

'He must never know the full truth of his father's death,' she thought. 'For that would kill him as surely as the hangman's noose.'

CHAPTER TWELVE

Margaret had been watching as Sir William and the lady made their progress out of the hall. She had been hiding just inside the door to the kitchens and was confident that the lady had not seen her.

It had been a shock to realise that the master's dinner companion was actually the witch called Justine. She had seen it immediately when she approached with the silver water bowl – the shape of the face, the line of the eyebrows – it would take more than some make-up and a French hood to have fooled her. So she already had her guard up in preparation for Justine's guilty reaction, and was able to keep calm and not react herself. Thereafter, she was able to ignore Justine completely while serving Lady de Beauvais, before sending a kitchen boy down to the village to fetch Hopkirk.

She had also made some discreet enquiries from the other servants as to the name of this lady. The one named Sarah had told her that she was called Mary Fox, had come recently from France and was staying while her father was away at sea. "I helped bathe and wash her, and I clothed her," Sarah had said. "What a gracious lady. Not too sure what to do, mind, but most gracious."

Once the couple had left and the guests had all taken their seats again, Margaret ran down the stairs to the kitchens, to find Hopkirk had arrived. He was sitting bolt upright on a bench at the edge of the kitchen, staring unblinkingly at the hustle and bustle going on around him, his black cloak drawn round him despite the heat of the fires.

Margaret approached with caution; she was still wary of this small grey man with his power as a witchfinder and a magistrate.

"Master Hopkirk," she said. "You are welcome here."

He did not turn, but carried on staring at the activity in the kitchens.

"Mistress Margaret. I came when I was called." Now he turned and fixed her with his grey eyes. "You have identified this witch?"

"Oh yes, Master Hopkirk." She took a breath to calm her nerves. "She has been changed from a serving maid to a fine lady called Mary Fox. She must have enchanted the master as she was his guest of honour at the banquet."

"And she is still in the hall with Sir William?"

"Oh no – the witch has gone upstairs with the master."

"Upstairs? To his chambers?"

"Aye – I fear for him, to be alone and unprotected in her wicked grasp."

Hopkirk paused in thought, his eyes boring uncomfortably into hers.

"I will need to gather some people from the village; we must have numbers if we are to restrain her. It will take me a few hours so I think we must agree that we will come to arrest her in the morning."

At that point the cook came over, straightening her cap and running her hands down her apron. "Master Hopkirk, as I live and breathe."

"Madam Cook," he replied, slowly turning towards her.

"What a pleasure to see you in my kitchens, Master Hopkirk. Is there anything I can do for you?"

Margaret could not contain herself. "It's that girl from this morning, Cook. The one that was put to turning the spit. She's like as not a witch! Master Hopkirk is here to see her brought to justice."

"A witch indeed?" The cook scratched her cheek. "Aye, now I think on it, she was right strange, that one."

"She knows things she didn't ought to know," explained Margaret. "She made the hearth clean by magic. And she blasphemed something wicked, as the Lord is my witness."

"Blasphemed?"

"Aye. She said – oh Lord forgive me – she wished…" Margaret gulped and crossed herself, "…she wished Christ in Hell." Margaret crossed herself again several times.

"She never!" responded the cook, crossing herself also.

"And she enchanted Sarah to bathe her and clean her from the soot of the kitchens, and to make her into a fine lady called Mary Fox," added Margaret.

"Well, Master Hopkirk," said the cook, "this one is no good and that's the truth. You must find her and test her."

"I will," whispered Hopkirk. "Indeed I will." He fixed them both with his unblinking eyes, now burning fiery red in the reflection of the kitchen fires. "We will test her for witchcraft and if we find her to be a witch…" His voice rose to a menacing growl, "If she is found to be a witch, we will condemn her to the flames of eternal salvation."

"Amen to that," said the cook. "Tell us what we must do to help."

"You must gather up the servants, and be ready to help me hunt her down and arrest her. At present she is with Sir William in his room – we will arrest her in the morning."

"I'll have them ready."

"Good. I will return at dawn." Hopkirk bowed. "By your leave, Madam Cook."

"Master Hopkirk."

Hopkirk turned and went out along the corridor towards the door which led out to the herb gardens, leaving the cook and Margaret standing staring after him. The cook looked at Margaret. "I thought there was something not right about that girl. Her dress… Her speech… Not right at all"

"And from out the parish, too," added Margaret.

"Aye, from out the parish," agreed the cook.

Margaret gasped as a thought struck her. "Why are we not arresting her this very evening? Why wait until the morning? She's with the master on her own – maybe she's enchanting him." An awful vision came into her mind. "Maybe even now she has turned him into a cat!"

At that moment Martha came down into the kitchen, carrying a wooden tray with some plates on it. "There is more to clear; we need some servants up in the hall." She stopped, seeing the cook and Margaret standing together looking very worried. "Is there something wrong?" she asked.

"The girl you brought down here this morning – she's a witch," announced the cook.

"A witch?" asked Martha. "Are you sure? She was strange in her speech and dress to be certain, but a witch?"

"Aye," said the cook. "She knew things she didn't ought to know, and she used an incantation to clean the hearth, and she blasphemed something horrible to Margaret."

"She blasphemed?" responded Martha, appearing suitably shocked. "What did she say?"

"Terrible things," said the cook, as she and Margaret crossed themselves repeatedly. "She said…" the cook hesitated before uttering the words. "She said 'I would that Christ rots in Hell.' Oh Lord forgive me."

Martha crossed herself as well. "She said that?"

"Those very words to Margaret here – as true as life."

"And she's with the master in his rooms – enchanting him as we stand here!" burst out Margaret.

"No," said Martha, "that is Mistress Mary Fox, the guest of honour."

"One and the same," said the cook grimly.

"Mary Fox, the fine lady, is Justine the witch?" asked Martha slowly. "But surely I would have recognised her?" She stared at them a moment. "But now I think on it, there is some sense in the girl Justine being this Mary Fox. Both appear as if from nowhere and both have strange mannerisms – and both are tall and red-haired…" She slapped her fist into her palm. "By the risen Christ, I should have seen it myself."

"Maybe she enchanted you," suggested Margaret. "Maybe she thought I was of no matter, so she did not enchant me and I recognised her, but you, as the housekeeper were more important and she thought to enchant you not to recognise her." Margaret was very satisfied with this; it was clear logic. The facts were in order.

"So, what is to be done?" asked Martha.

"Margaret has called Hopkirk, the witchfinder," said the cook. "And he has said he will call together a band of villagers to take her, and to test her for witchcraft."

"He says he will take her in the morning, but she could have turned the master into a cat or a bat by then," said Margaret, repeating her earlier concerns. "I say we should go up to the master's chambers and take her now."

"No," said Martha quickly, surprising Margaret with the hard edge to her voice. "The master can take care of himself. We will take her when she comes down in the morning."

"Master Hopkirk said we should get the kitchen servants to help," offered the cook.

"I will tell them," said Martha. She moved to the other side of the kitchen and climbed onto a stool.

"Hear me all!" she called out. "Hear me!"

The servants started to put down their knives, pestles and other tools. After a couple of minutes they were all standing still, listening.

"The guest of honour this evening with the master, was in fact the serving girl who came this morning into the kitchens to turn the spit. We have reason to believe she is a witch, so we will need to arrest her and test her for witchcraft. We will take her in her room or when she comes down to break her fast in the morning."

"How do you know she's a witch?" asked one of the servants.

"She knows things she shouldn't know," said Martha.

"She used black magic to clean the kitchens," said Margaret.

"And she blasphemed," added the cook.

"What did she say?" asked another servant.

Martha crossed herself several times, then answered, "She said she rejected Christ and all his good works, and she wished he would go to Hell for all eternity."

Margaret watched the servants cross themselves repeatedly and mutter darkly to each other. One decrepit and elderly under-cook even dropped to her knees to pray feverishly for a few moments, then had to be helped back to her feet by those either side of her.

"We will meet here at dawn," said Martha. Master Hopkirk, the witchfinder, will come with others from the village. With him to lead us, we will take this witch and we will bring her to justice." She paused for effect, looking along the line of servants in front of her.

"And may the Lord have mercy on her soul."

CHAPTER THIRTEEN

As Justine left the hall after the banquet, her mind was racing.

It was obvious that Sir William would only be interested in one thing when they got upstairs to his rooms – sex.

He'd been perfectly clear on that at dinner and his suggestion that he could wait was scarcely credible. No, there was no doubt that he would expect to sleep with her tonight.

A battle raged between Justine's head and heart.

Her heart fired the opening shot.

'Go on girl, sleep with him,' it said. 'You know you want to. You know you want to be in the arms of a strong, handsome man. Grab it, relish it, enjoy it, love it!'

Then her head cut in. 'Don't be so foolish. Lady de Beauvais was clear that he loses interest in girls once he's had them. Don't kid yourself that you'll be anything different in that. Let him have you and you won't just lose his interest; you'll lose his protection and his mother's as well.'

Her heart could see this was a strong argument, but it rallied. 'You came here by some freak chance, maybe you could leave by the same means at any time. You always fancied him in the picture – now you've met him in real life. Better not let the chance go.'

That was an easy one for her head to counter. 'The freak incident that brought you here was just that – a freak. The chances of it happening again are so remote as to be virtually impossible. So it's likely that you're stuck here in Tudor England as Mary Fox for the rest of your days. And the natives are not friendly – they think you're a witch. So you need the protection of Sir William and his mother and you can't risk letting him lose interest.'

Her heart had to concede that this was the clincher. Her head pressed home its victory. 'And anyway, he's a hunter. Let him have his hunt. That's the only way to keep his interest.'

'OK,' said her heart, 'you win – for now.'

Her mind made up, she smiled at him as they went upstairs, and was rewarded with a deep smile back.

"You are radiant, Mistress Justine Parker – or as I must now call you – Mistress Mary Fox. Your beauty makes my humble home seem to come alive."

"My lord," she said, inclining her head in recognition of the full acceptance of her new name, as well as the fine compliment to her beauty.

Her heart put in an extra beat and told her head it had better watch its step.

They reached the top of the stairs and walked past the portrait of Sir Thomas.

"My grandfather, Sir Thomas," said Sir William. "He built this house in the reign of the first Henry Tudor."

"A fine gentleman," observed Justine. "I'm sure he would be proud of what you have achieved."

"I do hope he would."

With that they passed along the gallery and through the door to the bedroom wing.

As they walked down the corridor, Justine glanced through the leaded windows. Dusk was falling and the summer sky was a deep fiery red.

Sir William opened a door at the far end of the corridor, bowed and stood back to let Justine enter.

"My humble chambers are yours," he said.

Justine knew that this was the master suite and they had set it out as such in her time. It consisted of an ante-room for dressing and a bedroom beyond. Once again she was pleased to see they had got it pretty much correct – except that they had set out the ante-room as a museum exhibit, whereas this was a room that was lived in. And it was a total mess.

The room had three large chests for Sir William's clothes, plus a wooden chair and desk under the window.

The desk was strewn with papers and had a large ink pot with a jar of quills on it. There were ink spills on the desk and several papers on the floor. The chests were covered in discarded clothing – doublets lying on top of crumpled hose, with several pairs of boots on the floor near the chair. Clearly Sir William had sat in the chair, pushed off each boot and left them where they fell. A sword in its scabbard was propped up against the wall, near to where a burnished silver breastplate was lying.

Justine realised she must have been looking at the mess in the room with some disdain, as Sir William suddenly leapt forward, gathered up the discarded clothes, boots and armour and threw them into one of the chests.

He then made a half-hearted attempt to sort the papers on the desk into a tidy pile. When he was done, he stood back with a weak smile, like a puppy who has sat on command for the first time.

"A thousand pardons, Mary; my servant has failed his duty. It is not usually such a mess."

"No, I'm sure it is not," she laughed. "Men," she observed. "They're all the same. Helpless. Always have been; always will."

"You have rendered me helpless, good Mary, with your beauty and your charms." He smiled and bowed deeply.

"Oh please, my lord," she replied, with a touch of amusement. "If you want to flatter me, you'll have to do better than that."

"Oh, I see," he replied with mock sternness, "I must first make love to you with words, like a Cheapside poet." He thought a moment, studying her intently.

Justine waited with high expectation for what she hoped would be some beautiful Shakespearean-style metaphors.

"Your lips are most wondrous," he began.

'OK start,' she thought.

"They are like… they are like…" He looked like he was running out of steam and Justine's hopes sank.

Sir William stared wildly out of the window for inspiration "Your lips are like… the um… red sky at night…"

She raised an enquiring eyebrow, interested to see where this was going and rather enjoying his boyish discomfort. "…as the… er… red sky betokens the promise of warmth and sunshine in the day to follow."

"Hmm," she responded, not wishing to hurt his feelings. "Not bad. Not great rhyme and meter, but I like the idea."

"Your eyes…"

'Wait up,' she thought 'there's more...'

"…are like cornflowers…"

"Cornflowers?" she enquired.

"Yes, cornflowers. Because…" again Justine raised an eyebrow and waited expectantly "…because… because I think cornflowers are the prettiest of flowers," he ended lamely.

Justine clapped her hands. "Thank you, that was a worthy effort," she said. "But I think the truth is that these Cheapside poets are safe just now."

He laughed, then started to unbutton his doublet.

"What are you doing?" she asked.

"I would not lie with you fully clothed," he answered. "Will you also remove your clothing so we can lie together?" He gestured the door to the bedroom.

"But I have not agreed to lie with you," she said, folding her arms decisively.

Sir William looked genuinely puzzled. "You truly would not wish to come to the bed of Sir William de Beauvais? Why would you not?"

"It's not you," she answered, thinking fast, "it's just that where I come from, it takes a bit longer. A man and a girl need more time with each other first."

He studied her intently for a moment, then burst out, "Poppycock! A wench is for the bed, no more and no less. It has always been so and always will be."

Justine considered this, then shook her head. "How can you say that? You might take a girl just because you can. But where's the satisfaction?"

"God's teeth," he answered, "I would show you if you'd let me…" He made a grab for her, but she dodged away behind one of the chests.

"But how much better to join with her in a warm loving embrace than to have to fight her every inch of the way," she answered, moving round the chest as he advanced on her. "Come on," she added, "I bet you've had to fight for a few of your girls, haven't you?"

"Aye, I might have," he answered, making a sudden change of direction to try and reach her from the other side.

"And there's hardly been much warmth afterwards has there?" she responded, making the opposite change of direction and keeping the large chest between them.

"So?" he asked, pausing a moment as he flicked his eyes left and right, judging angles of attack.

"So make her feel truly special… make her realise that she's the only one…"

For a moment, Justine thought she had scored a good hit with that shot. He stayed still, looking up and to the left as he did some quick mental arithmetic. "But if she is one of hundreds..?"

Justine groaned. "I know, but that is hardly what she wants to hear," she observed testily.

"In truth," he answered, ignoring her testiness, "what she wants to hear is of no consequence."

Justine could see she was getting nowhere with this. She decided to change her approach. "Listen," she said, "tell me what you like best in life."

"What I like best?" He looked nonplussed. "Why?"

"Because I want to know. Because I am asking."

"Yes, but why?"

"Tell me," she repeated "what you like to do best in life."

There was a moment's silence while he considered her thoughtfully. Then he seemed to make up his mind.

"That is easy," he answered. "The chase."

"The chase?"

"For the deer."

"And how do you feel when you've caught it?" she asked. "Do you marvel at its beauty, its nobility, its passion?"

"Nay, I kill it."

Again, Justine groaned with despair.

He laughed. "'Twas a jest! I respect the deer as a worthy foe, and I love it for its beauty, but surely you cannot draw comparison with a wench?"

"Yes, I can," she answered. "I'll demonstrate." She moved to the far corner of the room, turned away from him, then looked back over her shoulder with what she hoped was a 'noble deer' pose. "Pretend I'm the deer."

"This is unnatural."

"Go on." She shot him a look over her shoulder. "What happens now?" she asked.

"I laugh, because you look a fool." Again she shot him a look, challenging him to go with her on the pretence.

He sighed. "In faith, I see you across the clearing." He went down on one knee, then mimed selecting an arrow and fitting it to his bow, seeming now to humour her. "I kneel slowly, and prepare an arrow…"

His voice softened as he seemed to become absorbed by the scene.

"I slow my breath, because the smallest part of my scent in the still air could alert you to my presence… I draw slowly, looking for the spot where I can shoot true to your heart…"

She stared at him over her shoulder.

"I wait for you to be motionless, choosing my moment with care…"

He stopped; his breath as soft as the still morning air as he stared at her.

"…And then I wonder at your beauty, your nobility, as you stand proud in the morning mist, and I am sad for a moment to take such a life… but then I know that to make such nobility mine in conquest is… is a worthy pursuit… I steady my aim…"

He opened his fingers. "I let fly."

Justine fell back against the wall with a small cry.

He stood up and ran over to her.

"I run to her side, and I claim her as my own."

He took her hands in his and pulled her towards him.

"And now I look closely at her… I see how beautiful she is, how perfect is the line of her brow, the shape of her eye, the ruby softness of her lips…"

Still holding her hands, he dropped again to one knee in front of her.

"Mary Fox, the truth is you are the girl of my dreams and you have stolen my heart with your beauty and your charms. I have known you but a day, yet I feel I have known you a thousand years."

He raised her hands to his lips and kissed them.

"I cannot live another moment without knowing you are truly mine for all time," he whispered.

Justine's heart melted as she saw the sincerity in his eyes, and gently she raised him up until they were standing face to face.

She moved closer to him and he put his arms around her. "Oh my lord," she said, "kiss me."

Their lips came together and his mouth opened under hers. His tongue caressed hers gently.

She melted into his arms and into his kiss.

Time stood still.

Later, they broke off and stood back, looking into each other's eyes.

"Mary Fox," he said, "you are truly becoming the mistress of my heart."

"Sir William de Beauvais," she replied. "I think you have been master of mine for all time."

He took her hand and led her through to his bedroom. "Come, Mary Fox," he said, as he led her to the bed and laid her down, "I must know you completely."

Justine's heart went out to him. 'Oh yes,' it whispered 'I want this more than anything else in the world...'

And she would have submitted then and there, had not her head suddenly cut in.

'Just hang on one minute, young lady,' it said. 'Have you forgotten our agreement?'

'That's out the window,' said her heart. 'Were you not paying attention just now when he kissed you? That was a game changer. You won't get another kiss like that for oh... maybe 450 years. You can't ignore that kiss.'

'You can, and you will,' said her head. 'You must.'

Justine pushed him away and stood up.

"I am sorry, my lord," she said. "As I said before, this is too soon. We have been together for just one day." She tucked a stray lock of hair back under her hood and stood up as straight as she could, aware that her chest was now heaving right under his nose. "I am sorry. We cannot do this now."

'Well done, girl,' said her head. 'Good move.'

Her heart refrained from answering.

Sir William frowned. "But when we kissed... I thought that now we knew each other well?"

He looked enquiringly into her eyes, like a puppy who had sat on command but had not got a treat. "You would still refuse to lie with me?" he whispered.

"My lord," she replied. "My heart says I should, but my head says it is too soon."

He stood back, and stared at her for what seemed an eternity.

"I would have my way." He said finally. "With any other girl I would have my way. But you..." he leaned forward and touched her cheek, "...you are different." He stood back again, while she looked steadfastly at him, her eyes never leaving his face. "You have bewitched me; that I must bend to your will."

"My lord, this is not witchcraft," said Justine quickly.

"Nay, I have no time for such nonsense," he answered, much to her relief. "Witchcraft is most often born in the minds of the accusers, not in those they accuse. I see no proof of witchcraft in you – and without proof there is no basis for an accusation. And yet…"

He kneeled down in front of her and took her hand. "And yet, I am so enchanted by you, that I must bend to your will. No girl has made me do that before." He paused. "My lady, what would you have me do?"

She lifted his hand in hers, pulling him up from his knees till he was standing in front of her. "My lord," she said, looking up into his eyes "you are a huntsman. You must consider how to shoot your arrow true to my heart." She reached up and touched his cheek, stroking his golden beard. "And when the time is right, perhaps it will find its mark."

"Aye, I warrant it will," he replied, putting his hand over hers, holding it against his cheek. "But like as not the huntsman will be led a merry dance first."

She smiled. "Indeed, my lord." She was about to add something about it being a lively dance nonetheless, when she felt an involuntary yawn starting. Initially she fought to keep her mouth closed, but it was an unequal battle and very soon the yawn popped her ears and forced her mouth wide open. Sir William watched in amusement, waiting till she had finished, then gently took her hand off his cheek.

"My lady, you are most tired and must to bed this instant," he observed.

"Yes," she said, as another yawn, even bigger than the first, quickly followed. "It has been quite a day," she said. She hadn't realised till that moment just how totally exhausted she was.

"I shall call for Sarah to undress you and make you ready for bed," he said, moving to the corner of the room and pulling on a red cord. A faint sound of a bell could be heard in the distance. He turned back to her.

"You shall sleep in the room at the end of this corridor. It will be your room – for now."

"For now?" she asked.

"Aye, my mother's sister Katherine Mansfield comes from Nottingham on the 13th of August next. She is used to staying there. But it will be yours for the two weeks until then."

A small alarm bell rang in Justine's sleepy mind. Two weeks to the 13th August – that made this the end of July…

Suddenly she was wide awake again.

"My lord, what day is it?" she asked, trying unsuccessfully to keep her voice flat calm.

"Why, do you not know?" he asked, not seeming to notice the edge of panic in her voice. "It is the 30th day of July in the year of our Lord, 1565."

Justine felt her legs go weak. She staggered back with a small cry, as the realisation hit her like a steam train that she had found Sir William and was starting to fall in love with him – on the eve of the 31st of July, 1565.

The very day he was destined to die.

She remembered the leaflet that she had picked up, and even the words it had said; "Sir William de Beauvais - born 1539, died on the night of the 31st of July 1565 in a barroom fight. He was reputed to be something of a wild man."

"What ails you, my lady?" Sir William asked with great concern, dragging her back to the present. Justine shook her head, unable to speak and unwilling to explain. She stared at him with wild eyes, seeing him now, not as a future lover, but as a man with an imminent sentence of death hanging over him.

"Oh my lord," she lied, "I am tired, as you said. I feel faint." She fell back onto the bed.

The door opened and Sarah entered. She took in the scene – Sir William standing over Justine lying on the bed. "Shall I come back shortly, Master?" she asked with a knowing smile.

"Nay, Sarah, Mistress Fox is tired," said Sir William. "She must be undressed and made ready for her bed. Please go to it."

"Yes, Master," answered Sarah, the smile disappearing as quickly as it had come.

Justine stood up, nodded weakly to Sir William, and walked unsteadily over to the door. She turned and looked back at him standing by the bed.

"Goodnight, my lady," said Sir William.

"Goodnight, my lord," Justine whispered, then followed Sarah out into the corridor and along to her bedroom.

---0---

Once in the bedroom Sarah set to work; removing Justine's make-up and hood, unpinning her hair, helping her out of the Tudor gown, farthingale, kirtle and her boots, putting her into a nightdress and into bed.

Throughout this process Sarah found Justine to be a model of willing obedience; lifting up her face to have her make-up wiped off, raising her arms to have her sleeves removed, stepping out of the gown, farthingale and kirtle when asked and offering up her legs to have her boots pulled off – but Sarah could see that Justine wasn't seeing her, or the bedroom. Justine may have been like a willing child being undressed and put to bed, but mentally she was in a completely different place – her eyes focussed on dreadful visions that only she could see.

Sarah, who was a kindly soul at heart and who had developed an affection for this girl, tried to bring Justine out of it by engaging her in conversation.

"Did you enjoy the banquet, Mistress Fox?" she asked while unpinning Justine's hair.

Or, while pulling off Justine's boots; "Did the master have much to say? He is well practised in courtly conversation, so I am told."

But Sarah got no answer. With a sigh she tiptoed out of the room, leaving her mistress sitting up in bed, hugging her knees to her chest and staring blankly at the wall opposite.

CHAPTER FOURTEEN

As dawn broke the next morning and the first golden rays of the summer sun pierced the still mist of the forest, Matthew Hopkirk led a small militia of villagers along the path towards Grangedean Manor.

He was sitting on a small, grey, shifty-eyed donkey while the villagers followed on foot. There were just fifteen of them; Hopkirk had managed to recruit only those who were not working in the fields or in their houses, so his group mainly consisted of the elderly and a few of the young village girls.

The elderly men and women carried pitchforks, which they planned to use to make the witch keep her distance if things turned nasty. The young girls carried crosses as a shield against the malevolent power of the Devil.

The girls had been Hopkirk's easiest recruits; not only were they excited by the chance to cast a witch out of the village, but it was also an opportunity to prove how God-fearing they were in case anyone ever thought to accuse them of witchcraft in future.

One of the girls, a pretty fifteen-year-old with straw-blonde hair tucked up under her plain coif, hitched her skirts and ran up to Hopkirk as they walked up the lane.

"Master Hopkirk," she began, as she drew level with him. "How are we to know this witch when we get to the manor?"

Hopkirk turned his cold grey eyes and stared down at her without blinking. She swallowed nervously. "If she maybe turns into a cat, or a raven or suchlike?" she added.

"It is Agnes, daughter of Jake of the tavern, isn't it?" he asked coldly.

Agnes took a deep breath as she glanced back down the line of villagers to where her friends Ruth and Maggie were watching and giggling nervously. They had just now dared her to talk to Hopkirk.

"Yes, Master Hopkirk," she answered.

"We will know her, I assure you, Agnes. We are true God-fearing folk, so if she be a witch, we will see the blackness of her heart and the Devil that resides within."

Agnes shivered. She was a good Christian girl, to be seen in church every week and on all the saints' days. This talk of the Devil disquieted her greatly.

"But if she assumes a different form?" she asked, emboldened by the support of Ruth and Maggie further down the path behind her. Hopkirk seemed not to notice them.

"My child, we will have to hope she does not, so we may identify her and bring her to trial." Hopkirk paused and Agnes was surprised to see he went a little red in the face. "We will challenge the Devil by submitting her to a test. We will put her under water so we can see if she has the magic to save herself."

They walked a moment in silence, as Agnes pondered on this.

"But if she does not save herself, she will be drowned?" she asked.

"Aye."

"And if she does save herself, by magic or by turning into a fish or suchlike, what then?"

"Then we will banish the Devil with fire," he answered softly. "We will burn her."

"So she will be dead whatever happens?" asked Agnes.

"Aye. Such is God's will."

Agnes crossed herself. "Such is God's will, Master Hopkirk," she acknowledged, and ran back to tell Ruth and Maggie what she had learned.

---0---

A few minutes later the party passed through a gate under a brick archway into the stable yard of Grangedean Manor, just as Sarah the servant was walking along the narrow corridor in the top floor above, leading from her tiny bedroom to the main house.

Noticing the movement in the yard below, she stopped by a leaded glass window and pushed it open a fraction so she could hear what was going on. She bit her lip as she recognised the grey man on the donkey as Hopkirk the witchfinder. What could he be doing at Grangedean Manor with a collection of pitchfork-wielding villagers? Was there a witch to be found?

Sarah shrunk back into the shadows to watch and listen.

Hopkirk dismounted and a servant ran out and took the donkey's bridle, then led the angrily braying beast away to a stable.

Hopkirk placed himself squarely in the middle of the yard, as menacingly still as a stone gargoyle. He waited as the villagers gathered around him.

"We are here to arrest an alleged witch known as Mary Fox," he began, his voice carrying clearly up to the window above.

Sarah gave a small cry, then quickly shrank further back into the shadows in case she'd been heard. The witch was Mary Fox! There must be a mistake – the Mary Fox she had served the night before was a good and kindly girl. She was no witch – of that one could be quite certain.

Sarah crept forward again and looked down on the yard. All the villagers were listening to Hopkirk – by God's good grace her small cry had not been heard.

"We must proceed through to the kitchens, where we will meet with Martha the housekeeper, who will tell us where the witch Mary Fox is sleeping, so we can arrest her and test her by ducking."

The villagers growled and the elderly shook their pitchforks.

"Evil witch!"

"Cast out the Devil!"

"Mary Fox, servant of Satan!"

Hopkirk held up his hand and there was silence.

"We must proceed with caution; this witch may have the power of transformation and may escape arrest by changing her form to a cat or a raven."

"By what evidence do we have her accused?" asked one of the elderly women.

"By her blasphemy and her rejection of Christ and all his good works," answered Hopkirk. "She was heard to say this: that she would have Christ rot in Hell for all eternity." The villagers all gasped. "And that Christ is the Devil incarnate."

"Those words?" asked the elderly woman, sounding deeply shocked.

"Those very words," confirmed Hopkirk, "spoken to Margaret, a servant in the manor."

The villagers shouted, stamped their feet and worked up their righteous anger, then Hopkirk again held up his hand.

When there was silence, he said, "We will proceed now into the manor. Follow me." He turned and went into the building, followed by his enraged militia.

Upstairs, Sarah closed the window quietly and for a moment she stood rooted to the spot. Mary Fox accused of being a witch – it was not to be believed! But if Hopkirk were to arrest her and test her... oh, how could such a thing be allowed? Such a poor girl, so exhausted she could not speak or sleep, but who had been so kind and gentle... No – it cannot be allowed. She must be warned!

With a determined lift of her head, Sarah turned and ran down the corridor.

Soon she reached the bedroom door and knocked. There was no sound. She knocked again, louder.

"Hello?" came a sleepy voice. "Come in."

Sarah pushed open the door and peered in. Her mistress, the girl she knew as Mary Fox, was sitting up in bed, bleary-eyed and with tousled hair.

"Morning, Sarah," Justine said, yawning sleepily and stretching her arms out wide.

Sarah went quickly up to the side of the bed.

"Mistress Fox, you must fly now!" she blurted out. "Master Hopkirk the witchfinder is here to arrest you!"

Her mistress was wide awake in an instant.

"Hopkirk? Here? Now?" she asked, her voice coming out in a strangled squeak.

"Oh yes, Mistress," answered Sarah "I saw him enter the manor with some people from the village. They had pitchforks."

"Oh, Sarah, will you help me?"

"Yes, Mistress Fox," said Sarah. "Yes I will."

Justine looked searchingly into Sarah's eyes. After a moment she seemed reassured. "So what are we to do?" she asked.

"We must get you out of the manor to somewhere you can hide out."

"Oh, yes – but where?"

Sarah paused a moment, chewing on her lower lip. What she was about to suggest was highly risky – putting herself and her family in danger. But one look at the terrified girl in front of her, and she knew she was doing the right thing. She said, "My mother has a little cottage in the woods; I can take you there. You'll be safe a while."

"Thank you so much, Sarah," said Justine. "But I don't want you or your mother to suffer if I am caught."

"We can look after ourselves, Mistress, never you mind."

Sarah said the words, but in her heart she was not so sure.

Justine took both Sarah's hands in hers and said, "I cannot thank you enough. Really I can't." She swung her legs out of the bed and was about to stand up when suddenly she froze.

"What is it, Mistress?" asked Sarah, concerned.

"Sir William!"

"The master – what of him?"

"I have to stop him going to the tavern this evening!"

Whatever Sarah might have expected her mistress to say, it was not that. "But the master does not go to the tavern, Mistress Fox," said Sarah, frowning. "He prefers to drink wine in the manor."

"Trust me on this, Sarah – he'll go today unless I can stop him," said Justine grimly.

Just then they heard some shouts from downstairs. Sarah stopped, listened a moment, then grabbed her mistress's arm. "You must come now, we have no time to lose!"

"I'll need to put my boots on!"

"No, Mistress! No time – not for boots!"

She pulled Justine to the door, then opened it a fraction to listen for sounds downstairs. She looked back with her hand to her mouth in a gesture of silence.

To her horror, Justine mouthed "wait" and slipped back into the room. For a moment Sarah thought her mistress would try and pull her heavy man's boots on, but instead the girl pulled a bag from under the bedcovers, swung it over her head and onto her shoulder. Then she grabbed the bow and quiver of arrows that still stood propped up in the corner and threw them onto the bed. Still barefoot, she ran back to Sarah at the door.

Sarah raised an enquiring eyebrow. Justine muttered, "It's a clue for William – best I can do," then slipped out of the room after her.

They crept quietly along the corridor towards the door at the end that led out to the gallery.

As before, Sarah opened the door a fraction, listening for sounds of Hopkirk and his posse of villagers. Almost immediately they heard the tramp of boots and a hissed direction to proceed upstairs.

Sarah quickly closed the door and looked back at Justine, her heart pounding fit to burst.

"We must go the other way," she whispered.

Together they ran back up the corridor, Justine's nightdress billowing around her; her bare feet making little sound on the wooden boards.

They reached the door at the end that led to Sir William's rooms. Justine looked at the solid door surrounded by wood panelling.

"We can't go in there, Mistress," Sarah hissed.

"Why not?" Justine squeaked.

"Those are the Master's rooms."

"But he could protect us."

"And have Hopkirk accuse him also?" Sarah shook her head. "Nay, Mistress, we'll not go that way," said Sarah. She glanced back along the corridor, expecting to see the door at the far end open at any time and the figure of the witchfinder appear.

"Then where do we go?" Justine whispered, the rising panic in her voice matching Sarah's.

"This way, quick!" said Sarah.

She pushed on an intricately-carved rose decoration at waist height on the wood panelling on the right side of the corridor. Immediately a small low doorway swung open below the carving to reveal a black opening behind. Without waiting for Justine, Sarah ducked down and disappeared into the dark space.

Sarah glanced back out and saw Justine's feet staying still, while the hem of her nightdress twisted round. The girl must be stopping to look back down the corridor,' she thought, 'when every moment is vital!'

Sarah was about to call out, when she heard the sound she had been fearing the most – the door at the far end start to open.

With a startled squeak Justine plunged head first past Sarah into the black opening. Sarah leaned back and pushed the door quietly shut, enveloping the two girls in total darkness.

Despite her thumping heart, Sarah stayed absolutely still, kneeling on the rough wooden boards. Then to her horror, she heard a board creak as Justine tried to get up.

"Easy, Mistress," she whispered. "Be quite still. It is dark and the roof is low at the start. We must gather our breath before moving."

"Where are we?" came the whispered reply.

"Old secret passage. It leads down through a hidden door in the courtyard. From there we can get out through the rose garden. I found it one day when I was cleaning."

"Oh. Right."

Then they heard the dreadful sound of boots marching along the corridor.

Closer they came; Sarah's heart thumping more and more as the boots got louder and louder. Then the boots stopped.

Right outside the door to the secret passage.

"The bed was still warm," came a menacing, sinister-sounding man's voice. "She cannot have gone far."

"She did not come past us as we walked along the gallery," came another voice, sounding like that of an old man.

There was the sound of several other people agreeing, accompanied by a noise like pitchfork handles thumping the floor.

"Sarah," Justine hissed. "We must move away!"

"Nay, 'tis too late – they will hear us. Best to keep very still, Mistress."

At that moment there was a slight scuttling sound from the floor inside the pitch-black hiding place.

Then the sound stopped, and Sarah heard Justine draw in her breath sharply. "Sarah," she hissed with unmistakable panic rising in her voice, "there's something crawling up my leg."

"By all that is holy, Mistress, you must stay still," breathed Sarah. "Belike, it is just a mouse," she said hopefully.

"Too heavy," came the whispered reply. "It's a rat... I know it's a rat... I hate rats..."

Sarah strained her ears to hear what was going on in the corridor outside their hiding place.

"She has disappeared, Master Hopkirk!" This sounded like an old woman. "She has used the Devil's magic to vanish into the air."

"Perhaps she has passed through this door here," said Hopkirk.

Sarah froze, her heart now about to jump out of her chest. She expected any second for light to flood in to the hiding place and a triumphant Hopkirk to bend down and drag them both out.

At that moment she heard Justine give another gasp and the tiniest cry. "It's moving up my leg," she breathed. "Oh God, oh God, oh God…!"

"Be still, please, Mistress…"

"Now there's another one! It's on my ankle…"

"In the name of Jesus, Mistress, please…"

"One's on my knee! What if it bites me?"

"Give your leg a shake, Mistress," hissed Sarah. "Just a small one, mind."

There was small grunt as Justine moved her leg, followed by a noticeable thump as the first rat jumped off and scuttled noisily up the dark corridor, followed by another thump and scuttling as the second rat followed.

"What was that?" said the sinister voice. "Quiet. I heard something."

Instantly there was quiet from the villagers in the corridor.

"Is there a secret passage here? A priest's hole or somesuch?"

The silence continued. Sarah prayed that none would know of the secret passage.

"There may indeed be one," said the sinister voice. This was followed by a sound that made Sarah's blood freeze in her veins and drew a small squeak from Justine.

It was the sound of tapping across the panels as Hopkirk searched for a hollow area.

The tapping started high and to the left, returning the dull thud of a solid wall. Then it moved across to the right, but just above their low doorway, so it still returned a dull thud.

Then it moved down and back across, getting closer and closer, till Sarah knew that any second it would return the hollow sound of an empty space.

Just when Sarah was convinced that all was lost, she heard another noise – that of a door opening.

"What is the meaning of this intrusion?" came the loud, indignant voice of Sir William de Beauvais. "Who are you, sir, that would trespass in my private rooms? And who is this rabble with you? What is your business in my house?"

The tapping stopped.

"I am Matthew Hopkirk, magistrate," came the sinister voice. "And I am charged to arrest a woman accused of the vile practice of witchcraft."

"Nonsense!" came the reply. "I am Sir William de Beauvais, and I do not entertain such fanciful notions."

"But I believe you have 'entertained' this woman," answered Hopkirk. "She is a serving girl, or the daughter of a merchant, and is known as Mary Fox."

There was a long silence. Sarah could picture the master going red with anger.

Eventually he gave out an explosive roar. "How dare you, sir!" he bellowed. "How dare you suggest that Mary Fox is a witch! Be gone sir, be gone this instant, and get your peasants and their pitchforks out of my house!"

There was a pause, as Hopkirk must have stood his ground.

"I warn you, Sir William, do not harbour a witch. For we will find her, and we will test her, and if she be found to be a witch, we will burn her to banish the Devil. And if we find you have been harbouring her willingly and defending her, as you seem to suggest, then we will test you too, and the Lord will have mercy on your soul."

"Get out!" bellowed Sir William, "get out before I have you arrested for trespass!"

"I go now, Sir William, but I shall return."

"You do that and I'll have you hanged for it! Out!"

The two girls heard Sir William's door slam, followed by the sound of Hopkirk and the villagers walking away down the corridor, then the door at the far end opening and closing.

Then – silence.

Sarah let her breath out in a long, low hiss of relief. "Oh, Mistress, that was ever so close," she said. "We must be away from here quickly."

"We can't go back out into the corridor," hissed Justine. "He might be hiding and waiting. He wants to drown me then burn me!"

"Nay," said Sarah. "We must be away to my mother's cottage. He'll not find you there. We go forward. Follow me. You have to crawl to start, but it soon opens out to a place where you can stand."

Sarah crawled forward and heard her mistress do the same. After they had crawled for a short while, the echoes of their hands and knees scraping the floor changed to a deeper, higher sound. Sarah said, "You can stand here, Mistress. Watch your head as you get up."

Sarah stood up and walked forward. Then she heard a rustle, a bumping sound and a small yelp behind her. "Watch your head there, Mistress," she repeated.

Sarah ran her hand along the rough wall beside her till suddenly it curved away. "And the corner here, Mistress," she said.

A little later she took a step out into empty space and nearly overbalanced. Recovering, she said, "The stairs here, Mistress." She trod carefully down the stairs, feeling each step with her toe before committing her weight to it. When she felt the last step, she reached her hand out, feeling for the old iron handle. Finding it, she twisted it round a three-quarter turn and pushed. A sliver of light appeared as she eased the door open an inch and squinted out through the gap.

After a moment, she opened the door some more and peered right round it. Satisfied that no-one was watching, she opened it fully and together they slipped out. Sarah pulled the door closed behind her. There was a click as the latch caught and locked – committing them to their escape.

---0---

Justine stopped and looked around her. They had emerged into a narrow shadowy passageway between two brick walls. She looked back at the doorway. It had been cut so cleverly into the brickwork that now it was closed it was virtually impossible to see where it had been – there were just some faint lines running down that followed the line of the mortar. You really had to look to see them.

Rubbing the bump on her head with her hand, Justine followed as Sarah crept to the end of the short passage, then stopped as the girl gestured for her to wait. Again Sarah peered cautiously round the corner. Appearing satisfied that no one was there, she turned back and gestured for Justine to follow her. They ran out into the courtyard.

The morning sunshine burned into Justine's eyes after so long in the dark, but she put this out of her mind – it was nothing compared to the thought of Hopkirk and his tortures lingering behind her.

She lifted her leg to look for marks where the rats had been, and was relieved that there was nothing to see. Thank goodness they had not bitten her; she'd have screamed for sure if they had – and it had been hard enough not to scream when they were on her leg. She shuddered at the memory.

"Come, Mistress!" urged Sarah.

They ran across the courtyard to a solid wooden gate. Sarah opened it slowly, and they slipped through.

They were now in a beautifully laid-out garden, with rose bushes set in deep beds, surrounded by well-maintained lawns. The roses were mainly red and white varieties. 'It's a Tudor rose garden – how beautiful,' Justine thought as they ran through it. 'If I'm not mistaken, we have a tea room here in the 21st century.'

"Come!" called Sarah. Justine followed her quickly across the garden and through another gate at the far end under a wooden pergola festooned with large, colourful roses.

Now they were in a garden with herbs laid out in narrow rows. Justine noted rosemary, basil and thyme, plus a couple of plants she couldn't identify, before they had crossed this garden and arrived at another wooden gate under a brick arch. Sarah pushed the gate and it opened easily. They ran through onto a narrow lane leading out to open countryside.

Justine would have loved to stop and enjoy the view of the Tudor fields, with occasional little cottages, dense green copses and burbling streams rushing down the hills. But instead she had to focus on keeping up with Sarah and trying – unsuccessfully – to avoid sharp stones with her bare feet as they ran. As the air started to burn in her chest, she tried to remember the last time she'd been to the gym. She wished it had not been so long.

After they had been running down the open path for what seemed to Justine to be hours, but must have been no more than a few minutes, Sarah slowed down to an easier pace and Justine saw that they were now approaching a dark wood. Soon they were trotting in among the trees; picking their way through majestic oaks and tall elms and getting deeper and deeper into the forest.

After a while Sarah slowed to a walk, allowing them both to catch their breath – and for Justine to realise just how much her feet were now hurting. Her initial attempts to avoid the sharp stones and sticks had proved ineffective and she had ended up just running as if she had shoes on and trying to ignore the growing pain in her feet.

Sarah came up to a twisted old oak tree and she stopped altogether.

"How do you fare, Mistress?" she asked.

"Fine," panted Justine. She hopped onto her left foot and pulled the right foot up so she could study the sole. There was a fair amount of blood trickling from a number of cuts, making red channels in the black dirt.

"I'm just fine," she repeated.

She gingerly set down her right foot, then leaned back against a low thick branch of the old tree and lifted the other foot to see the sole. It too was blackened with the dirt of the forest floor and running with rivulets of blood that were carving red tracks through the blackness.

"We will bathe your feet when we arrive at my mother's cottage." said Sarah. "It's not far now." She left the path and started walking through the forest.

Justine put her foot down gingerly and loped along, wincing, after Sarah.

They went deeper and deeper into the forest, till eventually they came to a small thatched cottage standing alone among the trees. It had tiny windows without glass that were no more than slits in the wall and a solid slatted wood door. Smoke was rising from the single central chimney. Justine was surprised to see the smoke of a fire on a summer's morning.

Sarah pushed open the door and they went in.

It was dark inside the cottage; with the weak beam of sunlight from the windows joined only by the orange glow of the central fire. There were no internal walls – just one room. The fire was in a grate in the middle; a table and a couple of stools stood against one wall and a low pallet bed against another. The bare earth floor was covered only with rough straw.

An old lady sat by the fire, watching a pot which was suspended over the flames from a metal frame. Inside the pot was some bubbling liquid, which she was occasionally stirring. She was wearing a rough woollen dress and apron, and had a simple cotton coif covering her hair.

She looked up as Sarah entered, and her face lit up with a broad smile, to be replaced by a frown as Justine then appeared in the doorway.

"Hello Sarah, dear," she said.

"Hello, Mother," said Sarah.

"Who is this that comes to call on us?" asked the old woman, pointing a bony finger at Justine.

"It is my mistress from the manor," answered Sarah. "Mary Fox, the daughter of a London merchant."

"Why does she wear only a night dress?"

"We had to run from the manor."

Sarah was silent a while, as she stared at her mother. Eventually she said, "Mistress Fox is falsely accused of witchcraft by Hopkirk, the magistrate."

Fortunately the old woman merely nodded, looked Justine up and down and said; "I have experience of Master Hopkirk – he is all too ready to see witchcraft in God-fearing folk and I'll have none of his false accusations here. You are welcome, my child."

"Oh, thank you," said Justine with some relief. "You are most kind." She wondered what the old woman's experience of Hopkirk had been and decided that there would be time enough for that story later.

She hobbled in across the straw, grimacing with the pain in her feet. Sarah's mother looked down at the trail of blood she was leaving.

"Oh, my poor child," she said, "your feet are cut to ribbons. 'Tis no wonder if you must run all the way from the manor." She looked up at her daughter. "Sarah?"

"Yes, Mother?"

"Fetch some water from the stream and we will see to these poor feet."

"Yes, Mother." Sarah grabbed an old tin pail and went out of the cottage. The old woman stood and picked up a small three-legged wooden stool, which she placed near the light of the fire.

"Now, sit down here and let me see."

Justine hobbled to the stool and sat down, putting her bag down on the floor beside her. She held up her right foot. The old woman lifted it and peered at the sole.

"Hmm. There are many cuts, but fortunately none too deep." She put the foot down and picked up the other, studying it closely in the light of the fire. "This too. The water will take off the dirt, then we will let God's grace take care of the healing. And if His grace does not do the work, we will apply a poultice of mouldy bread. You will need to rest a while till God's blessed work is done and the wounds have been closed over. Then we can dress you, and decide how you are to avoid the zealous Master Hopkirk."

She took another look at Justine's foot.

"Indeed," she observed, "your feet are otherwise unmarked – they are those of a young girl who has only ever seen the softest of shoes." She looked up, studying Justine intently in the firelight. "You are a merchant's daughter?"

Justine nodded.

"From London?"

Justine nodded again.

"Then you have truly led a charmed life, that you have not been made to wear rough, ill-fitting shoes. We are most blessed to receive such a fine lady in our humble dwelling."

"I am the one who is humbled, by your kindness and hospitality," answered Justine, grabbing this as a perfect cue to confirm her gratitude.

"Aye, you are welcome to stay a while." The old woman put Justine's foot down. "Let us hope the Lord is also welcoming, and chooses not to let these wounds become rotten with pus or canker."

Sarah returned with the tin pail full of clean, fresh water from the stream. Her mother took a piece of cloth from the table, sat down again and started cleaning the dirt from Justine's feet. Justine tried not to wince as the rough cloth rasped across the cuts, but as the water became blacker and her feet became cleaner the pain began to recede – to be replaced by a steady throbbing in the warmth of the fire.

Justine studied the woman who was cleaning her feet as she worked, bent over her task in deep concentration. A few tendrils of grey hair had escaped from under her rough cotton coif and were swaying with the rhythm of her movements. The sleeves of her brown woollen dress were pushed up to reveal bare arms that were surprisingly youthful – very much at odds with the calloused, working hands she was dipping into the water and sponging off the blood and dirt from Justine's feet. With a shock Justine realised that Sarah's mother must be nowhere near as old as she had first thought; the bony hands, grey hair and pinched face were more a result of unremitting hard work in harsh winters than of old age. Justine decided that she probably wasn't more than 45 years old – although she did briefly wonder if reaching such an age in the Tudor countryside was itself something of an achievement.

Sarah's mother finally took another cloth and tore off a strip. She used it to dry Justine's feet, then looked up.

"The wounds are not as bad as I first thought. The bleeding has stopped and with God's good grace you will be walking without pain in a short while." She smiled. "Although a pair of shoes would help."

"Thank you," said Justine.

"You will lie on the bed and rest a while. I will make you a hot posset."

"Lovely," said Justine, wondering what a hot posset might be. It certainly sounded like something comforting.

Sarah's mother then tore the remaining cloth into two strips and used each to bind Justine's feet, enabling her to hobble across to the bed and lie down.

"Rest a while," Sarah's mother repeated. "Sarah and I need to fetch some milk and ale from the farm a few miles hence. We will be back after noon."

The two of them left, closing the door with a creak.

Peace descended on the little cottage.

Justine lay back on the rough mattress, her hands behind her head in the absence of a pillow. She took a deep breath and let it out slowly, forcing herself to relax. Her feet were still throbbing, but the lack of pain made that easy to bear.

The weak shaft of sunlight that had been beaming in through the thin window suddenly disappeared as the sun went behind a thick cloud. The fire had subsided to a dull orange glow, and the cottage was now quite dark inside, with strange, unfamiliar shaped shadows thrown up by the old Tudor furniture.

In the peace of the dim, cool cottage, she became aware of the many sounds of the forest outside. She tuned in to the birds calling and singing in the trees; then she switched her attention to the breeze rustling the thick summer foliage, before idly noting the clip-clop of horse's hooves approaching...

Hooves?

Quickly she looked around, desperately seeking somewhere to hide, but the small, bare cottage offered no real hiding places, and anyway, it was too late, as there came the unmistakable sound of a man dismounting and heavy boots walking up to the door.

The door opened. A man's figure was silhouetted in the light of the doorway.

"Mistress Fox?"

She gave a little cry of relief as she recognised the deep voice of Sir William.

He closed the door behind him and approached the bed.

"Mistress Mary Fox. I have given chase and I have found my quarry," he said, his voice warm with the sound of a smile.

"And now my arrow must find its path — true to your heart."

CHAPTER FIFTEEN

Thomas Melrose stared at his mother open-mouthed across the table, his piece of bread frozen half way to his lips.

"You mean to tell me," he said very slowly and deliberately, "that the reason my father killed himself was not because of the enclosure of his land?"

Jane Melrose looked down at her pewter plate and poked at her half-eaten piece of salted mutton with her knife. She didn't answer. She was tormented with guilt – only the night before she had vowed never to let her son find out the truth of his father's death, and now here she was, at breakfast the very next morning, on the verge of stupidly revealing it all.

It had been a silly, chance remark, said without thought, which had begun this unstoppable cascade towards a truth she'd kept hidden for many years.

A truth she'd intended to take to her grave.

It had started when Thomas, still angry from Sir William's insulting remark of the previous day, had observed dryly over breakfast that Sir William should have been grateful that he, Thomas, had actually pushed him to study harder when they were boys.

His mother, chewing absent-mindedly on a piece of mutton, had answered, "Aye, and a shame for you that it led to the death of your father."

She might have been able to bluff it out; maybe to come up with some plausible explanation, but she had stopped, looking absolutely horrified. Naturally he had picked it up.

"My education?" he had asked, puzzled. "What had that to do with my father's death? It was the forced enclosure of his land that killed him, wasn't it?"

Her continued silence allowed him to deduce that this was not the case.

So now Thomas put down the piece of bread, leant across and pushed her plate away down the table, then grabbed her chin in his hand and lifted it up. After a moment she raised her eyes and looked deep into his.

He repeated the question that was still hanging ominously in the air between them. "The reason my father killed himself was not because of the enclosure of his land?"

"No, Thomas, dear, it wasn't," she said, with some difficulty. "Let me go, you're hurting me."

His eyes bored into hers, his hand still gripping her chin.

"Then – why?"

"Let me go, Thomas."

"You'll tell me?"

"Yes. Let me go."

He released his grip and took a sip of beer. "Tell me," he whispered, his voice unnaturally calm, like the still air before a storm.

Jane rubbed her chin. "It's not so simple."

"It never is."

"Your father loved you very much…"

"And I him," cut in Thomas. "To the point, woman."

"That is the point, Thomas." She paused, choosing her words with care. "It was because he wanted the best for you that he agreed to the enclosure."

Thomas stared at his mother with complete incredulity. "How could he begin to imagine that cutting me from my lands would be in my best interest?"

"He made a bargain with Sir Henry de Beauvais."

"A bargain?"

"Aye."

"With that man?"

She nodded.

Thomas pushed back his chair and stood up, his eyes burning.

Suddenly he brought his clenched fists down hard onto the table, making her jump.

"Why, in the name of the risen Christ, did he do that?" he shouted.

"He agreed to the enclosure so that you may be educated as Sir William's classmate, and for your inheritance," she whispered, looking up at him with wide, fearful eyes. "Sir Henry would never have agreed to such a thing normally." She stopped, then added, "And your father accepted a fair price for the land."

"He was paid for the land so I could be educated?"

"Aye."

"Then what became of the money? My inheritance?"

"Some was spent on clothes and Arthur, your horse. Your education was paid in full. The rest was…" she swallowed nervously "…it was – lost."

There was an uneasy silence as he thought hard. Finally he whispered,

"Lost?"

"Aye. He… he gambled it away in the tavern mostly…" She swallowed again and looked up at him with eyes that were swimming with tears.

"It was the shame of that that drove him to take his own life," she said.

"Not the enclosure by Sir Henry?"

"No. Not that."

"And he agreed the enclosure so I could have an education? And some money to inherit?"

"Aye."

"And yet you say he was a gambler? My father?" Thomas thought a moment, "So how have we lived all these years? What money have we had in income if he gambled it away?"

"There was still some income from the lands that Sir Henry let your father work."

"But the money he received from the enclosure was gambled away? I will never believe the truth in that."

"I am sorry, Thomas," she replied. "The truth will be told by Jake, the landlord in the tavern. He saw your father in there many times."

"Then I must go to the tavern shortly and ask him – ask him to give the truth to your claim that my father was a gambler."

"I never wanted to tell you, Thomas. I know how much you loved your father."

"Aye, and you are so ready to tell me he was not the man I thought he was. That also hurts."

"Maybe it is good you know the truth of his death, Thomas." She paused. "My son, as I said, I would have kept this from you, but it was the truth, and maybe it is better for you to know it."

Thomas slumped back down in his seat with his head in his hands. After a few moments he looked up at his mother.

"William knew," he said. "When my father died I saw it in his eyes. He knew."

"He knew your father had made the bargain with Sir Henry," she answered. "But why would he have known your father gambled away the money?" She pressed her point. "He was your friend."

"A friend would have said something."

"What – that your father was a gambler? That would have been the worst thing to have said." Jane put her hand over his, stroking it gently with her thumb. "My dear son, I should not have told you this. I am sorry."

"Nay, woman. Do you know, I am glad you have told me," he answered, taking his hand out from under hers. "Now I value the truth in this."

He stood up.

"But I do not think Sir William de Beauvais is the innocent in this matter. He knew what my father was doing, and he did not share this news with me.

I saw it in his eyes that day. He knew. And he has never forgotten it – every day he must remind me with his slights and his taunts."

"You read too much into his words," she said quietly.

"Indeed I do not," he snapped. "They are as plain as the nose on his face."

"You do, my son. You see slights where none are meant. You use them to stoke the fires of your anger but they are mere pebbles not coals, and they do not burn."

"You use a pretty turn of phrase, Mother," he observed dryly, "but you are not there each day to hear the words he uses."

"I know enough of life, and of the ways of men," she answered, "to know that Sir William is a good man and means you no ill will."

"But I know what I hear," he said, his voice rising again, "and I hear words that are the very driest of coals! They are very eager to burn! They turn my anger white hot!"

"My son," she said, trying to speak calmly and evenly to cool his anger. She could see that it was real and all too likely to become physical. "I would you listen to me. You imagine these slights – they are real in your mind but not in his."

"Again, I say, Mother, you are not there and I am. You must let me be the judge in this matter. He swallowed the remains of his beer. "Now, I must be away."

"Where?" she asked.

"I have business to attend to in the town. Then this evening, I will go to the tavern. I will ask the truth of Jake. A fool such as he will tell the truth in his eyes, whatever his mouth may say. And I will have the truth in this matter – I will not have anyone stand in my way."

"Be careful, son," she warned. "You must keep your anger in check. This is none of Jake's doing."

"Nay, indeed. It is Sir William's doing, and that oaf of a father of his. He is the cause of my anger," he patted the hilt of his sword, "and he will feel the full force of it if I chance to meet him!" He strode out of the room, calling for a servant to saddle his horse.

His mother sat silent, still and alone at the table, a single tear running down her cheek.

CHAPTER SIXTEEN

In the dim light inside the cottage, Justine looked up at William as he leant over the bed, his dark shape silhouetted against the meagre light of the window. At any other place and time Justine would have found this to be quite menacing, with echoes of some black and white horror movie she'd seen as a child – but this was William leaning over her and she could just make out the twinkle in his eye and the smile on his mouth – and she was not afraid.

"My lord," she asked softly. "How did you find me?"

"Ahh," he said as he sat down on the edge of the bed, his leather boots and belt creaking gently as he moved, "you are asking the huntsman how he follows the trail?"

She nodded, then realised it was probably too dark for him to see. "Yes," she said.

"Indeed," he answered, and she could hear the warmth of a smile in his voice, "I would love to tell you of the skill with which I picked up your scent; how I sniffed the wind and determined your direction; how I tracked you down by the smallest clues that would be all but invisible to any other person…" he laughed. "But, I cannot."

"Then how?" she asked, her curiosity raised.

Just then the beam of sunlight burst back through the small window and added enough light to the cottage that they could now see each other.

"'Twas not so difficult," he answered her, reaching forward and stroking her hair. "First, I noted the quiver of arrows on your bed, and I realised you had told me to hunt for you."

"It was all I could think of in a hurry," she said.

"And it was most effective," he affirmed. "It told me you had run from your bed in great haste and were seeking my help. Knowing that little grey man, that witchfinder, had come up the stairs, I understood that you could not have escaped that way. So I checked the secret passage behind the corridor..." She raised an enquiring eyebrow. "Ah yes – I have known of it since I was a boy and used to delight in escaping from my mother that way..." He chuckled, then became serious again. "But this morning I noted the dust disturbed on the floor. So I knew to check the hidden door out into the rose garden – and sure enough there were footmarks in the dirt leading from it."

He laughed. "You are most resourceful, Mistress Fox, but I quickly deduced you had no time to put on shoes, for the man's boots you wear were still by the bed, and when I looked at the other shoes in the chest, they were all half the size of the boots and none would have fitted you anyway." He chuckled softly. "So do I take it you were wearing those boots under your gown last night at the banquet?"

"Yes," she answered. "You're right; none of the shoes would fit."

"How amusing. My mother would have fainted had she seen them. So, I could only assume you had escaped barefoot from the manor." He turned to study her feet in their bandages, sticking out from under the thin blanket. "As I thought," he said, examining them closely, "there is blood in no small measure coming through the bindings."

"There were sharp stones."

"Indeed," he continued, "so it was not difficult to follow your trail."

"You're very clever," she observed, genuinely impressed.

"Nay," he answered, with what sounded like a touch too much self-deprecating modesty. "You left many spots of blood on the path. I did not need the nose of a hound." He paused a moment. "Although I'll warrant that peasant Hopkirk would have missed it."

"Lucky he didn't know where to start looking," she said.

"Aye," he nodded. "And in truth, I was lucky, too."

"How was that, my lord?" she asked encouragingly, wanting to help keep his tale moving along. She guessed that in a world with few books and no TV or cinema, listening to a story would be as much of an art as telling it.

He nodded in approval. "I lost the trail by an old twisted oak tree," he continued. "The spots of blood so kindly left for me stopped abruptly. I looked all around; I even checked the tree in case it was hollow and you were to be found inside, but there was no sign of you."

"So why 'lucky'?" she prompted.

"I had dismounted while I was looking at the tree, and my horse started to walk into the forest to find the sweeter grasses. So, once I had determined you could not be hiding inside the old oak, I chased into the forest after him. He had gone some way."

"I see." Justine smiled to herself as she had a mental image of William desperately crashing through the undergrowth after his horse.

"When I reached my horse, with luck I spotted some broken twigs with yet more spots of your precious blood on them, and I was back on your trail." He leant back with some satisfaction as his story reached its happy ending. "And here I find you, with your poor damaged feet bound up so they may be restored to good health." He patted her foot.

"Yes," she winced. "They are a bit sore."

"A thousand pardons. And did you wash them yourself," he enquired, "or is there an owner of the cottage who has performed this necessary task?"

"Well, it was Sarah who led me here," explained Justine. "This cottage belongs to her mother, and it was she who cleaned and bound my feet." Then Justine added, "They have gone for some milk. They said they'll be back in a couple of hours."

"They have given you great help," observed William.

"Oh yes. They have been so kind, helping me get away from that dreadful man," said Justine, the words catching in her throat as she remembered the sinister snake-like voice she'd heard on the other side of the wall while crouching in the dark of the secret passage.

"Then they shall be well rewarded," said William, reaching down to touch Justine's cheek. "They have done you good service, and by that they have done me good service."

Justine put her hand over his and held it against her cheek. Suddenly she felt an intense heat flow from his hand and she gasped as it started a hot glow that quickly spread to her whole body.

He leant down till his face was close to hers and she could see clearly into his eyes. She lifted her other hand up behind his head and pulled him closer, until their lips touched. His mouth opened on hers and their tongues came together in a gentle caress.

This time, there was no conflict between Justine's head and her heart.

This time, her heart was the winner, and she knew she was going to give herself to William completely, because she knew she had to.

Slowly she moved his hand off her cheek and started to guide it down her neck, then across the soft cotton of her nightdress towards her breast.

---0---

A couple of hours earlier, Hopkirk had slid into the kitchens like a grey-black snake, followed shortly after by his motley collection of young and old villagers.

Martha, Margaret and the cook had been sitting in a small huddle by the fire. They had been speculating on how long Justine would take to burn, especially if the authorities denied her the quick release of a bag of gunpowder round her neck. Martha had been of the opinion that Justine would allow herself a quick death, whereas Margaret was convinced she would try all manner of magical trickery to quench the flames, thereby delaying the inevitable for much longer. The cook, who was of a more practical disposition, compared Justine to a large boar – which she said could brown nicely in half an hour and cook through in two. But she did concede that the fire for a boar was smaller and further away than Justine's would be.

They turned as Hopkirk and his followers entered.

"Master Hopkirk!" exclaimed Martha immediately, jumping up. "Do you have the witch?"

"Nay," said Hopkirk. "She has disappeared like a wraith in the mist."

The villagers stamped and muttered under their breaths, knocking the handles of their pitchforks on the stone floor. "She used her magic to disappear!" blurted out Agnes, the pretty blonde daughter of Jake the innkeeper.

"Her bed was still warm, yet she was nowhere to be found!" added her friend Ruth excitedly. She turned to Agnes and whispered, "With God's good grace we'll not find her too soon – or the chase will not be half so much fun!"

Agnes, meanwhile, started to look around the kitchen. "I would we undo her magic and find her presently," she whispered back, "as I have not had anything to eat for this many an hour – and I will soon faint away." Her eye lit on a tray of cakes nearby. "There's my prize," she muttered, and started edging towards them.

"Your master, Sir William de Beauvais, was, let us say, most unhelpful," continued Hopkirk, the menace in his quiet voice leaving no doubt to Martha as to his sinister interpretation of Sir William's actions. "He stood in the door of his chambers with much anger on his face and in his voice, and he bade us leave immediately." He looked Martha directly in the eye. "Indeed, I would warrant that the girl may have been found by a simple search of his rooms."

Martha nodded in full agreement.

Just then Simon, one of the servants, came down into the kitchens.

"Some manchet bread and a flagon of wine for the master – he's riding out," he called. He stopped, taking in the strangers in the kitchens and the inactivity of the cook, Margaret and Martha, then shook his head as if to clear such irrelevant images. Again he called out, "Some manchet bread and a flagon of wine for the master! In a saddlebag, now! He's riding out and must have them!"

The cook nodded to one of the kitchen girls who had been nearby. The girl fetched a leather saddlebag, into which she put in a loaf of creamy yellow-coloured bread. She then took a costrel – a shaped leather pouch with twisted rope handles – and filled it with wine from a silver jug before stopping it with a wooden stopper and putting it into the saddlebag. She handed the bag to Simon, who grabbed it impatiently with a muttered "thank you!" and ran back out of the kitchens.

There was a moment's silence, then Martha said casually "If the master is gone, I would suggest I see to the tidiness of his chambers..."

"Indeed," agreed Hopkirk with equal casualness. "Such a task is onerous in the extreme. I would warrant you'll need the help of myself and these good villagers in this task. You can never tell what... ah... filth... may be found hiding in a dark corner..."

"Aye," smiled Martha. "It is well we search thoroughly in case we find such a... dirty... thing. Come, Master Hopkirk, we must be swift." She marched out of the kitchens towards the stairs up to the Great Hall.

Hopkirk swept his cloak around his dark grey body and followed, with the villagers jostling to get out behind. Agnes, who had got close to the cakes but not close enough, reluctantly gave up her quest and followed them out.

There was silence. Margaret looked at the cook. The cook looked at Margaret.

"Like as not the girl will be found," said the cook.

"Aye," said Margaret. She reached for a carrot, a chopping board and a knife.

"Like as not she'll be tried," added the cook.

"Aye," said Margaret with satisfaction, as she lined up a carrot on the chopping board and poised her knife in the air above it. "As the Lord is my witness, like as not she will."

She brought the knife down hard, cleanly severing the top off the carrot.

"Like as not she will."

---0---

The still air hung softly in the cool dark cottage.

Justine and William were lying close together on the rough little bed, with William sleeping deeply. Justine gently stroked his hair as he lay with his head on her chest and his warm breath drifting across her breast. She knew she would have to wake him shortly, as Sarah and her mother would soon be back, but decided to let him sleep a few more minutes while she enjoyed the memories of their passion and the warmth of his body.

He had been a surprisingly gentle lover. She had been ready for him to be rough and demanding – interested only in his own pleasure – but she had been delighted to find he was in fact totally attentive to her needs above his own. He had spent what seemed like a lifetime exploring her body, finding where the softest touch, the lightest stroke or the warmest kiss would deliver her the most pleasure. Indeed, he was so skilful at applying this knowledge that the climax, when it finally came, exploded simultaneously for both of them with such depth and with such intensity that she thought she would surely die of happiness.

She stared up at the rough wooden beams, just visible in the darkness above her.

Making love with William had felt natural; completely, comfortably and totally natural.

They had been fully at ease with each other from the very first moment; there had been none of the shyness or awkwardness that you would expect from first-time lovers – none of the fumbling, the apologies, the mistakes…

Now she thought about it, it had been as if they had made love many times before, and William's explorations of her body had been more like him re-acquainting himself with her than if he were discovering her for the first time.

She moved her hand down to stroke his beard and was rewarded with the sound of his breathing getting even deeper as he slept.

'You've found your ideal man,' she said to herself. 'Don't lose him now…'

Her hand froze mid-stroke and William grunted softly in his sleep.

The unwelcome memory had suddenly come rushing back of the conversation she'd had with him the night before in his rooms in the manor.

"My lord, what day is it?" she had asked, to which he had replied, "It is the 30th day of July in the year of our Lord 1565."

So today was the 31st of July.

The very night that history had decreed he would die, stabbed in some fight in a tavern.

'Well, history has got to change,' she thought. 'It will have to, because I am going to do all I can to change it.' She stroked his beard again. 'If I can keep him here till tomorrow, then history will have to take a different course and he will not die.'

Justine smiled grimly. 'That's it. He has got to stay here tonight. Then I will have won and history will have lost. I will keep him with me and I will keep him alive…'

She let her mind follow the course that this would mean. If William did not die, then he would need a wife. And after their passion just now, perhaps she would be the one to secure his heart. 'Then I can become Lady de Beauvais, the very model of a Tudor wife.'

That happy picture danced in front of her eyes in the dim light of the cottage.

'I wonder what a Tudor wedding is like?' she thought. 'I bet it is absolutely beautiful.' Images of a magnificent wedding banquet in the Great Hall sprang to mind, with garlands of flowers, glorious wines, sumptuous dishes and many happy guests to welcome her to the life of a Tudor lady. She would look proudly at William as he made a warm, funny speech, and she would catch his mother's eye and receive a nod of approval in return. She would be wearing the most exquisite white gown and hood, with beautiful pearls in her hair and emeralds round her neck. There would be many servants moving round the tables; serving the food; pouring the wine; making sure the guests had everything they needed. In her imaginary banquet a servant approached her proffering a beautiful silver bowl of water so she could wash her hands, and as she washed them she looked up at the servant and the servant looked down at her and the servant was Margaret...

The banquet disappeared in an instant, like morning mist in a puff of wind.

It would never happen. It could never happen – because Hopkirk wanted to test her as a witch and burn her at the stake.

William grunted again and moved against her, as he started to surface from his deep sleep.

"I need to save you, my love," she whispered. "And then I have got to save myself."

She looked down at his head.

"And it's not going to be easy."

---0---

The search of Sir William's chambers and the bedroom used by Justine had been most thorough. Beds had been looked under, chests had been emptied and curtains had been pulled back, but no sign had been found of Justine. Some enterprising villagers had even opened the smallest of containers – such as jewelled boxes, desk drawers and china pots – in the possibility that Justine had somehow miniaturised herself by magic and hidden inside them.

There had initially been some reluctance to enter the chambers of the lord of the manor, let alone to search them thoroughly. Hopkirk had made it clear that his power as magistrate gave them full authority, enabling the villagers to overcome their feudal inclinations and enter into the search with increasing enthusiasm.

Their fear, however, was even more marked at entering the bedroom used by Justine. Someone observed that she may have left an enchantment on the room, so no one would touch anything in case they were suddenly turned into a weasel or a stoat. Again, Hopkirk had to provide reassurance, moving around the room and demonstrating that nothing he touched had the power to transform him into any particular creature.

Justine's room was then searched equally thoroughly, but again, Justine was nowhere to be found.

Finally the search was over and Matthew Hopkirk stood in the corridor outside Sir William's chambers. He addressed the disappointed group of villagers clustered in front of him.

"So the witch is not to be found." He licked his lips. "She has indeed vanished like a spectre, either by transformation into a cat or a crow, or by some spell of invisibility."

This raised many mutterings of deep concern.

"We have found no trace of her, save for these boots we found in her room." He reached down and held up Justine's worn leather boots. "They are as a man would wear; a sure sign she cleaves only to Satan in her worship."

There were deeper mutterings from the villagers and signs of the cross were made repeatedly.

"So, while we must follow due process and test her for witchcraft, we can be most assured we are dealing with a foul and evil witch in the person of the girl known as Mary Fox."

Cries of, "Burn her! Burn the witch!"

Hopkirk held up his hand for silence, and was about to speak again, when a voice came from the back of the group.

"Master Hopkirk? I'm hungry."

"Who is that?" asked Hopkirk. There was a further moment's silence, as everyone looked around curiously, then young Agnes shouldered her way to the front and faced up to Hopkirk.

"I'm hungry," she repeated. "I want to go home and eat."

Gasps of shock at such impudence gradually turned into mutterings of agreement from the villagers, as they each realised how hungry they were. Agnes looked round at them and drew strength and confidence from their apparent support. She looked back at Hopkirk.

"I want to capture the witch as much as I want anything, Master Hopkirk. She's evil, right enough, and must be stopped. But just now I'm awful hungry, and I want to go back to my pa's tavern and have some bread and ale." She looked back at the villagers and got more encouragement to continue. "We've been on the hunt with you since dawn, and we ain't had so much as a morsel of rye bread to eat."

Hopkirk stared at her with unblinking grey eyes and said nothing.

"We can carry on with the hunt after we've had some vittles," she observed.

Hopkirk continued to stare at her, still silent.

Agnes felt an uncomfortable need to fill the silence.

"We'll hunt better with food in our stomachs," she added.

"Indeed," said Hopkirk quietly, appearing to have come to a decision. He looked at the group, fixing them each in turn with his piercing gaze. "Is this the opinion of you all?"

At first there was an embarrassed shuffling of feet and some close studying of pitchfork handles, accompanied by scratching of ears.

Then, one by one, the villagers agreed.

"It has been a while…"

"Now I think on it, I do have a hunger…"

"Can't hunt on an empty stomach…"

"Better if we have a little food and ale…"

Hopkirk held his hand up again for silence.

"Then we must return to the tavern," he conceded, and there was a relieved muttering from the villagers.

"Come," he continued, "we will take bread and ale and make our plans for resuming the hunt."

The villagers stamped and voiced their approval. Hopkirk walked past them, along the corridor and through the door onto the gallery. They followed him down the stairs and through the Great Hall to the kitchens, where they could exit through the vegetable gardens.

He may have been prepared to search Sir William's bedroom, but not even Hopkirk would dare leave Grangedean Manor by the front door.

---0---

William swung his legs out of the bed, and stood looking down at Justine. She returned his gaze directly and steadily into his eyes.

He put his hand on her cheek and looked deeper into her eyes, as if searching out her soul. "Mistress Mary Fox," he said, "your beauty is a joy to behold."

They continued to hold each other's gaze for a few long seconds, then he sighed. "But I fear I have to forgo the joy for now."

He turned away and rummaged on the floor for the hose he had discarded so hastily earlier and started to pull them on. "For you have sore feet and cannot walk, and there is the small matter of that odious little man Hopkirk, who has an unhealthy interest in your whereabouts." He pulled his chemise over his head, then his breeches and doublet, before putting on his boots and cloak. "So I suggest you remain here and enjoy the hospitality of Sarah and her good mother till no doubt Master Hopkirk tires of your search and finds some other unfortunate girl to accuse."

Justine wished she could share William's optimism that Hopkirk would let her go so easily. "I would be so pleased if that were true, my lord," she said. "For I am innocent of all his charges."

"Then as God is your witness, you have nothing to fear," he answered, buckling on his sword belt. "But now, I must be away."

"No, my lord!" she said quickly, reaching out to grab him forcibly by the leg, then, worried he might think she was being too weird, turning it into a gentle stroking action at the last second. "I do fear he will not give up the hunt so easily," she added softly.

She deepened her stroking in the hope that this would make him change his mind about leaving.

"Then you must let me persuade him," he said, moving slightly closer to the bed to give her better access to his upper thigh.

"And let yourself be accused as well?" she asked, moving her hand higher.

"Hmmm. There is that."

"We must make a plan," she purred. "Why don't you stay here tonight and we can talk?" Her hand moved even higher, easing up under the hem of his breeches.

"Aye, for sure, we must…oh Heaven," he breathed, as her hand found its mark. She applied some pressure through the thin cotton material of his hose, and felt him stiffen once again under her touch. "Indeed we must… oh my love… to the left but an inch…"

The door opened and light flooded in as Sarah and her mother returned to the cottage.

Justine quickly withdrew her hand and stuck it back under the thin blanket. William stood quickly away from the bed, a look of studied innocence on his face.

Sarah was carrying a wooden bucket containing some milk and her mother was carrying a pair of rough-looking shoes. They both looked tired after many hours of walking, and relieved to be home.

The two women curtseyed low. "My lord," said Sarah, acknowledging her master's presence with a completely blank expression; as if finding him next to the bed of a semi-naked girl was not an uncommon situation.

"Ah, yes, Sarah," responded William, looking as if he was trying to take back control of the situation. "And this, I understand, is your mother, who I must thank for taking in Mary and bandaging her wounds?"

"My lord," said Sarah's mother, curtseying again. "I am honoured to have you in my humble home."

"Yes, well, it was but a brief visit," answered William. He glanced down at Justine in the bed, "though most rewarding. But now I must be away."

"No!" exclaimed Justine loudly. Everyone looked at her in surprise. "I mean, you must stay, my lord." She tried to sit up, clutching the blanket up to her chest. "We were going to make plans…" she hissed quietly at him, imploring him to stay with her eyes.

"Aye, but it is best if you stay here for now." He smiled, oblivious to her pleading. "I will return in the morning and we can talk more about how to secure your future."

"No, my lord – you should stay here tonight…"

"Mistress Fox," answered William with another smile, although now slightly forced, "nothing would give me greater pleasure, believe me." He reached down and stroked her hair, then stood back. "You remain here with these good people for your safety. I have outstayed my welcome and must be away till the morrow."

"But that's too late…"

"Too late?" asked William, quickly. "Too late for what?"

Justine sat up some more, thinking fast. "Too late for me, my lord. I cannot spend a single moment away from you."

"My sweet Mary," said William, firmly. "Nor I you. But I really cannot be with you tonight. You must know it is not seemly for me to stay here." Sarah nodded in agreement and looked enquiringly at Justine, as if she should have known that it would not be possible for the lord of the manor to stay in a worker's cottage. He bowed to Justine, then turned to Sarah and her mother. "I must bid you all farewell, good ladies." They both curtseyed low as William turned and strode out of the cottage. He was shortly heard mounting his horse and cantering away.

There was a long silence in the cottage after he had gone, with only the sound of the breeze in the trees and the insistent cooing of a wood pigeon outside.

"I will prepare the posset," said Sarah eventually.

"And I have secured some shoes for you in a large size," said her mother, putting a pair of rough leather lace-up shoes down on the floor. "It took us some time to find them."

"Thank you," said Justine quietly. "You must think me a poor guest..."

"Sir William is our lord and master," said Sarah, taking the milk over to the fire. She added some wooden kindling to the embers and stoked them with a stick, turning the wood till it blazed nicely. "We must all do his bidding," she paused and suddenly her face broke into a broad smile – "however 'hard' it may be..."

The tension broken, Justine flopped back on the bed. "It wasn't hard..." she paused. "Well it was, but it was... oh... you know... it was wonderful..." she started to laugh. Sarah joined in and soon they were both quite breathless.

"You are not a poor guest, Mistress Fox," said Sarah, when they had got their breath back. "It seems you have truly won the master's heart – and that makes you even more honoured than when we left you earlier."

Sarah's mother, however, was not joining in the laughter. She was looking curiously at Justine, clearly puzzled about something.

"But why 'too late'?" she asked slowly. "You were most concerned not to let the master go." She moved round the bed to look closely at Justine. "You wanted to stop him leaving because you knew something of his fate if he did not."

She leant over the bed and put her face closer to Justine's.

"Do you have the gift of second sight into things yet to happen?" she asked quietly. "Do you have the powers of witchcraft?"

Suddenly the atmosphere in the cottage turned very cold. The laughter of the moment before evaporated.

Justine stared at Sarah's mother, her mind racing as she tried to decide what to say. To tell the truth was the highest risk – she would be citing time-travel as her evidence that she was not a witch – which was hardly to be believed. Quite possibly she would be bundled off to meet Master Hopkirk quicker than you could say 'Abracadabra'.

Or she could deny everything and say she really was a merchant's daughter from London. But she could hardly back this up for much longer now that Sarah's mother was suspicious – there was simply too much she would give away through sheer ignorance. At best they would think her strange in the head.

But maybe, just maybe, the truth was a risk worth taking?

If she could find a way to get them to believe she was the innocent player in this amazing time travel saga, then at least she would have some allies to help guide her though the maze of Tudor England – and if that meant a better chance to save both William and herself, it was a risk worth taking…

As these thoughts rushed across Justine's mind, she became aware that there was a vital piece of missing information. It was just that she couldn't quite grasp it – it was sitting just on the edge of her consciousness, tantalisingly niggling away at her like an irritating little stone in her boot. She knew it was important, yet as she tried to remember it, it darted away just out of her reach…

Then suddenly in a flash of inspired revelation, it came to her.

Gift! Sarah's mother said 'the gift of second sight!'

Justine realised that to Sarah's mother 'second sight' was a positive thing! Maybe that was why she'd had a run-in with Hopkirk before! Maybe she was a witch herself?

Justine's heart leapt as another inspired thought came to her. 'Maybe there is a way I can convince these two women – with a reason that would actually make some sense to them…'

She took a deep breath and steadily returned Sarah's mother's gaze.

"I am not a witch," she said slowly and carefully. "I have no knowledge of any such powers. I cannot do spells or make anything happen by magic."

Sarah and her mother stared at her in silence.

"But I think that witchcraft was practiced on me, and that is why I am here."

Justine looked from Sarah to her mother to see how this was being received. From the alarmed looks on their faces, she could see that it was not going well.

"You are enchanted?" asked Sarah cautiously, starting to edge backwards.

"No," answered Justine. "But I think a spell was performed on me that made me travel to Grangedean Manor."

"So where did you come from?" asked Sarah. "What sort of witchcraft is necessary to make a girl travel to a house? Surely you could just be taken there on a horse or by foot?"

Justine knew she was committed to her story now – there was no going back. "It is not so much where I came from as when," she said.

Sarah's mother frowned, clearly not convinced.

"I think," said Justine, "that maybe a witch, or someone with magic, cast a spell on me that made me travel through time itself – even though I stayed in the same place."

"You have travelled across time?" asked Sarah's mother incredulously. Justine supposed that as a person who lived by the movement of the sun and moon and by the changing of the seasons, she would have no concept of time as an abstract thing – let alone a thing you could travel through.

"Yes," said Justine. She thought a moment, trying to construct an explanation of time-travel that would have meaning to these people. "It is as if you were to wake up one morning and find that instead of living in the reign of Queen Elizabeth, you were now living in the reign of her grandfather King Henry. You would be the same person, but time would have moved backwards around you, so that the world and the people and the events around you come from history."

"So you have done the same; you have come into our world – into our time," said Sarah's mother.

"Yes."

"But where – or when – did you travel from?" asked Sarah.

Justine looked at the two women in the dim light. She knew this was a make-or-break moment; that she had to make this work...

"I come from 450 years in the future."

There was a long silence. The wood-pigeon cooed loudly outside. The breeze rustled in the branches of the elm trees. Justine looked at each of the two women in turn as they tried to take in what she had told them.

Then Sarah's mother stood up and walked across the cottage. She turned and looked back.

"You are telling me that some witch, or some magic, sent you back by 450 years to our time and place?"

"Yes I am."

"And you expect us to believe this?" asked Sarah's mother, shaking her head.

"Yes," answered Justine. "It is true."

Justine saw looks being exchanged between Sarah and her mother – looks that begged a thousand questions – of truth, of lies and of madness; of the wisdom of allowing such a strange creature into the cottage, of witchcraft and sorcery. It fell to Sarah to voice the one question that needed to be answered before all others.

"But..." she said in a quiet voice "...why?"

Justine knew this was where her story needed to be at its strongest. "I was working in Grangedean Manor in the year 2015. For us it is a historical monument to your time – which we call the Tudor period after the Queen's family. I organised special Tudor banquets in the Great Hall. One of the guests must have been a witch or had some magic – and maybe she wanted me to save Sir William from his fate." Justine paused, to see how this was going down. The two women were still looking sceptical. "But when I got here I didn't know what to say, or how to behave, so I ended up working in the kitchens and saying the wrong thing to Margaret, so she thought I was a witch myself, and accused me to Hopkirk."

Sarah looked round at her mother, then back at Justine.

"There was many things you did not know when I bathed and dressed you," she said slowly. "Just now, you were asking the master to stay, when that was not proper." She thought some more. "And you were wearing the strangest clothes…"

She went over to her mother and pulled her further away from Justine across the cottage. They went into a little huddle, whispering quietly. Justine strained her ears, but could not make out what they were saying.

Would they believe her? Could they believe her? If they didn't, how would she escape, with bandaged feet and in her nightdress? And how could she get to William in time…?

After what seemed a lifetime, they both came back to the bed.

"Sarah and I have thought hard on what you have told us," said the older woman. "And strange though it is, we find ourselves inclined to believe your tale."

Justine realised she had been holding her breath, and let it out in a long sigh of relief.

"But…" said Sarah, "we need more information on what will happen to the master this day, and what we must do to prevent it. This is the reason we will believe you; if you are right and we can save the master's life, then we must make every effort to do so. We cannot take the risk that you are not lying and then the master loses his life."

"It is the very unbelievable nature of the tale that leads us to believe it may be true," said Sarah's mother, cautiously. "If you told the same to Master Hopkirk he would take it as proof absolute of witchcraft." She stopped, and was thoughtful a moment. "Or at the very least, of stupidity."

"You would not tell Hopkirk?" asked Justine quickly, her voice catching in her throat.

"Nay," said Sarah's mother, much to Justine's relief. "I have evidence of the man's accusations in the past, and as much as I am not yet convinced that you may have been sent here from times yet to come, as I look at you I do not believe you have the sign of witchcraft on your face."

"You had knowledge of Hopkirk and his accusations?" asked Justine. "Did he suspect you of witchcraft?"

"Aye. It was said, but he never made an actual accusation. I do have some of the arts; I have knowledge to make potions which can cure ailments. But I do not use incantations and I do not worship Satan," she paused. "You'll find we're God-fearing folk here."

"My mother would help cure people with her potions," explained Sarah. "But a child in the village died of sweating sickness, and Hopkirk looked to my mother as the possible cause. But enough of the villagers had been cured by her, that they would not entertain any accusation and eventually Hopkirk looked elsewhere."

Justine considered this – Hopkirk reacting to pressure from the villagers. "Do you think Hopkirk would ever withdraw the accusation on me?" she asked.

"Not if it was made by Margaret," answered Sarah's mother. She would have to withdraw it, not him."

"The villagers know you only as the accused witch," added Sarah. They will not fight for you as they did for my mother."

"No, only the Lord Jesus himself would get Hopkirk to change his mind," said the older woman. "So we will need to make our prayers for that."

"Thank you," said Justine.

She decided to change the subject. "You said you would have put a poultice of mouldy bread on my feet," she observed. "In my time we know that mould is a fungus and it kills the tiny little creatures that cause infection. That is just what we all know. It's not witchcraft."

"I am glad that my potions and my arts become commonplace in the future," answered Sarah's mother. "But right now I will continue to believe in their magical properties." She walked back to the bed. "And we have a task ahead of us – to save the master. You need to tell us what the future says will happen, and how you have come by this information."

"It is well documented in my time that Sir William was stabbed while in a tavern on the evening of the 31st of July," said Justine. "To us, it is part of history."

"So that is why you would have kept him here tonight," said Sarah.

"Yes," said Justine. "I don't know who kills him, or why, or what he was doing in the tavern, but I know that if I could have stopped him being there, then I would save him."

"So we need to plan our actions," said Sarah.

"Yes, and we don't have much time," said Justine. "We know the stabbing takes place this evening, but we don't know when. We must get to the tavern as soon as possible."

"Aye, and avoid Master Hopkirk, who will test you and condemn you to death by fire if he catches you," added Sarah.

Justine rather wished she hadn't been reminded of that. Hopkirk needed to be removed as a threat – or she would end of saving Sir William for some other girl to marry.

She swung her legs out of the bed and gingerly put some weight on her right foot, testing it for pain. She was pleased that it did not seem to hurt. She put her left foot down and did the same. Again, it seemed to be pain-free. She stood up with all her weight on her feet and did some little jumps. She turned to Sarah's mother and smiled.

"Yes," she said. "We need to avoid the attentions of Master Hopkirk. But I think I may have a plan for that."

CHAPTER SEVENTEEN

Bright sunlight flashed between the tall elm trees as Sir William urged his horse along the emerald green forest path at a reckless gallop, past the low branches and the high roots that emerged suddenly out of the deep shadows. But he was oblivious to any danger – he was in love, and love was to be celebrated.

It was to be celebrated with this joyful gallop at speeds more suited to the open plain than to a hazardous narrow path through a dense forest.

It was to be celebrated by encouraging his horse to soar gracefully over a moss-covered tree trunk; to land with pinpoint accuracy beyond and gather himself to gallop onwards towards Grangedean Manor.

It was to be celebrated by standing in the stirrups and whooping with elation as he emerged from the forest by the gnarled old oak tree, because he had finally found the girl he'd been searching for all his life, and she was just perfect – totally, wonderfully and completely perfect.

William turned onto the path back to Grangedean Manor and slowed to a steadier pace to collect his thoughts after his initial burst of lover's energy.

'She is most beautiful,' he affirmed to himself. 'Truly, she has a sweet, comely face, with a nose that wrinkles just so, and eyes that would make the fair Helen of Troy green with envy...' He chuckled. 'She does not defer to me, as all other girls do – and acts as if she is my equal. I should be repelled by this, but...' his mind went back over their passion in bed, and her hand running up his leg '...but to be sure, it is most refreshing.' This thought made him realise how thirsty he was. Rummaging in the saddlebag beside him, he found the costrel given to him by Simon earlier. It was empty. Now he thought about it, he remembered finishing it while he was tracking Justine's trail of blood spots through the forest. And anyway, it had been filled with wine – what he wanted for his thirst was beer – some refreshing beer.

He trotted into the stable yard at Grangedean Manor and leapt off his horse, as servants came out to take it from him.

He entered the building and strode through the corridors into the Great Hall.

"Martha! Martha, I say!" he shouted loudly, as he threw off his cloak and crashed down into his chair at the head of the table.

After a while he heard her leisurely and slow footsteps on the stairs from the kitchens, before she appeared through the door. There was once a time when she would have run up the stairs and arrived out of breath in her eagerness to serve him. He frowned. That time appeared to have passed.

"Sir William?" she asked, her voice and her expression staying just on the right side of insolence.

"Some beer!" he demanded, deciding to ignore both her attitude and her slow appearance – a man in love should not give mind to such things, however thirsty he may be.

"Yes, Sir William," she answered, giving a perfunctory curtsey and disappearing back down to the kitchens.

He relaxed back in his chair with a deep sigh and closed his eyes, letting his mind drift back on a wave of warm contentment to the little cottage buried deep in the woods. He was kneeling on the bed, looking down at Mary Fox as she lay smiling beneath him, her legs either side of him. Slowly, gently, he was stroking the warm, velvet-soft skin of her waist; feeling her moving in perfect time with the touch of his hands. She smiled as he broadened his strokes out so that his hands started to travel further and further up towards her firm, round breasts with their hard, red...

"Good day, my lord."

William opened his eyes, to find Dowland and Stanmore standing in front of the table.

"Well met, my lord" said Stanmore. "We are come for the hunt today."

"The hunt? What hunt?" asked William vaguely, much more interested in chasing after his memories as they slipped tantalisingly away.

"My lord," said Dowland. "Have you forgot? There is talk of the white stag up at Briar's Copse. We are keen to give it chase."

"I have no stomach to hunt a stag today," said William with finality.

"My lord?" asked Dowland, sounding confused.

"No stomach, my lord?" asked Stanmore. "Are you well?"

"Quite well, I assure you," answered William. "But I shall not hunt the white stag today. Another time, maybe. Good day, gentlemen." He relaxed back into his chair again and closed his eyes, seeking out the little cottage once again in his mind...

"But my lord, another time it may not be so easily found," spluttered Dowland. "It is a wily stag that we have oft chased but never caught." There was a silence, and William started to drift through the door of the cottage and towards the pallet bed. Then Dowland's voice pulled him back. "It has been seen at Briar Copse, my lord. This is our chance at last! We can approach from the west and push it back onto the woods."

William opened one eye and stared at the two men. "Nay, let it be," he said. "I have other things on my mind than that stag."

"But my lord, it is ours for the taking!"

"But my mood is not to take it today, Dowland," answered William curtly, opening the other eye. "So there's the end to the matter."

"As you wish, my lord," said Dowland, finally seeming to recognise that he was beaten. Then he sniggered and grinned in devilment. "Is it perchance a 'Fox' you are hunting instead, my lord?"

There was a heavy silence. Stanmore shifted uncomfortably from foot to foot. Dowland stared at William uneasily; his grin now starting to become more like a grimace.

William returned his stare, turning over the options in his mind as to how to respond to this insolence and intrusion into his private love. Anger was always an option – he could switch it on at will, and had been known to have men and women running for cover from his magnificent rage. But after a moment, he decided it would not be prudent. Anger would indicate that there was some truth to the suggestion made by his grinning friend in front of him, and while Mary Fox was still being sought for witchcraft by Hopkirk, he did not want to be accused by association. No, what he needed to do was wear a mask of innocence – and wear it until such times as she was no longer accused.

"Indeed, Master Dowland," he observed levelly, "I would hunt any creature I could give chase to."

Dowland let out his breath and un-fixed his grin. "As you say, my lord," he answered, sounding relieved. "Any creature indeed."

Just then Martha appeared at the door from the kitchens.

"Oh, Sir William," she said with a snide little smile, "the beer is spoiled – some rats have got inside the barrel and it has a most rank odour. I cannot serve it to you."

William stood up. "What?" he asked, dismayed. "But I have a raging thirst and must drink some beer now!"

"I am truly sorry, Sir William," answered Martha, not sounding sorry at all. "Some wine instead?" she suggested.

This was the last straw for William and he snapped.

"Nay, I have a thirst, woman!" he barked. "Wine does not satisfy my thirst – I need beer to quench it! By the Lord's wounds, is that too much to ask?"

"I am sorry, Sir William, but the smell is most rank. I truly cannot serve it." Then she added, "And the colour is, well… it is…" she looked down at her feet to cover her smile, "…it is green."

"My lord, why do we not repair to the tavern in the village?" suggested Stanmore. "There is beer to be had there." He laughed, then added, "Of the correct colour."

"Aye," said William. "That is the most welcome idea you have had today." He turned to Dowland, "Come, you also. We shall go to the tavern and drink our fill!"

CHAPTER EIGHTEEN

Agnes, the landlord's daughter, looked at Hopkirk as his grey eyes bored into hers from across the table in the dark, noisy tavern.

"I have known many witches," he said, in answer to a question from Maggie beside her. "And I have tested them all by putting them under water to see if they have the magic to save themselves."

Ruth, who was sitting on the other side of Agnes with wide, shining eyes, asked breathlessly, "Have any of them had that magic, Master Hopkirk?"

Hopkirk drank some ale and fixed the girl with his unblinking stare. "None chose to save themselves," he answered. "They may have decided to confound me by choosing to die instead."

Agnes considered this, her enquiring young mind spotting a flaw in Hopkirk's logic. "But what if they weren't witches at all?" she asked. "The outcome was the same in either case."

"Nay," answered Hopkirk. "They had the darkness in their eyes. You can always see the mark of darkness in their eyes." He broke off a crust of bread and ate it slowly, as they shivered with delicious fear. "The testing must be done, but in truth, I always know when I have a witch in front of me."

The three girls looked suitably impressed. "We'll find this witch, won't we Master Hopkirk?" asked Agnes. "Then you'll know when you see her in front of you."

"Yes, we'll find her," he answered.

"And will you test her by ducking?" asked Ruth. "Even if you can see the darkness in her eyes?"

"Indeed," he said, his tongue darting out of his mouth to lick his lips. "We must follow the process. She must be put under the water so we can be sure if she is able to save herself with magic."

"Aye," agreed the old men and women of the village, who were seated at a table next to them and listening intently. "She cannot have gone far," added an older man hopefully.

"The Lord will not guide her steps away from us – if she has rejected him and embraced the Devil then she will make mischief here," said an old woman.

"Indeed," said Hopkirk as he looked around the tavern. It had filled up considerably since he and his party of villagers had come in earlier, hungry and thirsty after their hunt. There had been much ale drunk and bread eaten, and the talk had all been about continuing the hunt in the evening – but Hopkirk had said they would resume it in the morning instead. He had suggested that the witch had clearly found a secure hiding place so she was unlikely to break cover before nightfall. A rough, cold, uncomfortable night, possibly without shelter, could well bring her out into the open and they could take her more easily in the morning. She would be tired, hungry and most likely unable to fight back with any spells or incantations when she was taken.

So he had bought ale and bread all round, and agreed to let his group of villagers have a relaxing summer's evening in the tavern before resuming the hunt at dawn.

He finished the ale in his tankard and beckoned to Jake, who was padding around with two pitchers, one in each hand.

Jake came over and refilled Hopkirk's tankard, then looked down at Agnes. "Come girl," he rumbled, "we are most full in the tavern this evening. You have sat with Master Hopkirk and these good men and women long enough. You will help me serve all these people."

"Yes, father," answered Agnes. She nodded to Hopkirk, got up from the table and joined Jake.

"Take this pitcher and serve those men over there," Jake said, handing her one of the jugs of ale and indicating a table in the corner.

Agnes looked where her father had indicated and saw four men sitting around a small table preparing to play cards. She went over and filled each of their tankards. Three of the men looked old and boring – she was not concerned with them – but one was younger and looked quite nice, so she decided to linger a moment and listen to their conversation.

"How is your good fortune?" asked the grizzled old man dressed in brown who was dealing the cards. His question was addressed to the younger man who was sitting opposite him. "We want no lucky man at our game."

"No lucky man? Why then you invite me to play but you expect me to lose?" responded the other. Agnes thought this was quite a good answer.

"Certainly. Do you take us for fools?" asked a fat man in a green doublet next to him. "You are a stranger to us – we would not have asked you to play if we thought you would win."

"In truth," responded the younger man, "I take for a fool any man who cannot use his wits in a game of cards." Agnes watched him pick up his cards and study them carefully, then take one out and put it back further along the fan in his hand. "You want only an unlucky man to play?" he continued equitably. "Well show me a lucky man, and I will show you a fool who lives upon his luck and never troubles to use his wits. Such a man can rarely win at any game."

The grizzled older man looked up from his cards, no doubt impressed by the younger man's quick mind. "Ah, but is not an unlucky man a fool also – for if he never troubles to use his wits, then he has only himself to blame for his luck!"

The younger man placed a card on the table, then looked up and winked at Agnes, drawing her into this verbal swordplay. "I say there is no such thing as an unlucky man – only a fool." She smiled back.

The fourth man, dressed all in black, looked at his hand and appeared to consider his options carefully. He had long grey hair and a trim beard, with bright blue eyes looking out from under a deep brow. Agnes thought he was probably the leader of the three older men. After a moment he calmly placed a card next to the first one on the table. "Aye, and a fool to say it," he observed, sitting back. "This taproom philosophy is as well in its place, sir, but I fear it is misplaced here."

"And what philosophy brings forth that conclusion?" asked the younger man crossly. "Or are you a knave in search of a fight?"

The challenge hung in the air a moment, as each of the other two players placed their cards on the table. The fourth man considered the cards a moment, then scooped them up and placed them face down by the edge of the table in front of him.

"Neither a knave, nor seeking to cross swords with any man," he observed calmly. "I say only that you presume too much. It is possible to have a man who is both wise – and out of luck."

The younger man then started to let his anger show, leading Agnes to think he may not be so nice-looking after all. "Show me such a man, knave," he growled as he slapped down a card to open the next round.

The man in the green doublet said, "We have an example here today. Are you acquainted with our esteemed magistrate, Master Matthew Hopkirk?" He inclined his head in the direction of Hopkirk and his villagers.

The younger man looked round, then nodded.

"Well, he is most decidedly a wise man who is out of luck."

"How so?"

"He is wise – he has identified a cunning witch who would kill us all with her wicked incantations. But he is out of luck," he paused as the grizzled older man in brown studied the card on the table, "for he has not found her so he can test her and if she is a witch, burn her."

"And drive out the devil that possesses her," said the man in brown. He placed his card down then drained his tankard, looking confident that he could not be beaten on this round of play.

The man in black, who had been mysteriously silent throughout this last exchange, placed his card down. The man in the green doublet barely glanced at it and reached out to scoop up the pile, only to find that the man in black had beaten him to it.

"Mine, I believe," the man in black said, and put the cards next to the first pile on his side of the table. Then he beckoned at Agnes to refill his tankard.

"I saw you earlier with this Master Hopkirk?" he asked her.

She nodded. The other three men paused to listen.

"And you have been with him this day, hunting for the witch?"

She nodded again. "Tell me," he said, looking her in the eye, "how was she known as a witch? Was she seen preparing a charmed circle, or brewing potions, or muttering incantations?"

"Nay, she blasphemed most foully," said Agnes, wide-eyed.

"She blasphemed?" The man looked at his companions with a raised eyebrow, then back at Agnes. "It must have been a foul blasphemy indeed for her to be so actively pursued."

"Yes, sir," answered Agnes earnestly. She put the jug down and crossed herself, then took a breath and said, "The witch was heard directly to say that she rejects Christ and all his works; that the good Lord should rot in Hell for all eternity, and that her one true lord is the Devil." She crossed herself again. "And that she would spit on the Host in Communion," she added.

The other three men crossed themselves. Agnes was pleased to see that the younger man visibly paled. "Aye, a most foul blasphemy indeed," said the man in black. "If she said that, then she should certainly be questioned thoroughly." The others nodded. "But," he continued, "as our Queen herself has observed, we should not make windows into the souls of men." He considered a moment. "Or, in this case, women. I believe we as a society are, in truth, more tolerant than this Master Hopkirk would allow." He got up from his chair. "Excuse me a moment, gentlemen."

Agnes followed him as he crossed over to Hopkirk's table and touched the grey man's shoulder. "Master Hopkirk?" he enquired.

The magistrate looked up without expression.

"Yes?" he answered quietly. "Who asks?"

"I am Master Robert Wychwoode, lawyer." The man in black paused, as if expecting some glimmer of recognition from Hopkirk, but only got a blank stare. "I am staying with my good friends here," he gestured back towards his table, "on my way to the Oxford Assizes." Hopkirk remained silent, so Wychwoode continued. "I could not help but overhear that you are in pursuit of a woman accused of witchcraft, but the evidence against her is for the sin of blasphemy. A strong blasphemy, I'll admit, but nonetheless, blasphemy."

Hopkirk stared at Wychwoode. "Are you suggesting that a blasphemer cannot be a witch?" he asked.

"Not at all," answered Wychwoode. "I am simply suggesting that the one does not necessarily lead to the other."

"Then you would need to conduct a trial to ascertain the truth?" asked Hopkirk.

"Indeed I would. That would conform to the principles of law and justice that I and my brothers in the law hold dear," Wychwoode said with apparent satisfaction.

"Then you and your brothers will be comforted to know that I will hold such a trial," said Hopkirk quietly. "Good evening to you, Master... Wychwoode, is it? Good evening." He turned back to Ruth and Maggie, who had been hanging on every word of this exchange.

Wychwoode stood a moment, his mouth working. "Master Hopkirk," he said firmly. "I understand you are a magistrate. You must have a care for the law and those who have reached greater positions of authority within it."

Hopkirk turned back slowly and looked Wychwoode up and down.

"I have such a care, believe me, Master Wychwoode," he observed. "But I have a greater care for the eradication of witchcraft. And if I find those who practice witchcraft, or those who appear to me to seek to protect them..." he paused, "...I will stop at nothing to destroy them. Whether they are a lowly maid or even a great lawyer."

Wychwoode's hand went to the hilt of his sword; his neck blotching to the colour of one of Agnes's prize red roses. "Do you threaten me, sir?" he barked.

Hopkirk stood up and faced the older man. His face was pale and grey, but there was no doubting his strength and power as he answered.

"I do, sir," he hissed. "I am the magistrate here, and my word here is the law. And I will not have it challenged by any man, least of all by a fancy lawyer from London. So, sir, leave me to my work and I will leave you to yours. Unless," he said, with a slight raise in his voice, "you seek to protect a witch, in which case..." he paused for effect, "...you become my work."

Wychwoode said nothing, but his mouth worked and more red blotches appeared on his neck.

Then he took a deep breath and very deliberately took his hand off the hilt of his sword. As he let the breath out slowly, Agnes noticed the whole tavern had become silent, watching this drama playing out in front of them.

"I can see you are a most determined man, Master Matthew Hopkirk," Wychwoode said slowly. "And I respect that determination." He looked around the room. "But I shall remember this conversation, Master Matthew Hopkirk, and I shall watch with great interest how you go about your work, and I shall be particularly interested in your respect for the law, and how effectively you cleave to the principles of justice." He bowed formally. "Good evening to you, sir." Then he turned and walked away.

Agnes watched as he walked back at his table, but did not sit down. He said something to the fat man in green, who nodded, then Wychwoode tossed a coin onto the table, turned and walked straight past Agnes and out of the door without looking left or right. The villagers, who were now crowded into the tavern in some numbers, watched him go in silence. His companions stood up, bowed to the young man they had invited to join their game earlier, and marched out also.

There was a silence in the tavern once the men had left, as the crowd of villagers looked at Hopkirk with increased admiration. Agnes could see they were deeply impressed that he had stood up to such a fancy London lawyer, and that it had been for a cause they held dear – their protection from an evil witch.

They turned to each other and there were mutterings of support for Hopkirk.

"He's right to be out seeking the witch," she heard one say.

"Can't be having meddling by London lawyers. He had no right to be telling our magistrate what's the law."

"Master Hopkirk won't be pushed off the hunt for this evil witch, for sure."

More and more villagers joined in, all of the view that Hopkirk had been right to send Wychwoode packing. Soon the hubbub was back to its earlier level.

The young man left at the card table gathered up the cards and sat idly dealing himself hands. Hopkirk and his villagers picked up earlier conversations. Agnes went back to circulating round the tables serving ale.

At one point she stopped by the table of a woman with two young boys who were not yet old enough to grow beards.

"Such excitement," she said with studied casualness, as she filled their tankards.

"Oh yes," said the woman. "My sons thought they might see a fight."

"As did I," said Agnes, with a smile.

She looked at the two boys, both dressed in the basic lace-up smock and open breeches of the field worker, with rough woven caps on their heads. They both seemed shy, looking down rather than catching her eye.

"I'm sure they'll see fights a-plenty in times to come," she observed, before moving on to the next table.

CHAPTER NINETEEN

Thomas Melrose walked up to the door of the tavern just as Wychwoode and his companions were leaving. He stood aside to let them out, then went in.

He was dusty and tired from the ride back from the town, and he was very thirsty. He caught sight of Agnes holding a pitcher of ale and gestured her towards him as he dropped heavily into a chair at an empty table.

"Some ale, girl, and presently," he ordered.

She fetched him a clean pewter tankard and filled it to the brim. "My thanks, girl," he said. He studied her a moment, thinking he recognised her from the last time he had been in the tavern. "You're Jake's daughter, aren't you?"

"Yes, sir," she answered. "Is there something you want?"

"Send your father to me," said Melrose. "I would talk with him."

"Yes, sir."

Agnes moved off round the tables towards her father. A few minutes later, Jake padded up to Melrose.

"Master Melrose, isn't it?" he asked in his deep voice.

"Aye, it is," said Melrose, studying the man closely. He noted the big, rough face with close-set eyes under bushy brows, and the fleshy nose crisscrossed with broken veins. "Sit down, Jake," he said. "I must talk with you."

Jake pulled out the empty chair opposite Melrose and eased his large bulk down carefully into it. "How can I be of service, Master Melrose?" he enquired.

"You saw my father in here by chance?"

"Aye, many times," answered Jake, settling back in his chair with a smile, as if he'd been expecting this line of questioning.

"And what was his purpose here?"

"As anyone's, Master Melrose," said Jake. "Good ale to drink and vittles to eat."

"For sure, for sure." Melrose took a deep draught of ale, and prepared to ask the question he needed to ask. And to hear the answer he would have preferred not to hear.

"And did he play, perhaps, at cards or the like?"

"Aye, that he did," was the unwelcome answer. "Cards, backgammon, draughts; he even would challenge others to a trial of strength – where he would sit opposite a man and they would each place their arms on the table, grasp hands and attempt to push the other man's hand to the table." Jake stared into space with a half-smile as if he was re-living the scenes of bravado, laughter and drunken merriment. "He was not a strong man, your father. He challenged many men and was beaten by most of them. But he was a man of great charm and ready wit." Jake laughed softly at the memories.

"But not for money?" asked Melrose earnestly, ignoring Jake's laughter. "He challenged for the fun and for the sport, not for money?"

Jake looked at him a moment, the smile dying on his face. "No, Master Melrose," he answered seriously. "Your father loved to wager on the challenges and games he played. He wagered big, and when he lost, he wagered again twice as much to try and get it back."

"He lost?" whispered Melrose. "Are you sure?" he asked, as if challenging Jake to say he'd made a mistake and that in truth his father had continually won.

"I am sorry, Master Melrose, he lost," confirmed Jake. "Near on a hundred pounds."

"A hundred pounds?" asked Melrose in total disbelief, blood draining from his face. "A hundred pounds, you say?" He sat back in his chair, quite beyond understanding. How could his father have squandered so large a sum?

"Aye, sir." Jake scratched his nose thoughtfully. "I know it was a lot, but he was a driven man. It was as if he would push himself always to his own downfall. I was saddened to hear he'd taken his own life. Deeply saddened."

Melrose fought down the sudden urge to jump up and strike this lumpen barkeeper. 'Were you really so saddened?' he thought furiously. 'My father must have put much of my money in your pocket too!'

Instead he leaned forward, put both his hands over Jake's large, rough, calloused paw on the table and said, "Thank you Jake, for telling me how it was. We were all saddened – he was a good man."

"That he was, sir, that he was."

"Tell me," said Melrose casually, keeping his hands over Jake's, "did Sir William de Beauvais ever play at cards with my father?"

"Sir William?" Jake asked. "Why no, sir. Sir William only came in once, as

I recall." He thought a moment. "It was the day before your father took his life."

"Oh," said Melrose in surprise. He had been expecting to hear tales of William gambling with his father and pushing him on to lose ever larger sums. "So he saw my father here the day before he died?"

"That he did, sir." Jake nodded his big head, making his beard flap like a flag in a breeze. "They were talking quietly – at this very table as I recall – but I was not privy to their talk."

Melrose took his hands away from Jake and sat back to absorb this news. So William had been talking to his father at this very table – and a day later he was dead by his own hand. What other conclusion could there be than William was inciting him to suicide? That was how he knew! The day of the hunt when the stag had charged them and William's father had told him of the suicide, William had known. He'd seen it in the man's eyes; how could he ever forget the image of William leaning against the wall, with the look that said he knew?

"Thank you, Jake. You have been very helpful." Melrose finished his ale and stood up. "What do I pay for the ale?"

"That's not necessary, sir. I am pleased to have been of use," said Jake, heaving his bulk out of the chair. "Good evening, Master Melrose. You are always welcome here."

"Thank you again, good Jake, and well met."

Melrose made his way to the door and opened it, then walked straight into a man coming into the tavern.

It was William.

Melrose reeled back, and stared wide-eyed at his master.

William rubbed his nose and laughed loudly. "Hello, Tom," he said. "You must look where you go with more care. Have you been enjoying too much of our friend Jake's finest ales?"

CHAPTER TWENTY

Melrose took a step back and William marched past him into the tavern, followed by Dowland and Stanmore.

"Come, Tom, you must join us," said William jovially, turning and clapping Melrose on the back with good-natured but somewhat excessive force. "We have abandoned today's hunt in favour of slaking our thirst with some of Jake's good ale and we shall make merry with the good company in this place. Although I may say," he leaned in towards Melrose's ear conspiratorially, "we would sooner have made merry on the beer from my own kitchens, but it seems the rats have been pissing in it!" He roared with laughter at his own joke. "So here we are!"

Melrose fought back the urge to find a cutting retort; a pithy put-down that would have shown his master just what he thought of him. Instead he gave a small formal bow and said through gritted teeth, "Nothing would give me greater pleasure, my lord."

"Good." William marched over to a table and sat down, followed by the other three men. Catching Agnes's eye, he smiled and beckoned her over.

"Four of your finest beers, girl!" he ordered.

"Yes, Sir William," she answered, her eyes down, and went off to fetch some tankards.

William watched her retreating back for a moment, with a puzzled expression. Turning to his companions, he said, "I have not been down to this place in many months, but that girl is familiar to me. I would swear I have seen her only recently. How can this be so?"

"Maybe she has been up at Grangedean for… some purpose," suggested Stanmore with a lewd smile.

"Nay," said Dowland, watching Agnes's bottom with serious

consideration. "She is a comely wench, and buxom with it. I would have recalled seeing her."

"You are not at Grangedean every moment of every day," said Melrose quietly. "She could have been there and yet have avoided your," he paused, as if searching for the right word, "your most thorough inspections."

"I would certainly have recalled her," observed Dowland. Melrose couldn't be sure if he was choosing to ignore the insult or simply did not understand it.

Agnes returned with four tankards and a jug of beer. She put down the tankards and filled them for the four men.

William stared intently at her, then banged the table making Melrose jump.

"I have it!" he cried, triumphantly. "I know I have seen you recently. You were in the party of that impudent magistrate Hopkirk, that would have trampled across my rooms this morning in search of the unfortunate girl he accuses of witchcraft!"

"Aye, my lord," she replied, her hand shaking slightly as she poured the last of the four tankards of beer. "We were charged by Master Hopkirk to seek out a most evil witch, that would enchant us all."

"Nonsense!" barked William testily. "I said this to Hopkirk this morning, and I say it again now; the girl is no witch!" He turned to his companions. "But this impertinent fellow would have her tested for witchcraft – and if she were found to be a witch, he would burn her at the stake!" Dowland and Stanmore made appropriate noises of shock and disbelief while Melrose held his peace. William turned back to Agnes, who was looking very uncomfortable to be in the presence of the master in full flow of his anger, and in defence of the witch Mary Fox as well. "You, girl!" he barked, and she flinched back, almost spilling some beer from her jug. "By what reason is she accused?"

Agnes curtseyed deeply and stayed down low. "Begging your pardon, my lord, but she was heard to blaspheme most foully," she said, finally looking up at him with wide, scared eyes.

"Get up, girl," he ordered. "Blasphemed most foully? What did she say, that has so offended the sensibilities of the precious Master Hopkirk and half the village?

"Oh, Master, she said..." the girl paused and crossed herself, then took a deep breath and let the words tumble out. "She said that she rejects Christ and all his good works; that the Lord should rot in Hell for all eternity; that her one true lord is the Devil; that she would spit on the Host in Communion." She paused, then added, "And she would condemn all who cross her to the everlasting torment."

"Blasphemy indeed," observed Stanmore drily.

"If it is true," snapped William. He seemed to compose himself a moment, as if letting his anger wash away like a retreating tide on the beach. "It does not have the ring of truth about it to me," he said. "I have sat with this girl at the banquet last evening, and have spoken much with her after, and I would not see it in her to hold such thoughts, least of all to express them in such a way."

"I swear upon my mother's grave she was heard to say this, Master," volunteered Agnes, with surprising boldness.

"An oath indeed," observed William. "But it was not to you that she said this diabolical litany?"

Agnes hesitated. "No, Master, not me. It was to Margaret that these words were spoken."

"Margaret? That little shrewish woman who works in my kitchens?" Now William laughed. "I doubt she is a reliable witness." He turned away from Agnes and back to his companions. "This is a frail case indeed," he said dismissively, the matter closed in his mind. "I give it no credence."

---0---

Agnes lingered for a brief moment, staring at William's back and coming to the conclusion that her audience with her master was over. She made her way back through the crowded room to Hopkirk's table, put down her empty ale jug and sat down, looking at Hopkirk with the bright eyes of one bursting to tell a desperately important story.

"Well met, girl," said the witchfinder absently. "Have you finished your serving duties already?"

"No," she answered. "I have been talking to Sir William de Beauvais."

"Sir William?" Hopkirk's attention was suddenly focussed very closely on her.

"Yes, Master Hopkirk," she answered, breathlessly.

"So what ails you, girl?" he asked. "You look as if you are sat on a burning coal."

"He says he gives no credence to the witch's blasphemy," she exclaimed. "He called it a frail case!"

"On what grounds?" Hopkirk leaned in and fixed her with his staring grey eyes. "What was his reason?"

Agnes hesitated. Deep down she knew she should not be telling tales against the master – it was not her place and it was against the natural order of things for her to be so bold. But there was something about the unblinking stare of the man across the table that mesmerised her, like a mouse before a snake about to devour it. She felt powerless to resist. "He said he has met her," she answered. "He said he knows her well." She paused. "He said she is under his guardianship."

Hopkirk leaned back and smiled. "Then he is indeed protecting her. I was correct in my assumption." He pushed back his chair and stood up. "He may be the lord of Grangedean Manor, but in this, I am his master."

Pulling his cloak around him, he pushed his way through the crowd, until he was standing at William's table.

---0---

William was talking to Stanmore as Hopkirk approached from behind. Seeing Stanmore's attention drawn to something over his shoulder, William stopped and turned round. Slowly, he looked the man up and down.

"Master Hopkirk," he observed drily. He found the sight of this grey man offensive, but decided to hold his temper. For now.

"Sir William de Beauvais," said Hopkirk, his sibilant voice grating.

"I warned you this morning to stay out of my affairs," William said. "They are none of your business."

"I believe they have now become my business," answered Hopkirk.

William's eyes narrowed. "How so?" he asked carefully.

"Because I have heard that you claim to protect the woman called Mary Fox, that we would test for witchcraft."

"I know her, that is all," answered William. "I do not deny it."

"So she is under your protection?" hissed Hopkirk.

"You mean, do I allow you to drown her for your perverse abomination of a trial?" growled William. "Then no, I do not."

"So, you do protect her." Hopkirk gave a small smile of triumph. "Then I must perhaps try you as well…?"

William let Hopkirk's question hang in the air, as he stared into the man's cold, expressionless eyes.

He became aware that the room had now fallen silent. Slowly he wrenched his eyes away from Hopkirk's and looked around him at the villagers' faces. They were staring intently at him to see how he would react; to see if the legendary de Beauvais temper would finally be unleashed by this monumental challenge to his authority and position.

As he looked from face to face, he considered his options. Would the villagers support him if he pulled out his sword and ran this impudent magistrate through? He may be lord of the manor, but in a tavern fight you could never be sure who would be for you and who against. That burly yeoman and the red-faced farmer – they looked as though they could be Hopkirk's men. The peasant woman with her arms around her two young boys – she may be for him, but neither she nor her boys would be of any use in a fight; indeed William could not even see the boys' faces – their heads were bowed, staring down at the rough dirt floor. The villagers now standing behind Hopkirk holding pitchforks – they may be elderly and young, but with those pitchforks they could be dangerous.

He decided he would try words and reason. For now.

He became aware that Hopkirk was looking with unhealthy interest into his eyes, as if looking for some sign or mark. Then the magistrate gave a cold smile and stepped back, as if he had found what he was looking for.

"Sir William?" asked Hopkirk, breaking the silence. "I would have an answer."

"You are asking if I practice witchcraft?"

Hopkirk gave a small nod of his head.

"Because I would not give up Mary Fox to your twisted justice?"

"Have a care," Hopkirk whispered softly, although his voice carried clearly to every person in the tavern. "It is God's justice I practice. To counter me is to counter God himself."

There was a murmur from the crowd in the tavern. William looked carefully round at all the faces. Many were nodding in approval and exchanging looks. William could see he was losing them to Hopkirk – they may have feared him as lord of the manor, but these simple folk feared God even more. William's blood turned to ice in his veins. If Hopkirk had the crowd, his cause would be easily lost.

He decided it was time to try and take God out of the equation.

"Nay, Master Hopkirk," William answered, slowly and deliberately. "I am as God-fearing as the next man, but right now…" he paused for effect "…I counter you alone."

There was a gasp from the assembled crowd.

Behind him, William could hear swords start to be drawn from scabbards, and he assumed it was Dowland, Stanmore and Melrose preparing to defend him.

He was only partly correct.

"You would deny my authority from God himself to test for witchcraft?" asked Hopkirk, his voice thick with assumed outrage.

"Yes, I would," William responded levelly.

"Then you give me no choice," snapped Hopkirk. "Take him!"

William's hand went to his sword hilt almost faster than the eye could follow, but even that was too slow. He had barely got his sword halfway out of its scabbard, when two strong hands gripped around his upper arms from behind and pulled him back. His sword dropped back into its scabbard. Someone unbuckled the belt straps and pulled it off him.

Hopkirk produced an evil-looking dagger from under his cloak, which glinted as it caught the light of a flickering candle. He thrust it up towards William's throat. William pulled his head back away from it, but could not move far enough, and he felt a sharp pain as the tip pierced the skin.

Hopkirk's eyes were grey and expressionless as he moved in closer. "So, you would deny my authority from God, Sir William?" he repeated softly. "You would deny God himself? That is the word of a witch indeed. The word of a man who would worship Satan." He pushed the knife a little deeper into William's throat. William squirmed and tried to lift his head further away. "And that must be tested, because, Sir William, you may reject God, but I do not, and neither do these good people, and God's justice must be served."

The crowd murmured their approval. William knew he'd made a terrible mistake – and had given all the momentum to Hopkirk.

Hopkirk looked past William at the man who was holding his arms and barked out an order. "Seat him. Bind him."

Hopkirk stood back and William saw there were bright red drips of blood on the blade of the knife. His blood! Seething with impotent rage, William was thrust down into a chair and his hands held down onto its arms. Two leather straps were produced and these were lashed several times around his wrists and buckled tight, securing his arms to the chair. William noticed with anger that they were his own leather belt straps that had, until a few seconds ago, held his sword and scabbard.

Hopkirk studied the man who had bound William to the chair. The man who had decided in a split second to grab William's arms and prevent him drawing his sword. "I must congratulate you for choosing to be on the side of God in this matter," he said.

"I do God's bidding," came the distinctive voice of Thomas Melrose from behind William.

For a moment William was totally speechless. He strained to look over his shoulder to see the man he had thought of as one of his closest friends, as Melrose tested the tightness of the straps, then moved round to stand next to Hopkirk, a look of quiet satisfaction on his thin features.

"Thomas?" whispered William, shaking his head in total disbelief. "Thomas? What, in the name of all that is holy, are you doing?"

Melrose said nothing; his thin mouth tightly shut.

"Dowland! Stanmore! To my aid!" William called out.

"They cannot help you," said Hopkirk.

"They are my men, and they must," answered William.

There was the sound of chairs scraping back and boots dragging on the floor, as Dowland and Stanmore were marched round into William's line of sight. Each one was held by another man, with a knife to his throat. They were both looking away, unable to meet their master's eye.

"Seat them and bind them also," ordered Hopkirk.

The two men were thrust down into chairs and held while some rope was sought. William noted with anger that neither man struggled, nor made any move to escape. The knives were being held loosely against their throats; their arms were being held down without much force onto the arms of the chairs – they could easily have made a bid for freedom and created a chance to fight for him. He was about to shout to them to fight back and escape, then he realised the hopelessness of their position. He could see the whole crowd was for Hopkirk, and without fresh loyalist fighters, the odds were against them.

With a sigh he sat back; waiting to see how this would play out and determined to seize any chance, however slim, to turn the tables on Hopkirk.

A couple of lengths of thin rope were produced and a sturdy yeoman bound Dowland and Stanmore's hands to the arms of their chairs. He pulled the rope as tight as possible – William could see it was cutting into Stanmore's wrists most cruelly. Stanmore winced but held his silence as the knots were made firm and tested by Hopkirk.

William looked the yeoman up and down. He had been right that this man would side with Hopkirk, but he was disappointed. "Geoffrey Smitheson, is it not?" he asked. The man avoided his eyes. "I helped you with a lowered rent last year, when the harvest was poor. Yet you are not for me in this matter?" Smitheson said nothing and stood back from the two men he had bound.

Dowland looked up at William with a defeated expression in his dark Hispanic eyes, like a guilty hound caught with the remains of the roast. "I am so sorry, Sir William," he muttered. "They were too fast for us, and…"

"Silence, fool!" screamed Hopkirk, suddenly stabbing his knife down into the wooden chair arm, just a hair's breadth away from Dowland's fingers. Dowland went white as he stared at the knife quivering upright in front of him, clearly imagining it slicing into his hand or severing the sinews of a finger…

"For the love of Jesus, man! What possesses you?" shouted William.

Hopkirk pulled his knife out of the arm of Dowland's chair and sheathed it carefully beneath his cloak. Then he turned slowly to William.

"What possesses me?" he asked, dropping his voice down so quietly that the crowd around would have had to strain their ears to hear him.

"What possesses me?" he repeated, this time louder, as he put his hands on the arms of William's chair.

"What possesses me?" he repeated a third time, winding up the volume and casting little glances to the crowd on each side as if to make sure he was pitching the anger at just the right level. From their rapt and horrified attention, it was clear that he was.

He leant forward and put his face close to William's. "It is not I that is possessed, is it Sir William?" he screamed.

William recoiled from Hopkirk's sulphurous breath as the magistrate's gaze flicked unblinkingly from one eye to the other, holding him in his mesmeric stare.

"It is not I," Hopkirk said, bringing his voice back down to its more usual hiss, "that has the darkness that I have seen clearly in these eyes; the darkness that speaks of sorcery and magic. The terrible darkness that possesses a man to worship not the risen Lord, but his eternal enemy, Satan!"

The crowd shivered and there were murmurings of shock and sorrow at the revelation that their lord and master – a man they had looked up to and respected – could now be so clearly exposed as a satanic witch.

"We must test him now, by immersion in water," commanded Hopkirk. He turned and saw Jake standing in the crowd. "Landlord, fetch a barrel or water butt. We will put his head under and see if he has the magic of witchcraft to save himself."

Jake turned and gestured with a flick of his head towards a couple of men, indicating that they should follow to help him fetch a barrel. The three of them went through a door at the back of the room.

Hopkirk turned back to the crowd.

"And if he does have that magic, then we know what action we must take!" He lifted his arms and spread them wide above his head. "We must let God's justice take its course!"

The crowd roared their approval.

"We must not suffer a witch to walk this earth!"

The crowd roared again.

Hopkirk picked up a candle and lifted it high over his head, where it flickered and cast deep shadows across the faces of the villagers. "And we will put him to death!" he shouted. "Death by fire!"

The crowd roared and chanted "Death to the witch! Death by fire!"

Hopkirk turned and looked down on Sir William de Beauvais, bound in the chair. As he caught William's eye, his face became quite expressionless – as if the rabble-rousing of a moment ago was no longer needed.

"You played by the rules, Sir William," he said quietly, leaning in. "And I respect that in a man."

Hopkirk leaned in closer.

"But, Sir William, do you know what? I have you now. I have you in my power." He moved closer still and whispered in William's ear. "So in the end, my lord, it was the rules that gave the game away."

He shook his head, almost in sorrow, then straightened up and once again addressed the crowd.

"Bring the barrel! We test him now!"

CHAPTER TWENTY-ONE

William stared into the oily black depths of the water as it rippled slowly to and fro across the top of the barrel in front of him. It stank of rotten eggs, dead fish and pond weed, but he knew that was now the least part of his problems. Standing before the barrel with his hands bound behind his back and his feet bound together, it was only a matter of time before he would be forced into the stinking water head first and be drowned in the name of Hopkirk's perverse justice and the satisfaction of the hostile villagers all around him.

Hostile villagers? What in God's name had he done to cause them to turn so easily against him? Had he not been an honest landlord, charging fair rents and avoiding the enforcement of widespread enclosure of common land? Had he not supported the church and provided a living for the priest? Had he not often attended services in the village instead of restricting himself to the chapel at Grangedean Manor as his father had done? Had he not provided much employment for servants and staff in his house, and for labourers on his land?

Yes, he had demonstrated himself to be a good and beneficent master to many, if not all, of the villagers who had happened to be in the tavern this night – yet Hopkirk had managed to turn them so completely against him so that not one had come to his aid, or that of Dowland and Stanmore, who were still bound to their chairs beside him.

And Thomas Melrose – what had he done to explain the man's abominable treachery? They had been friends since they were boys – they had learned their Latin together, learned to hunt together. Damn it all, they grown up together virtually as brothers – so what had caused Tom to turn into a murderous Cain? William searched his memory but could not settle on any particular instance or sign that could justify Tom's change towards him. For sure it could not be down to his relationship with Mary Fox; Tom had not been at the banquet last night and seen them together – in fact he had not seen Mary since yesterday morning, when he offered to take her as a servant but William had refused…

Was that it? Was it that refusal that had turned his friend against him? Surely not – no man could willingly turn traitor for the refusal of a strangely-dressed girl as a servant…

A strangely-dressed girl indeed, and yet – such a beauty.

Despite his situation, William smiled as he saw again her lovely face looking up at him in the gloomy darkness of the forest cottage, breathing softly through parted lips as he moved slowly inside her, reaching her arms up behind his head to pull his mouth down onto hers…

The image faded, and now he saw her running out into the grounds after she had knocked into his mother, flapping her hands and crashing to the grass in such a comic and endearing fashion…

Then she was beside him as they walked into the Great Hall for the banquet; her face glowing in the light of a thousand golden candles as she took in the scene with such a look of joy and wonder that he knew, then as now, that he would love her for all eternity…

An eternity that was about to begin very soon.

In truth, he would not see Mary Fox again in this life. Although he hoped that maybe, eventually, he might see her again in the next one. By God's good grace she would have a long and happy life first – oh, how he wished for that with all his heart.

With luck she would be well away from the village by now, helped by Sarah and her mother to seek good fortune in some new place; somewhere where she could be at ease without the threat of a trial for witchcraft.

He imagined her arriving at some new village, settling herself into a small cottage somewhere; maybe finding a new man she could love – a man whose love would be worthy of her; who would make her happy. Would he make her as happy as he, William, would have done? Would he look after her, care for her, make sure she felt loved and valued till the day she died?

As William stared into the dark waters that would shortly take him to eternity, he again hoped with all his heart that this would be so.

Then slowly, reluctantly, he looked up.

Hopkirk was in a corner conferring with Jake, Tom Melrose and the yeoman Smitheson. As William watched, the witchfinder came over towards the barrel and held his hand up for silence.

Looking around the expectant crowd with a grim face, he called out, "Are we all ready?" There was a murmur of assent. "Then let the trial begin!"

"I do not recognise the competence or the authority of this court to try me," said William levelly, hoping to take the momentum away from Hopkirk.

"Nor do I recognise that there are any grounds." He lifted his chin and added a hard edge to his voice. "By what right do you dare to hold me prisoner and threaten me with drowning?"

"I do not need to justify myself to you, de Beauvais," answered Hopkirk with a thin smile. "I am appointed witchfinder in this parish, and I will do my duty by these good, honest, God-fearing people."

William shuddered. It was 'de Beauvais' now, was it? Did he no longer have sufficient respect from this dreadful little magistrate that he deserved to be called 'Sir William'?

"What are the charges? Who speaks against me?" he asked belligerently.

"I myself will prosecute," said Hopkirk.

"That does not surprise me," said William. Some people in the crowd laughed.

"And who speaks for you?" asked Hopkirk.

"Since you seek to open mine own heart and soul to your examination," said William, "then I will have to speak for myself." He looked at the hostile faces crowding in around him in the candle light. "And to be fair," he added, "I doubt if any of these good people would risk their own necks to speak out for me." He gave a little snort of derision. "That would not be bravery – it would be reckless foolhardiness."

"Have a care, de Beauvais," hissed Hopkirk. "Your fate rests with these good people – they will judge whether or not in truth you must face the test by ducking, once they have heard the case for you and the case against you. Do not presume upon their judgement."

"I presume nothing, Master Hopkirk," answered William, glancing down into the black waters awaiting him. "But I recognise when a decision is already made."

"Then let us see if you are correct," answered Hopkirk. "I will begin my questions."

He pulled his cloak closer around his grey body and advanced right up to the barrel, positioning himself opposite William.

"I shall seek to understand whether you are protecting the witch known as Mary Fox, and by doing so, are complicit in her own evil-doing." Hopkirk leaned his hands on the edge of the barrel as if he were standing at a pulpit. He stared at William. "I shall seek to prove that there are strong grounds to believe you are yourself a witch – and that we must submit you to the test of ducking for final proof."

"You are already making the assumption that Mary Fox is a witch," said William, seeing his opportunity to undermine Hopkirk's argument. "You have not yet tried her. What if she is not a witch? Then your case against me folds like a paper castle."

"She was heard to blaspheme most foully," said Hopkirk. "Such ungodliness cannot be ought but worship of Satan – and that is next to witchcraft."

"This is a tired argument," countered William. "She was heard by one person only, and that person a most unreliable witness who is not even here tonight to attest to it. I give her testimony no credence whatsoever." He looked at the faces around him to see how well this was being accepted, and was rewarded to see some beginning to look a little doubtful.

But Hopkirk countered swiftly. "I have heard tell of the witch's behaviour," he said, "and it endorses the accusation that has been made." He turned to the crowd. "This girl is from out of the parish. She uses unnatural magic powers to clean a hearth, she dresses as a man, she wears man's boots and she goes by different names – I have heard that she calls herself Justine and yet she also calls herself Mary Fox. These things are not in dispute." There were nods of heads and mutterings of assent – even those who had looked doubtful earlier were now nodding vigorously. "Such facts may be evidence enough, but then we have an accusation of blasphemy – an accusation made by a woman of our village of exceptionally good character." He put strong emphasis on the last three words, as if to counter William's earlier dismissal of Margaret's reliability as a witness. Then he looked across the crowd, holding the gaze of each man or woman in turn. "That is enough for me, and it should be enough for you as well!"

The crowd cheered and Hopkirk turned back to William with a silky smile.

"So I think we can all agree that the witchcraft of this woman Justine or Mary Fox, or whatever her name might be, is not in any doubt," he said.

William decided to try a different approach. "But you have no possible evidence of satanic arts on my part," he countered, "even if I am protecting her as you say, that is not witchcraft or anything close to it."

But Hopkirk didn't answer as William would have expected.

Instead he stayed silent, drumming his fingers on the edge of the barrel and appearing to be lost in thought as he stared down into the dark waters.

William was wondering whether Hopkirk had even heard him, and was about to repeat the point when the magistrate looked up and said, "I call on Master Melrose to come forward."

William watched with anticipation – and barely concealed loathing – as the gaunt figure of Thomas Melrose picked his way through the crowd and came to stand next to Hopkirk on the other side of the barrel.

Hopkirk turned to Melrose and said in his most polite and conciliatory tone, "You are Thomas Melrose, son of the late Walter Melrose, yeoman farmer?"

"I am."

"And you have known Sir William de Beauvais since you were both small boys?"

"I have," answered Melrose, looking at Hopkirk and not catching William's eye.

"You were schooled together at Grangedean Manor?"

"We were, by Master Frobisher."

"Master Frobisher?" Hopkirk feigned mild surprise. "A worthy pedagogue. You were both well taught."

"We were," agreed Melrose.

"So you know how de Beauvais thinks, and how he conducts himself?" Hopkirk paused and looked across the crowd for effect. "The values he lives by?"

"I do," answered Melrose.

"Tell me about these things." Hopkirk said, his voice now like flowing honey. "Tell me how Sir William conducts himself."

Melrose considered his answer carefully. "He has always had the ability to shoot straight with an arrow," he said, sounding as if this was a great wonder, rather than a skill patiently learned. "Even as a small boy, he could split a leaf off a branch by shooting through a stem no bigger than a few human hairs."

"And this is a trick…" Hopkirk let the word hang in the air a moment… "a trick born perhaps – of magic?" he purred.

"Of magic!?" shouted William. "Have you taken leave of your senses? It is the result of many hours' practice!"

"But Master Melrose has stated that you demonstrated this ability even as a small boy," suggested Hopkirk with what sounded like disarming reasonableness. "You cannot have had sufficient hours to practice by then."

"Maybe it was luck the first time," said William. "But I can swear to you, on my oath, it is the result of much diligent practice." He added, "It is a skill that any man here could perfect!"

"Indeed?" said Hopkirk. "These men are well practiced in archery." He looked across the faces of the men in the crowd. "Can any man here do the same thing?"

The men looked down and shuffled their feet uncomfortably. William stared at them in disgust. No man would boast of their prowess, lest they ended up joining him at the side of the barrel.

Hopkirk looked round the room with satisfaction, then back at William. "None of these men would claim the same level of skill. Truly, it appears your 'talents' are not of the natural world, de Beauvais."

"This argument is spurious!" shouted William. "I give it no credence!"

"The credence you give it, or don't give it, is of no consequence," snapped Hopkirk. "It is the one that these good men here give it that matters."

He turned back to Melrose. "And I believe you have further proof of Sir William's powers?" he asked, with an encouraging raise of his eyebrows.

"Aye," answered Melrose. "He commands beasts."

There was a collective gasp of shock from the crowd at this allegation. William clenched his fists behind his back. This could put him in the highest jeopardy if it were proven to the satisfaction of the crowd; the charge of witchcraft would be beyond question. He waited to see how this charge would be made.

Hopkirk kept silent a moment, watching the crowd and waiting as the groundswell of shock started to build the volume and intensity of their mutterings.

He raised a hand and after a moment the noise of the crowd settled back to a low rumble. "How is this so?" he asked softly.

"Yes, how is this so?" burst out William. "I too am keen to hear how this can be claimed!"

"Quiet!" snapped Hopkirk. "I am certain Master Melrose can clearly explain his statement."

"Aye, that he can – because you and he have collaborated on this nonsense!" muttered William, loudly enough for the crowd around him to hear. One or two laughed nervously.

Melrose looked directly at Hopkirk, and said, "We were out hunting a great stag, and William shot an arrow that failed to kill it…"

"So maybe my powers are not so magical, if I failed to kill it?" demanded William. "How is that, then?"

"Silence!" barked Hopkirk at him. "Your supernatural skill with bow and arrow has already been proven." Hopkirk turned back to Melrose. "So what happened then?"

"The stag was charging us, and would have gored us both on his antlers. I threw a spear but I was scared, and my aim was off." Melrose, paused and swallowed hard, as William snorted in disgust. "I knew we would both be killed the next instant," continued Melrose, "but Sir William called out to the beast."

Again, there was a gasp from the crowd.

"He called out? What did he call out?" asked Hopkirk encouragingly.

"He called out, 'Die, beast, die!'" answered Melrose.

"And then what happened?" asked Hopkirk.

"The beast was dead in an instant, and crashed to the ground in front of us."

"Dead in an instant?" said Hopkirk, sounding surprised.

Melrose nodded. "It crashed to the ground and such was its speed that it carried on moving towards us. The tips of its evil antlers stopped but an inch from Sir William's chest."

"Indeed? That is most… shall we say… fortunate." Hopkirk gave a little smile. "And how did Sir William react then?"

"He laughed and joked, as if this was the greatest sport," answered Melrose.

This was too much for William. He had held his anger in check during this exchange by further clenching and unclenching of his fists behind his back, but now his blood was up and his heart was racing. "By the Lords

Wounds!" he shouted. "This is arrant nonsense! It was your spear that killed the beast, and I laughed in relief! The rest is wicked lies and misinformation!" There was silence. William took some deep breaths and tried to calm his wildly beating heart.

He looked at Melrose, who finally met his eye for a second, then looked away — as if the sight of William sickened him.

"Why, Tom?" he pleaded. "Why are you conspiring against me this way?"

"This is no conspiracy, de Beauvais," cut in Hopkirk before Melrose could respond. "This is just a seeking after the truth."

"The truth?" asked William. "The only truth I am now interested in, is the truth of why this man has turned traitor." He looked again at Melrose. "What have I done to you, Tom? What could I possibly have done that turned you so deeply against me?"

Melrose looked back at William. "You caused my father to die," he said softly.

"I? What had I to do with it?" William asked, genuinely confused. "He took his own life."

"You encouraged him. You spoke to him the night before in this very tavern, and the next day, when I was told, you knew. I saw it in your eyes."

"Tom, please, believe me," pleaded William. "If I never speak another word, know that this is God's honest truth." He paused, collecting his thoughts. He knew this was his main opportunity; if he could turn Melrose back to his side, there was a chance — albeit a slim one — of maybe winning round the crowd.

"Your father was a good man," he said firmly, "and I was trying to stop him taking his life. I was trying to talk him out of it. He had lost a lot of money, and he was full of guilt for you and your chances in life. I was telling him that I would help where I could."

Melrose opened his mouth to respond, then appeared confused and closed it again. Some in the crowd looked puzzled. William pressed his advantage. "I was trying to make him see he had everything to live for — in you. That's how I knew the next day. I knew that he was planning it, and I was only sorry I had not been successful in stopping him."

"A pretty speech, de Beauvais," cut in Hopkirk quickly, as again Melrose appeared about to speak, then again stopped, looking unsure. "But this is not to the point. The point is that Master Melrose has affirmed that you have an unnatural skill with the bow; that you command beasts and they act upon your command, and that you have been protecting a known witch." He signalled to Smitheson and a couple of his men who were standing behind William. "Prepare him for the trial!"

Smitheson and another man positioned themselves either side of William and at a signal from Hopkirk grasped his thighs and lifted him up.

"We will test him!" shouted Hopkirk, raising his hands above his head.

"Test him! Test him!" responded the crowd, turning it into a chant that built and built, echoing off the rafters of the old tavern.

"The people have delivered their verdict! We will put his head under the water! We will see if he has magic!"

Smitheson and the other yeoman lifted him higher over the barrel.

"For the love of God, Hopkirk!" shouted William against the din "What kind of man are you?"

Hopkirk leant across the dark waters of the barrel and looked deeply into William's eyes. "I am the soothsayer of your darkest fears, Sir William de Beauvais," he said quietly, so quietly that only William could hear against the shouting of the crowd. He put his hand on William's chest, as if to draw out his heart. "Let me reach out and touch your deepest dreams. Come to me, I must deliver your soul to the people before me who chant and cheer."

He stood back, leaving William suspended over the edge of the barrel, then he signalled to Smitheson.

"Duck him!"

The crowd roared as Smitheson and his companion started to tip William face first into the barrel. William fought with all his might, but having his feet and hands bound, he could only wriggle and flap like a fish in a net, and against the combined strength of the two burly yeomen, it had little effect.

As he struggled, he saw one of the two young peasant boys start to run forward – he assumed to help the yeomen drown him in the stinking water, but he quickly dismissed them from his mind as he saw the water rushing up towards him and knew that in a few seconds it would fill his mouth and his nose and then be drawn down into his chest and cause him choke and suffer an agonising death…

"Stop! Stop I say!"

The shout rang out loud and clear against the sound of the crowd. With a sense of shock and relief William felt the yeomen check and his movement towards the water stop.

"Stop now! Set him down!" The voice had such authority that William found himself being lowered to the floor again. The shouting died down and silence descended on the tavern.

Everyone, including Hopkirk, turned to look at the man who had shouted. It was Melrose.

He was standing with his hands on his hips, his thin face flushed red and his eyes wide and staring.

"Master Melrose?" said Hopkirk. "What is the meaning of this?"

Melrose took a gulp of air as if to steady himself, then said quietly, "I was wrong. Sir William does not command beasts – my spear was thrown true and it was that that killed the stag." He looked at William. "I am sorry, my lord, for doubting you. You are no more a witch than is Master Hopkirk." He turned to Hopkirk. "Release this man, who I now believe has spoken true.

156

He is my oldest friend, who tried to help my father and would have helped me if I had but let him. Let him go – he is innocent of your trumped-up charges."

"Thank you, my friend," said William, a glimmer of hope in his voice. He tried to shrug off the yeomen's grip. "You heard the man. Let me go."

But Smitheson and his fellow yeoman held him firm. "Let me go, I say!" demanded William.

"Not so fast, de Beauvais," said Hopkirk. "Keep him tightly held." He put his hands on the edge of the barrel. "This changes nothing. The case is sufficiently proven for the ducking test to take place!"

There was a muttering from the crowd and Hopkirk glanced quickly around. William could see that the mood had changed with Melrose's change of heart and that many of the villagers in the crowd were now looking shocked. He hoped that it was because they had been about to do something which went deeply against the natural order of things – they had been about to kill their lord and master. Hopkirk must have seen this as well, and he raised his arms.

"Listen, good people..." he began, then stopped.

There was a commotion at the door of the tavern, with loud shouting, heavy boots thumping and armour clanking. Then there was the unmistakable sound of swords being drawn.

There was a gasp from the crowd as they stared towards the door. Then they began to part as men forced their way into the tavern and advanced towards Hopkirk, William and the barrel.

Finally the crowd around Hopkirk parted and a man in black with long grey hair appeared, accompanied by a dozen militiamen with drawn swords.

The man stopped in front of Hopkirk and slowly looked at the tableaux in front of him – William held by two yeomen and bound hand and foot by the barrel; Hopkirk standing on the other side like a grey statue; the crowd all around with their faces eerily lit by the flickering yellow candles.

"This is ill-judged, Master Hopkirk," he said. "Ill-judged indeed." He looked at William. "This is Sir William de Beauvais, I believe, and I take it you would have drowned him in your pathetic search for your proof of witchcraft?" He paused but got no answer from the furious Hopkirk, who didn't look capable of speech.

The man nodded. "It is as well I decided to follow my instinct that you were planning something like this and return with these militiamen," he said. He gestured towards William. "Release this man immediately!"

Hopkirk turned to Smitheson. "You will do no such thing!" he shouted, then turned back to the man in black. "Robert Wychwoode, by whose authority do you presume to defy me?"

"By the authority of Her Majesty the Queen, in whose service I practice the law," answered Wychwoode. He turned to Smitheson. "Now release him!"

Reluctantly, Smitheson and his yeoman colleague set William down and stood back.

"No!" shrieked Hopkirk, his voice rising to a strangled scream. "Duck him! Duck him now! See if he has the magic!"

Smitheson hesitated. He looked at Hopkirk, who was mouthing and screaming with spittle gathering in little white strings at the corners of his mouth; then he looked at Wychwoode, standing solidly in the middle of the room and backed by armed militiamen. It was clear that the power now lay with the lawyer, so he reached round and started to undo William's hands.

"No!" screamed Hopkirk again.

Then everything happened very fast.

Hopkirk reached inside his cloak and suddenly the evil-looking knife appeared in his hand.

Before Wychwoode or a militiaman could stop him, he was running round the barrel towards William with the knife raised up in in his hand, clearly intending to stab him.

As Hopkirk ran, one of the young peasant boys suddenly darted out and flung himself at the magistrate, knocking hard into him and throwing him off balance. Hopkirk fell into the side of the barrel, causing foul-smelling water to slop out over the other side. The knife clattered away under a table as Hopkirk sprawled out beside the barrel, and the peasant boy, carried on by his momentum, lost his balance and crashed into the legs of the table himself.

The boy struggled to his feet. William saw he was now holding Hopkirk's knife, which he must have retrieved from under the table.

The boy rushed to William's side and quickly cut through the straps binding his hands and feet, then turned and grabbed Hopkirk. Forcing the magistrate to stand up, he held the knife up to Hopkirk's throat.

Hopkirk stood unsteadily, straining his head back away from the knife, his eyes staring wildly around the room for help. But the boy was standing with his back against the barrel, making it difficult for anyone to come at him from behind.

"What would you do, boy?" snarled Hopkirk over his shoulder. "Would you kill me? Would you kill a man of godliness and purity? Have a care for your immortal soul, boy!"

The boy didn't answer, but pressed the knife harder against Hopkirk's throat, drawing a little blood.

"Is that your reply, boy?" Hopkirk demanded hoarsely. "Then if you would dispatch me, do it now." The boy didn't move. "You do not have the will to do it..." said Hopkirk; a calculating edge creeping into his voice.

William wondered why the boy did not answer or make any further movement. He had Hopkirk under his control, but if he did not make a move soon, Hopkirk would take advantage. Sure enough, Hopkirk then made his own move, driving back with his elbows into the boy's ribs.

The boy let out a high-pitched scream, dropped the knife and staggered back against the barrel, causing his head to flick backwards over the black water. The movement made his cap come off and fall into the barrel. It lingered on the surface a moment, then filled with water and disappeared into the depths.

But William could see that no one was looking at the water in the barrel.

They were looking at the boy's long, russet-coloured ringlets that had been tucked up and hidden under the cap and now fell freely down to his shoulders. They were looking at the soft curves of a face that was not that of a young boy, but of a woman in her twenties. They were looking at the heaving chest pushing against the rough lace-up farm-worker's smock.

There was a gasp from the crowd.

"Oh my Lord," said one of the villagers. "It's her! It's the witch!"

CHAPTER TWENTY-TWO

For a brief moment everyone in the village tavern was frozen still, like a tableaux in an oil painting.

Justine took in the scene; Hopkirk standing beside her at the edge of the barrel with a look of amused satisfaction on his grey features, as if he'd known all along that she would eventually appear; Wychwoode and his men standing a few feet away with their hands ready on the hilts of their swords; William standing just behind Smitheson, his eyes flicking down to the sword hanging at the yeoman's hip; Dowland and Stanmore still bound in their chairs, with the tall, thin figure of Melrose just by them; the crowd of villagers all around, staring at Justine with expressions ranging from horror to fear to fascination. And at the back of the crowd, she could just see Sarah and her mother slipping quietly towards the door.

The silence was broken by Hopkirk.

"Mistress Fox," he said silkily, massaging his shoulder where he'd hit it on the barrel, then putting his finger to his throat and examining closely the fresh blood he found there. He rubbed his finger and thumb together to remove it. "What a pleasure it is to see you properly."

"So you're Hopkirk," Justine said. "I have heard so much about you."

"And I you, Mistress Fox," he replied. "I have so much I want to ask you."

"And none of it to the point, I'll warrant," said William.

"Now then, de Beauvais," said Hopkirk, still watching Justine like a snake watches a mouse, "we are asking questions of Mistress Fox, not you." William snorted in disgust and edged a little closer to Smitheson's sword.

Hopkirk continued. "So, you have been here all evening, masquerading as a farm worker, as a boy?"

"Certainly," replied Justine. "I wanted to hear what was said about me."

"No doubt you did. You were here with another farm worker and a woman," Hopkirk looked around for them. "Are they also not what they seemed? Another girl dressed as a boy, perhaps? A man dressed as an old woman?"

Justine smiled sweetly. "I don't know what you mean, Master Hopkirk."

"'Tis no matter," said Hopkirk, "we will catch up with them later. For now, more important matters concern us." He touched his throat again and examined the amount of blood on his finger – appearing satisfied that it was less than before. "Yes, we have much more important matters. Like the list of blasphemous oaths you have been heard to utter."

"A list?" asked Justine. "I don't recall more than saying the words 'Christ' and 'Hell' one after the other and not in a connected way at all. I certainly didn't mean any harm by it, although Margaret did seem rather shocked."

"So you deny saying that you would have Christ rot in Hell for all eternity and that He is the Devil incarnate?"

"Of course I do," answered Justine. "Deny it, I mean. What an incredible thing to suggest."

"But you would not deny that a Satan-worshiping witch may hold such foul and despicable views?" continued Hopkirk.

"If such a person did exist, I suppose she might," answered Justine carefully "but…"

"So, as such a proven witch, we must therefore assume that you do hold such views." interrupted Hopkirk, with a hint of triumph in his voice.

"No," said Justine, "I never said…"

"Silence!" cut in Hopkirk, fixing her with his basilisk stare. "We must now turn to the matter of your dress. Is it not true that when you were first seen yesterday, you were wearing a badly-finished doublet, unfinished breeches and man's boots?"

"A jumper and a skirt, if that's what you mean."

"The names of the garments are unimportant. It is the purpose behind them that is of most consequence – disguise and confusion to ordinary folk."

"I did not mean to confuse anyone," said Justine, then stopped. "I mean…" she hesitated, realising that the evidence of her disguising herself as a boy was now overwhelming.

"Indeed," said Hopkirk. "I think we have all the proof of disguise and confusion in front of us. So we'll move on…"

Just then Wychwoode cut in. "I am not happy with you questioning the girl in this manner, Hopkirk," he said tersely. "I do not recognise this line of questioning about clothing and blasphemy and suchlike. I warrant she has attacked you with a knife, but she was justified as you were attacking de Beauvais. I would prefer that both these matters were dealt with through the proper legal channels."

Hopkirk gave a deep sigh. "Master Wychwoode," he said, "I am quite weary with your constant interference in my business." He turned slowly and faced the lawyer directly. "I would have you remove yourself and your men from this tavern, before I have you removed myself."

"You talk as if you have a militia of your own," answered Wychwoode confidently. "Whereas you have a rag-tag collection of villagers with pitchforks. I would suggest you have a care when you make such claims."

"The only care I have now is to see these good, honest folk here free of the threat of sorcery and incantations," said Hopkirk. "Which is why I was following the line of questioning before your unwelcome interruption."

He turned back to Justine and again he stared at her, his eyes narrowed as if he was looking for something in her face. She stared levelly back, wondering what he was doing and if he was ever going to blink. Eventually he gave a small grunt and stood back. "The mark of darkness," he said, "as clear as I have ever seen."

He turned to the crowd. "The mark of darkness is there!" he said "She is proven to be an evil witch!" The crowd gasped at this revelation.

Hopkirk walked quickly to some women a few feet away and stopped just before them. "Do you fear for the lives of your children if there is a witch present in the village?" The women nodded vigorously. "Oh yes, we do indeed Master Hopkirk!" one of them confirmed.

He turned to some men standing further along and asked in a raised voice, "Would you fear your sons and daughters won't work in the fields and mills if there is a witch among them? A witch casting spells to make them sick?" The men nodded their heads and shouted that they would.

Hopkirk went over to Agnes and Ruth and asked, "Would you suffer a woman to live if she clearly has the darkness of evil in her eyes?" They shook their heads violently. "No, sir, not if she has the mark!" Ruth shouted back.

Despite her rising terror at the situation she had put herself in, Justine couldn't help thinking that Hopkirk was certainly showing his skill at working the room up to fever pitch; he would probably have made a good game show host if he'd been born 450 years later.

Hopkirk then leapt up onto a bench and addressed himself to all the villagers crowded into the tavern. He lifted his arms and turned to each part of the room, shouting, "Do we now test this woman, who has been proven a liar and a deceiver and who has the mark of darkness in her eyes?"

"We do!" returned the crowd, clapping their hands and stamping their feet.

"And do we test her now?" roared Hopkirk, clapping his hands in time with the crowd, encouraging them; goading them on; keeping the temperature red-hot to get the crowd ready to do whatever it took to kill Justine. "Do we duck her in the water and see if she has the magic?" he yelled.

"We do! We do!" shouted the crowd. Hopkirk jumped back to the floor and they started to surge forward.

In terror, Justine looked to William. But William was focused on Smitheson; she saw him casually drawing the sword at Smitheson's belt as the yeoman went past him, then, when the man was ahead of where William was standing, she saw the silver sword tip emerge from the front of the man's chest, then disappear again.

She saw Smitheson's face go ashen white, cough a gobbet of bright red blood down his chin, then he disappeared from her view as he dropped to his knees.

Oblivious to Smitheson's fate behind them, the crowd continued to surge forward, shouting and yelling, buoyed up by Hopkirk's rhetoric and full of bloodlust to get to Justine and duck her in the barrel; their pitchforks raised and their snarling, hate-filled faces behind the evil-looking points.

Justine was desperately hoping that now William had a sword, he would fight through and rescue her, but then she was shoved to one side by a man drawing his sword and in panic she screamed – until she saw it was Wychwoode himself putting his body and his sword between her and the crowd. She looked quickly to one side then the other and saw his militiamen now taking up positions around the barrel, their swords drawn and points facing the crowd.

With rising relief, she realised that William was not going to have to save her single-handedly; she was now inside an effective ring of steel formed by Wychwoode and his men.

Hopkirk and the crowd faced the ring of swords.

"Let us through, Wychwoode!" shouted Hopkirk. "This is our matter, not yours!"

"Go home, Hopkirk!" said Wychwoode calmly. "You have had your say, now I have mine. You have no authority here and this 'court' is a travesty of true justice. I am a servant of Her Majesty the Queen and in her name I tell you to desist from this nonsense! Leave this girl to me and the proper authorities."

Hopkirk shook his head. "No, I will not. We outnumber you many times – we will have our way."

"Not if I have ought to do with it," came a strong voice from behind them.

"Or I," confirmed another voice.

"And I," said a third

"And I, too," said a fourth.

Hopkirk turned and let out an oath. William, Melrose, Dowland and Stanmore were standing in a wide line behind them with drawn swords.

Hopkirk looked at the four swordsmen, then he glanced down and checked as he saw the sprawled body of Smitheson in front of them; a pool of blood spreading out from under the chest and soaking into the sawdust on the tavern floor.

"He must have got in the way of a sword in the rush," observed William casually. "Most unfortunate – he really should have been more watchful."

Justine was gratified to see Hopkirk go white and lick his lips nervously as he stared at the body, then look up wide-eyed at the four swordsmen. Then Hopkirk looked across from these four to the thirteen armed men in a ring around Justine. He could clearly see that his rag-tag army of elderly men, women and children were surrounded by men prepared to kill.

"Come, my friends," he said grimly. "It seems we are not going to complete our trial this evening. These men, who would protect witches, do not allow justice to be served." He turned to Wychwoode. "You have not saved these evil-doers, lawyer. You have but delayed the inevitable. For one day soon I will test them and if their evil is proven, as the Lord Jesus is my witness, I will send them to Hell by fire!"

"As you say, Hopkirk, but not tonight," answered Wychwoode. "Goodnight to you."

With that, Hopkirk marched towards the door. The villagers looked at each other, unsure of what best to do. One or two went straight out after Hopkirk. The others milled around for a moment, muttering and enquiring of each other, then they too drifted to the door and left into the night. Only Jake and Agnes stayed; Jake dragging Agnes to the serving table and stationing her there, while he stayed by the door to see the final villagers out.

Eventually there was just Wychwoode and his militiamen, William and his three friends, and Justine.

A blessed peace descended on the tavern.

Suddenly Justine felt the room start to spin. She gave a little cry as her legs gave way and she found herself slipping down into an all-enveloping darkness.

---0---

William sheathed his sword as Justine fell and ran over to her. He picked her up in his arms and carried her like a child over to a table. He swept aside some tankards, then laid her tenderly onto the table.

"Some ale, landlord, for the love of God!" he called out to Jake. "She has fainted!"

"I'm not sure I like her being here, Master," began Jake, "she being a witch and all…"

"By the Lord's Wounds, man," snapped William, "you cannot give credence to that nonsense after all that has passed tonight!" He touched Justine's cheek tenderly. "She is a mere girl, which is all – and has had some adventures this night. She is now safe and has fainted from relief. Some ale, man, and presently!"

Jake nodded to Agnes, who filled a tankard with ale and carried it over to the table where Justine was sitting. Agnes stopped before she got to the table, stretched out her arm to its fullest length and gingerly put the ale down on the bench, then picked up the fallen tankards and ran quickly back to her station.

William put his arm under Justine's shoulders and lifted her into a sitting position, then held the tankard to her lips.

The feel of the cold liquid seemed to bring Justine back to a hazy consciousness, and her eyes fluttered open. She looked up at William with wide eyes.

"It's the 31st of July," she said in wonder. "You would have been stabbed by that man and died. But I was in the right place at the right time. I have saved your life." Then she shook her head and smiled slowly.

"I have changed history."

"Aye, my angel, so you did," answered William, thinking this was indeed a strange thing to say. "I shall forever be in your debt for that." He held the ale back up to her lips again. "Come, my sweet Mary, drink some ale."

Justine had a few more sips.

"I would have killed him – that Hopkirk," she said quietly. "I wanted to push that knife into his throat and…" She trembled as she relived the moment, as if staring at the dreadful scene again in her mind's eye. "I couldn't do it. When it came to it, I just couldn't do it."

"I know," he answered. "It is not easy to kill a man. You were most brave to attack him at all."

"I didn't think about it – I just ran at him."

"And I am still here because you were in the right place at the right time." He gave a little chuckle. "And well-disguised, I warrant. I had seen you a number of times before you revealed yourself, and I took you as we all did – as a young peasant boy."

He stopped at a sudden memory. "You would have tried to save me the first time they made to put my head under that stinking water. I recall now – you ran forward."

"Yes," she answered. "I wasn't sure what I was going to do, but I had to try and do something. When Melrose stopped them, I just shrank back into the crowd. I think people thought I was just a rash young boy running forward in the heat of the moment."

"A rash young boy!" He laughed. "'Twas a disguise well made."

"It was easy to do."

"Aye, but why?" he asked. "Why put yourself in Hopkirk's way, even with a disguise? Not that I am complaining, mind," he added.

Justine took some further sips of ale and looked away in deep thought, as if she was choosing what version of her story to tell. Eventually she seemed to have made up her mind.

"We have a saying where I am from," she said. "Know your enemy. I wanted to see what that man was doing. I wanted to understand him better – to find his weakness so I could defeat him." She looked up at William and shook her head. "But when I had the chance to defeat him – to kill him – I couldn't do it."

"Then we must find another way, and that we will when the time comes," he answered, trying to sound reassuring. "Come, finish this ale." He held the tankard back up to her mouth and she drained it.

"You have more colour," he said, putting the tankard down. "We must get you back to the manor" he added. "My mother can see to your well-being. She will be most concerned for you."

"Yes, I want to go to bed."

Melrose came over. "I must away, Will. I have much to think on this night."

"Aye, Tom." William stood up. "I must apologise if I ever gave you cause to doubt me. You have been my truest friend since we were boys, and my soul is tortured to think I gave you reason to turn against me. I can only thank the Lord he saw fit to show you the truth before it was too late."

Melrose did not answer immediately; he put his hand on William's shoulder and nodded. "We have had good times together," he said after a moment. "Good times indeed. I would have done well to have thought more on that, but I was blinded by my own thoughts on my father. When they made to drown you, I realised it was wrong – I was wrong. If they had carried their purpose through, I could not have made that a burden for my immortal soul." He nodded to Justine, then turned back to William. "Goodnight, my lord," he said, then walked out of the tavern.

William watched him go, then turned to Wychwoode. "I must thank you, sir, for your integrity and foresight in this matter," he said. "I owe you much. I would you and your men come to Grangedean Manor this night and enjoy some wine and some food, and a well-earned sleep as my guests."

"I must away to the Oxford Assizes on the morrow," replied Wychwoode. "But I will take up your kind offer this night, and I will make these men available to you for your protection for the next few days – or weeks if needed," he paused, then, like Melrose, he also put his hand on William's shoulder. "You are a lucky young man, possessed of a brave and loyal woman," he said. "But I fear this troublesome magistrate will not let the matter rest here. I fear he will shortly return and try once more to test your woman and yourself. You must be ready for him." He continued grimly, "For next time he may have more than a rag-tag army of ill-matched peasants with him."

"Aye," answered William. "I have had the same thought. But I will be ready – and I thank you for the loan of your men. They too are welcome to my house."

He turned to Dowland and Stanmore. "Will you come to my house too, my friends? We must drink some wine and relive the glorious rout this night of Master Hopkirk and his rag-tag army. For though he may return, for now we have sent him away with his tail between his legs, whining like a miserable cur! And that is worthy of a barrel of my finest wine!"

He paused and gave a rueful chuckle.

"Although in truth I'll not want to see a barrel again, as long as I may live."

CHAPTER TWENTY-THREE

It was very late one night around two weeks later, that Martha the housekeeper hobbled stiffly into the kitchen, put down the tray of empty wine goblets she was carrying and collapsed with a groan onto a small wooden stool in a dark corner. The cook and Margaret were already there, sitting on a couple more old stools, talking quietly and drinking ale. Other than these three, the kitchens were dark and empty; the usual bustle and noise gone for the night. The only light came from a couple of fat old tallow candles sinking softly into clay plates, plus the eerie glow of the previous day's fire as it smouldered gently in the grate – ready to be stoked back into life in the morning.

Martha reached down and pulled her shoes off, then rubbed her toes to ease the pain from running up and down the stairs over the last few hours with wine for the men in the Great Hall.

"They have been drinking so much," she said, shaking her head bitterly. "Master Dowland, Master Stanmore, Master Melrose and Sir William. It will soon be morning and they show no signs of stopping or retiring to their chambers."

"It is more than a fortnight since they sent Master Hopkirk about his business in the tavern, and still they celebrate wildly each night," observed the cook, lifting her head as the sound of raucous laughter drifted down from the Great Hall.

"And that woman – that witch – is all but mistress of this house now," muttered Martha. "They say she felled Master Hopkirk in the tavern with just the power of incantation." She stared into the fire. "He was cast down to the floor before he could attack the master."

"An incantation?" asked Margaret, "By the Lord's good grace I was not there, or maybe I would have been felled also."

The cook considered this. "Does an incantation thrown at one body work on another also?" she queried. "I would have believed an incantation is made for one body alone."

"Nay, it is like an arrow fired through a cotton sheet; it could fly on and hit any number of others," said Martha, pretending confidence. "That is a well-known fact of incantations."

"Aye, and now she is living among us as bold as you like, as the Lord is my witness," said Margaret bitterly.

"She is all so sweet and full of kindness, and she acts like she would be mistress of my heart, but I can see that she is but masking her evil ways and biding her time to cast a spell of sickness on me." Martha rubbed her feet absently, still staring into the settling embers of the fire. "She would have me believe she knows nothing of the ways of a great house – she asks me at all times of day how this must be done or how that must be done; she says it is not how they do things 'where I come from', then she smiles at me like a soft-headed child and thanks me over and again," Martha gave a soft bitter laugh. "Truly I would slap her in the face if I could."

"She came to my kitchens and offered to help with kneading the marchpane," observed the cook. "A girl not capable of turning the roast a few weeks past, now she comes to help knead the marchpane."

"What did you say?" asked Margaret.

"I smiled, right enough, and showed her what was to be done," answered the cook. "As you have said, she is all but mistress of the house now."

"And what is more, two days ago she offered to help me organise the next banquet," said Martha indignantly. "She said she had some experience of that 'where I come from'. Naturally I thanked her but refused. She appeared defiant and made some spiteful remark about only wanting to help."

"She cannot have come from a great house," said Martha, "or the fine expensive sugared foods she would have eaten would have blackened her teeth."

"She is most particular to keep them white," observed Margaret, looking down at the circles she was making in the dusty floor with her toe. "Simon says she asked him to make her a tool for cleaning them. She had him take a stick and whittle a flat end, then push in many pig hair bristles to make a small brush. Then she took some chalk, mint leaves and some oil and beat it into a paste, which she keeps in a jar. He says she will spend much time in cleaning her teeth with this concoction on the brush, two or three times a day."

Martha and the cook sat in silence, pondering this behaviour.

The cook shook her head. "They say it is only a matter of time before the master takes her to be his wife," she said bleakly.

"The Lord help us," said Margaret, crossing herself. "The witch will be the next Lady de Beauvais." The three of them stared desolately into the glowing embers of the fire; each considering the dire prospect of life under Mary Fox as their mistress.

The cook eventually broke the silence, saying out loud what the other two were thinking. "We must do all we can to stop that happening," she said. "Has Master Hopkirk been heard of these past two weeks? He must be pressed back into the downfall of this dreadful witch."

"I have heard tell that he is moving about the county," said Martha. "Maybe he is seeking support and will return with forces behind him."

"Aye," said the cook, nodding. "There is much to hope upon."

"He will have to call the witch and the master out, and there are still the militiamen here to guard them," said Margaret. "They will defend the witch."

"Perhaps we can find a way to let Master Hopkirk in?" suggested the cook hopefully.

"All the gates are secured daily," said Martha. "No person is allowed in or out of the estate without one of the militiamen agreeing it. I myself have to ask permission." She gave a derisive snort. "The mistress's sister, Alice Mansfield, is expected to stay shortly, coming all the way from Nottingham. How will we allow her in if the gates are all barred? I cannot imagine Lady de Beauvais will suffer her to remain outside. It is quite ridiculous that we must have such measures."

"There must be a way to get Master Hopkirk and his men in unseen," said Margaret thoughtfully. She paused a moment then looked up with bright eyes. "Maybe out of the woods to the south?"

"It is possible, for sure," said Martha. "It is a long stretch of land for the militiamen to guard and I believe there is a path through the trees into the parklands." She leaned forward and stared into the glowing embers of the fire once again as she considered all the options. Then suddenly she leant back and slapped her leg, causing the other two to jump. "I've been a fool!" she exclaimed. "There is no purpose in finding a way for Hopkirk and his men to gain entrance to the estate, unless we can tell him what it is! We must first get ourselves out – or one of us must – to find Hopkirk and show him the way back in!"

Martha turned to Margaret. "It must be you!" she said. "Tomorrow you must go to the south side woods and see if, or where, they are guarding it, then find the path so you can lead Hopkirk in."

"And if they are guarding it?" asked the cook.

"Then we will think on ways we can disable the guard," said Martha, practically. She turned back to Margaret. "Take the path yourself, then you must go to the village to wait for Hopkirk so you can guide him back."

Margaret was silent a while, staring into the fire. "I might have to disable a guard – oh Heaven, will that need some sort of seduction? What if he is pig-ugly or has foul breath? What if he makes to kiss me and I can do nothing but submit? How would I then disable him? Would I have to kill him – or just tie him up?" She turned to Martha. "Can it not be you that goes to the village?" she asked, with a forced-looking smile. "You could ask permission and be granted leave."

"As housekeeper I would be expected back presently," said Martha, "and we do not know how long Hopkirk will be. No, it must be you."

"Maybe you could find the path first?"

"No," answered Martha, "how would you lead Hopkirk in, unless you knew exactly where the path was to be found? And the best person to do that is the one who found it."

"Oh." Margaret swallowed hard, then straightened her back a little and said in a small, but brave voice, "Yes, I suppose it must be me."

"Good," said Martha. "We must act swiftly. Explore the south side tomorrow. Tell no one what you are doing – especially the witch or her tame handmaiden Sarah – and make sure you are not seen. Look particularly for a path out of the forest where Master Hopkirk can lead many men into the estate – by God's good grace he has been able to raise sufficient."

She paused as another roar of laughter was heard from upstairs, followed by the sound of chairs being pushed back, then boots tramping unsteadily out of the Great Hall and up the stairs.

"Then by the will of God this evil witch will be banished from Grangedean and gone from our lives for ever."

CHAPTER TWENTY-FOUR

Justine sat bolt upright, her eyes wide with the shock of a sudden awakening.

Slowly she looked around her, expecting to see the sight she had woken up to every morning for these past two weeks; her room in Grangedean Manor. She looked for the deep red velvet drapes on the magnificent four-poster bed, the metal-bound oak chest of Tudor gowns at its foot, the carved and painted fireplace with the welcoming fire dancing in the grate...

Instead she saw something she was not expecting – the grey plastic steering wheel of her little Ford car in the flickering orange overhead lights.

Above it she could see dark cedar trees at the edge of the park through the now cleared windscreen. She looked down at her lap; her phone was lying there in its battered old case, with a Mary Fox story still showing on the screen.

In panic she felt the wheel – it felt solid enough. She became aware of a low rumbling noise; it was the little engine chugging away, powering the whirring demist fan.

Justine gave a small cry of anguish.

It had all been a dream – a very vivid, very real dream, but in the end, just a dream.

She was still in her car – on the night of the banquet for the Americans.

She must have dropped off to sleep while reading on her phone, waiting for the windscreen to clear. And she'd been reading a Mary Fox story, so it was not surprising she had become Mary Fox in her dream, having a wild, exciting, Tudor adventure...

Desperately she put her head back in the seat, trying to drop back off to sleep so she could get back into the dream again. But it didn't work – after a few minutes she was still wide awake.

And what was worse, the dream was now starting to fade.

As she tried to remember what had happened, it all became confused and jumbled. People and conversations started to drift out of her mind, and when she tried hard to reconstruct them, she couldn't be sure if she had them correct, or if she was just making them up. What had William said at the banquet? Was it at the cottage or at the manor that they had made love? Why was Wychwoode disguised as a peasant boy in the tavern?

Justine turned to her side in the seat, put her elbow on the armrest and leaned her head on her hand to get more comfortable. But sleep now seemed further away than before.

What was that horrible man called? Hopkraft? Falkirk? Why was he chasing her?

Was she even being chased? If she was, surely William would have protected her?

William? Was that William de Beauvais, the lord of Grangedean Manor? The one who had been killed in a fight in a tavern in 1565?

But hadn't she saved him...?

For a moment she clearly remembered knocking into a grey man trying to stab William, so she'd saved his life. Or had she? That was silly – it was all just a dream – you don't change history in a dream. He was stabbed in a fight; historical fact.

She stared out of the windscreen at the cedars in the distance, hoping to buy herself a few more minutes to try and remember the dream. A barrel flashed into her thoughts, and a knife. She knew they were important, but why? It all seemed further away than ever.

A man... a lover..?

Then her phone started ringing; the opening bars of The Phantom of the Opera.

Justine looked down at the screen. There was a caller ID picture on the screen.

It was her mother.

Justine looked at the clock on the dashboard – 1.33am. In amazement she swiped to take the call.

"You all right, Mum?" she asked cautiously. "It's really late. It's past half-one in the morning."

"Hello Justine, dear." Her mother's voice was as bright and chirpy as ever.

"Why on earth are you calling me at this time?"

Her mother did not acknowledge the sharp tone. "I just wanted to say, don't forget you're coming down for the weekend."

"You wanted to remind me of that at half past one in the morning?" Justine was incredulous.

"You weren't in bed."

"How did you know that?"

"You had a banquet. You're never in bed before two after a banquet."

"How did you know I had a banquet?"

"I'm your mother. I know everything about you." Her mother sounded smug. "I know you had forgotten you're coming for the weekend."

"I hadn't forgotten," Justine lied. She must have agreed to the visit at some point, but she couldn't for the life of her remember having done so. "Any special reason?" she asked cautiously.

"Just that we like to see our little girl occasionally," replied her mother, shifting into her 'I'm trying not to be wounded by my daughter's indifference' voice. Justine suspected there was a big 'and…' still to come.

"And… it's your father's birthday."

"Of course." Damn – she'd completely forgotten that.

"So we're having a party." That, too.

Her mother paused. "Are you bringing anyone?" she asked, casually. Too casually.

The loaded question hung in the air.

"I mean," her mother continued sweetly, "it's been quite a while now since you last brought a boyfriend down."

"No Mum, I'm not bringing anyone," Justine said with finality.

"OK dear, just asking."

"Well don't. I'll find someone when I'm good and ready."

"OK dear." There was a pause. Justine could virtually hear her mother choosing her words with care. "Actually, one of my friends has a nephew she thought you might like to meet…"

Justine sighed. Her mother was so predictable. "Your friends always seem to have nephews," she snapped. "And they always seem to want to meet me. Only, they all turn out to have buck teeth, a squint and terrible personal hygiene."

"Yes, but apparently this William is absolutely charming and very good-looking. He has land in the country, and he farms and he hunts. Mary says you'll love him."

"William?" A picture of a smiling man in Tudor clothes suddenly appeared in front of Justine's eyes, holding out his hand to her as she descended the last step of a magnificent stairway. She shook her head as the image faded quickly. "He hunts in the country?"

"Yes. And the way my friend, Mary Fox, describes him, he sounds very handsome."

Justine's breath caught in her throat. Mary Fox? How did her mother know about Mary Fox…? Another picture jumped into her mind – an elegant Tudor lady. Then some words; the lady was talking "…you will be Mary Fox, the daughter of my old friend, Richard Fox, a London merchant…"

"No!" Justine gave a strangled yelp.

"What is it, dear?" asked her mother, sounding concerned.

"But I'm Mary Fox!"

"Mary Fox? You're Mary Fox?" Then, completely unexpectedly, her mother sniggered.

Justine had never known her mother to snigger, but there was no other word for the strange sound that she had just heard.

"That's funny!" her mother snorted. "That's unreal!"

Justine looked at the phone. Somehow, the normally static caller identification picture of her mother had come to life. It was actually laughing.

"Stop it, Mum, you're freaking me out…"

"Mary Fox? That's the funniest thing I've heard in years!" As she laughed, her mother's voice started to change; it became deeper, harder and yet more sibilant – in fact it started to sound more and more like… then the name jumped into Justine's head, accompanied by a dreadful sick feeling in the pit of her stomach… it was the voice of Hopkirk.

Justine's eyes opened wide as a series of images suddenly crowded unbidden into her mind.

A terrible storm, resolving itself into a bright summer's day…

A cook with foul breath making her turn the spit…

A dark passageway with a rat crawling up her leg while Hopkirk tapped on the other side of the wall…

A beautiful man smiling at her in the dim light of a humble cottage in the forest…

Planning to be at the tavern with Sarah and her mother – and disguising themselves as a peasant woman with two young sons…

Coming back to the manor on horseback – so tired that she would have fallen off had William and Wychwoode not ridden on either side of her horse…

Being put to bed by Lady de Beauvais and sleeping a deep, dreamless sleep…

Now, she remembered everything – it all came flooding back as if it had never gone away. As if the dream were absolute reality.

And now Hopkirk was forcing his way back into her life, his horrible hissing voice coming out of her phone.

As Justine looked at the screen with sick fascination, Hopkirk's laughter was clearly coming out of her mother's mouth.

Then the laughter stopped and the picture of her mother started to change; it melted and shifted; the nose started filling out, the brow jutting, the hair shortening – until it was the grey, unblinking basilisk face of Hopkirk himself that looked triumphantly out of the screen at her.

As she watched in horror, Hopkirk gave an unpleasant smile.

"Oh, Mistress Fox," he hissed. "You know I will not be defeated again – not by you, or that self-opinionated lawyer Wychwoode, or by de Beauvais.

You know that I will find a way to get to you and de Beauvais, and try you both for sorcery!"

"No, Hopkirk!" gasped Justine, staring at the screen in horror. "No!"

"So why did you not kill me when you had the chance?" sneered Hopkirk, his face now coming out of the rear-view mirror as well as the phone. "How long will you regret not pushing in that knife..?"

Justine swung round to see if he was sitting behind her, but there was no one there. "I couldn't do it!"

"You are weak. You are useless!" said Hopkirk, now looking in at the side window as well. "You and de Beauvais will never be together! I will hunt you down and I will not stop until I have you both in my power. I shall test you both under water and then I'll burn you both for sorcery!"

"No!" shrieked Justine. "Leave me and William alone! Leave us both alone!"

The phone slipped from her nerveless fingers. Then she felt the car seat was no longer supporting her weight; it was becoming soft and liquid, like chocolate melting in a hot pan. She grabbed at the steering wheel but it too seemed to melt in her hand and then the seat gave way completely and she felt herself falling and falling, as if down a long dark liquid tunnel, slipping and sliding with nothing to hold onto, dropping down faster and faster, then her mother's voice came back and could be heard, saying "Mistress Fox? Mistress Fox?" over and over, while Hopkirk's laughter filled her ears, and she was sliding and falling faster and faster, then her mother reached out and grabbed her shoulder and shook it, repeating "Mistress Fox?" only now it wasn't her mother's voice any more, now it was Sarah's voice, and her shoulder was being shaken harder and harder...

"Mistress Fox?"

Justine opened her eyes.

"Oh Mistress, you were having ever such a nightmare – you were calling and crying – I had to awaken you."

She was in her four-poster bed in Grangedean Manor.

Justine sat up slowly and tried to gather her wits; trying to comprehend where she was and what was real.

"Sarah?" she asked, nervously. "Where am I?"

"You're safe in your room here at Grangedean Manor, Mistress."

"Am I? Am I really?" Justine looked desperately around the room. The four-poster bed looked solid enough, as did the clothes chests. She reached out and felt the nearest post of the bed, hung with a red velvet drape. It definitely felt real as she stroked the soft, thick material. Out of the diamond-paned window she could see the tops of the trees swaying gently in the summer breeze. The regular morning sound of the wood pigeon coo-cooing could be heard from outside.

"Are you sure this isn't a dream?" Justine asked in a small voice.

"Nay, Mistress, not a dream," answered Sarah. She reached down and shook Justine's shoulder again. "There, Mistress," she said. "That felt real enough, didn't it?"

Justine flopped back onto the bolster.

"Oh, Sarah," she said, staring up wide-eyed at the serving girl. "I had such an awful dream. I'd gone back to my original time and although it was good to talk to my mother again, I felt I had abandoned William and you and everyone."

"Oh, Mistress, no."

"Yes – except Hopkirk – he came after me to taunt me for not defeating him."

"I did think you were dreaming of Master Hopkirk, Mistress," said Sarah. "It sounded like he was attacking you – you said 'No, Hopkirk, no!' I heard you quite clearly. I hope I did right to wake you."

"Thank you, yes," said Justine. "Just knowing he's still out there and wants to try me and Sir William…" Justine shuddered. "Such a horrible man."

"Well, he's not here now, Mistress," said Sarah with a reassuring smile, "but the master and Lady de Beauvais are down in the hall, and they would have you join them presently to break your fast." She started rummaging in one of the oak chests. "Which means I must have you dressed and have your hair set and your face lightly painted; so you can make your entrance this morning and stun them all to silence with your natural beauty."

She produced a blue velvet gown and held it up for inspection. "Here Mistress," Sarah said, "I'll warrant this will be just the thing."

"The master and his mother are in the hall?" asked Justine.

"Aye, Mistress, although I cannot answer as to how Sir William has managed to be awake and in control of his humours this hour – he was drinking again with Master Dowland, Master Melrose and Master Stanmore till but a few hours since. I saw him going to his bed just as I had risen from mine for the day's labours." She chuckled. "Any other man would have stayed abed till sundown with the amount of wine he looked to have had."

"Then I had better get up," said Justine.

She swung her feet out of the bed and stood up, taking a deep breath in and out – to clear her head of Hopkirk and put the nightmare out of her mind. "Right, Sarah," she said, forcing herself to be bright and cheerful, "let's get dressed!"

A short while – and much tight lacing – later, Sarah was finished. She stood back to admire her handiwork. "There, Mistress, you are truly a beauty. I'll warrant your friends in your future time would not even know you! Stay here withal and I will let the master know you are ready to come down to the hall." With that she curtseyed and trotted out of the room.

Justine stood still, trying for a few minutes to adjust her breathing to the tight corset of the heavy gown. She had found that if she focussed on relaxing her shoulders and straightening her back, she could maintain some sort of control of her breathing. But she still hadn't got used to the way the clothing pinched in her waist and prevented her from eating more than the tiniest amount of food. 'If I do ever get back to 2015,' she thought, 'I'll make my fortune with the Tudor Costume diet. "Look great and lose weight!" – I'll clean up.'

There was a knock on the door. "Come in," she called.

The door opened and William strode in.

"My sweet Mary," he said, looking her up and down. "Each morning these past two weeks I have marvelled how you grow ever more beautiful." He bowed. "I would be honoured if you would accompany me back down to the hall to break your fast."

"Good, my Lord," answered Justine, then winced as she realised she sounded like a bad Shakespearean actor, "I would be most honoured."

He held out his arm and she slipped her hand onto it. They stepped out of the room and made their way down the great stairway and into the hall.

Lady de Beauvais stood as William led Justine to her place at his side. As they all sat down, servants ran out from the kitchens with plates of bread, meats, cheeses and cups of beer.

William immediately set about loading his plate with as much of the food as he could fit on it. Justine watched in wonder – she and Lady de Beauvais were both much more restrained, taking only as much as they could manage in their tight gowns.

"I would have you accompany me on a tour of the estate this morning," said William between mouthfuls of bread and cheese. He gave a small sidelong glance at his mother as he said it, giving Justine the distinct feeling that there was some unspoken message passing between them.

"That is a fine notion, William," said his mother. She smiled at Justine. "I am sure Mary will appreciate seeing more of the lands you own." She took a small piece of bread and a sip of beer. "Although I would have you keep a close eye on Mistress Fox, my son, lest she once again loses her horse."

Justine glanced at the older woman to see if this was a joke or if she was serious, and was relieved to see a twinkle in her eye.

"I would like very much to see more of the lands, Lady de Beauvais," she said, feeling that, as ever with this fine older lady, humility was probably the best policy.

"Good. I shall see to it that you have a steady mount for the ride." Lady de Beauvais turned to her son; her voice taking on a more business-like tone. "Now, my son; you still have men placed at all ways into the manor and the lands?"

"Aye," he answered, equally business-like. "Wychwoode has made them available to us for as long as we need them."

"But this matter needs to be settled for good, and presently," she answered. "Otherwise we are in a state of siege, awaiting the pleasure of that odious little magistrate to make his move."

"I am expecting Wychwoode back this day from the Oxford Assizes," said William, cutting a large piece of beef with his knife and putting it in his mouth. "We will consider our options and make our plans."

"Yes. We need a clear plan. I believe this dreadful little man will continue to chase after you and Mary whatever we try to do to stop him. He will not be diverted."

Justine had a flashback image of Hopkirk's face coming out of her phone and the rear-view mirror, as well as the side window of her car. "You and de Beauvais will never be together! I will hunt you down and I will not stop until I have you both in my power. I shall test you both under water and then I'll burn you both for sorcery!"

"What say you, Mistress Fox?"

"Eh?" exclaimed Justine, quickly putting the image out of her mind. Lady de Beauvais was looking expectantly at her. She paused a moment to gather her thoughts. "I was thinking that we should find his weaknesses and use them against him." That sounded good – she even impressed herself.

"Go on," said Lady de Beauvais. "What are his weaknesses?"

"He is an arrogant peacock," William suggested, "so sure of himself and his mission from God."

"Yes," said Justine, her mind racing. "He is arrogant and sure of himself. He also needs to command respect from his followers – he cannot bear to be made to look a fool. If we want to beat him, we have to discredit him completely."

"Indeed," said Lady de Beauvais, "that is very sound thinking." She glanced at her son, as if to ensure he had noted that Mistress Mary Fox had brains as well as beauty.

An idea started to form in Justine's mind – an idea of how to exploit the chink in Hopkirk's armour. She considered it a moment and decided it definitely had potential, although it was only a rough idea. She decided to park it for further consideration later.

"We will make plans later today when Wychwoode returns," said William. "I have also asked Tom Melrose to join us. I value his council."

"Even after he has betrayed you?" asked his mother.

"Aye," answered William, "but we have talked much on that. He was angry and Hopkirk recognised it. That is how Hopkirk was able to turn him against me."

"In the tavern you said his father had lost money," prompted Justine, keen to get more of the background. Even though she'd been hiding among the villagers in disguise, like everyone else in the tavern that night she'd followed the exchanges between Melrose and William with great interest.

"He had gambled it away," answered William. "It was the money my father paid him for the enclosure of his lands. It was Tom's inheritance, and his father lost it at gambling." He paused a moment, considering. "I know it was hard for Tom to understand – his father was a great force in his life.

"How much land was it?" Justine asked thoughtfully.

"It was enough for a man to plough and earn an honest living."

"And how much compared to your lands?" she asked.

"Around one tenth part of one tenth," he answered cautiously.

"Only one percent?" Justine looked at him in surprise. "Then you must return it to him! It is the best way to secure his loyalty. It means nothing to you, but everything to Tom."

"You would have me give away my lands?" William asked incredulously.

"If it secures his service to you, then yes, I would," she answered. "It seems to me to be a small price to pay."

"Yes, perhaps I could offer him a good price..." suggested William thoughtfully.

"No," Justine said firmly. "You must give the lands to him for free. It's the right thing to do."

William opened his mouth to try again, then seemed to think better of it. He turned to his mother. "What say you?" he asked.

His mother looked from one to the other as she considered her reply. "Mary makes an interesting suggestion," she said, "and not one I would have thought of myself. But you would do well to heed it, my son. With the house likely to face attack, you need to know you can count on the loyalty of all your men. Thomas Melrose has betrayed you once before and could do so again. Giving him one tenth part of one tenth still leaves you nine and ninety."

William looked like a man who knows he is outvoted by two strong women, but one who would not want to back down too easily. "I will think on it," he said eventually. "In time, I'll think on it."

"Good," said Justine brightly. "Then let's go for that ride in the park!"

CHAPTER TWENTY-FIVE

The militiaman watched idly as the steady stream of urine splashed around the base of the tree, spraying off the side of the trunk and sending a lazy plume of steam into the morning air. He raised the stream high to see if he could hit one of the leaves, and was pleased to see it buffeted in the arc of liquid. After a few moments he gave a final shake, pulled up his hose and breeches and walked back a few steps to where he had left his halberd. He picked it up and resumed his position, guarding the entrance to a path that wound through the forest towards the village.

It had been an uneventful morning, just like every other morning in the two weeks since he had been placed here on duty by Master Wychwoode. His orders had been very clear – no one comes into or goes out of the parklands. Just like every other morning, he had arrived at dawn to relieve the previous guard and had then stood – or sat – at the edge of the forest until dusk, before handing over to the next guard.

It was a lonely watch – no one to talk to and nothing to do except observe the birds in the sky and the occasional coney or squirrel in the forest. Once he had nearly managed to kill a coney as it ran out in front of him; his aim with the sharp tip of his halberd had been close, but not close enough. That was a shame – a coney would have supplemented his meagre rations nicely. He licked his lips at the thought of how he would have skinned the coney with his dagger, then built a small fire and roasted it on a stick. Much better than the few cuts of cold ham and a hunk of rye bread that was all he was given each day, along with a flagon of ale.

He wondered how long this guard duty would last – another week, another month, another year? All to keep that little grey magistrate and his forces out of the Grangedean estate. Quite right too; the man was obsessed and had to be stopped – just as, with God's good grace, they had stopped him that night in the tavern.

His mind drifted back to that eventful night. He could scarcely believe that Hopkirk had the presumption to try Sir William de Beauvais for witchcraft – that was going deeply against the natural order of things. Even if the plucky girl Mary Fox had not run out to stop Hopkirk stabbing Sir William de Beauvais, then he would have done so himself. Or at least he would have tried, even though he had been the other side of the barrel at the time…

Ahh, Mary Fox – now there's a girl…

Despite being accused of witchcraft, she hadn't run away; instead she had disguised herself as a boy and put herself right in the lion's den, like the prophet Daniel – and just like Daniel, God had saved her – He had shown that she was a good person and not an evil witch, for all Master Hopkirk had accused her.

So if he had to stand guard here for a year, or even two, to keep Mary Fox from the grasp of Master Hopkirk, then that's what he would do.

He looked briefly to his left across the parklands. The east wing of Grangedean Manor could just be seen among the dark cedars. Nothing out of the ordinary caught his eye, so he turned to the right and looked along the edge of the forest. Again, nothing.

He resumed his guard position.

---0---

Margaret ran silently out from behind a tree a few yards from the militiaman's back and darted lightly to the cover of the next one. Her shoe scraped slightly on the soft earth as she ran, and it made the smallest of sounds.

The militiaman glanced round, his small eyes staring suspiciously into the forest, but nothing caused him to raise the alarm. He did not appear to see or hear Margaret hiding behind the tree in the dappled shadows; she was breathing as quietly as she could, despite having run from tree to tree all the way from the manor. After a few moments she peered out and saw the militiaman shake his head and turn back to look across the parkland.

Checking again that his back was definitely turned, she darted like a small flickering shadow towards the next tree. This time she was less fortunate – a dry twig snapped under her foot with the sound of an exploding firecracker in the quiet morning air.

The militiaman was up on his feet in an instant, turning towards the forest; the wicked tip of his halberd dropping into the ready position.

Margaret froze between trees, camouflaged by the confusing patterns of light and shade in the forest.

"Stand, ho!" shouted the militiaman, his eyes scanning from tree to tree. "Who's there?"

Margaret held her breath and stayed silent.

"Who's there?" he repeated and advanced cautiously into the forest, his halberd sweeping in front of him. Then he spotted her. With a grunt of satisfaction he walked forward until the sharp steel tip of his halberd was at her throat, while the curved axe-head blade pointed down at her feet.

"'Tis I, Margaret," she answered quickly, stepping back with her gaze fixed on the tip of the halberd. "I am a servant at Grangedean Manor."

"What is your business out here?" he demanded.

She looked anxiously around for inspiration and saw some mushrooms growing on the forest floor.

"I am, er, collecting mushrooms," she answered.

"Step forward so I can see you fully and walk out into the sunlight."

"Raise your halberd first," said Margaret, with more strength in her voice than she felt. "I cannot walk further or I will impale myself."

He grunted in acknowledgement and pulled the point back. She walked forwards while he backed away, his halberd held in the ready position in case she made any sudden moves.

She stepped out of the forest shadows into the sunlit parklands, and stopped.

"Margaret – a servant?" he said, studying her. "Collecting mushrooms?" She nodded.

He looked her up and down. She was wearing a simple dress and plain woollen apron. "Then why do you not carry a basket?" he asked suspiciously. "You would need a basket to pick mushrooms."

"I would carry them back to the manor in my apron?" she suggested.

He shook his head. "That is too great a distance," he said. "I will not credit that."

She was silent, considering him.

So the moment had arrived; the moment she had been dreading, when she must do whatever must be done to get Master Hopkirk into the manor.

This coarse peasant stood between her and the success of that plan – so he must be removed.

And if it must be done, it must be done this moment.

Margaret straightened her back. "Oh, good sir," she said with what she hoped was her most alluring smile, "you are indeed a most observant guardsman." She put her hands on her hips and pushed her small chest out towards him. "You have found me out."

"Found you out?" He sounded deeply suspicious. "What have I found out?"

"That I am not in truth picking mushrooms – you are quite right." She moved closer to him and smiled up coquettishly. "That I have come out here for a much larger prize."

He looked down at her and laughed. She caught a whiff of his sulphurous breath and forced herself not to recoil. "What prize is that, Mistress Margaret?" he asked, chuckling.

"Why," she said, moving closer "it is you, you big ninny."

"Me?" The smile froze on his face.

"Yes, you. I have seen you in the manor, so big and strong, and I thought 'that is the man for me'…" She looked carefully at him to see how he was taking this nonsense in. "So I asked the sergeant and found out you were on guard duty here each day, and I thought I would come out to see just how… big…" she moved closer still and pushed her chest virtually into his stomach "…and strong… in truth you are."

He stepped back. "You have seen me and wanted to meet me?" he asked incredulously.

"Aye," she answered, moving closer again and putting her hand on his cheek. She stroked it up and down against his coarse beard.

He reached up and removed it. "I am on duty," he said. "I am to guard this path through the forest. We can meet and talk about this later."

"So you are minded to meet with me?" she affirmed, then reached up again and ran her finger gently along his lip.

"Aye," he answered, his breath catching as she pushed her finger into his mouth.

"Then why wait?" she said, in her softest and silkiest voice. "We are alone. We can get to know each other here…"

"Nay…" he muttered, but this time he did not remove her hand.

Margaret moved even closer still and put her left hand up to stroke the side of his chest.

"Good sir," she purred, "we must take our chances while we can…"

That was when his resistance crumbled.

He put his hands on her tiny waist, and pulled her into a close embrace.

It was the move Margaret had been waiting for. Her left hand moved smoothly down his side and her fingers wrapped around the hilt of the dagger at his belt…

---0---

Justine urged her horse to a gallop to try and catch William as he thundered across the Grangedean Manor parklands, his challenge to out-ride him still hanging in the air behind them.

"William!" she called out. "You started before I was ready!"

"Come, Mary!" he called back over his shoulder. "You must catch me!"

Justine gripped harder with her knees and urged her mount on, her hair flying out behind her, moving as one with the magnificent animal as it

186

strained to catch up with the rider ahead. William was on a big, heavy war horse; Justine's lower weight and nimble, eager mare meant that she had a speed advantage, and soon she drew level.

For a few exhilarating moments they rode side by side at full gallop. Justine couldn't help but laugh out loud with joy as the horses flew along together in the morning sunshine.

William looked across at her and laughed as well. "Bravo!" he called out. "You have skill at riding a horse!"

"Aye, my lord!" she called back. "It was as well I took the mare and not the sumpter!"

It had been earlier that morning in the stable yard that the choice had been made. William's mother had been as good as her word and had produced what looked to Justine like a steady old cob horse, together with a primitive-looking side-saddle. Lady de Beauvais called the horse a 'sumpter', which Justine took to have been the Tudor name for it. She must have looked surprised, for Lady de Beauvais asked if she were not happy with the choice.

Justine hesitated. She didn't want to offend Lady de Beauvais, but the thought of riding out side-saddle on an old plodding horse on such a fine summer's day made her feel like someone's aged aunt.

At that moment a beautiful young mare was brought out for exercise, skittishly prancing across the yard with her groom hanging onto her like grim death. On a sudden whim, Justine asked if she could take the mare instead.

"You would ride out on this one? asked Lady de Beauvais in surprise.

The mare pulled her head back, nearly pulling the groom's arm from its socket. "She is indeed quite difficult to manage," Lady de Beauvais said doubtfully.

"I have ridden lots of horses, many just like her," said Justine. She approached the mare and reached up to stroke the soft velvet muzzle, making 'shhh' noises to reassure the animal. The mare whinnied, but brought her head down and kept it still, so after a moment, Justine moved her hand up the side of the horse's head. She carried on whispering to the mare – more 'shhing' noises and 'there, there' – which seemed to have the calming effect she wanted. Soon the mare was quiet and still.

"What is her name?" asked Justine, still stroking the horse's cheek and muzzle.

"Juno." Lady de Beauvais paused a moment, considering. "You have a way with a horse. That is good."

Justine cast her mind back to Pony Club camps as a child; how she'd always found that ponies responded to her calm voice and touch, while the other children were often told 'that pony is too hard to handle; leave it to Justine Parker'.

"She is beautiful," she said.

"You may ride her," said Lady de Beauvais, suddenly and decisively. Then she turned to the groom. "Fetch a saddle for Mistress Fox, she will ride astride."

Justine looked at her, surprised. "You may have a way with a horse, but not even you can control Juno from sitting aside her."

"Thank you," said Justine, with a big smile.

"And you must change your clothing. We cannot have you trying to ride with full skirts. I will have you dressed in something more suitable."

Which is how Justine came to be riding Juno at full gallop alongside William, dressed in a special split skirt. She also had men's hose on underneath – mainly to maintain her dignity, but also to help avoid chafing against the high backed wooden saddle.

William sat up in his saddle and started to rein his horse in; they were approaching the edge of the forest.

Justine pulled up as well, and soon they were trotting gently alongside each other, their horses snorting, whinnying and throwing their heads around in appreciation of the gallop; steam rising from their sweaty flanks.

"You ride well, my sweet Mary," said William, when they had both got their breath back.

"I was well taught, my lord," she explained. "We had a club for young children and their ponies, and I rode every day as a young girl."

"What an interesting notion," he observed. "You are ever full of surprises."

He pulled his horse to a stop, so she did likewise. He turned to her, and looked her deep in the eyes. "And I have a surprise for you, too," he said softly.

She took a deep breath, smiled and replied "A surprise? What is that, my lord?"

"It is more that I have something I would ask of you…"

She looked into his eyes, searching behind them – trying to see if he was being serious, or if this was the build-up to some joke.

He leant across and took her hand in both of his. She realised he was trembling. He took a deep breath. "I have met many women, and none have had your beauty, your charm or your ready wit. In truth, I have never met a woman such as you, sweet Mary, and I would have you with me for all time. Mary Fox, will you…"

But he never finished the sentence. Instead he was cut off by a chilling sound in the still morning air; a long, drawn-out, blood-curdling shriek from the forest ahead, that ended in a terrible gurgling death-rattle – then silence.

William gave Justine a brief look of shock – and was that also a small amount of relief? – then he kicked his horse into an immediate gallop and sped off towards the place where the sound had come.

"Yes… oh yes…" breathed Justine. "Of course I will…"

Then with a sigh she kicked Juno into a gallop and once again chased after

William across the parklands.

She arrived at the edge of the forest to see that William had dismounted and was on the ground, bent over the body of a man. He looked up as she reined in and dismounted.

"It is one of the guards," he said. "He has been stabbed." He stood up and moved back; Justine could see the man had the hilt of a dagger sticking out of his chest.

She knelt down beside him and studied the dagger. It looked as though it had gone in deep, just below his breastbone. She put a finger to his neck. The pulse was there but it was weak. The man was still breathing, but only just, and with great difficulty.

She wished she could do something for this poor man, who had been guarding the estate for her protection. She wished she could get him to A&E at a 21st century hospital – with immediate surgery he might possibly have a chance. But out here, with no real medical practices, there was nothing she could do – except give comfort.

She lifted his head onto her lap and stroked his cheek. The man looked up at her with pinprick black eyes and coughed. A fine spray of blood hit her skirt.

"Mistress Mary?" he whispered. "Is that you?"

"Yes," she said.

"I have failed you."

"No, of course you haven't."

"I would have protected you. No one is to leave the park, Master Wych…" he coughed again and gathered what little strength he had left. "…Master Wychwoode said, but that bitch has got out. I let her go. I failed you." His eyes closed.

"Not at all." She stroked his cheek again as his breath got weaker. "I'll be fine. Who got out?" she asked.

He was quiet a moment, then his eyes opened and he looked up at her. "I'm cold," he said.

"Shh. We'll get help and you'll be fine."

"Nay," he answered, so quietly she had to lean right in to hear, "that bitch has killed me."

"Who's that?" she asked.

"She said her name was Margaret," he coughed again. "A serving wench at the manor."

"Margaret?"

"Aye, she said she loved me…"

The man gave another cough, then his breathing slowed and stopped. As she watched, his eyes lost focus, then rolled up into his head.

Justine looked down at the body and felt regret for the waste of this man's life. But then she frowned.

Why was it only regret she felt? There was a dead body on her lap – why was she not feeling fear and revulsion? With a start she realised that her attitude was becoming much more Tudor – she was becoming hardened to death as an ever-present part of life. The old Justine – the one from 2015 – would have been sick, or would have screamed at the man's death. Mary Fox, the Tudor adventuress, on the other hand, simply laid the body on the ground and stood up, smoothing down her skirts.

William looked at the body. "Who did this?" he demanded. "Who has killed one of our guards?"

"It was Margaret," she answered calmly. "The serving girl who first accused me of witchcraft. She stabbed him and got out of the park."

"That shrewish little woman?" he asked. She nodded.

"I should have cast her out before now!" he muttered. "I should have cast her out the moment we returned from the tavern." He walked away, thinking hard. Then he turned back. "I'll warrant she has gone to fetch Hopkirk – to lead him in on this path!"

Justine could now see clearly what had to be done. This was the moment when she had to take charge. Whatever happened, Hopkirk could not prevail; the memory of Hopkirk's challenge from her dream came back to her and she wasn't prepared to let him defeat her now.

She mounted lightly onto her horse, then wheeled round to face William.

"We have to get back and prepare ourselves," she said firmly. "We have men to organise and plans to put in place."

Then she wheeled Juno round towards Grangedean Manor and kicked her into a gallop. "Come on!" she called over her shoulder. "No time to lose!"

William walked over to his horse, who was calmly eating grass a few yards away.

"By the Holy Cross," he observed softly to the animal, "she is as much a leader of men as is our own glorious Queen." He mounted up. "I would I had completed my offer of marriage, for now I fear she'll not spare me the time!"

He kicked his horse into action and galloped off after Justine.

CHAPTER TWENTY-SIX

As William and Justine rode back to the manor, Margaret was running blindly along the dark path, picking her way through the deep forest under low branches and over high roots by instinct alone. In her conscious mind there was only one aim – to get as far away as possible from that awful thing back there – that awful thing that she had done.

Her breath punched in and out of her chest in great racking sobs as she ran; every breath accompanied by a fractured prayer to God or to Jesus for forgiveness.

She had killed a man. She had committed the most heinous of mortal sins – murder.

Suddenly a massive wave of nausea hit her. She stumbled to a large tree for support and leaned against it, waiting for the nausea to pass. But it didn't pass; instead her body contracted as her gut went into spasm and she leant over and she retched, again and again and again. Even when there was nothing left inside her, still she continued to retch. She thought she would surely die.

Eventually the nausea passed and the retching stopped. Wiping her mouth with her apron, she stumbled on a few more yards and collapsed down onto the forest floor with her back to the trunk of another tree.

She stared across the forest.

But the scene in front of her eyes was not the trees, branches and woodland path; it was the scene that had played continuously in front of her, without mercy, ever since it had happened.

She was looking at the militiaman as she grasped the dagger at his waist.

She was mouthing 'I love you' as he smiled at her.

She was staring into his eyes as she eased the dagger out of its sheath and in one smooth movement, thrust it deep into his chest.

She was seeing his eyes widen as the dagger went in; the smile turning to disbelief and then to shock; his eyes contracting and his knees giving way as dropped.

She was hearing the long, chilling shriek as he then flopped over onto his back and writhed on the ground with blood soaking into the front of his tunic; eventually ending when he lay still, staring hopelessly up at the sky.

She was recalling her panic as the full realisation of what she'd done thundered into her, the realisation that she had committed the mortal sin of murder.

After that, she did not recall, except that she must have run into the forest and started her headlong flight along the path, before the nausea made her stop and retch.

After many minutes sitting against the tree, her head started to clear. She looked about her, as if seeing the forest for the first time.

The path, barely more than a track between the trees, ran in front of her, winding its way from the parklands through to the road to the village.

She remembered now what she had to do – to get to the safety of Hopkirk's protection and lead him back along the path towards the manor. That was why she had to dispose of the guard; it was for the greater good.

Margaret gasped as the realisation hit her. In truth it was actually God's good work she was doing! She was helping Hopkirk to get to the witch and to burn the Devil! If she was doing God's work, then God must have wanted her to kill the guard! Maybe the guard had been a sinner – she had seen him shamelessly pissing up into the air towards the Heavens, which must surely be a sin – maybe he had sinned greatly in other ways too!

That was it! She was not the sinner – no – she had in truth been a tool of Lord Jesus, being used by Him to cut out the canker of sin by committing a mercy killing on an evil man who deserved no better…

Margaret stood up, put her shoulders back and took a deep breath.

She was God's chosen servant, and she had His important work to do.

She looked up at the morning sun as it filtered down through the trees and used it to get her bearing, then she turned and set off south along the path towards the village.

---0---

It was a long walk, and the sun was nearly overhead when Margaret staggered, dry and dusty, into the cool, dark tavern.

Jake was padding around with his pitcher of ale so she asked him, as she sank onto a bench by an empty table, if Hopkirk was anywhere to be found.

"Right enough, Mistress Margaret," said Jake as he filled a tankard for her, "he's expected back this very afternoon."

"Where has he been?"

"'Tis said he has been around the county seeking men to join his cause."

So Martha and the cook had been correct – Hopkirk was recruiting forces. Margaret permitted herself a moment of quiet satisfaction. God was most assuredly looking for her help in His work!

"They say he has gathered some four dozen men," continued Jake.

"Four dozen? Does that mean he plans to attack the manor?" she asked.

"I'll warrant it does," replied Jake. "He's talked of nothing else since that night when the witch was revealed right here in my tavern."

"I have heard much about that night," said Margaret. "They say the witch threw an incantation at Master Hopkirk and he fell down to the floor."

"An incantation?" Jake did not look as if he was bothering to hide his surprise.

"That's what I have heard from folk who were there."

Jake let out a deep guffaw. "Nay, she threw herself bodily at him, and struck him with some force, like she were a ball from a canon."

"Oh." Margaret considered this doubtfully. "Are you sure?"

"I was one of the folk who were there. I was as close to her then as I am to you now." Jake chuckled. "I'll warrant she may be a witch, but I know what I saw with my own eyes – and it was no incantation. She hit him with her body, with the force to knock ten men off their feet!" Still chuckling to himself, Jake padded off to serve others, leaving Margaret sitting alone with her thoughts.

So the witch had not used an incantation to fell Hopkirk – that much was clear. Did that mean she was supposed to think that maybe, the witch was not such a powerful sorceress as everyone was saying? Or was God testing her; deliberately trying to sow doubt in her mind, so He could see whether she had the strength of will to resist?

Well, if that was so, then she would prove to Him that her will was as strong as iron. She would prove she was resolved to carry through her mission. After all, God had commanded her to commit murder in His purpose – and she had risen to obey His command.

Margaret straightened her bony little shoulders and stuck out her chin.

Let the witch do her worst. With Hopkirk – and God – on their side, Margaret knew absolutely that the righteous would prevail.

---0---

At about the same time that Margaret was sitting nursing her pitcher of ale and contemplating a long afternoon waiting on the arrival of Hopkirk, Sir William de Beauvais was striding into the Great Hall at Grangedean.

He had decided to change out of his riding clothes and was now resplendent in a blue doublet and breeches, grey hose and black boots. On his head was his favourite grey velvet cap with a peacock feather protruding from the brim.

Justine and Lady de Beauvais were sitting at the long table. Melrose was standing opposite them, along with a man in black with long grey hair that William recognised as Wychwoode.

"Ahh, William," said his mother, "good of you to attend our council."

"Mother," he acknowledged, with a little bow. He then turned to Justine and bowed again. "Mary." She inclined her head at him, then broke into a mischievous smile. "What were you going to ask me when we were out riding, William?" she asked, her voice as innocent as a child asking for a comfit.

His mother looked at William and raised an eyebrow. "You have not...?" she began.

William gave a warning cough. "Um, no – we were disturbed..."

"Oh really, William!" said his mother, "Could you not at least...?"

"Has anyone thought to call for some beer?" asked William quickly, wanting to cut her off. "A council such as this cannot be run on a dry throat." He stood and shouted "Martha! Martha! Here I say!" then he sat down again.

"Really, William," scolded his mother, "must you bellow like an enraged bull in my ear?" He noticed her catch Justine's eye momentarily, and they exchanged a small but knowing smile. William sighed inwardly – what must a man do to keep the women of his house in control?

Wychwoode cleared his throat, bringing the meeting back to order. "I understand one of my guards has been murdered?"

"Yes," said Justine. "And by a forest path that may lead from the village to the estate."

"This is a clear sign that we are soon to be under attack," Wychwoode grimly. "Who has done this? Do we know?"

"Aye," answered William, relieved to be back on more important matters. "He named his assailant before he died. It was one of our serving maids – the one who first accused Mary of witchcraft and called in Hopkirk."

"Then she is most assuredly in league with that man."

"She has run off; we think to the village," said Justine. "It is most likely she has gone to find Hopkirk and show him the way in."

"And he will come stealing in like a wolf in the night," said the lawyer. "We will need to be ready for him."

Martha appeared through the door from the kitchens.

"Yes, Sir William?"

"We will have some beer and some manchet bread."

"Yes, Sir William." She turned and disappeared back through the door to the kitchens.

"We must put men by..." began Wychwoode, but stopped in surprise when Justine raised her finger to her lips and shushed him quiet. Everyone turned to look at her. "Martha," she whispered, indicating the door to the kitchens.

William could see it was still slightly ajar.

Justine got up and walked carefully and very quietly over to the door, then wrenched it suddenly open. Martha was revealed standing behind, the expression on her face alternating between shock at having been discovered listening, and pretend innocence.

Justine kept her composure. "And a flagon of wine, if you would, please Martha," she said levelly – as if the housekeeper had been correct to hang back in case of further orders.

William saw Martha shoot a look of the purest loathing at Justine, before assuming her customary mask of subservience. "Yes, Mistress Fox," she muttered. Then she deliberately turned her back on Justine and walked slowly down the stairs.

Justine waited until Martha's footsteps could be heard reaching the corridor below, then she closed the door fully and returned to the table.

Wychwoode, Melrose and Lady de Beauvais were staring at her open-mouthed. William, however, was smiling with quiet pride. Truly this Mary Fox was a remarkable and ingenious girl.

"We can't be too careful," Justine observed as she sat down. "I have my doubts about Martha's loyalty."

"It looks as though you have good reason," observed Wychwoode dryly. "We must be most diligently on our guard."

"Aye," agreed Melrose. "This man Hopkirk is full of cunning. He will use whoever he can to further his ends."

William looked at Melrose and nodded. "He used your anger to turn you against me, Tom. You, who was schooled alongside me from a boy."

"I was angry – that is true," agreed Melrose, with a rueful shake of his head.

"And I am truly sorry, Tom," said William. He paused a moment as he considered his next move. Mary Fox had suggested he should return Tom's lands. Without payment! It went against his every instinct – but look how Mary Fox truly seemed to understand the minds of others. She had seen so clearly how Martha would behave – she knew the housekeeper would be listening at the door. If she was right in this, he must give her other advice much credence.

He took a deep breath and looked up. "If we get through this, Tom, I will restore your family lands to you and yours. In perpetuity. It is the least I can do."

"My Lord…" exclaimed Melrose in surprise. "Are you sure?"

"Aye," said William. "You have come back to me and shown your loyalty. I value that above all else."

"My Lord!" Melrose touched the hilt of his sword and bowed. "You have my loyalty indeed!" William thought that as he stood up again, he stood a little taller; his eyes looked less hooded and his shoulders more relaxed. 'Good,' he thought, 'Mary Fox was right in this matter also. And it has secured Melrose for our cause.'

Once again, William observed a small glance between his mother and Justine, as if he had passed a test and the two women were now ready to move on.

Justine stood up.

"How many men do we have?" she asked, her voice sounding so business-like that Wychwoode briefly glanced up at her in surprised admiration. "I still have eleven of my militia," he answered.

"Plus Melrose, Dowland, Stanmore and you, Master Wychwoode," added Justine. "So we have fifteen men."

"And I, my sweet girl…?" said William with a small smile. "I also have a sword – and the wit to use it…"

"Yes, William, but you're a marked man," answered Justine. "If it comes to a fight, Hopkirk will target you directly, and if he kills you, he has won. We can't let that happen."

"You speak the truth, Mary," acknowledged Lady de Beauvais.

"And I would that I am not killed, more than I have a concern for Hopkirk's victory," pointed out William.

"Which is why we have to plan properly," answered Justine. "You and I will conceal ourselves in the secret passage and emerge only when Hopkirk is defeated. That way his whole cause is compromised – if he cannot take us both and try us for witchcraft, he has failed in his mission."

William stared at her in amazement. "You would have me skulking in the dark like a thief, while my own house is under attack?" he asked incredulously. "While my comrades fight on my part?"

"It's not skulking," answered Justine. "It's…" she paused a moment "…it's a tactical withdrawal."

"What if we are discovered?"

"We shouldn't be, but I suppose you should have your sword with you, just in case."

"Most assuredly!" exclaimed William, nodding sharply, so that the peacock feather danced wildly on his cap. "I will have my sword so I can burst forth and skewer that troublesome magistrate like the scoundrel he is."

"Nay, William" said his mother. "You will do as Mary commands in this matter. I will not have you killed by that vile little man. You know he would have stabbed you himself had it not been for Mary's brave action in the tavern. She is trying to stop history repeating itself."

"In any event, we will not let him get as far as the manor, Sir William," said Wychwoode, leaning forward with his hands on the table. "We will place men each night near the path where my man was killed, concealed in the trees. Then we will have the element of surprise when Hopkirk and his men come upon our ambush."

"We had best start this very night," said Melrose.

"We will," said Wychwoode. "Each night from now we must be ready for an attack."

"And must Mary and I sleep each night in the secret passage?" asked William, attempting to make this sound like a joke.

"No, William," said Justine. "But we must be ready to run to the passage the moment we hear a sword being drawn."

"But if Hopkirk comes in the dead of night…?"

"I will set a guard on the door from the gallery," said Justine. "Hopkirk cannot get to the bedrooms unless he comes along the gallery, so a guard will see him in good time to slip through the door and alert us."

"We cannot spare any of the men," said Wychwoode "Who will you use?"

"I will use my maid Sarah," answered Justine. "She has already agreed to help us in this way."

"Then that is settled," said Lady de Beauvais.

The door from the kitchens swung open, and Martha appeared with a tray of beer, wine and bread. Everyone was silent, all eyes on her as she walked across the room towards them. Martha placed the bread on the table and poured each person a tankard of beer, apart from Justine. She took a fine silver goblet off the tray and presented it to Justine with exaggerated deference, before filling it with wine from a small pitcher. She then put her nose in the air, turned and walked out of the room and slammed the door behind her.

The silence continued after she had gone, until eventually it was Lady de Beauvais who spoke.

"When we have removed the threat of this odious magistrate, we must look to our household staff," she observed carefully. "I would that we can rely on their unquestioned loyalty."

"I would do it now, Mother!" challenged William, scraping back his chair and leaping to his feet. "I will turn her out this instant for disloyalty and insolence!"

His mother raised her hand to calm him down. "Nay, my son. Now is the time for planning and preparation, not for concerns about servants. Let us settle the bigger matter first."

"But I will not have such behaviour in my house…"

---0---

While the argument continued between Sir William and his mother on the merits of removing Martha, Justine was definitely of the opinion that William was right. Keeping Martha in place was more of a risk than throwing the girl out; she had seen enough spy thrillers to know that as an 'inside person' Martha could be very valuable to Hopkirk in an attack.

So, once the argument was settled in Lady de Beauvais' favour – and William had stopped sulking – Justine decided to have a word with Martha. She slipped quietly down the stairs and made her way into the kitchens.

There were servants bustling all round; stuffing joints of meat, rolling pastries, slicing fruits and preparing dishes. Justine spotted Martha chopping some herbs and walked over to her.

"Hello Martha," she said pleasantly.

Martha carried on chopping, giving no indication she'd heard.

Justine tried again. "I wanted to thank you for bringing me the wine." As conversation-starters Justine knew it was lame, but it would have to do.

Martha scraped the choppings into an earthenware bowl. "'Tis no matter, Mistress Mary Fox," she said without looking up. "I serve the master and Lady de Beauvais, and they have ordered that I serve you also – so that I do."

"And I am grateful."

"Are you?" Martha finished scraping the chopped herbs and suddenly looked up with cold blue eyes.

"Of course."

"I should like to think you were, but I can scarce credit it, Mistress Mary Fox." Martha paused, studying Justine carefully. "Or should I call you Mistress Justine Parker – for is that not also your name?"

Justine was silent, shocked at hearing that name spoken aloud after so long.

"I recall that was your name when you arrived here, some two weeks since, as a vagrant who should have been turned out." Martha reached for some more herbs and started chopping, her blade moving almost faster than the eye could see. "But you weren't turned out, were you, Mistress Parker? You were put to service in these very kitchens as a scullion to turn the spit, which was no better than you deserved – and yet here am I, these two weeks later, ordered to serve you as the master's consort." Martha stopped chopping and stabbed the knife brutally into the wooden board, then looked up again. "And you would tell me there is no witchcraft in this?"

"No, Martha," replied Justine as steadily as she could, "there is not."

"Well, I do not believe that, Mistress Justine Parker, truly I do not." Martha pulled the knife out of the board and started chopping again. "And when Master Hopkirk catches you, do you know what he will do? He will take you to the fine brick well in the courtyard close to this place and he will try you there by ducking. And if you are proved as a witch, he will burn you at the stake."

"Then I will do all I can to stop Master Hopkirk catching me," said Justine levelly.

"Nay. He will catch you, and he will try you," said Martha with full confidence, "because he has the Lord Jesus on his side." She put down her knife and again stared at Justine with cold eyes. "His authority comes directly from God and from Jesus, whereas yours comes from Satan, may the Lord forgive me for uttering that name." Martha crossed herself. "With God and Jesus behind him, Master Hopkirk cannot fail, and your destruction is most definitely assured." She smiled coldly.

Justine, however, was staring wide-eyed at the housekeeper. Martha's words had brought back the idea she'd had that morning at breakfast for the downfall of Hopkirk – only now Justine knew in a flash exactly what she had to do to make it work.

The plan was clearly highly risky, but if she could pull it off, it would spell the end of Hopkirk's dogged pursuit.

Justine smiled back at the housekeeper.

"Thank you, Martha. You have opened my eyes to the truth," she said, and turned to run out of the kitchens and up to her room to put her plan into action.

Martha watched Justine go, then resumed chopping. "The truth will be your downfall, Mistress Justine Parker," she said aloud.

"Master Hopkirk will see you find it in the very fires of Hell."

CHAPTER TWENTY-SEVEN

Margaret yawned as she swilled the dregs of ale around the bottom of the tankard and chewed on her last crust of bread. The long, slow afternoon had dragged by; the sun was moving lower in the sky and the shadows outside the tavern were starting to lengthen – but there had been no sign of Hopkirk. The only highlight of the afternoon had been a conversation with Agnes, the young daughter of the landlord Jake.

"It's Mistress Margaret, isn't it?" Agnes had asked, as she stopped by to refill Margaret's tankard and give her a crust of bread. "I recall you from the day we searched Grangedean Manor for the witch."

"Yes, I am Margaret."

"You waiting for someone? I see you sitting here a while."

"Yes," Margaret replied, glad of some conversation. "As it happens, it is Master Hopkirk himself I am waiting for."

"Master Hopkirk? You're not a moment too soon. He is expected back this very afternoon."

"So your father has said." Margaret studied the younger girl and decided she would be a useful source of information – if the past looseness of her tongue was anything to go by. "I am told he has been about the county, gathering men."

"That's what he said he would be doing." Agnes sat down and made herself comfortable opposite Margaret. She poured herself a tankard of ale and leaned forward, bright-eyed, ready to tell her tale. "He came back in here the next night after the witch revealed herself and he vowed on all that is holy that he would find the witch and destroy her. And Sir William too, for being her protector." Agnes took a deep draught of ale. "But he knew he could not take them without some good fighting men, so he set off to go round the county, pressing men to his cause."

"But why not recruit men from the parish?" asked Margaret. "Why recruit outsiders?"

"Lord love us, Mistress Margaret!" exclaimed the girl. "He needed men who could not possibly be loyal to Sir William! So he must seek them from further afield."

"He is certainly dedicated to his task," observed Margaret thoughtfully. "It cannot be easy to recruit men to a stranger's cause."

"That is no matter to one such as Master Hopkirk," answered Agnes, with the fervour of a true disciple. "He can persuade any God-fearing man to his cause because it is the Lord's work he does."

"Then the Lord must have blessed his endeavour, for your father said he has gathered some four dozen men," said Margaret.

"Yes! We had word back from his party that he has been greatly successful, and that we should expect him back any day now with the men. There is much excitement in the village – nobody likes the thought that the manor is a godless place with a witch in residence." Agnes looked serious. "We pray for deliverance from her wicked grasp."

"She is all but mistress there now," said Margaret eagerly. "They say the master will have taken her to wife soon – or at least before All Saints Day is out," she added. She was rewarded with a gasp of amazement from the younger girl.

"The witch has enchanted him for certain," Agnes said breathlessly, "there is no other way of it."

"It does seem that is so," agreed Margaret. "I am come here to meet with Master Hopkirk and offer help to him and his men."

Agnes stood up. "Then you are well met here, Mistress Margaret. As I said, we expect him here soon, so you can offer your help to him directly." She took her pitcher and moved off to serve at other tables.

But there had still been no sign of Hopkirk by the time Margaret had finished her bread. She was just deciding that Agnes had been wrong and he would definitely not be coming this day – and was preparing to ask Jake for a room for the night – when she heard the sound of marching boots and jingling sword-belts outside.

Her heart lifted as the door opened and the familiar – although rather dusty and travel-weary – figure of Matthew Hopkirk walked in, followed by what seemed a never-ending procession of armed men.

"Master Hopkirk!" Margaret exclaimed, jumping up from her bench, "You are come!"

But Hopkirk did not respond, as his attention was focussed on seeing all his men into the tavern and seating them. He did not even seem to notice the excited Margaret leaping up from her table in the shadows.

Margaret ran over and tapped him on the arm, causing him to turn in annoyance.

"Well met, Master Hopkirk!" she said breathlessly.

"Who asks?" he snapped, barely glancing at her

"'Tis I, Margaret, from Grangedean Manor!" she answered with a smile. He looked blankly at her. "That first called out Mary Fox as a witch!"

"Oh, aye. Now I recall."

She gestured to all the men, who were seating themselves at tables while Jake and Agnes were running out with tankards and pitchers of ale for them. "You have gathered forces to take the witch?"

"That I have," he said, "and I must see to them." He started to turn away.

"Good," she said, reaching out and taking hold of his dusty sleeve. "But the manor is well guarded. I have come to help guide you in."

He stopped and turned slowly back, his unblinking grey eyes now boring into hers. "You have information on the defences?" he asked carefully.

"Oh yes, I do, Master Hopkirk!" She let go of his sleeve.

"Then you will share this information." He gestured to a table. "Sit and tell me what you know."

Margaret's heart swelled with pride as she sat down opposite Hopkirk. God must be pleased with her work, that he had put her in such a position of trust to this powerful man.

"The manor is well guarded?" he prompted her, once she had a fresh tankard in front of her and he had paid Agnes to fill it with ale. She took a sip to steady her nerve. "Aye. There are militiamen provided by Master Wychwoode posted at all the main entrances to the parklands."

"Master Wychwoode? That meddling lawyer?" Hopkirk made an annoyed hiss between his teeth. "I will take great pleasure in dealing with him in the course of this action." He considered Margaret. "How many men does he have – is it all that were here in the tavern?"

"Yes," Margaret paused for effect. "All except one – who is dead."

"Dead? That is convenient. How came he by that happy state?"

Margaret gave a slow smile. "I killed him," she said quietly.

Hopkirk looked at her in genuine amazement. "You?" he asked.

"Yes, it was me!" she said proudly. Then she added seriously, "But I was doing God's work, Master Hopkirk, God's good work."

"But how in Christ's holy name did you accomplish this deed?" he asked, looking Margaret up and down, clearly trying to imagine how this tiny woman could overpower a well-armed guard.

"I gave him to believe I was in love with him, so I could get close enough to grasp the dagger at his belt – then God guided my hand and gave me the strength to plunge it deep into his chest."

Hopkirk shuddered at this, but then stared at Margaret with a look of new-found respect.

"That is great work," he said. "I am... that is, God is... well pleased with you."

"God was looking for me to make a way open for the forces of righteousness to come in to the manor and take the witch," she answered. "The path that the man was guarding – it is now open to you and your men." She sat back, pleased that she had done her work.

"A path is open?"

"Yes, I have cleared a way in for you – through the forest." She was shocked when Hopkirk did not thank her for this critical action.

"But Wychwoode will undoubtedly know what you've done, assuming he's found the body. You did not hide it?" he snapped.

Margaret felt a cold dread – not only was Hopkirk not praising her, but he appeared to be chastising her instead. "No, the moment the deed was done I came straight here to tell you all, and to offer my help."

Hopkirk considered his options. "So they will know that we know of the path. They will expect us to use it. They will most likely conceal men about the end of it to ambush us." He looked up and gave a cold smile, making her heart sing. "You have done well, Margaret. They are expecting us to take the path." He paused. "So perhaps that is what we will not do."

"What will we do?" she asked, her pride in her deeds now fully restored. Truly God had heard her prayers. She added, "All the other gates are guarded."

"They won't put their best fighting men on the main gates," he answered thoughtfully. "They'll need them for the ambush. The main gates will only be guarded by servants. We need to find a reason to get them to let us in."

A thought occurred to Margaret, remembering something Martha had mentioned the night before. "Lady de Beauvais's sister is expected any day soon, from Nottingham. She will demand to be allowed in."

"Perfect," said Hopkirk, looking like a man with plan taking shape. "Absolutely perfect. We will attack them with all our force."

He drained his tankard.

"And we will attack when they least expect it."

---0---

Robert Wychwoode paced along the edge of the forest, studying each tree carefully in the deep orange glow of the evening sun. In particular, he noted the trees that lined the entrance to the path as it wound its way out of the parklands and into the depths of the forest.

The militiamen standing in a line behind him watched, as Wychwoode's strategic mind calculated the best position for each one; the best angle of crossbow fire; the best shadows for a man to melt into and become invisible.

There was a palpable air of anticipation as the men waited to be given their positions for the ambush – excitement crackling like an approaching electrical storm. Two weeks of uneventful guarding had made them bored and listless; it had dulled their wits and left their spirits dampened. But the murder of their comrade in cold blood at the hands of a serving woman had deeply enraged them and now, like fighting dogs about to be released from their cages, they were eager to be at the throats of their enemy.

Wychwoode turned and started issuing his orders.

"You," he said, pointing to the first man, "station yourself behind this tree here." The man moved quickly into position as directed. Wychwoode walked over and stood beside him, scanning the section of path visible from his cover, then stepped out onto the path. He looked back to see if the man could be seen, then grunted to himself in annoyance, returned and pushed the man deeper into the shadow of the tree. Then he walked back out onto the path and looked again at the man's position. Satisfied that he was now invisible, he said, "You stay in this position. Cover this section of the path and be ready to bring down anyone moving along." The man nodded briskly, cocking his crossbow, selecting a bolt from the pouch at his belt and slotting it onto the breech of the weapon.

Wychwoode walked back to the line to select the next militiaman, and placed him in the next ambush position.

Eventually all the men were in their places.

Wychwoode walked thirty yards along the path into the shadowy depths of the forest, then turned and walked slowly back out to the parklands, looking carefully about him as he went. A couple of adjustments were made to the position of some men, before he declared himself satisfied.

"Note the position of the shadows," he ordered. "When the sun sets you will have deep cover, but if they attack at dawn, the shadows will be on the other side of the trees. Make sure you move with them." The men nodded, studying the tree they were using as cover; looking to see where the shadow would most likely appear at dawn. "Now, prepare for the night, and stay alert. I want no man to fall asleep on this watch."

The men grunted their agreement and settled themselves by their trees. Like the first man, the others with crossbows made sure their weapons were cocked and ready. Other men had halberds which they leaned carefully up against the trunks next to them, ready to be snatched up the instant feet were heard approaching. The men whose main weapon was the sword gave a few practice draws of their blades from scabbards, thrusting into the air in front of them as if visualising how their blades would punch deep into the bodies of the enemy.

Wychwoode took a roll of wire from his belt and tied it between two trunks, one foot above the forest floor, as a tripwire. He tested it for tautness, re-tightening it until he was satisfied. He then tied a second one between two trees around ten feet further along the path. The nearest militiaman raised an eyebrow in enquiry.

"They will be expecting a tripwire," explained Wychwoode as he crouched down and squinted at the two wires to ensure they were all but invisible, "so they'll be proceeding carefully, feeling ahead." He stood up. "When they find the first one they'll think they have outwitted us – so they'll cut it and rush forward. That's when the second one will bring them down." The militiaman nodded, but said nothing.

Wychwoode walked back out to the parklands, to where William and Justine were waiting patiently on their horses.

"The ambush is secure, my lord," he said. "No man will pass through unharmed. If they attack in the night or at dawn, my men will stop them."

"You have done well," said William. "We are most thankful for your diligence in this."

"My men are pleased to have this chance to avenge the death of their comrade."

"And I, too, would have that magistrate stopped. For good, if possible," said William. "He is a thorn in my side that annoys me, with his fanciful notions of witchcraft and the like."

"There is no arguing with the man's conviction that he is on a mission from God," answered Wychwoode. "The only point he will accept now is the point of a sword." He patted Juno's muzzle, causing the mare to raise her head and whinny. "You and Mistress Fox should return to the manor and rest for the night."

He bowed. "My men and I will receive Hopkirk if he comes this night. We will put an end to this matter."

CHAPTER TWENTY-EIGHT

It was the darkest hour, just before dawn the next morning, when a lone hooded figure on a dark horse trotted up to the main gates of Grangedean Manor.

The clip-clopping sound of the hooves alerted Simon, the servant on guard duty, who had been dozing beside the gate inside the grounds. He staggered to his feet and picked up the heavy halberd resting against the wall. Lifting the point with some effort, he poked it though the gate and stammered out a challenge. "Who... who goes there?"

The rider made no move to rein in the horse – perhaps they had not heard him. He challenged again, trying to put a little more authority in his voice. "Halt now and show yourself!" He lifted the point of the halberd a little higher to show how serious he was, as he could hear the horse and rider trotting ever closer.

Just when he thought the horse must soon run onto the tip of the halberd, it clattered to a stop of its own accord.

As he stared hard, Simon could just make out the horse standing outside the gate, with its rider as a black silhouette against the night sky above.

"Identify yourself!" he demanded.

The rider spoke in a muffled voice. "Alice Mansfield."

"What is your business?"

"My sister, Lady de Beauvais, has invited me to stay at Grangedean Manor."

"Alice Mansfield?" asked Simon dubiously. He recalled being told that Lady de Beauvais's sister might be arriving, and that if she did, he was to let her in. He had naturally assumed, however, that she would arrive during the daytime.

The first light of dawn started to appear, softening the harsh night sky with a pale glow creeping upwards from the east.

Simon scanned the path leading up to the gate. There was no one else to be seen – just the line of hedges and bushes casting long shadows in the gradually emerging light. He decided it must be safe. Cautiously he unhooked a great metal key from his waist and unlocked the gate, then pushed it open. It swung heavily on its hinges with a creaking sound that was unnaturally loud in the still air, causing several pheasants to whir noisily up from nearby trees. He stepped through, pushed the gate back behind him and walked up to the horse and rider, still holding his halberd.

"Alice Mansfield?" he repeated. He could now see that the rider's face was hidden inside a deep hood. "Why do you not show yourself?" Another thought struck him. "And why are you alone?" he asked. "Why do you not have cases and servants and suchlike?"

"I became separated from them."

"They did not stay with you?" Simon asked in disbelief. He stared at the figure on the horse above him. There was something decidedly odd about this woman…

A cold flush of fear suddenly flowed through him. Now he thought about it, perhaps opening the gate might have been a mistake. He glanced back nervously – he could see in the strengthening dawn light that it was still slightly open behind him.

"Why do you not show yourself?" he asked again, raising the halberd.

There was a pause, then the voice came from within the hood. "I am tired with a long ride from Nottingham. I need to paint my face before I would have people see me, as the Lord is my witness."

Simon started. That phrase, 'as the Lord is my witness' – there was only one person who often said it in that way…

Suddenly he recognised the voice.

It was not the voice of a rich lady from Nottingham – no, it was the voice of a servant at the manor. A servant missing since the foul murder of a militiaman in the parklands…

"Margaret!" he exclaimed. "It is you, isn't it? What are you…?"

But he never finished the sentence. As he spoke, the bushes along the path seemed to erupt, spewing forth armed men. Where there had been only Simon and the horsewoman, alone in front of the gate, now there were upwards of fifty men, all brandishing swords and daggers, surrounding the poor bewildered servant. Simon spun round in surprise, and in doing so, he dropped his halberd. With rising panic, he scrambled to pick it up, but a well-aimed boot from the nearest man sent him flying back towards the brick wall next to the gate. He landed with his back to the wall, his head hitting it with a bone-jarring thud that sent stars spinning before his eyes. As he slumped against the wall, dazed and confused, he became aware of a man in a grey cloak approaching.

The man crouched down in front of him and a pair of unblinking eyes stared into his.

"A poor guard indeed," said the man. "To open the gate on such slender evidence. Truly the Lord has guided my hand in this deceit."

The man took out an evil-looking knife and held it up in front of the dazed servant's face. "I would let you run free, but I fear you may raise the alarm when we have passed into the manor to do the Lord's good work." The man studied the blade, appearing to consider his options. "So the Lord will forgive me for what I am bound to do now in His name..." He shifted his grip on the handle, then thrust it forward.

Simon felt what seemed like a heavy punch in the throat. Then he found he couldn't breathe.

Then he felt nothing.

---0---

Margaret stared in horror as Hopkirk pulled his knife from the neck of the lifeless body and wiped it clean on the rough woollen jerkin. He stood and turned to address his men.

"The Lord has blessed our plan with success thus far," he said. His voice was soft, but his words still carried clearly to all the men gathered around him. "Your silence in concealing yourself before Margaret rode to the gate was enough to ensure that this simpleton," he gestured to the body of Simon slumped against the wall, "did not hear your approach. And Margaret," he looked up at her, "you played your part well."

Margaret pushed her hood back as she stared white-faced at Simon's bloody body. 'It must have been necessary,' she told herself. 'He had to die. It is truly God's work we are doing here.' But in her heart she was remembering what a friendly companion he had been since they had started working together in the manor as children. She remembered the good times they had shared, how they had laughed and joked as they worked in the kitchens; how they exchanged stories in the servants' rooms; how they giggled and whispered together behind the cook's back...

Maybe he did have to die in God's name – but maybe God was being unbearably harsh in demanding his sacrifice.

"He was a good man," she said sullenly.

Hopkirk glanced up at her sharply. "Aye," he answered. "But a man who may have endangered our mission. God's mission." He considered her a moment, appearing once again to be calculating his options. He gave a small grunt, as if he had reached a decision. "You can dismount now," he said. "I will take the horse."

One of the men reached up and lifted Margaret down. Hopkirk climbed up into the saddle, adjusted the leathers, then leaned down and said something quietly to the man that Margaret couldn't hear.

The man nodded, then suddenly he grasped Margaret by the waist and lifted her bodily off the ground.

"What are you doing?" she yelped. "Put me down!"

Hopkirk leaned down again, and addressed the struggling serving woman. "You have been of use to me. Yes, to God, even. But your usefulness has passed. Go with the Lord, Margaret. We must be away."

"What?" she cried in total disbelief. "You would discard me now, when I have helped you this far?"

"Aye, that I would. We have the Lord's battle to fight to rid us of witchcraft. You are no longer part of that fight, Margaret. You have killed a man," he observed, without a trace of irony. "Now go and make your peace with the Lord." He nodded at the man holding Margaret, then turned the horse and headed through the gate, followed by all his company.

The man holding Margaret let her down, then quickly put his hands round her throat and squeezed hard, until she stopped struggling and her body went limp.

He let her body fall to the ground and hurried through the gate after his companions.

---0---

Sarah came awake with a start, nearly falling off her stool at the end of the gallery corridor. She knew that some sudden sound had caused her to wake up, but she wasn't sure if it was real or part of a dream. She thought it might have been the sound of pheasants whirring up from the trees, but she couldn't say for certain.

Anyway, it was no matter – she could only have been asleep for a few moments since Mary and Sir William had gone to their rooms after bidding her goodnight, and she had settled down at her guard post to keep watch for Hopkirk's potential attack.

She shifted to get more comfortable on her seat. It was a wobbly three-legged milking stool that she had pushed hard up against the wall to stop it falling over – which was useful as it meant she was hidden in the deepest shadow at the end of the corridor, just beside the main door through to the bedrooms.

She yawned and stared at the nearest portrait painting – of a stern-looking old lady in a fine green silk dress.

She looked idly down at her own dress – an old woollen one in a dull brown colour. She scratched her leg, wondering what it would be like to have a fine silk dress to wear that didn't itch so...

Suddenly she stopped. Was it not the middle of the night – only a few moments since she had started her guard duty? So how could she see the painting when the gallery should be in pitch darkness? How could she could make out the colours of the woman's dress in the picture and her own?

She looked to the window – and then under her breath she uttered a short, sharp curse.

The first glow of dawn had started to lift the total blackness of the night. There was no doubt – the sky was glowing orange when it should have been pitch black.

Which meant it was now the morning.

Which meant she had actually been asleep for many hours on her watch.

Sarah's hand went to her mouth as an awful thought hit her. What if Hopkirk and his men had crept past her while she slept and murdered the Master and Mary in their beds?

With a growing sense of dread she stood up, took a large black key from the pocket of her apron and unlocked the door to the bedrooms. The key turned sweetly and silently in the lock, thanks to the oil that Mistress Mary had insisted was poured into the old iron mechanism the night before.

With her heart pounding, Sarah crept as quietly as she could along the corridor to her mistress's room. Slowly she opened the door and looked in. The curtains were still drawn around the large four-poster bed, and if she stood very still and listened intently, she could just hear the gentle sound of her mistress's deep and regular breathing.

With a long sigh of relief she closed the bedroom door, then padded back along the corridor and slipped through the main door to resume her guard.

She sank gently down on the stool, taking comfort in a small prayer of thanks to Jesus for keeping guard over her mistress while she had been so wantonly asleep. The night-time silence of Grangedean Manor once again settled around her.

The image of her smiling mistress hovered in front of Sarah in the dim light.

Such a strange, but warm-hearted girl, this Mary Fox – appearing at the manor these two weeks hence and making such a mark that now she was all but the mistress of the house. So full of ideas – like the quiver of arrows to help the master come after her, or the disguise in the tavern. Could she truly be from times yet to come – times so distant that it was beyond the capability of a simple soul to understand? Sarah thought of the strange things that Mary had described to her mother and her, as they had all sat together in the gardens one evening. She recalled the images that Mary had conjured before them, to try and help them understand the things of the future world.

"Imagine a large covered cart made of iron, like a beetle's carapace, that can travel at twice the speed of a galloping horse, yet without a horse to pull it!"

"But why would you want that, Mistress?" Sarah had asked, confused.

"To get to somewhere else – somewhere you want to be."

"But I don't want to be anywhere else. I'm happy here."

Then there were the large flat black stones, shining and smooth like the surface of a still pond, yet which were hung upon a wall and lit up brightly with moving pictures of people in other places and at other times.

This idea had fascinated Sarah. "You would see on one of these stones what other people were doing? Belike you were spying on them?"

"I suppose so, yes. But most times they know they are being watched. Sometimes they might put on a play for you to see, or show you events that are happening in faraway lands."

"And you say that this is not done by magic?" Sarah's mother had asked suspiciously. "It is as a crystal ball that a mystic might use."

"Not at all," had been the reply. "They work because clever people have understood how to make them, and other people have assembled them using special machines." Mary had thought a moment, as if considering how best to explain. "You make bread, yes?"

"Yes," they answered.

"You know that if you grind the wheat into flour then add yeast and cook it in the oven, you get a loaf of bread?" They nodded. "Then turning wheat into bread is not magic?"

"No, that it is not," Sarah's mother replied.

"So the people who make the black stones know that if they take all the right pieces, and put them together in the right way, then the stones will show the pictures. That is not magic." Mary sat back, satisfied.

There was silence while the Tudor women digested this information.

"Ah," Sarah said, spotting the flaw in Mary's argument. "But if you can see what others are doing by staring into a flat stone, why do you need the covered carts? You can see other places without having to go to them."

"But what if you simply have to be somewhere else? Like if you're having a baby, or if you're sick? Then you need to go to a large building where sick people are healed by trained apothecaries."

"There are special buildings full of apothecaries to cure the sick?" Sarah's mother asked, intrigued.

"Yes, there are," Mary said with a smile.

"But not the common people? These buildings must be only for the nobility?"

"No – every man in the country, even ones with no money at all, can go there and the apothecaries will do all they can to cure him."

Sarah could not accept this. "But surely not a beggar?"

"Absolutely – every man can get help."

"But why would they do that?" Sarah exclaimed.

"Because we believe every man deserves help in their time of need…"

Sitting alone in the dark corridor with these memories, Sarah smiled to herself. 'Maybe Mary is just a great storyteller,' she thought. 'Although Mother seemed to accept that such strange future things could happen.' Mother had even said to Mary that she dearly wished she could see one of these black stones – which had made Mary smile in such a strange way…

A stair creaked.

Sarah froze.

With fear turning her stomach to ice and blood starting to pound in her ears, she forced herself to hold her breath and listen. Maybe she'd just imagined it…?

It creaked again.

This time there was no mistaking it, nor the muffled whisper of command that followed, nor the soft brushing sound of leather sword belts against woollen breeches.

These were the sounds of men entering the hallway and starting up the stairs.

Despite legs that felt as wobbly as a fruit pudding, Sarah stood up as quietly as she could and slipped back through the main door, quickly locking it behind her. She then ran along the corridor to Justine's room.

"Awake, Mistress! Now! Please!" she hissed in Justine's ear, as she shook the girl's arm through the sheets.

Justine grunted and turned over.

"Awake, Mistress! Oh, in the name of sweet Jesus, awaken!" urged Sarah, shaking harder.

Justine opened her eyes, unfocussed and vague in the dim light. She looked sleepily up at Sarah.

"They're here, Mistress!" hissed Sarah. "Oh my Lord, they're coming up the stairs!"

Now Justine was wide awake.

"They're here?" she squeaked.

"Yes, Mistress! You must hide now!"

Justine threw back her sheets and stood up. "We must get William!" she whispered.

Together they ran to the door and peered cautiously along the corridor, now bathed in an orange glow as bright beams of dawn light shone through the leaded squares of the window panes.

As they looked, the handle of the door at the far end started turning.

Justine gasped and was about to retreat back into the bedroom, when Sarah put a hand on her arm and shook her head, holding up the key to show she had locked the door. Justine smiled grimly and nodded, and together they ran out of the bedroom and along to William's rooms.

---0---

Justine opened the door carefully and peered round. At first she thought William had been abducted after a struggle – there were clothes strewn all about the room, armour pieces on the floor and papers fallen off the table. Then she remembered that this was just the usual mess. She signalled to Sarah and together they went to the door to the bedroom.

Justine carefully opened it and peered round.

The curtains around the magnificent ornate four-poster bed were pushed back and it was quite empty.

Justine ran to the bed in panic. Had Hopkirk somehow got in already and taken William?

"'Tis no matter," came William's voice.

Justine turned with a squeak of relief, to see him standing behind the door, already dressed and buckling on his sword. She threw her arms around him. "I thought they had taken you," she said, taking comfort from the feel of his hard chest on her cheek and his strong arms around her.

"I was awoken by the sound of someone putting up pheasants," he explained. "Then I heard you two running around, so I knew something was amiss." He unclasped Justine and looked down at her. "Are we under attack?"

"Yes, Master," said Sarah. "I heard them coming up the stairs so I locked the door. We must hide immediately!"

At that moment there was the unmistakable sound of an axe thudding into the door at the end of the corridor.

There was a brief moment as they all looked at each other in shock, then they turned as one and ran out of William's rooms. They emerged into the corridor just as another blow was heard and the silver head of an axe suddenly appeared next to the black iron lock.

William quickly put his hand to the intricately carved rose decoration on the wall. The low door to the secret passage swung open by their knees, revealing the dark dusty space within.

"In, Mary, now," he commanded.

For a split second Justine hesitated. The memory of the rat on her leg was all too clear, and she had no wish to renew its acquaintance – but then she saw the axe head disappear with a grinding sound from the protesting wood of the door as the man wielding it prepared to make another blow, and she popped down into the void like a rabbit down a hole, quickly followed by Sarah.

Justine stopped once they were far enough inside for William crawl in after them. But there was no sound of him coming in. She wriggled round and looked back out of the hole, then yelped in fear.

William's boots could be seen planted squarely, facing down the corridor. Then there was the sound of his sword being drawn.

"Oh, for goodness' sake!" she hissed as she poked her head back out. "Get in here, you silly man!" She reached up and grabbed his hand to pull him in.

"Nay!" he said, pulling his hand away, "I'll not hide like a coward when there's a fight to be had!"

"Get in here and don't play the hero!"

The axe came down again by the lock and the door start to bend inwards.

"Get in!" she yelled.

William hesitated only a second longer, then sheathed his sword, dropped to his knees and scrambled through the door. Justine leaned back and pulled it shut, just as another axe blow could be heard, followed by a crash as the door was thrown open.

The three of them froze as boots came running along the corridor, stopping right outside their hiding place.

Justine fought to control her breathing as a very familiar and most unpleasant voice spoke in a commanding tone on the other side of the wall. "You there, and you – search the bedrooms." Justine pictured Hopkirk in his grey cloak singling out the men for this task. "Make sure you search most thoroughly – leave no corner unchecked. Look in every chest, right to the bottom; under each bed, check even above the canopy of each one."

There were grunts of acknowledgement as the men split to search both rooms.

"You," Hopkirk must have indicated some further men, "guard the corridor. They may try to flee from the search. If so, take them as they come out." Justine heard the sound of boots moving back towards the door and swords being drawn.

There was a short silence, broken only by the sound of Hopkirk pacing up and down outside the hiding place. The three fugitives stayed as quiet and still as they could, scared to move a muscle in case it made a creaking sound to alert Hopkirk. They could hear the sound of his boots getting louder as he paced towards them, then fading as he paced away.

Then there was the sound of boots coming out of William's room.

"Nothing, Master Hopkirk. We have searched most thoroughly."

"He must be there. He must!" Hopkirk's voice was starting to sound pinched and high. "Go again and seek him out! I want him found!"

"Yes, Master Hopkirk," said the man, with a doubtful edge to his voice. The boots went back towards William's room and a door slammed.

A moment later more boots were heard, this time coming out of Justine's room.

"There's no sign of the witch, Master Hopkirk," said a voice, "for all we have looked in every place it is possible to hide a body."

"She's there! She's there!" Hopkirk was screaming now. "I know she's…"

Suddenly he stopped. There was a moment's silence, then he spoke more softly. "She's here, isn't she? She's right here. There's a priest's hole or suchlike – I knew it before…"

He started tapping the wall.

Tap tap tap. Tap tap tap.

Tap tap…

Thud.

There was no point worrying about making a noise now. "Quick!" Justine hissed. "Get to the door outside!"

The three of them scrambled onto their knees and started crawling quickly away from the entrance to the priest's hole. Sarah led the way, with William and Justine crawling behind.

Immediately Hopkirk heard them. "Quick!" he screamed. "Quick! They're in there!" There was a thumping sound as he frantically prodded and pushed at the carvings, and by luck he quickly hit on the correct piece. The door swung open and light flooded into the hiding place and along the passageway.

Hopkirk bent down and peered in triumphantly, just in time to see Justine crawling along the low passage, then standing as she reached the place where it opened up to full height.

"Get them!" she heard Hopkirk yell. "Get in there and get them!"

The man who was with him immediately dropped to his knees and shuffled into the hole.

"Men here, men here!" screamed Hopkirk, his voice rising almost to a falsetto. A man must have appeared from the bedroom. "In there!" Hopkirk shouted, pointing down at the hole. "They're in there! Get them!"

The man scuttled into the hole and started shuffling along behind his fellow.

Sarah, William and Justine ran along the passageway, then round the corner. Immediately the light from the open doorway was cut off, and they were back in pitch blackness.

Justine slowed down, feeling her way cautiously along the wall with one hand, and listening out for Sarah and William to start down the stairs ahead of her.

Then she heard footsteps closing up behind her.

Finding herself making small cries with each step, she tried to increase her pace – but the total darkness meant she couldn't go much faster for fear of falling.

The footsteps got closer.

Now she could hear heavy breathing as well.

She tried to run faster, but it was too late.

A hand suddenly clutched at her nightgown from behind, forcing her to a complete standstill.

"William!" she screamed, trying unsuccessfully to push the hand away. "They've got me!"

Another hand grabbed her around the waist and held her tight. She heard a throaty chuckle behind her shoulder. "Yes, we got you, witch!"

"William!" she screamed again, just as she felt the man release her nightdress and instead clamp his rough, calloused and foul-smelling hand over her mouth.

"Hold your tongue, witch!"

Then he started dragging her backwards; her bare heels trying to get grip on the rough wooden floorboards.

Justine did the only thing she could think of doing in the heat of the moment. Hoping desperately that she wouldn't catch something nasty, she bit down as hard as she could on the man's hand.

It was like biting on a rotten stick. There was a foul taste and she felt warm, metallic blood flood her into mouth, but she had the satisfaction of hearing the man yelp in pain and release her. She spat the disgusting substance out and started to run forward.

She didn't get very far – the man reached out and managed to grab her foot. She fell heavily with a shriek, just managing to put her hands out blindly in front of her at the last moment to break her fall.

Then she felt the man tighten his grip on her foot and start to drag her backwards. She heard his menacing voice from above her. "Best not to have done that, witch," he growled.

"William!" she shrieked again, as she scrabbled with her fingernails to find some purchase on the floorboards.

Then she heard William's voice. "Here, my love," he said quietly. "Stay low."

There was a whooshing, swishing sound above her, followed by a grunt from the man. Then her leg was released and she heard him make a long drawn-out groan. A moment later, she screamed as she felt his body – presumably now dead – flop down hard across her back and pin her to the floor.

"Get him off me!" she yelled in uncontrollable panic, trying to crawl forward but unable to move from the dead-weight on her back. "Get him off!"

"Hold still," came William's voice, and she felt the man being rolled slowly off her.

"Oh God, William!" she exclaimed "Is he dead?"

"I truly hope so." He grabbed her hand and helped her stand up. For a moment he paused, listening. Footsteps could be heard coming fast down the passageway.

"Come," he said, "let us get out of this place before his companions arrive to finish his task." He quickly pulled her away from the body and they started running forwards. "With luck he will cause them to trip and fall in the dark," William said.

Almost immediately they heard steps coming round the corner, then a shout of surprise, and a loud thud as a man hit the floor hard. William chuckled. "As good as a trip wire," he observed.

They ran a few more yards, then William spoke again. "Here are the stairs," he said.

Together they clattered down, then out through the secret door into the shadowy corridor leading out into the courtyard.

William pulled the door closed behind them, hearing the lock click shut. Almost immediately the faint sound of a man hammering on the other side of the door could be heard.

William smiled at Justine. "Are you well?" he asked.

"Oh God, William!" she looked at him wide-eyed. "I bit him! I bit the man and tasted blood!"

"Aye – you do have some blood on your chin. Here…" He took a handkerchief from his sleeve and carefully wiped it away.

The banging on the door behind them got louder.

"Come, my love," he said, "we must run for the cottage before they discover the way to open to door."

They ran together across the courtyard, making for the wooden gate out into the rose garden. William reached it a pace or so ahead of Justine, threw it open and ran through.

They ran across to the rose-covered pergola, then through the gate into the herb garden. The wooden gate out to the country lane was just ahead, promising escape and freedom.

Triumphantly, William threw open the gate and ran through.

Straight into the arms of two of Hopkirk's men.

---0---

As he struggled to free himself from their grip, William saw Justine run past him. Before he could shout a warning, another man appeared and grabbed her from behind, holding her tight around the arms.

A third man appeared from behind an ornamental bush. He pulled Sarah out from behind it with a look of triumph, then started tying her wrists behind her back.

"Let me go, you impudent fool!" shouted William, struggling to free himself from the men holding him. The men said nothing, and William could feel his wrists being bound behind his back; the ropes cutting deep into his skin. "Do you dare bind me?" he yelled. "Do you not know who I am?"

At that moment Hopkirk himself slid into his line of sight with a thin triumphant smile that did not reach his unblinking grey eyes.

"Aye, we know exactly who you are, Sir William," he said. "A man accused of harbouring a known witch and suspected of witchcraft himself on firm grounds. A man shortly to be tested alongside her, and this serving girl, for magical powers." He sniffed. "A man to be tested by ducking in the deep water of his own well to see if he has the magic to save himself." Hopkirk gave a small, hollow laugh. "We have no need of a barrel this time, de Beauvais." Then he turned and walked slowly up to Justine.

He studied her closely a moment, his grey eyes boring into hers. Then, as she watched in terrified silence, he reached up and touched her hair. William could do nothing to stop this sickening act; he could see that Justine was fighting the urge to scream, as Hopkirk's cold, reptilian hand rasped down her ringlets. Despite herself, she let out a small gasp of revulsion as his hand touched her cheek, then started moving slowly down towards her neck. "Nay," he said. "Do not flinch from me, my pretty. You are being touched by the hand of God this day and I will see his work done through to its conclusion." He stared deeper into her eyes. "Such a sweet face, but I see the mark of evil, as clear as a bolt of lightning crosses the night sky."

He let his hand drop and turned back to William, his voice taking on a more business-like tone. "Such a fortunate chance that I had men stationed at all the side gates for just this opportunity," he said. "Although I do believe that the lawyer Wychwoode had himself put a man here to stop me." He glanced over to a bush where a pair of feet in rough leather boots could be seen protruding. "'Tis a pity he did not choose one with the capacity to fight, though." William glanced down at the feet and with some difficulty, managed to hold his tongue.

"And where is this precious Master Wychwoode, I wonder?" continued Hopkirk. "Busy waiting to ambush us on the far side of the park, I'll warrant." He laughed. "Aye, a fool's errand. But he and his men are too great a distance away to hear us, and nor will they ever come to your rescue. I have detailed a handpicked group of my best fighting men to march out and engage them directly. I'll warrant we will outnumber them considerably – so you can expect no help from that quarter." He paused. "Nor from your mother, in case you were wondering. She is even now being guarded in her rooms by a couple of my ablest men – and as she is a lady of such fine standing, I have told them to be on their best behaviour at all times. Of course," he continued with a sickeningly innocent expression, "I cannot guarantee they will obey me in this. Your mother is still a magnificent woman for her age…"

William struggled against the ropes binding his wrists and fixed Hopkirk with a burning stare of hatred. "I'll see you in chains for this, Hopkirk!" he snarled.

"Nay," said Hopkirk. "You no longer have any chance to make good on that threat. For all you tried to evade me, my plans have run exactly as I expected. I wasn't sure of which direction you would come, but I was sure you and your companions would be flushed out somehow. Indeed, it was just like picking fish from a barrel!" He gave a dry chuckle. "My apologies, Sir William. There – I have once again talked of a barrel! I know you are not greatly enamoured of these. Just my little jest."

Hopkirk turned and looked in satisfaction at the two girls; Sarah standing with her hands tied behind her back and Justine grimacing as one of his men tied her hands also. He turned back to William.

"So now I have you. I have the witch and I have a serving girl as well. What a perfect start to a summer's day." He turned to the men holding the captives.

"Take them to the well."

---0---

Martha turned over on her pallet bed in the dormitory room above the courtyard that she shared with the cook, Margaret and a few other servants.

She settled on her back, folding her arms under her head, and looked up at the rough wooden roof beams rising up to a sharp point high above, festooned with cobwebs. The dawn sun was streaming in through the single open window, throwing deep shadows behind the beams. Martha sought out one particular shadow – her 'morning sundial'. It had nearly reached a particular broken slat in the roof that would mean it was an hour after dawn; time to arise and begin the day's labours.

Another day under the cruel regime of the witch! How was this to be borne by anyone of goodness and purity?

Martha offered up her regular morning prayer. 'Sweet Jesus, you who are forgiving, kind and gentle, make this the day that the evil witch vanishes from my life; make her go away, or better still, gentle Jesus, make her meet a truly unpleasant death. Please, Jesus, as you love me, make it happen. This very day. Amen.'

She rolled out of bed and stood up, yawning and stretching her arms.

Just then she became aware of a commotion in the well yard outside the window – some shouts and cheers, with the words "Witch! Witch!" coming through. With sudden hope rising, she ran over to the window and peered out to see what events were taking place in the yard below.

Hopkirk (she recognised the top of his hat) was leading three bound prisoners towards the well; one was Sarah, one was the master, and – oh glory to God! – the third was the witch herself! Bareheaded and in her night gown, there she was, being led towards the well!

Jesus had heard her prayer! Truly, he had heard her!

With an excited squeak, Martha leapt back from the window and ran to the cook's bed. She shook the sleeping woman's shoulder.

"Awake, now – they are about to try the witch at the well!"

The cook stirred sleepily and gazed bleary-eyed at the housekeeper.

"What is to do?" she asked, her voice still thick with sleep.

"Hopkirk is here! He has the witch and the master and Sarah. He has them by the well! My prayers are answered! He is to try them for witchcraft!"

The cook sat up, now wide awake. "Hopkirk is here to try the witch? You are sure?"

"I'm sure!" Martha grabbed her dress and threw it over her head, sliding her feet into her shoes. "Come – we must go down there now!"

The cook heaved her bulk off her bed and started to dress also. Martha, meanwhile, was running round waking the others. She stopped a moment by the one empty bed and smiled – it looked like Margaret must have been successful in getting Hopkirk into the manor. With luck they'd shortly have her back with them – particularly now that it looked like the witch's time at Grangedean was coming to an end and everything would be back to blessed normality.

Soon everyone was up and dressed. Martha led them down the narrow wooden stairs at a run, almost tripping and falling at one point in her haste to get down.

Emerging into the yard, she ran across to the crowd that was now starting to gather around the well. She recognised several of Hopkirk's original followers from the search of the manor two weeks before, some of whom had again brought their pitchforks. Agnes and Ruth were there, giggling excitedly. Martha supposed Hopkirk had sent word to the village that the witch was found, and they had all come up to see her tried. Jake had even brought a cart with some casks of ale up from the tavern, which he was selling to the thirsty crowd at a farthing a pint.

Martha elbowed her way through to the front of the crowd to get a better view.

As she emerged she saw Hopkirk standing on the raised dais in front of the well talking to one of his men. Next to him, in the shadow of the large tiled roof above the well, were standing the master, the witch and Sarah the serving girl, each with ropes binding their wrists and the ends tied to one of the roof posts.

Martha looked at the witch. The girl was still in her nightdress and Martha thought she must be freezing. If so, she gave no sign of it. Martha tried to catch her eye, but the girl steadfastly refused to look at the people in front of her. In fact, Martha thought she was searching the faces in the crowd, trying perhaps to see if a particular person was there? Maybe she was expecting someone to rescue her? Martha sniffed. That was definitely not going to happen – particularly after the Lord Jesus has so clearly answered her prayer.

"Mary Fox!" Martha called out to get the witch's attention above the noise of the crowd.

Slowly the girl lowered her gaze and met Martha's eye.

"I told you this would come to pass, did I not?" Martha shouted. "I said that Master Hopkirk would come for you and would try you by ducking at the well! Did I not tell you?"

The girl remained impassive.

"And what is more I prayed to Lord Jesus for this to happen, and he has heard my call! Truly he has forsaken you!"

At this, the girl smiled and slowly shook her head.

"Nay, you cannot deny me this," Martha responded. "You are forsaken and will burn in Hell!"

Sir William shot an angry look across at Martha. "Hold your peace, woman!" he shouted. "This is as much your doing as anybody's. As soon as I am able, I will have you turned out of my house!"

"You will be in no position to do that, Sir William," responded Martha triumphantly. "Soon you will no longer be the master of this house – you will be a witch condemned to burn or you will have perished by drowning in the well."

William shook his head sorrowfully. "What have I done to make you hate me so, Martha?" he asked.

"There was a time when I would have done all for you, Master," she answered. She stepped up to the dais next to him, and her voice became warmer, more reflective. "A time when you took me to your bed and made my heart feel so alive. Then this witch came and enchanted you and took you from me."

"Martha," he said. "Are you deluded? You must know your station. I would never take you to wife."

"Yet you took her," Martha pointed at Justine, "a mere scullion girl! You must have been enchanted to take her and not me!" Her voice rose. "You knew happiness with me in your bed, yet she took you by magic!"

"Martha, for the love of Christ, hold your tongue!" snapped William. "I am sorry if you thought I might have cared for you, but…"

At that moment he was interrupted by loud shouting from the other side of the yard. As one, the crowd turned to look. There were gasps and growls as they saw three men with drawn swords running into the yard, howling like wolves and making straight for the well. They were being pursued by two of Hopkirk's men, also with swords out.

---0---

Justine strained over the heads of the crowd to see who these men were, as Martha ran back into the crowd and started elbowing her way towards the action.

Justine heard William groan, just as she also recognised the bright silk doublets of Dowland and Stanmore and the more sober clothing of Melrose. They were running for the well, appearing intent on fighting their way through and rescuing the accused captives.

As they approached the well, three more of Hopkirk's men emerged from the crowd, drew their own swords and started running to meet them. Within seconds, Justine could see that the would-be rescuers were completely surrounded. Clattering to a stop, they quickly arranged themselves defensively back to back, each with their sword facing out towards the ring of armed men now encircling them.

"The damned fools," muttered William. "They have not even had time to put on armour. What did they mean to accomplish by getting themselves killed or taken?"

"They are brave – and loyal," said Justine, then added under her breath, "Athos, Porthos and Aramis – to the life."

"Eh?" asked William.

"Nothing, my lord."

She saw Hopkirk push past and march out towards the unfolding drama on the edge of the crowd.

"Well met, good sirs," he announced in a brusque tone, as he elbowed his way into the circle of swordsmen and faced William's three friends. "What mean you to achieve here?"

Melrose looked at the magistrate with what Justine thought was a very determined expression on his thin face.

"You have trespassed on Sir William's land and have unlawfully restrained his person and two of his household," he said defiantly, jabbing the tip of his sword towards Hopkirk to emphasise the point. "We would free them and restore the natural order."

The men either side of Hopkirk stepped forward half a pace, raising their swords towards Melrose's neck.

"Then you and I share the same sentiment," observed Hopkirk silkily, waving his men back to their places.

"How so?" Melrose asked dubiously.

"I would free them also," said Hopkirk levelly, "but only if they be not witches."

"Which you will test by drowning them in yonder well?" This was Stanmore, looking briefly over his shoulder, giving the man opposite him the chance to step in closer.

"That is the correct way of these things."

"Thereby rendering them quite – dead," snapped Stanmore, forcing Hopkirk's man back with a few warning sweeps of his blade.

"Unless they are indeed possessed of magic," said Hopkirk.

"In which case you will burn them at the stake, you piece of carrion!" shouted Dowland.

"Tsk tsk," admonished Hopkirk. "Their immortal souls must be freed of the Devil." Hopkirk waved his men forward one step, closing the ring tighter.

"So," said Melrose, raising his sword so it was almost touching the sword of the man opposite, "they die in either case."

"Indeed they do." Hopkirk shook his head regretfully. "Such is the way of these things."

"Then we will not allow it," said Melrose defiantly. "While we have breath in our bodies and swords in our hands…"

"Fie!" cut in Hopkirk suddenly "You waste my time!" He stepped out of the ring and marched back to the well.

"You have loyal friends," he snapped to William and Justine as he stepped up onto the dais beside them. "But their loyalty is misplaced."

"They have right on their side," answered William. "God will guide their hands."

"No!" shouted Hopkirk, turning and facing William, and now Justine could see the mask of civility stripped away to expose the zealotry that drove him. "It is I! It is I who has God on my side! It is I who fights for truth, for purity and justice – a fight you could not hope to understand! I am the one whom God favours, not you, nor her, or her!" he pointed at Justine and Sarah. "And certainly not them!" he shouted, pointing at Melrose, Dowland and Stanmore.

"In the name of God!" he screamed at his men. "End this nonsense!"

As the crowd yelled and whooped, his swordsmen moved in and started to engage with the three would-be rescuers.

Justine held her breath as she watched the fight over the heads of the crowd, seeing it quickly develop into a desperate melee with Dowland, Stanmore and Melrose circling back to back as the attackers came in and pressed them hard with their relentless swords.

She could see Stanmore's blond head above the fray; a look of grim determination on his face as he fought desperately against repeated attacks.

"Come on, Stanmore!" she yelled, forgetting her own predicament for just a moment. "Oh, do come on!"

She watched as he parried sweeps from two attackers, before turning a third on his hilt. Then he stepped to one side and let the man's own momentum carry him past, giving him the space to pull back his sword and thrust it deep into the man's side. The man went down like a sack of corn. William yelled "Huzzah! Well done, Richard!"

"Silence, imbecile!" snarled Hopkirk over his shoulder. Justine noticed he was gripping the upright well post with knuckles that were bloodless white.

As Stanmore turned to face his next attacker, Dowland was locked in fierce hand-to-hand combat with another. It was clear to Justine, even with her experience of sword fighting limited to cautious re-enactments, that he was coming off worse in the encounter. The attacker was pressing him hard with a sword that moved almost too fast for the eye to follow, driving him back towards the edge of the crowd with fierce cuts across the chest, great lunges towards the head and wide sweeps across the legs. It was all Dowland could do to defend himself against such a fierce onslaught – let alone make any attacking move of his own.

Then Justine saw his attacker make a feint with his sword to the left, which Dowland swung to his right to parry – leaving his chest wide open. Justine screamed as, with a vicious smile, the attacker lunged forward and buried his sword in up to the hilt.

Dowland dropped to his knees, then his head fell forward and he slid from view.

At this there was an agonised roar from William. "Oh my God, Oliver! No!" He rounded on Hopkirk like a wounded lion. "By all the Heavens, Hopkirk, I'll see you pay for that!"

"Strong words, de Beauvais," snapped Hopkirk, "for a man in your position."

Justine could see William struggling against the ropes that bound him, his face red and his eyes fixed on Hopkirk's neck.

A sudden roar from the crowd brought their attention back to the fight.

They saw that Stanmore was now standing still, face to face with one of Hopkirk's men. The two of them were staring deep into each other's eyes, almost as if they were lovers. Justine bit her lip, uncertain as to whether they had just locked swords or one had run the other through; hoping against hope that it was not Stanmore who had taken a mortal hit. The two men stared at each other a moment longer, then, to Justine's horror, Stanmore gave a little cough and a trickle of blood appeared at the side of his mouth. Like Dowland before him, he too dropped slowly out of sight.

William's head fell forward with a deep groan of despair and Justine saw his shoulders shaking as he tried to control the great sobs that racked his body.

"Courage, William," she said, as much to reassure herself as him. "It's not over yet."

"Richard and Oliver, both dead in my cause," he muttered bleakly. "I am truly cursed."

Then Justine became aware once more of the sound of clashing blade on blade and the roar of the crowd, and she looked back at the fight.

"Not totally, my lord," she said. "It looks like Thomas Melrose is holding his own."

"Thomas?" William's head came up in surprise.

Looking across the crowd, Justine saw the most magnificent sight.

Melrose was not only holding his own against the four remaining men, he was dominating them. His blade was moving lightning fast, with practiced sweeps, cuts and parries against those who came at him from all sides – he was keeping them away from his front, turning and protecting his back, and when openings occurred, he was exploiting them ruthlessly.

"Belike Oliver and Richard will be avenged," William said, "Tom will send them all to hell." Justine noticed just a tinge of pride in his voice. "I taught him well, eh?"

But Justine was remembering the promise that William had made the day before to return Melrose's lands – and she thought that perhaps this was what was also spurring Melrose on to ever greater feats of swordsmanship.

And there was no doubt he was fighting like a man possessed.

As Justine and William watched, one of the attackers left his chest unguarded and Melrose unerringly picked his spot at the point where the man's breastplate was buckled, thrusting his sword deep into the chink. Turning and withdrawing his blade as his opponent went down, Melrose parried a sweep from behind him, turned this man's sword on his hilt and pushed it away to expose the man's neck. Justine quickly screwed up her eyes in horror, as Melrose flicked the tip of his sword down. When Justine opened her eyes again, the man was clutching at his blood-covered neck, his eyes wide in shock, before he fell forward out of her sight.

"Oh golly, William, I feel so sick," she muttered.

"Be brave, my love," said William. "Thomas has fight enough for us all just now."

"I can't watch," she said. "They'll kill him like the others." She turned away. "Then they'll kill us."

"Nay," he said, with the smallest note of triumph in his voice.

Justine heard the crowd give a sudden gasp, then a deep roar of appreciation, followed by booing and hissing. It reminded her of a pantomime crowd.

If only this was just a pantomime...

"Thomas has felled one more man!" yelled William, breaking into her thoughts. "And the other has slunk away like a miserable cur. He has triumphed!" William stamped his boot. "God speed, good Thomas! He has run to get help!"

Hopkirk stepped across and slapped William across the face with his open palm. "Be quiet, dolt! Your foolhardy friend may have escaped but there is no help for miles."

Justine looked across at the six bodies lying dead on the cobbled stones of the yard. Most were dressed in the drab woollen uniform of Hopkirk's militia; but two were clearly distinguished by their brightly coloured silk doublets, expensive ruffs and fine boots.

"And your other two friends will be of no help to you now."

---0---

William rubbed his jaw where Hopkirk had hit it, but even Melrose's triumph could not mask the pain he felt at the sight of his friends lying dead, their foolhardy bravery come to naught.

No more would he hear Oliver Dowland's drunken boasts of the magnificent chest size of his latest conquest, or witness Richard Stanmore's unerring ability to locate a hidden stag as if by smell alone. William could see them now, sitting across the table with goblets of wine, Oliver in full flow on the latest girl he'd found, while William and Richard laughed so hard at his use of his hands to describe her assets that they would nearly choke on their wine; or out on the hunt with Richard pointing at a patch of forest and swearing blind there was a stag in there – and his quiet satisfaction when proved right.

William looked back at the grey man standing next to him. "My good friends Richard Stanmore and Oliver Dowland fought this day with great courage and honour," he said firmly. "Each one of them had more goodness in the smallest part of their smallest finger, than you will ever have in your heart, Master Hopkirk." He took a deep breath. "But what is done is done. If you must have this travesty of a trial, then let us begin."

---0---

Hopkirk stood squarely on the dais and looked down at the sea of faces around him. Despite William's resigned agreement to start, he did not want to begin until the crowd was sufficiently fired up to become the single-minded mob that he needed to drive his trial to a satisfactory conclusion. His life's mission – to seek out and destroy witchcraft wherever it lurked – always required the support of a mob; to make sure that the fear of witchcraft was kept alive at all times, but also to ensure that more witches could be identified later by individual members of the crowd who had been present.

So he waited, letting the momentum build after the excitement of the sword fight.

"Witches! Evil witches!" called out a voice at the front.

"Burn them!" came another voice in response.

"Worshipers of Satan!" came a third.

This was picked up by more voices; more angry shouts and cheers of support.

Hopkirk spread his hands out wide in front of his body, his open palms facing the mob. This generated even more shouts and louder roars – but now they became incoherent, with no single words being clearly heard.

He crossed his fists up high in the sign against witchcraft and the mob went wild – screaming, waving their arms and pitchforks.

He uncrossed his hands and punched the air: the mob gave a mighty, tumultuous roar that could have been heard in the next county – a roar of hatred born of fear coming from hundreds of throats but from a single collective mind.

Hopkirk punched the air twice more, each time producing the same momentous roar, before he decided the mob was ready. He made a sweeping motion with a flat palm and in response, the crowd fell silent.

Every eye was on him. Every man, woman and child, waiting expectantly for the show to begin.

"Good people!" he began. The mob roared its appreciation. He let them shout a moment, then held his hand up for silence.

"Good people – you who worship the Lord Jesus, and who fear God – we are here today to seek God's truth about these three." He waved at William, Justine and Sarah. Again the mob roared, and again he let them a moment, then held his hand up and waited for silence.

"These three are accused of witchcraft and we must test them to see if they have the magic powers! The powers of Satan himself!"

These words worked the mob into its loudest screaming frenzy yet. When silence was eventually restored, Hopkirk continued.

"We will tie each one by the feet and hands and lower them into this well, until they are fully under the waters. If..." he paused for emphasis, "if they have the magic to save themselves, then we will know them truly for a servant of Satan! And what does the Lord Jesus want us to do with the servants of Satan – his bitterest enemy?"

"Burn them! Burn them!" responded the mob.

"Aye, we will burn them! We will banish the Devil with fire!"

Hopkirk turned to some of his men standing nearby and pointed at Justine. "She will go first. Prepare her for the trial!"

---0---

Justine tried hard not to shout out in fear and pain as the men tied ropes around her, binding her arms close to her chest, then secured the free end of the rope that usually held the bucket onto them. Then they tied her feet together with another length of rope, before lifting her up and carrying her over the lip of the well – so she was hanging just above the edge of the well, swaying over the waters far below.

The rope supporting her went up to the capstan in the roof which was attached to a pulley that could be turned by a handle at the side of the well. Justine looked up; there was many yards of rope wound around the capstan – plenty to drop her all the distance down the deep well. It was held by a pin that stopped the pulley wheel from turning.

She looked down at her feet swinging over the black void and tried to fight down the terror of the cold dark waters waiting for her down below.

She heard William's voice from over her shoulder.

"Courage, my love – we will meet again this day in heaven and have all of eternity together."

"I'm not ready for that just yet, William," she muttered, but was not sure if he heard her.

Hopkirk leaned down and picked up a stone from the cobbles, then he held it by Justine.

"Let us see how far down to lower you," he said quietly to her, and let go of the stone.

There was an agonising few seconds as it fell, then they both heard it splash into the dark waters far below.

"Quite a fair way down, my pretty one," he said with a sickening smile, "before the waters test your purity. We will make sure you have sufficient time down there for the test to be most effective."

He stood back and addressed the crowd.

"This woman has blasphemed the Lord, has dressed as a boy in order to confuse, and has caused alarm and fear amongst good, honest God-fearing folk. We will test her now…" he paused and turned to Justine, "unless…" he said quietly.

"Unless what?" asked Justine querulously.

Hopkirk smiled. "Unless you are prepared to confess your witchcraft, and that you worship the Devil."

"What then?" Justine asked, although she knew exactly what his answer would be.

"You will be burned at the stake as a witch."

"As I thought. Well, you know what, Master Matthew Hopkirk," she said, with much more strength than she really felt, "I wouldn't give you the satisfaction."

"Aye, well – I thought not," Hopkirk sighed. Then he turned back to the mob.

"She will not confess! Then let the trial begin!" As the crowd roared, he gestured to a man standing by the handle. "Let her go!"

The man knocked the pin out of the pulley wheel.

Justine screamed, "No, wait!" But it was too late. She felt a sickening lurch in her stomach as the capstan started to spin and she dropped just like Hopkirk's stone, plummeting towards the deathly dark waters below.

With her screams echoing off the black slime-covered walls and the circle of light above her shrinking quickly to a small disc, she fell so fast that she hardly had time to prepare herself. The water came up and hit her with an almighty splash, punching her in the soles of her feet, then knocking the air from her lungs. Immediately, the weight of the ropes pulled her down and the freezing black waters closed over her head.

She felt the water trying to force its way into her nose and mouth and found herself grunting in the back of her throat as she flopped and writhed on the end of the rope like a fish on a line, her chest starting to burn and stars starting to dance in front of her eyes, as the effort to hold her breath became harder and harder, but still she hung on, her grunts ringing louder and louder in her ears until she started to think there really was no hope and maybe she should just let the water in and end it all, and surely it wasn't death that was scary – but rather it was the process of dying that petrified her – and anyway, she'd been dead for all eternity before she had been born, so how hard could it be to do it again – except that she hadn't been dead for all eternity before her birth, she had been alive 450 years before, for two glorious, exciting, momentous weeks, and she'd met William and could have been the next Lady de Beauvais, if only she didn't have to die, if only, if only – oh, sod it, sod it, sod it, sod it, just open your mouth, and end it now, girl...

There was a sudden tug on the rope.

Then another. And a third.

Then the rope started moving jerkily upwards, and then, wonderfully, her head broke clear into the air – the beautiful, glorious, life-giving air that Justine sucked in by the lungful as she found herself being winched slowly up the well, gasping, coughing, retching...

And alive.

She looked above her. The circle of light was becoming larger and larger as she was winched slowly and jerkily up the well shaft, until the light was strong enough to make out the green glistening slime-covered bricks lining the top of the well. Finally she had to screw up her eyes against the bright sunlight as her head emerged over the edge.

Into a scene of stunned silence.

Hopkirk was staring at Justine with a look on his face that she could only interpret as total shock.

William was staring at her open-mouthed, while Sarah looked at her pale and wide-eyed.

Even the man operating the pulley wheel was paper-white as he made the last few turns, then replaced the pin and reached over to pull her back over the side.

It took some time to get the sodden ropes undone, but eventually Justine was standing free by the side of the well, shivering in her soaked nightdress.

"By the Risen Christ, man!" barked William at Hopkirk, as he and Sarah were being untied. "Do you not see how she shivers?"

Hopkirk tore his gaze from Justine and turned slowly to William, as if seeing him for the first time. "Eh?" he muttered.

"She is cold!" said William. "And she is – wet." He indicated her chest. Justine looked down and realised in shock that her soaked nightdress was virtually transparent.

"Aye, aye... indeed," said Hopkirk vaguely. It was clear he had not registered Justine's condition at all. He looked to the silent crowd. "Someone – a cloak or... somesuch." A woollen cloak was found and passed up to Hopkirk, who carefully wrapped it round Justine's shoulders. She pulled it tight to re-establish her modesty – as if her heaving chest had not just been on show to the whole crowd.

She turned to William. "Thank you," she said quietly.

"'Tis no matter." He was equally quiet.

"William," she asked, "what has happened? I nearly drowned down there."

"My love – it was without doubt the strangest thing I – or I believe any man – has ever witnessed. As you descended, a voice was heard.

"A voice?"

"Aye. It was as loud and as clear as the voice of the finest orator – but no man could be seen speaking." He studied her closely, then he whispered, "My sweet Mary, it was the voice of our true Lord Jesus Christ."

"Christ?" She was suitably shocked.

"Aye. Christ himself."

"What did he say?"

"He said – and I'll remember these words till the day I die – he said, "Matthew Hopkirk – I am the Lord Jesus Christ and I say before these people that you do not act in my name. Mary Fox is my loyal handmaiden – she is not now, nor has she ever been, a witch. Matthew Hopkirk, you are a servant of Satan and I call upon you in the name of God my Father, to end this trial now."

"He said all that?"

"Those very words, in front of me, Hopkirk and this whole crowd."

Justine smiled. "That was nice of him."

They became aware that Hopkirk had started to address the people gathered round the well. "The trial is over," he said. "We have heard from the Lord Jesus himself that there is no witchcraft here. Go to your homes, go to your church, and worship him who has spoken to us this day."

But the crowd did not move. Instead Justine could hear some angry murmurings starting amongst them.

"Go now!" commanded Hopkirk. "The trial is over."

The murmurings swelled and became louder. Angry exchanges were starting within the crowd. Justine watched as the anger built amongst them and within them, growing and building, feeding on itself as more and more heated exchanges took place. All it needed was a spark and the crowd would once again turn ugly.

It was Hopkirk himself who provided that spark.

He raised his hand to try and silence the crowd, just as he had before Justine had gone down the well. But the power he had wielded earlier was gone – stripped away by a divine accusation of Satanism – and instead of placating and silencing the crowd, it reminded them of the hold he'd had over them.

And they didn't like it.

"You are a worshipper of Satan!" shouted a voice.

"We thought you were a man of God!" said another. "You had us for fools!"

"You would lead us on the path to Hell!" said another.

Hopkirk tried again. "Good people…" he began.

"We'll not be called good by you!" shouted a further voice, which was followed by a cheer from the crowd.

Once again they were starting to become a single-minded mob – but not one that Hopkirk could control.

And as a single-minded mob, they surged forward towards the dais.

"Stop them!" screamed Hopkirk to those of his men who were nearby. But they, too had heard the voice – and they too held their positions.

The crowd surged further forward and several sturdy-looking peasants ran up onto the dais with their pitchforks held forward as weapons. Hopkirk was pushed quickly backwards against the side of the well.

Justine, William and Sarah stood to one side, watching. "I fear Master Hopkirk now knows what it is to be the accused," observed William with a smile.

"Aye, Master," said Sarah. "But why do they not skewer him now? He is in their power."

"Belike they will shortly," said William. "Have patience."

They saw Hopkirk retreating from the pitchforks as far as he could, then it looked as if he was going to try to get in a position to address the crowd again. Keeping a close eye on the pitchforks, he reached up with one hand and grasped the roof post of the well, then used it to pull himself up, until he was standing on the edge of the well itself with his back supported by the roof. The pitchforks were raised up accordingly, to keep him under threat.

"My people…!" he began.

At that moment a loud, piercing scream came from within the crowd.

It was a long, drawn-out scream of pain, rage and anguish, and it made Justine shiver despite the cloak drawn around her shoulders.

Hopkirk stared into the crowd from his vantage position up on the well, and his face paled as he watched.

The screaming continued, and it was getting closer.

Justine saw the crowd turn to look at the screaming person, then part like the Red Sea before Moses to let them through.

A small hooded figure emerged out of the crowd.

She thought it was incredible that such a small person could make such a noise, but there was no doubt where it was coming from.

Then the screaming stopped. The figure stepped up onto the dais, pushing pitchforks aside to get to where Hopkirk was perching on the side of the well. The figure stood in front of him a moment, looking up, before pushing back the hood to reveal itself.

It was Margaret.

Hopkirk went even whiter than before.

"You would have killed me, Master Hopkirk!" she said, her voice carrying clearly across the silent crowd, "when I had done all for you."

"Margaret!" Hopkirk managed a watery smile, blinking furiously. "How good it is to see you well!"

"Aye, and no thanks to you – it is thanks to Lady Alice who found me on the road and gave me care and water after I had all but died at the hands of your man."

"Lady Alice – indeed – how wonderful…"

"And now we have heard the word of God himself, that tells us that you follow Satan!" Margaret reached across to the villager next to her, snatched the pitchfork out of his hand and brandished it at Hopkirk.

"So Matthew Hopkirk, I would you join your master!"

She thrust the pitchfork violently forward. It caught Hopkirk squarely in the stomach, forcing him to double up and his head to drop down below the edge of the well roof, so that he had nothing now to support him.

He lost his balance.

For a moment he scrabbled at the roof of the well above him, but he could not get a grip and with a despairing yell, he dropped backwards like a felled tree.

His head hit the far wall with a sickening crack that drew a collective gasp from the nearest villagers, before he slid down into the hungry black mouth of the well.

For a split second he appeared to be suspended there, then, with a swirling of his grey cloak, he disappeared from view.

The crowd held its collective breath as the body plummeted down the long well shaft, thumping and bouncing off the walls.

Then a loud splash echoed up from the depths.

Shocked, no one made a sound.

Then a lone voice shouted out, "Hopkirk is dead! The servant of Satan is gone to meet his master!"

Another voice responded "Yes! Christ has saved us!"

"The Lord has blessed us!"

"Now we are freed from Satan's grasp!"

Then a cheer went up, and soon everyone was shouting, throwing their hats and pitchforks in the air and shaking their fists. There was much congratulating and clapping of backs, as well as some dancing round in jubilation. Many villagers ran over to Jake's cart and started filling their tankards with celebratory pints of ale.

William turned to Justine and Sarah and shouted, "This is a most welcome outcome! We are well rid of that monster!"

"Indeed, my lord," yelled Sarah, "he has truly gone to meet his master!"

"I warrant Satan will welcome him with open arms, even while devising some eternal torture," yelled William.

"Yes, Sir William, I warrant he will!"

"Christ has forsaken him – and this we have heard in his own voice!" William shook his head in wonder. "That I have lived to see this day – that is the true miracle." He looked at Justine. "What say you, Mary, my love?"

But Justine was not listening to him, instead she was staring across to the far edge of the crowd.

Sarah's mother – whose name she now knew was Ruth – was standing apart from the rest of the villagers and was studying something in her hand that looked like a small, rectangular black stone. As Justine watched, Ruth dropped the object into her apron pocket.

Justine smiled to herself.

The plan she had devised to humiliate Hopkirk had worked out spectacularly in the end, even if not exactly in the way she had envisaged.

The plan had required some preparation, as well as the phone, speaker and solar charger she had kept securely hidden in her bag. It had also taken all her powers of persuasion on her secret accomplice – Ruth.

They had met the evening before in a quiet corner of the rose garden. Justine had shown Ruth the phone and Bluetooth speaker, both on full power thanks to the solar charger, and had explained her plan.

At first it seemed that for all her earlier interest in seeing a 'black stone' – and her general open-mindedness – Ruth was still very much a woman of the 16th century.

"This thing, that you call a 'phone' – you are telling me it is not magic?" Ruth had asked dubiously, as she turned it over and over in her hand.

"No," said Justine. "Because it can only do what it has been made to do, and it only responds to set commands. Many hundreds and hundreds of these phones are made every year in my time, and each one is the same – each one does exactly the same thing if you give it the same command. That is no different to the bread that rises if it is made and baked correctly, or the gown that looks the same as another gown, if you cut it to the same pattern and sew it the same way. As I said before, these things are not magic."

"And you want me to command this stone to speak in the voice of the Lord?" Ruth looked up at her with worry written into every line on her face.

"Yes, I do, if it will make Hopkirk look a fool and stop him doing his trial, assuming he does get past our defences and into the manor."

"And if I touch the stone in a special sequence, as you say you will instruct me, then the voice of our Lord Jesus will issue forth from this other thing?" Ruth gestured at the speaker. "That is surely blasphemy and I will suffer eternal damnation."

"It is not the real voice of Jesus," said Justine, thinking fast. "As you say, we could not command Him to speak. But we can make Hopkirk think it is Him, which is not blasphemy if we're doing His work, is it?"

"Perhaps." Ruth studied the phone. "Perhaps not. Show me how it makes pictures that move."

Justine took the phone and found a music video. "There." She handed it back.

Ruth watched in amazement. "And these are not people as small as beetles who inhabit the inside of this phone?" she asked.

"No, look." Justine turned the phone horizontally and the image resized bigger. "There – it makes the picture bigger when you turn it. The people are not there, their actions were captured once before and can be shown on any phone like this one, whenever you command it." She pressed the stop button and sighed briefly, as Howard, Jason, Gary and Mark disappeared from the screen.

"Hmmm." Ruth looked up. "So how then, do I command the voice of our Lord?"

Justine took the phone and patiently instructed Ruth on the sequence of swipes to open the voice app, find the text file she'd previously written, and play it through the Bluetooth speaker.

"And you will have secretly placed this thing you call a 'speaker' in the roof of the well?"

Yes, I'll secure it up in the roof out of sight. I'll do it tonight and check it again each day in case Hopkirk gets in."

"And I am to make the voice of the Lord speak out when Hopkirk is about to start his trial?"

"Yes." Justine smiled nervously. "Please don't leave it till William or I go down the well – that will surely be too late."

"I will try," answered Ruth. She looked up with a frown. "But I must remember the sequence of commands with my finger, and start to perform them in good time. How should I know when to begin? And I must not be seen tapping on this black stone by honest folk, or they will think I have taken leave of my senses and carry me away."

"Ruth, I am really grateful that you are helping me," said Justine.

"Aye, well, you are a good woman, or at least my daughter tells me so," said Ruth, then she added with a sly smile, "and as I have seen with my own eyes, very much enamoured of the master. 'Tis enough for me."

"Thank you," said Justine. "I hope we never have to put this plan into action, but if we do, I know you'll get the timing just right."

'And she very nearly didn't,' thought Justine, as she stood on the dais the next morning, watching Ruth drop the phone in her apron pocket and hurry away from the celebrating crowd in the well yard. 'One more second – just one more second fumbling with the phone and it would all have been too late.'

She turned to William.

"You spoke, my lord?"

"Aye. I would know your thoughts?"

"My thoughts, my lord?"

"On how it is a miracle that I have lived to see this day."

Justine looked at Sir William de Beauvais and suddenly it was as if she were seeing him for the very first time.

This handsome, charming, strong, sensitive man from history, whose portrait she had so often gazed at in the Great Hall, who she now loved and who truly loved her back; this man had been destined to die some two weeks before.

It was not a miracle that caused him now to be standing in front of her, very much alive.

He was here now because of her; because of Justine Parker.

Because she had somehow fallen through a freak time portal and abandoned her own time in favour of his.

Because she had known what would happen to him on that fateful night, and was there in disguise to try and do something to save him.

Because she was able to use her 21st century technology to convince a murderous mob to switch their anger onto the very man who would have killed her and William.

"No, my lord," she said with a shake of her head, "it was not a miracle."

She smiled warmly, with love dancing in her eyes.

"I think it was fate."

CHAPTER TWENTY-NINE

The wedding of Sir William de Beauvais and Mary Fox was celebrated on a glorious October Saturday, eight weeks later.

The ceremony took place in the little chapel at Grangedean Manor that sat a hundred yards away from the house down a path through the gold and brown autumn trees.

It was along this path that the bride and her entourage processed towards the chapel to the sound of its pealing bells, past cheering crowds of well-wishers who had come up from the village to see Mary Fox become the next Lady de Beauvais.

Her entourage consisted of the ten-year-old twin sons of Alice Mansfield as page boys and three small girls as her bridesmaids. She had picked them specially; Amy and Elizabeth Stanmore aged five and seven, and eight-year-old Olivia Dowland. Their job was to hold up the hem of Mary Fox's gown and stop it dragging in the dusty track, and it was a job these girls performed with great enthusiasm and rather too much giggling.

Walking nervously alongside was Sarah, once Mary Fox's maid and now elevated to the position of her lady-in-waiting. Sarah looked uncomfortable in an elegant pale blue velvet gown with blue and white patterned sleeves and matching underskirt. Her long dark hair flowed down to her waist and round her head was a thin wooden band garlanded with lilies of the valley.

Without a break in her stride, or in her smiling and waving at the villagers, Justine inclined her head towards her lady-in-waiting and whispered, "Keep your chin up, Sarah, you have every right to be here and to be looking so lovely in that dress."

"Mistress Mary, you are most kind," answered Sarah, her cheeks starting to flush. "But I cannot help but wonder if every villager's eye is on me, asking how a lowly maid has been so elevated that she wears such finery and walks by the side of such a noble lady as yourself."

"Nonsense," replied Justine. "They are very happy for you, and rightly so." She smiled at the cheering crowd. "It seems to me, Sarah, that they are as pleased to see me wed today, as they once were to see me drowned."

"Aye," replied Sarah. "They know you are favoured by Jesus, and revile Hopkirk as a servant of Satan."

Justine spotted Jake and Agnes, who were serving tankards of ale off their cart by the side of the path. She gave them a cheery wave, then chuckled to herself as she thought she must look like minor 21st century royalty. Agnes waved back, dancing round on the tips of her toes with joy.

"Truly, Sarah," said Justine from the side of her mouth, "now they wish us well."

"You are a vision of beauty, my lady," answered Sarah.

"Thanks to you. This dress is magnificent – and I would not have known how to go about having it made if you had not been there."

"You have learned so much these last two months, my lady. You've not once mentioned 'where I come from' this many a week."

Justine stopped and turned to Sarah. "No, I don't suppose I have," she said slowly. Then she turned and pointed back at the manor house still visible beyond the cedar trees behind them. "I suppose that is where I come from now."

"Yes, my lady," said Sarah firmly. "It is."

They walked on a few more yards and stopped at the door of the chapel.

"Let me check the dress, my lady," said Sarah, and made some small adjustments. After a moment she stood back and looked Justine up and down.

Her mistress was clothed in a gown of the finest ivory silk, made by the best team of seamstresses in London that Sarah could find. The bodice was bordered with silver thread, embroidered with a thousand tiny seed pearls and lined with white sable fur. The underskirt was visible from the front and was of pale blue satin and embroidered with intricate floral patterns in silver. Her sleeves were of ivory silk, slashed to show the pale blue satin lining beneath. A single pearl on a silver chain hung at her throat and on her head was a simple, elegant French hood in white velvet surmounted by a double row of pearls.

"Perfect, my lady," said Sarah. "Just perfect."

---O---

Sir William and Thomas Melrose were standing together in the front pew of the small whitewashed chapel, with the curate standing holding his prayer book in front of them.

William looked round towards the door.

"My lord, you will strain your neck if you keep turning so every minute," muttered Thomas. "She will be here soon, upon my oath."

"Aye," answered William. "But I would catch sight of her the instant she appears."

"You will see her shortly, then you will have a whole lifetime to gaze like a love-struck youth upon her fair face," said Thomas with a smile.

"Aye. And I would it would begin soon," said William, staring down the chapel.

Every row of pews was crammed full of guests. He picked out Robert Wychwoode, Jane Melrose and Sarah's mother Ruth, who was now excelling herself as the manor's new housekeeper.

An ancient man hobbled in, leaning heavily on a stick, almost doubled over so his forked beard trailed on the flagstones. He pushed in to sit at the end of one of the rows.

"Dr. Frobisher! I had no idea he was still alive," said William.

His gaze moved to the row directly behind him, and he caught sight of his own mother. She gave him a teary smile as she played with the diamond on the chain around her neck.

"My mother is so pleased to see me wed at last," said William as he turned round again to Thomas, "that she would cry like a babe."

"She is pleased to see you settle yourself as a husband, and no doubt soon a father," answered Thomas. "Or maybe she is crying because she fears your beautiful bride may choose not to arrive here today."

William heard some sounds coming into the chapel through the slightly-open door and lifted his hand to silence his friend.

"I'll warrant from the sound of cheering outside, that she is arrived now," he said.

There was movement as the door was pulled open, then suddenly he saw his bride standing at the end of the chapel, silhouetted against the autumn sun so that she looked like a ghost with a golden halo. Then she stepped forward a couple of paces and the door was shut behind her.

Beams of light from the high windows shone down on her. William caught his breath. "By all that is holy," he whispered, "there is not another girl in the whole of England more fair."

"She is a true beauty," agreed Thomas. "You are a lucky man indeed, my friend."

The bride glided slowly up the aisle, with Sarah beside her and her attendants following behind. As she drew level with William, she held up her hand, and he took it, then stepped out beside her, facing the curate.

---O---

Justine held her breath a moment, resisting the urge to gaze up at William. Instead she gave a little squeeze of his hand and was rewarded with a squeeze in return.

The curate looked at each of them and nodded.

"Dearly beloved friends," he read from his prayer book, "we are gathered together here in the sight of God, and in the face of his congregation, to join together this man and this woman in holy matrimony, which is an honourable estate, instituted of God in Paradise, in the time of man's innocence, signifying unto us the mystical union that is betwixt Christ and his Church: which holy estate Christ adorned and beautified with his presence, and first miracle that he wrought, in Cana of Galilee, and is commended of Saint Paul to be honourable among all men; and therefore is not to be enterprised, nor taken in hand unadvisedly, lightly, or wantonly, to satisfy men's carnal lusts and appetites, like brute beasts that have no understanding: but reverently, discretely, advisedly, soberly, and in the fear of God, duly considering the causes for which Matrimony was ordained. One was the procreation of children, to be brought up in the fear and nurture of the Lord, and praise of God. Secondly it was ordained for a remedy against sin, and to avoid fornication…" the curate looked up and gave both bride and groom a significant stare, "…that such persons as have not the gift of continence might marry, and keep themselves undefiled members of Christ's body. Thirdly, for the mutual society, help, and comfort, that the one ought to have of the other, both in prosperity and adversity; into the which holy estate these two persons present come now to be joined."

He paused and coughed loudly, as if to make sure the congregation were aware he was coming to an important bit. "Therefore if any man can show any just cause, why they may not lawfully be joined together: let him now speak, or else hereafter for ever hold his peace."

The curate looked up and glowered at every member of the congregation in turn, but thankfully no one spoke.

"I require and charge you," he continued, "as you will answer at the dreadful day of judgment, when the secrets of all hearts shall be disclosed, that if either of you do know any impediment, why ye may not be lawfully joined together in Matrimony, that ye confess it. For be ye well assured, that so many as be coupled together otherwise than God's word doth allow, are not joined together by God, neither is their Matrimony lawful."

He turned to William. "Sir William de Beauvais, wilt thou have this woman to thy wedded wife, to live together after God's ordinance in the holy estate of Matrimony? Wilt thou love her, comfort her, honour, and keep her in sickness and in health? And forsaking all other keep thee only to her, so long as you both shall live?

William looked at Justine, then back at the curate.

"I will," he answered firmly.

The curate turned to Justine.

"Wilt thou have this man to thy wedded husband, to live together after God's ordinance, in the holy estate of Matrimony? Wilt thou obey him, and serve him, love, honour, and keep him, in sickness and in health and forsaking all others keep thee only unto him, so long as you both shall live?"

She took a breath, knowing that the next two words she uttered would mean her life could never be the same again.

No more Justine Parker, the girl from 21st century Hammersmith.

Now she would forever be Lady Mary de Beauvais, the loving wife of a Tudor knight. Maybe the mother of his children.

She said, "I will."

---0---

The rest of the ceremony passed in something of a blur for the new Lady Mary de Beauvais.

She remembered Sarah stepping forward to give her away and the vows being exchanged with her and William agreeing to 'have and to hold from this day forward, for better, for worse, for richer, for poorer, in sickness and in health, to love, and to cherish, till death us depart'. She thought how little the service had changed in over 400 years – and with a small tinge of sadness – what a shame it was that her parents were not there to see it.

But the future that her parents inhabited was now firmly in her past; her role now was to live her life to the full as the new Lady de Beauvais, and to make a new family with William. Her old family from 2015 would have to be kept secure in the hidden recesses of her mind, just like the phone, charger and Bluetooth speaker that were safely locked away in a little jewelled box in her room.

So when William put the ring on her finger, she thought it was so beautiful she could not stop looking at it, all through the dull prayers that followed and which seemed to go on for hours.

Eventually the prayers were over and she and William emerged together from the chapel into the glorious autumn sunshine, and were greeted by the sound of the villagers cheering them to the tops of the golden brown trees.

CHAPTER THIRTY

The CEO stood in the middle of the hall, his hands thrust deep into the pockets of his jeans, looking around him. He looked in his mid-forties, tall with short grey hair and small round glasses. His gaze stopped on the picture of the blond knight with the white stag.

"Who's that guy?" he asked

"That's Sir William de Beauvais, the owner of Grangedean Manor from the 1560s," said Mrs. Warburton. "A very interesting man indeed."

"Why so?"

"He married late by Tudor standards, after he had been accused of witchcraft and nearly drowned in a ducking trial."

"The guy was the lord of the manor? Why was he accused of witchcraft?"

"It's unusual, I agree. He was accused by implication, trying to protect a girl. The girl that, in fact, he later married."

"A romantic, huh?" The CEO looked at the picture. "Did they give witches a rough ride in Elizabethan times?" he asked. "I thought that was later – in the 1600s. Salem and all that."

"Salem was in America, but we had our fair share here as well. But you're right – in Elizabeth's reign many people didn't believe in witches; there was none of the mass hysteria of the later Puritan era. Witchfinders would have to whip up the hatred and fear in order to get the mob on their side."

He moved to the next picture, a portrait of a handsome smiling Tudor woman in her mid-50s. "Who's this dame?"

"That's Lady Mary de Beauvais, Sir William's wife. She, too, was a remarkable woman. She was accused of witchcraft and tried by ducking in the well – but it is said that the heavens opened and Jesus himself appeared, claiming she was his chosen one and not a witch at all."

243

"That has gotta be mass hysteria."

"For sure. The interesting thing is that there are several accounts that corroborate the story, so it must have been a mass hallucination that felt very real to the people who were there."

The CEO studied the picture of Lady Mary. "She was a fine-looking woman."

"Indeed – she was known as a real beauty in her youth." Mrs. Warburton moved closer to the portrait and gave it deeper inspection. "But she was also known as a very progressive, forward-thinking woman – and prepared to fight for what she believed was right."

The CEO walked on, his Converse sneakers squeaking on the flagstones. He stared at each of the tapestries and the leaded windows in turn.

"Place like this has gotta be haunted?" he demanded.

"Certainly," said Mrs. Warburton. "An old house such as this has to have its ghosts."

"Cool. What's the ghost here? A headless woman?"

"Oh no. It is the ghost they call the Grey Man. He is sometimes seen in the bedroom wing; people have seen him standing in the corridor as they come through the door from the gallery, but as they get closer he disappears through the wall." She paused a moment. "But most often he is seen out in the car park by the old well. They say that every year just as the sun goes down on the 14th of August, the Grey Man can be seen standing by the well in the courtyard and holding his hands out as if addressing a crowd. Then he turns and glides through the side of the well and disappears. The local people will tell you that if something bad is going to happen around here, then it invariably happens on the 14th of August." She shook her head ruefully.

"They say it is always the fault of the Grey Man."

---0---

It was early the following evening as Rick the catering manager stamped up the stairs from the kitchens and into the Great Hall. A massive storm was coming and he wanted to get home before it hit.

He was also in a foul mood. The night before he had had to fire one of the actresses hired as a serving girl for the banquet, and now she had put in a formal complaint.

The girl had come down the stairs carrying too many pewter plates and had missed her footing on the bottom step; she had fallen headlong and thrown all her plates into the air, so that they had crashed down to the flagstone floor causing breakages and mess everywhere.

Rick had let his annoyance show, barking out, "Oh effing hell! What the frigging heck was that?"

The girl had been insolent, saying. "Sorry, Rick," like she didn't mean it in the slightest.

"Sorry?" he had said grimly. "Sorry? You'll be effing sorry if you don't clear up that effing mess. You'll be out on your effing ear!"

"Sorry," repeated the girl, and went forward to pick up the first plate. But then she had clutched at her leg, muttered something about being hurt, and had just started to walk out of the kitchen, leaving him to clear up.

So he'd stopped her and told her she was fired, and to get out for good.

Now he'd had an email from the agency telling him she'd complained and saying he was out of order. They were threatening to withdraw all their staff before the next banquet.

Rick went through the low door and into the hall. Out of the windows he could see the sky was so dark with the approaching storm, it was almost as if it was a winter's night. It looked like he was too late – it was going to hit any second.

A few of the electric candle lights were on in the Great Hall, and Rick's eye caught the picture of Lady Mary de Beauvais on the wall. He glanced at it, and as he did so a flash of lightning lit up the room with a burning intensity that seared a negative of the picture into his brain. Immediately afterwards, there was a deep blast of thunder that made the windows shake and the whole room resonate like a giant drum.

At the same moment, the lights went out.

With the image of the picture dancing in front of his unseeing eyes, he turned and made his way by feel and force of habit to the main doors, as another roar of thunder shook the room and a searing flash of lightning lit it up as if it were broad daylight. He reached the main double doors and pulled – but they remained stuck. He pulled again and again, as yet another flash of lightning lit up the room, followed by another crash of thunder. This one was so loud, that Rick thought his ears had burst. He pulled at the door again, but it remained stuck firm. He pummelled on it, shouting, but was sure no one would be able to hear above the sound of the rain and the echoes of the thunder.

Another bolt of lightning lit up the room and he ran to the door to the kitchens that he had come through only a few moments ago. He knew it couldn't be locked – it didn't have a lock on it at all. But like the main doors, it too was firmly closed. He beat on it till his fists hurt, but no one came.

Another bolt of lightning.

Another immediate massive crash of thunder – the loudest yet.

After the massive crash came further loud secondary rumbles. They rolled on, one after another, but seeming to get louder and louder so that soon he was sure they were louder than the original crash.

Then he heard the voices...

THE END

BY THE SAME AUTHOR

The Witchfinder's Well story continues!

Part 2 - The Alchemist's Arms

Lady Mary de Beauvais seems to be the perfect 16th century woman, but she hides a dark and terrible secret - she is actually a time-traveller from 2015. So when she discovers there's another traveller from her own time, she sets out across Elizabethan England to find him.

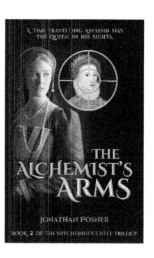

But it's a search that leads her into dreadful danger - threatening not just Mary's own future, but the life of Queen Elizabeth as well. So Mary is forced to face her fears and take control - if she wants to save herself and those she loves, in this "gripping adventure thriller".

Part 3 - The Sovereign's Secret

Lady Mary de Beauvais's past finally catches up with her, bringing her to the attention of Queen Elizabeth's calculating spymaster, Francis Walsingham.

His daring plan then plunges her into a world of intrigue, espionage and danger. Can Mary save herself once again, and in doing so, will English history have to change?

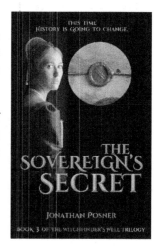

Both books are available on Amazon.

Printed in Great Britain
by Amazon

80650526R00144